PLAYING JAMES

PLAYING JAMES

JAMES

SARAH MASON

BALLANTINE BOOKS
NEW YORK

A Ballantine Book
Published by The Random House Publishing Group

Copyright © 2002 by Sarah Mason

All rights reserved under International and Pan-American Copyright Conventions. Published in the United States by The Random House Publishing Group, a division of Random House, Inc., New York.

Ballantine and colophon are registered trademarks of Random House, Inc.

www.ballantinebooks.com

Library of Congress Control Number: 2004090461

ISBN 0-345-46955-0

Originally published in Great Britain by Time Warner Paperbacks, London, in 2002

Designed by Joseph Rutt

Manufactured in the United States of America

First American Paperback Edition: June 2004

10 9 8 7 6 5 4 3 2 1

For my husband and
my parents, with love.

acknowledgments

T, you've been thoroughly amazing. I could tell you how much and in what ways but I've only got a page.

Enormous thanks to my agent, Dinah; you've been wonderful in every way possible.

I am indebted to my editor, Tara, not only for her continual support and enthusiasm but also her complete acceptance of excuses such as "the dog ate that chapter" and "I wasn't feeling particularly creative that day . . ."

Thanks also to everyone at Time Warner Books for making me feel entirely at home and not having sense of humor failures when they clearly should have done.

I am grateful to my parents, for when they weren't being an unending source of material for me they were liberally pouring alcohol down my throat. Most supportive.

Thanks to all my friends for absolutely nothing—you were all completely useless. But it was nice to have you there anyway.

Lastly my very grateful thanks to everyone at Lansdown police station who put up with my persistent questioning when they obviously had much better things to do. Thank you.

PLAYING JAMES

one

⁓

"Hello, Casualty Department?"

"Hello? Is that Casualty?" Now, please don't think I'm being stupid, I know the woman *said* Casualty. But I am double-checking. To be sure. If you were in my predicament then you would check too.

"Yes, this is Casualty, how can I help you?"

"I have a problem."

"What sort of problem?"

"I have a condom. Stuck."

"Stuck where?" she asks politely.

I glare at the phone. Now who is being stupid? "In my, er . . . my, er . . ." I frantically search for the appropriate medical term, ". . . whatsit."

"Vagina?" she asks.

I cringe at the blatant use of the word. "Yup. That."

"Please hold," she says briskly.

Please hold? PLEASE HOLD?! That's the bloody problem, HOLDING. Holding doesn't seem to be the issue, letting go does.

Actually, maybe I ought to explain something here. I don't have a condom stuck. Anywhere. Absolutely not. No way. I would know if I had.

So why am I on the phone to Casualty? Well, it is *sort* of true. It's just not me. It's Lizzie, my best friend, who is sitting on the sofa opposite me, crying into my kitchen roll.

"I'm holding!" I say brightly over the top of the mouthpiece. I think about telling her she ought to try and relax a little and the condom might just slip out but wisely decide against it. You would have thought that at the grand old age of twenty-five we'd have grown out of these sort of dramas and moved on to the bridesmaids'-shoes-don't-match-the-dresses ones instead. Don't misunderstand me, I don't mind, I was just expecting something different. At least it's an excuse to eat Jaffa Cakes at nine in the morning (me) and quaff medicinal brandies (Lizzie).

Lizzie was utterly distraught when she turned up on my door-step this morning. I thought something absolutely awful had happened, but obviously this isn't so great and probably won't be up there on her "Special Days" list. Poor Ben, my boyfriend extraor-dinaire, was shoved out so quickly he was still carrying the spoon he was trying to eat his cereal with.

I won't go into gory details because presumably you can guess what's happened. Lizzie's boyfriend of six months, Alastair, has in the meantime sodded off to work, pleading an important meet-ing, leaving little old moi to sort it out. I didn't have the heart to make her telephone Casualty herself and then I really couldn't be bothered with the whole "my friend has" stuff when they always presume it's you with the problem anyway.

Lizzie and I have been best friends since the age of thirteen and grew up together down in Cornwall. Two friends couldn't come from more contrasting backgrounds. With Lizzie's family it's all doilies and the best dinner service. Nothing like my Bohemian family, where not one plate matches the other and all the dogs eat off them anyway. We love each other's families, probably for the differences. I used to revel in the coziness of her household. She similarly loved the chaos of my home—we would sit on the stairs, eating apples and watching them all (I have three brothers and a sister to boot) charging about in the midst of some drama or other. I would tut and raise my eyes heavenwards, but she would be sitting forward slightly, avidly watching the proceedings, simply soaking up the atmosphere.

It would be much easier if the condom thing really was my problem and not Lizzie's because I am very comfortable in a crisis situation. I mean, how many families do you know who have the number of the local hospital on the speed-dial of their telephone? It is in there at number six, after Auntie Pegs and before my father's first wife, Katherine. She and my father are still on speaking terms. Katherine and my mother are downright pally and I send her Christmas cards for goodness' sake! I have had this pointed out to me as peculiar.

The lady from Casualty comes back on to the phone. I sincerely hope she has been talking to a sage, condom-removing professional and has not instead rushed through to the staffroom shouting, "Come and listen to this! I've got a right one here!"

"Hello?" she says.

"Hello!" I answer in a bright, I've-got-a-johnny-stuck-and-I'm-OK-with-that kind of way.

"I've been to talk to one of the nurses . . ."

"Yeeesss . . . ?" I say encouragingly, unwittingly imitating her rather annoying habit of traversing an octave in one sentence.

"She says you should come straight down to Casualty and they will remove it for you."

"Thank you so much. I'll do just that." I hang up gratefully. At least they weren't going to talk me through a DIY removal course. I was wondering how Lizzie and I were going to deal with that.

Lizzie stares at me questioningly. "We've got to go down there, Liz," I say in answer.

She buries her face in her hands and breaks out in a fresh bout of weeping. I pat her back rather ineffectually for a while, then say, "Lizzie, are you all right? Don't you want to go?"

OK, OK, stupid question to ask, but we have to start somewhere and we don't look like we're moving toward Casualty.

"I . . . I . . . I might meet someone." Her shoulders heave with the effort of getting the words out.

"At-ta girl, Liz! That's the attitude! There's nothing like a new boyfriend to get you over the last!" I leap up and grab my bag; Lizzie stops crying and starts glaring at me. I sit back down.

"Oh, as in someone you know. Sorry." I bite the inside of my cheek to stifle a giggle and try to study my shoes.

"If my mother finds out, she will never forgive me."

I look back up. "How would she find out? She lives in Cornwall, for heaven's sake!"

"What if someone sees or overhears us, and it gets back to her?"

"Like who?"

Lizzie just gives me a long, hard look. I sigh. "Oh." We went to school in Cornwall with a girl called Teresa, who now also lives here in Bristol and unfortunately makes a great show of doing volunteer work down at the hospital. She pretends to be terribly Christian and has an awful lot of those little fish symbols everywhere, but in actual fact she is one of the most horrible people I have ever met. When Lizzie and I were at school, Teresa's sole aim in life was to land us in as much hot water as possible, an ambition which used to be regularly met. If anyone could take this particular little incident back to Lizzie's mother it would be Teresa the Holy Cow, and my how she would feast on it.

"I'll register for you in my name. My parents probably wouldn't get to hear about it." Not that they'd care if they did. My mother would doubtless mishear anyway and think it quite an achievement to have London stuck up me, and if my siblings found out they would wink and say "Nice one" as they passed me in the hallway. My father? My father wouldn't look up from the newspaper.

"Will Alastair tell your work that you've had to go to the hospital if you don't turn up?"

Lizzie works with Alastair. In fact, he's sort of her boss. She nods miserably.

"Do you mind if we pop into the paper en route? It is on the way and I ought to tell them where I am. We could be hours in Casualty."

"You won't tell them why, will you?"

"Lizzie, I may work as a reporter but discretion is my middle name."

I escort Lizzie out of my flat, carefully holding her elbow. She is walking gingerly and looking a little bow-legged. She couldn't catch a pig in a corridor, as they say. We stop suddenly.

"Off. We. Go!" I cry, urging her in the general direction of the hospital just in case she has got cold feet again. I look across to find her glaring at me.

"What?" I ask.

"I am not ill, an OAP or pregnant! Please let go of my arm!" Narky or what? I drop her arm and we start off once more on our snail's journey toward the car. Now and again we both look over our shoulders in the vain hope that the condom may have dislodged itself and is lying on the pavement. No such luck. Never mind! I quite enjoy trips down to Casualty. It's the drama queen in me.

Lizzie has a tricky time getting into my car, but then everyone does because it is quite tricky to get into. There are only two ways to get in and out of an MG Midget sports car—the elegant way or my way. The elegant way is how you see the film stars do it on TV when they arrive at the Oscars. To get in, put your bum inside first and then swivel legs round. Similarly, to exit, swivel legs out, bum last. My way is to get everything *but* bum in first, leave bum out in the cold for a bit while struggling with other appendages, and then bum can come in. To get out, I simply fall onto the pavement.

I call my car Tristan. I know it's unbelievably naff to give inanimate objects names and I don't normally, but he has so much character and such delicate sensibilities that I feel depersonalizing him might be an additional hex on his already rather volatile nature.

I try praying to Allah this time that Tristan won't let me down (God wasn't feeling terribly benevolent on the last occasion). I hold my breath as the starter motor chugs over and exhale as he suddenly growls into life. Relaxing completely is out of the question however, because Tristan can stop at any point for absolutely no reason. I have spent many a happy evening on the hard shoulder of the motorway en route to Cornwall, waiting for the RAC to turn up. Because I am a lone female, I am a priority call for the police to sit with. I know all the boys on that particular beat quite well now and they all cheat appallingly at gin rummy. I think I would be quite sorry not to see them if (a) Tristan ever starts to behave or (b) I replace him with a reliable Volvo called Brian.

Lizzie reads the rabid gleam in my eye correctly and straps herself in. She plants a foot firmly on either side of the passenger well and hangs on. I rise gleefully to the challenge of an "emergency" situation and at last have the excuse to stretch my wings and drive in a manner akin to *The Dukes of Hazzard*. We bounce over speed bumps, go the wrong way around roundabouts and have a distinct tendency to maneuver, signal, mirror.

Ten minutes and several road-rage incidents later, I pull up at the paper's offices with a screech and, saying to Lizzie that I won't be a sec, skip through the front doors of the *Bristol Gazette*. I fight my way through the jungle of triffid-like plants to the lifts and give a cheery wave to one of the security guards (who I think are also there for aesthetic purposes only as I have never seen them do anything of a security-minded nature).

The lift doors open on to the third floor where the features department is based and I take a swift left toward our editor's office. I knock and am answered by a bellowing, "COME!"

Joseph Heesman is in his habitual position as I walk through the door. He has his feet up on the desk (stereotype of an editor but nonetheless true), he is talking on the phone and smoking what looks like his tenth cigarette of the day. His loud tie is lopsided and obviously trying to make a run for it as it is teamed with a rather bright turquoise shirt. It's so bright that it's a question of whether the tie or I can make it to the door first. He is a giant of a man and you don't argue with him. Ever. His joviality can flash into a tempest with simply the phrase, "But *I* thought . . ."

He replaces the receiver. "Holly, will this take long? We have a few problems today."

"A friend of mine needs to go to the hospital for, er . . . for, er . . . some reason and I really have to go with her."

He takes the cigarette out of his mouth and balances it precariously across the top of a coffee mug. He narrows his eyes suspiciously as he exhales a long stream of smoke.

"What's wrong with her?"

"Wrong with her?"

"Yes, wrong with her."

"Wrong with her?"

"Holly! Stop sounding like a demented parrot and tell me what's wrong with her. Presumably she is going to the hospital because something is wrong with her?"

"Of course something is wrong with her," I say in a strained voice, uncomfortably aware of the absolute whiffiness of the situation. I wish I had spent my time in the lift a little more constructively and actually thought this through.

"This isn't *you* we're talking about, is it? Is there really 'a friend'?"

See? Nobody ever buys the friend stuff. "Yes, there is! It's Lizzie and she's waiting in the car!" I say indignantly.

"Well, what's wrong with her then?"

"It's, er, women's stuff," I say shiftily. That just about covers it. Luckily the mere mention of gynecological problems gets Joe to dramatically shift into reverse gear. He wearily waves me away as though fighting a losing battle. "Try not to be long," he says resignedly.

"Thanks, Joe!"

I make to walk out, but just as I get my hand on the door handle he stops me with a question.

"Did you say you were going to the hospital?"

I blink nervously. Is he trying to catch me out or something? "The hospital. Yes."

He frantically starts shuffling through a pile of papers in front of him. "There's a story you could cover while you're down there."

"What is it?" I ask with interest, coming back toward his desk.

"A suspect in a fraud case tried to make a run for it and ended up in a car accident. The police are down there now waiting for him to be treated."

"Shouldn't Pete go?" Smug Pete is the paper's crime correspondent and therefore this is his beat.

"Pete's out on another story."

"OK then!" I say eagerly. Crime correspondent is hardly a coveted job as our relationship with the police is far from ideal, but such is the lowliness of my position on the features team, by virtue of my age, that I rarely get to cover anything of interest. I grab a notebook and the brief and make a run for Tristan and Lizzie before Joe changes his mind. Anything makes a welcome change from what I'm working on at the moment.

"Got to cover a story," I gasp to Lizzie a few minutes later as I shove all my limbs into the car at once.

"Eh?"

"A story at the hospital. Joe wants me to look into it while we're there." I reach for my seat belt and simultaneously turn on the ignition.

"Holly! You're supposed to be there with me!"

"I *will* be with you. It's just one itty-bitty story I have to do."

We set off again at breakneck speed and race around the streets. We arrive far too soon at our destination and spy a parking space which I manage to beat a BMW to. Resisting the urge to execute a handbrake turn into it, I enthusiastically parallel park (I am mustard at parallel parking).

"Gosh!" I exclaim breathlessly, "that was fun, wasn't it?"

"You should have just shaken me upside down by my ankles and had done with it," Lizzie mutters mutinously.

"I needed to get you here quickly, Lizzie! You might die of toxic shock syndrome or something!" I cheerfully release my bones from their seat belt sling.

"As opposed to dying of just plain old shock, I suppose," she snaps, heaving herself out of the car.

I stroll into the building and up to the front desk with Lizzie limping frantically behind me. We get into the queue behind a small boy and his mother. The small boy rather disturbingly seems to have swallowed a plastic dinosaur. Apparently it is his third this week. A stegosaurus, followed by a raptor and now finally a tyrannosaurus. Lizzie and I wait while the lady behind the desk painstakingly writes all this down.

Lizzie looks anxiously about for spies in the form of would-be do-gooders called Teresa and I have a good stare around the

Casualty ward while the spelling of "tyrannosaurus" goes on. It hasn't changed much since my previous visits. I've been to Casualty a couple of times. Last time it was because I'd hit myself in the face with a tennis racket and needed six stitches in my eyebrow (which was very fortuitous on the scarring front). My wound, which positively gushed with blood, meant I went to the front of the Casualty queue.

As a double bonus, the doctor who treated me was ab-so-lute-ly gorgeous, a real-life version of George Clooney from *ER*. His dark, smoldering looks nearly made me forget why I was there. The blood all over my face made my natural charms a little hard to see, so I tried to show off my feet as they are my second-best feature (so I've been told). I don't believe he really noticed them though, and when I offered to take my plimsolls off he said he didn't think that was necessary. I remember his name quite well. It was Dr. Kirkpatrick. I think it is an absolutely magnificent name and I rather fancied being Mrs. Kirkpatrick at the time (although that is quite out of the question now because I am in love with Ben and intend to stay that way).

The small boy is finally led off, being cuffed round the head by his mother all the way, and Lizzie and I step up to the reception desk.

"Hello!" I greet the receptionist cheerfully.

"How can I help you?"

"Well, I called earlier and was advised to come down. I have a bit of a delicate problem."

The lady raises her eyebrows inquiringly and purses her pink-frosted lips accordingly, so I lower my voice to a whisper and continue. "I have a condom stuck inside me."

We gaze at each other for a second. She looks as though she has swallowed her lips, then reaches over for a form and asks me to fill it in. I do so and Lizzie and I go through to the waiting room and take a seat.

I pat Lizzie's knee; she is looking a little strained, poor thing.

"See?" I whisper. "Easy."

"When I'm called, will you come with me?"

I take a quick look around and spot two official-looking blokes talking animatedly in the corner—they might be the police officers on my fraud case. "Well, I really have to go and cover this story," I say, staring at them.

"Please?" She turns puppy eyes on me.

I sigh. "All right. But look, I think those men over there must be police officers, so I'm just going to go and make a few inquiries while we wait. But I'll be back," I say with a fake Arnie accent, "and the dinosaur will take at least ten minutes." And with this I scurry over to my suspects.

"Hello!" I greet the two men cheerfully. Both are dressed in shirts and ties, with their shirt sleeves rolled up but no jackets. The one I am facing smiles lazily; he's rather nice-looking with dark, thick hair. The other one swivels round. The greenest pair of eyes I have ever seen bore into me suspiciously. The green eyes, I can't help noticing, belong to the head of an immensely attractive young man. And the head is atop a rather splendid physique.

It takes me by surprise somewhat. "Yes?" he snaps.

"Er . . ."

"Well?"

"Are you police officers?"

"Do you need to report something?" he asks with, I fancy, a soupçon of derision.

I am tempted to refer to my notes, but I bravely plough onwards instead. "I understand one of your suspects from the Stacey fraud case has been involved in a car accident?"

"Do you indeed? And which newspaper are you from?"

"*Bristol Gazette.*"

"And what do you want to know?"

"Anything you can tell me?"

"Go and talk to our PR department. They'll be issuing a press release."

"But has the suspect been badly injured? Were you about to arrest him? And on what charges? Have you arrested anyone else in connection with the case? Or—"

"What's your name?" he cuts in. I'm starting to wish Old Green Eyes' manner could match his looks.

"Holly Colshannon."

"Well, Holly Colshannon," he says grimly, "as persistent as you seem, you will have to wait for a press release." And taking me firmly by the elbow, he escorts me to the front desk.

"You can't do this!" I protest as he frogmarches me across the waiting room. Lizzie watches in horror. He doesn't answer.

"Please don't admit this young lady again," he says to the woman on the desk.

The woman looks at me. "But she's here to be treated, Officer."

"Yes! I'm here to be treated, Officer," I indignantly echo.

"Really?" He lets go of my elbow and looks me up and down. "And what exactly is wrong with her? She looks pretty healthy to me."

Oh shit. Both the lady and I hesitate.

"Well?"

"It's, er, personal."

"Big coincidence, isn't it? That you happen to need treatment and then, lo and behold!, one of the suspects from the story you need to cover is admitted too!"

"Well, I am terribly sorry for being a coincidence," I say in my best sarcastic voice.

"Holly?" A voice interrupts us from behind. It's Lizzie. "They're calling you," she says acidly, with eyes open wide and teeth gritted. She jerks her head pointedly.

"Excuse me, Officer. But I have to go through for my treatment now." And with this, I draw myself up, hold my head high and march over to Lizzie.

"Of all the pig-headed, nasty, sly rats," I rave at Lizzie as we follow a nurse down some corridors.

"Er, Holly?"

"Bad tempered, odious, repellent worm . . ."

"Holly?"

"Lily-livered, vicious, detestable—"

"HOLLY!!"

I jump. "What?"

"Do you mind if we concentrate on me for a second?"

"Of course not, Lizzie." I rub her arm comfortingly. "After all, we are here for you. Do you know," I continue, "that he was practically accusing that poor lady of—"

"HOLLY! STOP IT!"

"Right. Sorry. I'm one hundred percent here."

We follow the nurse toward a bed, where she draws a curtain around us and says that the doctor will be here shortly. We wait for a few seconds and I fume silently to myself.

Finally I say, "Lizzie, would you mind if I just had a little poke around to see if I can find the bloke who's been injured? He must be in here somewhere and I can't stand the idea of that slimy git back there getting the better of me. I'll just be a couple of minutes . . ." Lizzie waves her arm at me impatiently and I slip out into the ward.

I start walking past the beds, wondering exactly how I'm going to find this person when I don't even know his name (not released in my brief) or the type of accident he was involved in. I stop short as I spy something in a far corner.

It's an old-fashioned English bobby, dressed in the habitual black and white uniform and wearing a considerably more friendly expression than his plain-clothed colleague. He's sitting next to a bed which is shrouded by curtains, sipping a cup of tea. I quell the desire to run over squealing with joy, which may alarm him somewhat, and instead execute a more steady pace.

Ten minutes later I have all the information I need to make an excellent story. I have to cut short my jolly conversation with PC Woods as I spot my green-eyed friend striding up the ward toward me, and from the look on his face he has spotted me too. I nip out of a door behind me, resisting the urge to flip a V-sign, and then, with a smile I can't wipe from my face, cut back round to Lizzie.

"Lizzie?" I call from the other side of the curtains. "Can I come in?"

"Yes, Holly."

I poke my head around the divide to find Lizzie sitting on the edge of the bed, gloomily staring ahead of her. "Been seen yet?"

"No."

Before I can tell her about my news story, the curtain is flung to one side and a nurse asks, "Which one of you is Holly Colshannon?"

"I am," I say automatically, before my brain engages itself.

She points at me and says to an approaching figure, "This is the patient." The gorgeous Dr. Kirkpatrick stands before us.

I have never been so embarrassed in my entire life. Never. The emotional scars from the last hour or so will be with me for a long time. I will probably never be able to have sex again without at least a year in therapy.

Dr. Kirkpatrick was still gorgeous. I know I said that I am in love with Ben and I am, but that doesn't stop me admiring other people and, even worse, craving their good opinion. I think it would be quite fair to say that Dr. Kirkpatrick's good opinion and I are destined never to meet. The first thing he said was, "You've been here before, haven't you? I recognize the name."

Damn and blast it forever. The nurse was looking at me in rather a strange manner, as though I was a serial condom-bagger and did this on a regular basis.

I went bright crimson and was completely incapable of saying anything. Unfortunately he wasn't.

"No need to be embarrassed. Pop your knickers off and get up on the bed."

Aaaarrgh! I could have killed myself! How mortifying is that! And what was my best friend doing in the midst of all of this? A very good question. She, too, was apparently struck dumb by his sheer beauty and was not quite ready to own up to her predicament. One wonders how far everything could have got before she had felt ready to own up.

At this point I still hadn't uttered a single word (charming or otherwise). I glared at Lizzie so viciously I expected her hair to go up in flames. It's fair to say our friendship was hanging in the balance in those few seconds. She knew exactly what my look was saying—it was the business. Squinty eyes, the works. It wasn't saying, "Could you give me a hand up on to the bed?" It was shouting, "OWN UP NOW!!"

Things got worse. A minor tussle ensued between me and the nurse. She was trying to hustle me toward the bed with a, "Come, come, the doctor hasn't got all day," when at long last I found my voice. My face still burning, I bellowed, "LIZZIE, TELL THEM NOW." At this point Lizzie simultaneously found her conscience and the ability to speak and told them that it was her with the problem and not me. I sank, absolutely exhausted, into the chair by the side of the bed. It's not every day that you have an over-enthusiastic nurse tugging at your knickers.

We were then treated to a lecture from the nurse about practical jokes and wasting hospital time. She moved swiftly on to the state of the NHS for which, it seemed, Lizzie and I were solely to blame. Darling Dr. Kirkpatrick bustled around; he probably hadn't seen such pandemonium since the last time I was in and I'm certain I will be the talk of the hospital staff room for some time. I can almost hear it now. I will become one of those stories that starts, "And do you remember the time when . . ." Cue raucous laughter.

Now and then he patted a freshly weeping Lizzie on the arm and said, "It's not that bad."

I felt like roaring, "Au contraire, Monsieur le Docteur, it *is* that bad. And don't pat her,
she
doesn't
deserve
a
pat."
But it might have seemed a little uncharitable. Why I was worried about what would seem uncharitable in front of Dr. Kirkpatrick after what he had just witnessed I will never know.

Excuse me, but I don't want to talk about this any longer. It's eleven o'clock in the morning and I have already been in a ruckus with a plainclothes police officer and been manhandled by a nurse who believed me to be harboring a condom with intent.

Sod the Jaffa Cakes. I'm just going to have the brandy.

two

The *Bristol Gazette* wasn't my first choice of newspaper when I started work fresh out of university four years ago. I had planned to live in London and was desperate to get on to one of the national newspapers, but applicants needed some really good work experience. My only work experiences were picking strawberries in the holidays (and I must be the only person alive to actually be fired from that) and some waitressing work. I realized I would have to lower my sights when I opened my twentieth rejection letter, and I would have taken ANYTHING by the time this job in Bristol popped up. And I was very lucky to get it because you have no idea of the sort of lies I had to tell to bag the position of sports correspondent. Really. You just don't want to know.

When Joe made the lightning deduction that I knew absolutely nothing about sport, which may have been at the same time I asked if Tiger Woods was seeded in Wimbledon, he put me on to features. I am the most junior of the junior members of the features team, which basically means I get all the jobs no one else will do. I seem to specialize in pet funerals at the moment. But it's very hard to show off one's superior writing skills when waxing lyrical about a cat: ". . . and Persil's virgin white coat looked like driven snow against . . ." Yes. Exactly.

It's Friday and I am late into work as usual. Even though the paper's offices are only a ten-minute drive across town, I just can't seem to bring myself to make it there on time. As I stand waiting for the lift which will take me to the third floor, I try desperately not to think about yesterday's hospital incident. The mere sight of white coats starts me twitching nervously. The lift arrives and the doors open. I zip in, only to run full-pelt into Smug Pete, the crime correspondent. He is carrying a large cardboard box. Such is the force of our collision, I nearly invert my own breasts.

Smug Pete and I don't get on. I think he is smug and he thinks I'm annoying (fair enough, I probably am). Luckily we don't go through the pretense of liking one another.

"Pete!" I gasp with a wince, resisting the temptation to sink to my knees clasping my mammaries, "what's the box for? You're not leaving, are you?" I add on hopefully.

Smug Pete has a self-satisfied smirk on his face. I don't do it very often, but this time I seem to have inadvertently banged the nail square on its proverbial head. Damn.

Pete smiles a smug smile. "Just handed in my notice. Got a job with the *Daily Mail*. They've said I don't need to work my notice so I'm off."

"Right. Well. Best of luck with that," I spit out.

"Thanks."

We shuffle around each other as he gets out of the lift.

"By the way, Holly," he says as the doors start to glide shut, "Joe wants to see you." He smirks once more and the lift doors clunk home.

I take a swift left toward Joe's office on arrival at the third floor and knock on his door, just below the "Editor" sign. I am answered, as usual, by a bellowing, "COME!"

He's on the telephone and so I gaze round his office while he continues to lambast some poor bugger. It is the most impersonal room I have ever seen. It never ceases to amaze me how a man so large in life, metaphorically and physically, can have so little effect on his surroundings. He has no photos on his desk, just mounds and mounds of paperwork. There are no pictures on the wall or indeed any evidence of personal effects whatsoever. Ironically, I think this is because he loves his job so much. He puts the receiver down.

"Joe, hi."

"Holly! How's that cousin of yours? I looked for him in the Spanish Open last night."

While I was trying to get the post of sports correspondent, I made up an imaginary superstar sportsman cousin called Buntam. I was about to call him Bunbury after Oscar Wilde's fictitious invalid in the country, but as soon as the first syllable was out of my mouth I realized Joe might get the literary connection. Buntam, bless him, clinched the job for me. The problem is that he plays championship golf (I'm nothing if not ambitious).

"He was ill. Couldn't play."

"Too bad! What was wrong?"

"Er . . . flu."

"Flu?" Now he says it, flu doesn't sound serious enough to keep Buntam out of a major championship.

"Well, flu-like symptoms. It was typhoid actually." I nod vigorously.

"Typhoid? In Spain?"

"Well, he didn't catch it in Spain," I hedge.

"Of course he didn't!"

"That's right! You know your tropical diseases, don't you?" I beam at Joe. It's just a pity I don't know mine. Or where to catch them. "He caught it in, er, Africa?" Poor old Africa seems a large enough continent to harbor all manner of epidemics and Joe seems to be nodding sympathetically at this so I add more firmly, "Yes, Africa."

"What was he doing out there?"

"In Africa?" I ask needlessly to buy some precious thinking seconds. Joe nods.

"Er, well. He was playing golf, of course. For charity." An

unlikely vision flashes before me of the rugged plains and forests of Africa interspersed with twee little golf courses.

Happily, the same vision doesn't appear to Joe. "Gosh, that was unlucky!" he exclaims.

"Well, you know Buntam. Disaster seems to dog his every footstep!" I resist the temptation to fan myself with one of the wads of paper from Joe's desk.

"He's certainly jinxed! I mean, he's played how many tournaments this year? Two? And both times I was away. And the things that have happened to him! Shame. Maybe I'll catch him next time."

"Maybe!" But don't count on it, I add silently to myself.

I am so exhausted after the effort of my verbal gymnastics that it takes me a few seconds to remember why I am actually here. "You wanted to see me?"

"Yeah. That was a good article you wrote yesterday on the Stacey fraud case."

"Oh, thanks."

"Is your friend OK?"

"Lizzie? *She's* OK."

"Good! Your story is part of the reason I wanted to see you. Pete is leaving."

"Yeah, I know. I just met him in the . . . er . . . in the . . ." I stumble as I remember that I shouldn't be in the lift at a quarter past nine. I should be in the actual building. Joe waves my amnesia to one side.

"But it's good news for you! What's the phrase? A foul wind that blows no fair? A fair wind that . . ." I think he may have got it right the first time. This is a nasty habit of his, mixing his metaphors. It's quite tricky working out what he actually wants to say. I stop the agonizing.

"Is it?" I ask warily.

"Yeah, yeah, great news!"

"It is?"

"Yes, because do you know who the new crime correspondent is going to be?" Old Colshannon here may be slow on the uptake but I'm getting a pretty good idea. I blink nervously. Crime correspondent is a despised position and Smug Pete was on it in a last-ditch attempt to improve relations with the local police department (why Smug Pete would seem the obvious candidate I will never know). From what I can make out, the police are really aggressive toward us, we're aggressive back and write bad stuff about them and so it goes on. When the police post becomes vacant, folks hide under their desks for days. It is a career black hole and I'm about to be sucked into it.

Joe gets out of his chair, walks around to the front of the desk and perches on the edge of it. Do I feign enthusiasm for the moment and get out of it later? Or do I try and do it now?

A girl's got to eat so I opt for the former and give a little gasp of joy. This seems to please Joe and he positively beams at me. Good decision, Holly.

"It's you! I'm giving you this chance!"

"That's great! But, but . . . do you think I've got enough experience for something like the police beat?" Mock horror. Please say no. Please say no.

"Yes! Of course you have!" Rats. "I'm giving you this chance! You deserve it!" He tilts his head and adopts a more serious note. "Holly, I want you to make a go of this role. In the past we have always had the best people on it . . ."

OK, OK, what's he saying?

". . . but they have been too aggressive, too pushy. I want you to build a better relationship with the police force. Pour oil on, er, you know, murky waters. Eat humble tart. Don't upset the apple pie. Do you understand what I'm saying?"

Er, no, not really, but I'll nod my head anyway.

"The *Journal* has always had a really good relationship with the police and it's been showing recently in their crime stories." The *Bristol Journal* is the second largest paper in the region and our main competitor. We've taken it personally ever since they called our paper "a debauched office party that can't tell the difference between Tony Blair and Tony Bennett." I would dispute that wholeheartedly if only I knew who Tony Bennett was. They retracted the comment the next day under threats of litigation but steam still comes out of Joe's ears every time their name is mentioned.

He frowns deeply and continues, "They always seem to be one step ahead of us when it comes to crime leads. I think they must have someone on the inside. Anyway, I need you to take the bear by the horns on this one."

He pats my shoulder. "I'm pleased we've had our little chat. I feel better now. Much better."

Well, I'm glad someone does.

"Start Monday. Have a good weekend if I don't see you. Give Buntam my regards," he adds breezily as he waves me out of the office.

Last year we had a swear box in the office for six months and all the proceeds went to charity. It had only been going for three months when we received a letter from The Guide Dogs for the Blind Association thanking us for our donations and saying that the money was now supporting four golden retrievers. Well, I was responsible for at least two dogs and one leg of the third. As much as I am in favor of such a worthy cause, my salary only goes so far and apparently swearing is not an attractive quality in a woman. So I devised a new swearing system using fruit and vegetables which, I am happy to say, caught on here in the office. Fruit and veg you hate are bad stuff, and those you love are good. So, my new position on the police beat is TURNIPS but Pete leaving is something like apples (obviously not strawberries or anything *really* yummy because that's reserved for the absolutely brilliant stuff). Now the office is littered with phrases such as, "Can you believe it? That is really, like, swede, you know?"

Clearly the system is open to interpretation. There is one girl here who always yells, "That is so kiwi!" down the phone. We wondered if we ought to explain the system to her again until someone pointed out that she has a lifelong allergy to kiwi fruit. I really have got to find something better than this to put on my CV.

So, the police beat is SWEDES, MARROWS, BRUSSELS SPROUTS and anything else horrible you care to mention.

"How's your day been?" Ben asks earnestly.

I look at him sardonically. There's a loaded question. We're sitting in Henry Africa's Hothouse for a Friday drinks-after-work thing. The giant palms are annoying me as one particularly troublesome leaf keeps scratching my head, and the setting sun is streaming through the windows and causing me to squint unattractively. Funnily enough, I'm not in the best of moods.

"Oh. You know. A bit peculiar." I take an almighty suck of vodka through my straw. I have wafted a little orange juice under its nose but that was only to show willing.

"How peculiar?" He leans closer to me so that we can hear each other better in the excited, humming atmosphere of a bar on Friday night.

I pause and rest my chin on top of my glass with the straw still in my mouth—no point in being too far away from it. I've never really seen the use of straws before tonight but suddenly I understand. Do you know you don't have to move your head at all?

"They've made me the new crime correspondent for the paper!" I say with my new straw friend to one side of my mouth, and try to smile brightly through my glass.

"Is that good? I mean, didn't you say it was an awful job? What happened to Percy or whatever his name was?"

"Pete." The giant palm tickles the top of my head again.

"What happened to Pete?"

I sigh deeply, breathing in vodka fumes. "Left for a job with the *Daily Mail*."

"Oh well. It's a sort of promotion, isn't it, really?"

I look at him sideways. If he only knew. "That's one way of looking at it."

"Holly Colshannon, crime correspondent on the *Bristol Gazette*." He sketches out my new job title in the air with his hand.

"I suppose it sounds all right," I say, returning my gaze to the cross-eyed examination of my ice cubes.

"It sounds great!" Ben says boisterously. Normally a punch in the arm or a slap round the back would accompany this. This is his jollying-her-out-of-it tone. Not terribly jolly when you realize that the slap/punch in question comes from a six-foot-three rugby player.

"Joe said he gave it to me because I did a good job on the Stacey fraud story." The giant palm is looking for trouble now and I swat it away, trying not to lose my temper. I don't want to be remembered in here forever as "that girl who got into a fight with a palm tree."

"Was that the one down at the hospital? With the shitty police officer?"

"The very same."

"That was probably just a one-off. You said the other officer seemed quite nice."

"Well, I didn't exactly get the opportunity to speak to him."

"Anything else happen?" he asks.

"Isn't that enough?"

"I mean, anything interesting?"

I toy with the idea of telling him about my Buntam conversation with Joe, but decide, as I always do, that Ben wouldn't see the funny side of Buntam. Ben is occasionally completely bemused by me and my scrapes and spends his time asking, "But how did . . . ?" and "Why did you . . . ?" in a puzzled sort of fashion.

I shake my head and ask, "Who are you playing tomorrow?"

"Bath."

"Oh," says I in a knowledgeable sort of way. "Bath. That'll be a difficult game." I honestly haven't got a clue, but I find that if I stick to ambiguous comments then I can't come a cropper. "And will you be wearing your red shoes or your blue ones?" I ask, bringing the conversation back to more comfortable ground.

"Holly. I have told you a hundred times. They are not shoes. They are boots. And it depends on whether the ground is wet or dry, not on what color the other team are wearing." He smiles, leans over and kisses me affectionately on the forehead.

Ben is boyfriend extraordinaire. He is simply perfect. I met him at an awards dinner. It was when I was the sports correspondent for the paper (before Joe found out I couldn't tell one end of a cricket bat from the other). Ben was there to collect the "Player of the Year" trophy for the local rugby team. He gave a little acceptance speech and told *the* funniest joke about a Labrador, a vicar and a skateboard. Now what was the punch line? Yes. Well. Maybe you had to be there.

I couldn't take my eyes off him. He was dressed in the obligatory dinner jacket, his sandy hair was flopping over his face, he had the bluest eyes I'd ever seen and he glowed with the remains of a golden tan from a week's sailing. I didn't take one single note for the paper all night, and the next morning I had to frantically phone round the other sports correspondents and promise them all sorts of lewd acts if they would just let me borrow theirs.

Now, I can look OK when I want to. In fact, quite nice-looking. I am not like the advert people, of course, who wake up looking good, do a cross-country run, get the kids to school, rescue an old person and still look exactly the same. But when I take the trouble to do my hair and makeup the results can be pleasing. I am tall (about five-foot-nine, to be exact), have blond, longish hair (natural in places), freckles (yuk! Have tried lemon juice, doesn't work), and a huge smile which I don't think is very elegant but Lizzie assures me it is extremely jolly (which is sure-fire proof that it isn't very elegant at all). Ben is very tall which is fantastic as I am a sucker for tall men. It is nice to slob around in his clothes and feel petite. I have always been really tall for my age. Once, at school, I went to a fancy-dress party as a flower fairy. I flounced and pirouetted around in what I imagined was a fairy-like fashion and then won second prize! For being the Jolly Green Giant . . .

But the gods must have been smiling upon me the night I met Ben, because I sashayed up to him and not only scored a try but converted it as well.

I, the Jolly Green Giant herself, won the jackpot.

Still to this day, I don't quite understand how. Because he is, as Lizzie would say, "a catch." And now, wonder of wonders, we've been going out for a while; in fact, nearly a year. So, life is very good. Not perfect, but then whose is? I mean, the rugby games every Saturday do get tedious, and then of course there are the constant training sessions. Oh, and the team-bonding male thing after the games . . . But I know loads of girls who would love to go out with him so that just makes me the luckiest person ever. And I don't want to be one of those girlfriends who is constantly nagging that I don't see enough of him because, to be honest, it is lovely to see him at all and I know his sport is important to him. I can put up with the rugby and all that goes with it because he is near enough perfect for me. He is charming, witty, funny, great in bed . . . the list just goes on and on. And although I am not thinking about it right now, I think he is The One because what else can a girl ask for? Right?

"Come on, Colshannon," says Ben as he drains his pint glass, "let's go home."

I resist the urge to give the palm tree a swift kicking as we leave and instead wave to the barman across a sea of people and get stuck in the revolving door for two turns before Ben pulls me out.

Ben and I drunkenly meander back to my flat, singing rowdy rugby songs to which I don't know any of the words but prefer to make up my own anyway.

I live in a darling little flat in Clifton (posh part of Bristol). It's small, but I love it so. It's situated on the first floor of a gorgeous old Regency house and my sitting room has huge sash windows that cost me over half a month's salary to curtain. The bedroom is at the back of the house and thankfully has smaller windows which look out over our neatly boxed communal gardens. I also have a tiny guest room which just about fits a small double bed and nothing else.

I live alone at the moment but I am hoping that in the not-too-distant future Ben will live here too. I choose to live on my own— if you had grown up in my household then you would too. There are obvious advantages to single occupancy, one of which being, as every self-respecting hermit knows, the freedom to eat toast for supper without the many questions that accompany eating toast for supper. (Is that all you're having? Why don't you put some ham on that? How many vegetables have you eaten today?) Also, I don't have to endure cohabitation with my family, who manage to take living together just those few steps closer to hell. They overstep the boundaries even nightmare flatmates respect. You have no idea how blissful it is to find everything in the fridge just the way I left it. It is a constant surprise to me to find my car still parked outside, money still in my purse and my eyebrows still intact every morning. I suppose I was a bit of an accident as I am the youngest out of five. The rest of them have been a bit pesky and although I didn't exactly have a haloed childhood, I think, relatively speaking, I didn't give my parents a huge amount of trouble. My brothers in particular gave my mother a lot of headaches. I remember her buying a book called *How to Deal With a Troublesome Teenager*. When I asked her which brother she had bought it for, she said, "All of them. I'm either going to smack them over the head with it or stand on it so I can reach while I smack them over the head with something else."

We buy kebabs at the top of Park Street. Ben has everything and I have everything except the meat bit because it always looks dodgy and someone from the paper was sick for five days after he had one. But Ben has the digestion and constitution of an ox so he is never sick. We leave a Hansel and Gretel trail of salad in our wake and wander up the hill toward Clifton.

I decide I want a piggyback halfway up one of the hills, but can't manage to leap up on to Ben's back. God knows how someone as uncoordinated as myself has ever managed to go out with Ben for so long. After the third attempt, Ben runs up the hill carrying one leg while the other one drags behind us and I hang halfway between.

We fall, giggling madly, into bed.

"Now," says Ben, "I have an important issue I want the new crime correspondent to look into . . ."

I am awake very early on Saturday morning, and lie in bed wondering if something awful happened to me yesterday or whether I've just had a bad dream. Slowly it all comes filtering back and I remember that I have been given the police beat. In view of its reputation, I don't quite know how to feel about it. Leaving Ben sleeping, I slip out of bed in order to make some tea to quench my raging thirst. Yesterday's events are still weighing heavily on my mind half an hour later so I go back to the bedroom to see if Ben is awake and perhaps might want to talk about it.

He's not. I bounce around on the bed for a while, open and shut drawers and curtains and generally make a nuisance of myself. I then check again on Ben's slumber situation. He opens one eye and mumbles, "Holly, go away."

I wander back out to the hall and, in a pathetic bid for attention, pick up the phone. My finger hovers over the first digit of Lizzie's number. Remembering her reaction last time I called so early, I redirect my finger to a different number.

"Hi, it's me," I say as my mother answers.

"Who?"

"Me, Holly."

"Holly, Ho-l-ly." She plays with the name thoughtfully in an it's-familiar-but-I-just-can't-place-it kind of way. This is my mother's idea of humor and her not very subtle fashion of telling me that I haven't called for a couple of weeks. I impatiently prompt her, "Your daughter, Holly."

"Ohhhh, *that* Holly! How nice of you to call, darling!" Despite being on the other end of the telephone a couple of hundred miles away, I smile at the long, drawling, emphatic tones of someone more accustomed to the West End than the West Country. It's rather like talking to a demented Eliza Doolittle.

"What's the weather like with you?" I ask while eyeing the rivulets of water streaming down my windows.

"Ghastly, darling. Absolutely ghastly. All this terribly healthy sea air. I nearly gag every time I take a deep breath. I'm having to smoke twenty a day now just to make up for it. Can you imagine? TWENTY a day. It's going to drive me to an early grave." Despite her protestations and passionate soliloquies on London smog, I have a fancy that my mother actually enjoys the country-side, but of course she couldn't possibly admit to it.

"How's the play?" My mother has managed to persuade the entire cast of the latest play she is starring in to start rehearsals down in Cornwall. The director, a longtime friend, agreed only because it stops her causing chaos elsewhere. One of the problems of starting a new play is that she partly assumes the identity of whichever character she's playing. This time it's Lady Bracknell in *The Importance of Being Earnest*. The whole family breathed a collective sigh of relief when the last run of Daphne du Maurier's *My Cousin Rachel* ended.

"Your father came to the last rehearsal and one of the new actors asked him if he had any advice. He told him to say his lines and not fall over the furniture."

"Well, that's quite good advice."

"It is, isn't it? How's the delectable Ben?"

A silly smile comes over my face at the mere mention of him and I wind the telephone flex around my fingers.

"Oh, he's fine. Really good, in fact. He's still asleep at the moment. How are Dad and Morgan?" Morgan is my mother's Pekinese. He is absolutely ancient and only has two teeth left at the back of his mouth. This is very amusing when he tries to bite other dogs as he has to sort of suck them for a while first.

"He's a little flatulent." I sincerely hope she is talking about Morgan and not my father. "How's work?" she asks.

"You're talking to the new crime correspondent on the *Bristol Gazette*! It's a kind of promotion, I think!"

My mother gives a very suitable gasp of admiration and says, "That's wonderful!" I grin down the phone. One of the advantages of having an actress for a mother is that you always get a good reaction. "But what happened to the, er, Possum bloke? Didn't he have the police thing before you?"

"Pete. Although Possum would have been a better name for him. He got a job with the *Daily Mail*."

"Serves him right." Sometimes my mother's idea of a person's comeuppance doesn't quite tally with my own.

"Crime correspondent is not a great post."

"Darling, you can turn it around. I am sure you will do brilliantly. Shit MacGregor! Stop it, Morgan! OFF! Darling, I have to go. Morgan is on the table eating the Stilton."

The only way he would have got on to the table is when she put him there while she answered the phone. I say goodbye.

"Love to Lizzie!" she says and rings off.

three

On Monday I try to delay the inevitable by spending the best part of an hour tidying my in-tray, sending e-mails to friends and gassing with the people in accounts. I really ought to be making a move down to the police station to take up the mantle of my new position but I just can't face it yet.

I have been reflecting on my rapid shift in job direction over the weekend and from a positive viewpoint I suppose there will be no more pet funerals and maybe "Crime Correspondent on the *Bristol Gazette*" does sound quite good. Sexy, even. And I will be on more high-profile stuff which is obviously great.

With uncanny timing, Joe pops his head around the partitioning. He frowns.

"Holly, what are you still doing here? Have you got a death wish? You know a stationary stone gathers lots of stuff. Get. Down. To. The. Police station! There could have been ten robberies, kidnaps or arson attacks while you have been sitting here!"

I leap up, make lots of "I was just on my way" sorts of noises, gather a notepad and pencils, pick up my bag and set off. I feel like Maria out of *The Sound of Music* when Mother Superior sends her off to the Von Trapps for the first time. Perhaps a quick chorus of "My Favorite Things" will help.

Maybe not.

I rev Tristan up and we depart in a cloud of carbon monoxide. I have to say I am feeling nervous. I hate being the new kid on the block—not knowing your way around or who everyone is. Not knowing that the coffee machine always gives you soup instead of hot chocolate or never to talk to your boss after Arsenal have lost. Those little nuances of familiarity that make everyday life comfortable.

The police station is a large, ugly, concrete building on the edge of the city center. I haven't been in it before—well, that is to say on a professional basis. I have been in there on a nonprofessional basis. Lizzie and I were arrested once for taking a shortcut through someone's garden. It was the dead of night and we were staggering home from a nightclub. As we were scrambling down the other side of a large wall the owner of the garden had rather selfishly built, we were highlighted by a set of headlamps, duly arrested and carted off down here to the police station. A little harsh perhaps for what was, after all, just a spot of garden-hopping, but it turned out that the one we had been hopping through belonged to the local juvenile home and the police thought we were escaping reprobates. As soon as they realized their mistake, by checking with the appropriate authorities, we were rather hastily dusted down and thrown with great alacrity back out onto the streets. I could have done without the rather enlightening hour in the police cells beforehand though.

I'm not too sure what the procedure is (the professional police reporter procedure that is, not the common criminal one). Normally the last correspondent talks you through it but Smug Pete has already left, and in view of my relationship with him I think it would have been distinctly unwise anyway. He would probably have had me parking in the High Commissioner's parking space and giving everyone Freemason handshakes. I could just imagine him trying to convince me that comments from reporters are always welcome in a court of law, and if silence is called for when I start to speak it's just to make sure I can continue uninterrupted.

I think I will just have a chat with someone in the police PR department, be charming, play the "I'm new around here" card and maybe they'll give me a clue on what to do next.

As I enter the hallowed portals of the station there are a few people milling about in the reception area, but I head for the front desk and wait patiently for the desk sergeant to look up from his work. He doesn't. I can tell we're going to be good friends. He is dressed in uniform. A white shirt and black tie and one of those rather attractive navy blue fisherman-like jumpers.

Still without looking up, he snaps, "Yes?"

"Er, could you tell me where the PR department is please?"

"You are?" he barks, continuing with his work.

"Holly Colshannon, new crime correspondent for the *Bristol Gazette*." At this point I am nearly prostrate on the desk with my head in his lap in a bid to get him to make eye contact with me.

"ID please." I hand it over and at last he looks up to check the physical likeness to my mugshot.

He frowns as he stares down at the photo and then looks back up. I helpfully scrape my fringe forward, tilt my head to one side and pull a face.

"Now I see it," he snaps, dropping the ID card disdainfully back over the counter. As always when faced with disapproval, my mouth goes into overdrive.

"I know it doesn't look much like me, but you see, you'll laugh at this . . . well, maybe not . . . anyway, my paper had just won 'Local Newspaper of the Year' which of course caused a hell of a strop from the *Journal* and naturally I'd had one or maybe two drinkies and—"

He interrupts my rambling by barking, "Have you been here before?"

I jump. There is no way I am going to own up to the escaping juvenile debacle. Especially to him. My voice leaps up at least an octave with nerves and I stammer, "First time, actually, inside any police station. Not terribly jolly is it? I mean, a couple of pot plants here and there and perhaps a sofa with a few scatter cushions would soon—"

An acerbic voice behind me breaks my monologue.

"I really hate to interrupt your *Changing Rooms* appraisal, fascinating as it is, but . . ."

I turn around with a nervous apology hovering on my lips, only to find a pair of very familiar green eyes looking at me.

"Oh. It's you," he says in the same way Churchill would have greeted Himmler if they'd happened to meet while holidaying on the Riviera.

He had me there. "You're absolutely right. It is me."

"What do you want?"

"I happen to be the new crime correspondent!"

"Oh, wonderful. That's all we need."

He turns toward the desk sergeant, who almost becomes animated. Almost.

"Morning sir."

"Morning Dave. How are you? The wife and kids OK?"

"Fine, thank you, sir." Yuk! I think I'm going to be sick. The desk sergeant hands over some papers to him and Green Eyes moves away. He must be someone reasonably important as (a) he was called "sir" and (b) he is dressed in mufti. Terrific. I haven't even gained entrance to the building and I have managed to annoy someone I shouldn't have. I go back to the desk sergeant and say in a very small voice, "Could you tell me the way to the PR department please?"

He duly snaps out a couple of loose directions, buzzes me through the security door and I scamper away as fast as I can. My encounter with Green Eyes has unnerved me a little. What a complete boiled cabbage.

I scuttle up several flights of stairs and along some corridors. This place reminds me, not a little, of a school. Maybe it's the faintly dodgy smell of canteen food wafting from somewhere or the impersonal gray rooms. I can tell it's not going to be anything like the offices at the *Bristol Gazette*. No cozy gossips around the coffee machine or long boozy lunches.

The PR department is situated on the second floor and has nothing to distinguish it from any of the other wooden doors that line the corridor except for the smallest sign I have ever seen for a PR office. I knock and wait patiently. No answer, so I knock again and poke my head around the door.

"Hello?" There is no one visible in the room, so I say again, "Hello?"

I know I said there was no one in the room, but they could be hiding in a cupboard or something. And you know what? I'm going to hide in a cupboard as soon as I find myself a comfy one.

There are some muffled noises coming from underneath a desk and a woman pops up and triumphantly holds out her finger to me. She is drop dead, stuff-it-up-your-jumper glamorous. She is dressed in what looks to my distinctly unpracticed eye to be Versace, Chanel or something else with a many-zeroed price tag. Something you wouldn't want to be scrabbling under desks in anyway. She balances on six-inch heels. If I tried to wear shoes like that I would be in Casualty before you could say, "Holly, you don't look very stable." Her dark hair is scraped back off her face in a neat little chignon and her freshly manicured nails are painted a sassy red. Her makeup has an elegance that would take me hours to achieve. And maybe not even then. She looks hopelessly out of place among the shabby office furniture. Her outfit looks as if it cost more than the yearly department budget. My first thought is what on earth is someone like this, who should be running multi-million campaigns from a flashy London agency, doing heading up the PR department of a police station?

"There it is!" she exclaims. "Dropped one of my pills! I'm Robin! I'm the new head of PR. Well, relatively new anyway."

As I step forward, I glance down to her desk and try to catch the name on her pills. Not that I'm horribly nosy—it's just a reflex action, as automatic as a dentist checking out your teeth. "Holly Colshannon," I say, just managing to catch the word "Prozac" before having to look back up.

She gives me a firm, brisk handshake. "Delighted to meet you, Holly. I only came down from London a couple of months ago and I'm still getting used to everything so you'll have to show me the ropes a little."

"Er, actually, I'm new as well."

"Do you fancy a coffee?"

"You've found the canteen then?"

"Sweetie, it was my first port of call," she says, leading the way out of the room.

I think I have found the origin of that school dinner smell which determinedly hovers in the air. The canteen is in the basement of the building and seems to be run mainly by extras from *Prisoner Cell Block H*. Despite the less than salubrious surroundings, my eye is instantly drawn to a shiny new coffee machine which sits proudly on a stainless steel surface behind the counter. Coffee heaven.

"I'm afraid it's quite *basic* here," Robin whispers loudly as we make our way toward the counter. "When I first arrived they had no idea what a skinny latte was! It was as though I was talking double Dutch! I had to make a hell of a row to persuade them to buy a proper coffee machine!" I think "hell of a row" would be somewhat of an understatement looking at the mutinous faces before me. I fervently hope my coffee will arrive intact and without additions of spittle, razor blades or boiled cabbage water.

"We're a bit *stuck* on cappuccinos at the moment," Robin adds. "Whatever type of coffee you ask for, you always seem to get a cappuccino. I suspect it's the novelty factor for them."

I suspect it is a small mutiny against the formidable Robin.

We order and pay for two cappuccinos and walk slowly toward a small table at the back of the room, carefully balancing our cups of frothy coffee. We sit down.

"So," Robin says briskly, shaking down a sachet of sweetener, "which paper did you say you were from, Holly?"

"*Bristol Gazette*. It's the largest local paper."

She immediately looks wary. "I met your predecessor. What was his name?"

"Pete."

"Yes, that's him. Where's he gone?"

"He's left for another job. With the *Daily Mail*," I add.

She raises her eyebrows and her mouth forms an "oh."

"It's OK. You needn't be polite about him. We didn't get on."

She looks relieved. "Oh, good. I mean, he was just a bit . . ."

"Smug?"

"Yes. Smug." We both sip our coffee.

We chat about various things until I get around to asking the question I have been dying to ask since we met. I drop it casually, bang into the middle of the conversation.

"So, what brought you to Bristol?"

It might be my imagination but I am sure there is a sudden wariness in her eyes.

"I worked in London. In advertising," she says shortly. A-ha! "I just thought I needed a change."

"Quite a change. And to join the police department as well."

"Yes, it was."

We both nod our heads energetically for a bit. For the first time a small silence ensues and I know for whatever reason she doesn't want to talk about this. One of the major rules of reporting is to let silences run and never break them yourself, the theory being that people hate gaps in conversation and will very often say anything to fill them. But my annoying and boring sense of fair play asserts itself. I am not interviewing Robin for the paper, I am just being nosy about her life. I decide not to further compound her discomfort and say, "It was a bit of a shock to find out I'd been given the police beat."

"Why?"

"Well, it's not been, that is to say, historically speaking, the best post in the world."

I go on to explain about the past situation and what a terrible job crime correspondent is supposed to be. She frowns into her coffee and says slowly, "Well, we're just going to have to do something about it, aren't we?"

"I don't really know what can be done because it has been like that for as long as I can remember. Once there was this guy, Rob, who inherited the beat and he actually hid in the back of one of the patrol cars. I mean, he only wanted to see a crime scene first-hand. But you should have heard the *fuss* . . ."

While I am speaking, I am busy scooping the froth off my coffee and sucking it from the spoon. At this not very attractive point in my existence, Green Eyes marches into the canteen holding a pile of paperwork. I have only just managed to extract the spoon from my esophagus and close my mouth by the time he has nodded at Robin and situated himself at the other end of the room. Robin sits there, staring at him.

"Robin?"

She looks at me distractedly. "You've given me an idea. We could turn this whole thing around, Holly. We could. Imagine what it would do for us! You could have your own column and I could go back to London in a trail of glory sooner than I ever dreamed!"

You can tell Robin works in PR, can't you? And why does she want to go back to London in a trail of glory? But I am anxious to hear any advice about my rapidly submerging career at this point and her obvious enthusiasm is a little infectious.

"What? What is it?"

"Good-looking isn't he?" She is staring over at Green Eyes.

"Er, yes, yes, he is. What is this idea?"

"Very boy-next-door."

I take another look at Green Eyes. What sort of boys did she live next door to? I don't know about you but I always got spotty skateboarders obsessed with Adam Ant, certainly no resemblance to this beauty. Not that I would have liked him living next door to me, especially after savoring the delights of his lashing tongue. God knows what he would have said about my legwarmer phase.

Robin swiftly starts to gather up her stuff. "Come on, I'll show you the ropes and then I'll talk to the Chief about my idea."

Back in the PR office, she shows me the report basket where all the press releases detailing crimes committed get placed for the reporters. We simply come up here and help ourselves to a copy. She absolutely refuses to say anything more about this idea of hers, except for winking and asking if I will be back tomorrow, and after a while I give up my line of questioning altogether. I gather three press releases from the basket and make my way back to the car park and Tristan.

Back at the paper's offices, I peruse the reports. Not terribly exciting; one act of car vandalism by students (now I am not a student myself I take enormous delight in raising my eyes heavenwards, tutting and saying, "Students, tsk, would you believe it?"), one joy-rider and one bank-note scam. Picking the most interesting of the lot, the bank-note one in case you're wondering, I start to make a few phone calls. It gets interesting and, before you know it, it's half-past five when I file copy. Maybe crime correspondent is going to work out OK. I take great care to be polite to the detective on the case even though he makes it clear I am bothering him, and I don't make one disheartening reference to the police in my report. Robin's positive attitude is catching. Maybe I,

Holly Colshannon, can turn this around. Maybe I can make them like me.

We're back to *The Sound of Music* again, aren't we? Carrots.

Lizzie is coming over tonight. We usually spend Monday nights together as a sort of a solace. A tribute to the start of the working week. We have a bottle of wine, maybe some ice cream. Sometimes we watch a video, sometimes we just talk. Ben is normally at rugby practice on Monday nights and Alastair is always working (but that's not just Monday nights).

Lizzie is fine after the condom incident. In fact, we both had pretty much forgotten about it by the next morning, although one tub of Ben & Jerry's ice cream and numerous videos on Thursday evening did help. There was still no sign of Alastair over the entire weekend although Lizzie did claim he had been called away to an important meeting in London. It does make me wonder how serious he is about her. I am completely prejudiced though because who wouldn't want to be with Lizzie? It is a mystery to me why he spends so much time working and lets her loose in my debauched company. She is mad about him and I am hoping this is just a natural cooling-off of the relationship on his side, which always happens after the initial can't-keep-my-hands-off-you phase.

As I buzz Lizzie in, I swing my head around the front door of my flat and wait for her to climb the stairs. She appears a couple of seconds later, grasping a bottle of wine in one hand and two Kinder eggs in the other. Her long dark hair hangs in a gleaming sheet on to her shoulders and her D-cup breasts jig about as she jogs up on her long, gazelle-like legs to the top step. Lizzie has an extra cup size on me which I would be very glad of, but she complains about it a lot. Do you know the test where you're supposed to be able to clasp a pencil underneath your breasts? Well, Lizzie grumbles that she can not only clasp several pencils but also a ruler, a protractor and a large eraser too.

"Hello!" She gives me an exuberant kiss on the cheek. "How are you?"

"Fine, how are you? Feeling OK now? Did Alastair get back on Sunday?"

She nods. I have only met Alastair a couple of times, which is a little strange in itself, but he is working so much he doesn't see Lizzie very often, let alone me. He is good-looking in a studious kind of way and wears a pair of those very trendy wire glasses.

"Have I said how sorry I am about that?"

I grin. "Yes. I believe you have mentioned it. But I'll let you say it one more time if you want to. I like the way it rolls off your tongue."

"Sorry."

I take the wine off her and lead the way into the lounge. She flops down on one of the sofas while I go through to the kitchen for glasses and the corkscrew.

She shouts through, "How was your first day?"

I reappear and start to open the wine. "OK, apart from the fact that the first person I met down at the police station was that police officer from the hospital."

"The really nasty one?"

"Yep!"

"Did he recognize you?"

"Immediately, but the new head of PR was nice so at least the day wasn't terrible."

I splosh the wine into the glasses and Lizzie and I happily take a slurp.

"So, did you see Alastair at work?" I ask.

Lizzie works with computers. Hmmm, yes, very bright. But then she says she doesn't understand them either, she just bandies a few well-heeled words like "bytes" and "hard drive" around and no one seems to notice she is more at home in French Connection than a computer software company. Alastair was senior to her when she started there. She ignored him for months, presuming he was just the usual spoddy geek who ends up working in a computer company. But then they started to work together on a project and she said there was something about him that made her start to fancy him. And not just fancy him but *really* fancy him.

"Oh, boring. Alastair didn't speak to me once all day, he was in a stuffy old distributor meeting for most of it. God, what a difference from the start of our relationship! Do you remember it, Hol? He used to drag me into stationery cupboards. Now he only just manages to drag himself away from work."

I do remember it well. I practically lived it with her. They finally got it together one night when they were working late. I personally breathed a huge sigh of relief as the tension had been unbearable (lots of hot steamy looks over the photocopier) and I wasn't sure whether it was going to be like one of those novels where nothing turns out quite how you want it. For example, *The English Patient*. Couldn't she have survived the plane crash and just been camped out in the cave waiting for him when he got back? Like an Arab version of a Girl Guide, with her yashmak out on the line and humming "Kum Ba Yah"? Anyway, I digress. Things between Lizzie and Alastair have definitely not stayed as they started out.

Lizzie continues. "So I went into town at lunchtime to console myself and guess who I met?"

"Who?"

"Bloody Teresa! And wouldn't you believe it—she took one look at my shopping bags and proceeded to tell me about how Jesus Christ gave the shirt off his back for his neighbor and would I do the same thing."

"No!"

"And I know it's blasphemous but I told her obviously JC didn't have Jigsaw in his time and I was *sure* he would understand that my new little crossover top was very hard to come by and I wouldn't like to part with it. I know it was awful of me but I simply couldn't resist it."

I laugh at this which is probably blasphemous by default, but then, according to Teresa, Lizzie and I blew our chances with Him a long time ago. About the same time we discovered boys and alcohol.

At school, Teresa was the most pious teenager you could ever meet. She never wore makeup or discussed clothes or wolf-whistled at boys. She read the Bible in break times and ran the local Christian Youth Group. She always dressed perfectly. Absolutely pristine. Even now she is the perfect M&S woman, complete with a little gold crucifix. Her hair is a dark, glossy chestnut, softly wavy and cut into a bob. She is actually a very pretty girl, but absolutely ruins any effect she could have with her very sour, squashed lemon facial expression. I don't think her holiness is a result of some entirely natural I-just-love-the-world-and-everyone-in-it viewpoint because, believe me, she is an ab-solute grade A bitch. There is some other, more complicated psyche at work which I can't even begin to fathom. Once, at school, she spread this really vicious rumor that I had been caught shag-ging my amour-du-jour, Matt, on a snooker table! Considering my only up-close-and-personal incidents with Matt at this stage in our relationship had usually taken place in a bus shelter with at least three layers of clothing between us, this was indeed a spec-tacular accusation. Especially since at that age I didn't have enough confidence to play snooker on a snooker table, let alone shag on one. Not very Christian of Teresa in my opinion.

Lizzie sploshes some more wine into our glasses and curls her feet up under her.

"So, what terrible fate has befallen Buntam lately?"

four

———

A t work the next morning, I receive a message to call Robin urgently. I am connected to her extension by another charming member of the Bristol Constabulary.

She answers.

"Robin, it's Holly Colshannon from the *Bristol Gazette*. We met yesterday."

"Holly! I was just about to call you! Stop the press! Have I got news for you!"

"Have you?" I blink in surprise.

She is jabbering madly like a demented typewriter. "It just came to me! It is a PR opportunity to die for! I don't know why I didn't think of it before! This is the one, Holly! It took a hell of a lot to persuade them, but they have actually agreed to do it. It's only for six weeks though."

"Who are they? What have they agreed?"

Robin leaves a dramatic pause and then says, really slowly, "I. Have. Got. You. Assigned. To. A. Detective!"

She breathes heavily down the phone, presumably waiting for the applause to come. The problem is Miss Thickie here doesn't quite understand. I frown to myself.

"To a detective? How do you mean?"

"Hol-ly," she says impatiently. "Instead of using the usual channels—you know, I write up the PR releases, hand them over and then you report on them for the paper, usual stuff, blah,

blah—you can actually go out with a detective and then write up the experiences yourself!"

"Like a sort of diary?"

"Yes, yes, a sort of diary. You can accompany the detective all day and tell your readers firsthand how it feels. Everywhere he goes, you go. A fly-on-the-wall documentary."

It's brilliant. Simply brilliant. And I, Holly Colshannon, get to do it. It's my big break and it's all I can do not to get up and dance a jig around my desk.

"Robin! You're wonderful!" I breathe down the receiver. Steve from accounts gives me a strange look as he passes my desk.

"Darling, I *know*. There are obviously some rules which will accompany it though."

"Why me? Why not the guy from the *Journal* or a freelance?"

"Well, you are from the region's largest paper. Besides which, we women should stick together."

Hurray for the sisterhood! I bombard her with questions.

"When can I start?"

"Immediately." I blink. This is quick, even by our standards.

"Do I need to meet the Chief?"

"Of course!"

"When?"

"This afternoon."

"Can I write about everything I see?"

"Yes, except confidential case details, certain parts of police procedure and the identities of anyone involved in a case. We will need you and the *Gazette* to sign various confidentiality agreements and indemnities."

"What do the police get out of it?"

"The best PR boost this region has ever seen. You have to write favorably, another part of the agreement."

The big question then occurs to me. "Who am I going to be assigned to?"

"You remember the man in the canteen yesterday?"

"Green Eyes? The boy next door?"

"Yep! Him! You're assigned to him!"

My little cloud of euphoria bursts with a small PHUT! because, although I do not know Green Eyes, my one brush with him tells me that he won't like this. Not one little bit. But I don't want to appear ungrateful to Robin and presumably this could still be given to someone else if I object too strongly. On the other hand, being on the receiving end of his sarcastic comments for over a month isn't looking too attractive. I say in a small voice, "Why him?"

"Well, he's getting married next month. You've got six weeks and an immediate start. We thought it would give some sort of finite timescale to the diary since this is experimental. Also, it's likely that he won't be assigned to any dangerous cases from now on so nothing bad can happen to him before his big day. The Chief thought we could keep an eye on you both at the same time. So you see, he is the obvious choice." Yeah, right. Obvious.

After lunch I have to go to the police department as that is when the Chief is breaking the news to Green Eyes. That is Robin's turn of phrase, by the way, and not mine. "Breaking the news." That's what you do with news people don't want to hear. Hmm, doesn't bode well for a good reception by Green Eyes. He has a name, too. It's Detective Sergeant James Sabine.

I barge into Joe's office. He is, surprise, suprise, on the phone and frowns heavily at this breach of etiquette. I need to tell him that he has to call the Chief immediately to discuss the finer points of the agreement. He puts down the phone and before he can even say, "Here's your P45" or "How's Buntam?" I jump in with both feet, negating the need for such piffling chitchat.

Joe is thrilled. In his excitable state, he mixes his metaphors more than ever, telling me gleefully that "This will knock the

Journal's crime page into a hen cap." He gets on the phone straightaway to the Chief. After about twenty minutes of discussion and a promise from Joe to send a signed copy of the faxed agreement back with me this afternoon, he whisks me out for a celebratory lunch (merrily chortling about the *Journal*'s reaction all the way) on a nearby canal barge called The Glass Boat. Truth be told, the slight swaying motion of this restaurant always makes me feel sick, but it is a favorite in the office so I unfortunately come here a lot. This time, however, I firmly keep any thoughts of vomit out of my mind and order the second most expensive thing on the menu, not caring if Joe thinks I'm a lunch tart. While we wait, I manically munch on a bread stick, eyes focused firmly on the shoreline over Joe's shoulder like a hypnotized hamster. Joe doesn't seem to notice though.

"This is good stuff, Holly. Really good stuff. How did you persuade them to let you do it, by the way?"

At this point I manage to drag my eyes back to his and give a modest shrug of the shoulders. Well, he doesn't need to know, does he? And besides, if he did know it was Robin's idea and not mine, he might be tempted to try and put someone with more experience in my place. "Contacts, contacts," I murmur airily.

"So much for the *Journal*'s guy on the inside!" Joe claps his hands together. "This is really going to upset them! Just think how it will look for us! Exclusivity and a person from our paper actually with the police while they work! You know, Holly, I really didn't think you could turn this around. I thought we'd never get ahead of the *Journal* on this score. They've been edging up the ratings ever since their new crime correspondent started!"

"Well, we should be the first ones on the story now!"

"The Chief tells me a detective normally has quite a few cases on his hands at once, so only pick a couple out and make sure they're ones that look likely to be solved within the six-week period, OK?"

"OK," I mumble, looking doubtful. How the hell am I supposed to know whether a case can be solved or not?

"We'll print your diary every day. The first episode won't start until next week, which will give you a chance to get used to everything and write a really good introduction in the meantime. And we'll need a title. A really catchy title. How about 'The Real Dick Tracy's Diary'? Yes, yes, I think I like that. 'The Real Dick Tracy's Diary.' It has a kind of ring to it. We'll trail it for the rest of this week. File the introduction by Thursday, first installment by Friday."

The Real Dick Tracy's Diary.

Detective Sergeant James Sabine isn't going to like this. Not one little bit.

It's just past two o'clock by the time I get back to the police station. The same place in the car park is free and I maneuver Tristan into it. The very same desk sergeant as yesterday is on duty and I give him a cheery wave and a resounding "Hello!" on my way up to the PR department. He looks at me and glares. Making progress, definitely making progress there. I get to the PR office in double-quick time and for some reason my heart is running overtime. I have no idea what I am so nervous about.

Robin looks as though she has been waiting for me; her eyes are shining and there is an unmistakable air of fidgety excitement. She is wearing a different but equally stunning outfit from yesterday and her hair is now loose, which calls for a frantic amount of head-tossing. Without saying a word she grabs my arm, takes me down the hallway and then into a set of open-plan offices that I have never seen before. It is an eruption of activity. There are people zooming all over the place. Files are piled high on every desk, people are yelling into phones. The air buzzes with animation. No one is in uniform which is rather unexpected in a police station. They are all dressed in shirts and ties and there is a surprising lack of women around. The odd one stands out like a nun in a nightclub. At the end of the room there is a small square of partitioning with frosted glass windows. Presumably the Chief's office. As a stranger (and a woman) I invite a few curious stares as we cross the room to it. Robin knocks on the door, and in the brief moment that we wait to enter she whispers, "The Chief wanted to know all about you so I'm afraid I had to fill in some gaps." Before I can ask her exactly which gaps, we are bidden to come in. Green Eyes, or James as I had better now call him, is pacing up and down. Call it my developed sense of intuition but I think the news has been broken to him. He stops pacing as soon as we come in and glares at us. Even the sassy Robin seems to shrink a little under his Medusa-like scowl.

The Chief stands up from behind his desk with a jovial smile as we enter. He is obviously a PR man at heart. He reminds me of a benevolent bank manager (not that I have met many of those in my time, it's just how I think they ought to look). He is a large man with a mustache and a spreading waistline. He says heartily: "Aah! Here they are now!"

He walks round from his side of the desk and pumps my hand.

"You must be Holly!"

"Er, yes. Nice to meet you."

"We're so pleased to have you on board! Robin tells us she knows you from the London circuit and I have been hearing all about your journalistic adventures! She says you're used to ground-breaking assignments! Say, you must tell me sometime about being undercover in Beirut. That sounds quite something!"

"Hmm. Yes. I must," I say in a voice that doesn't actually sound like mine at all. I haven't been to Brighton, let alone Beirut. I manage to shoot a look at Robin, who smiles brazenly at me with a warning look in her eye. I have a feeling she usually gets what she wants.

"This is Detective Sergeant James Sabine. James, meet your new shadow!"

James grimaces. "We have met," he says through gritted teeth, but nevertheless he steps toward me and, with pursed lips that I presume are supposed to pass for a smile and without meeting my eyes, shakes my proffered hand. Hell, he damn near throttles it. I try not to wince.

"Holly, I have arranged for a desk to be cleared for you up here so that you can write your stories while James writes up his paperwork," the Chief continues. "That's something you'll have to learn about! The huge amount of paperwork these officers have to deal with! But I expect you found out all about patience on the Arctic expedition!"

The closest I have been to an Arctic Expedition is getting an Arctic Roll out of the freezer. An expedition of sorts, I suppose.

"I'm sure I'll have a lot to learn!" I say in a conciliatory manner, anything to get us off the subject of expeditions and anything else from my fictional career.

"Do you have the signed agreement from your editor?"

I fish into my bag for the faxed wad of papers that the *Gazette*'s lawyer had been poring over at lunchtime. Joe's hasty signature is at the bottom of the last page and I bend over the desk to add my own next to his. As I do so, I feel James Sabine's eyes boring into my back. I shift uncomfortably. As I straighten up and hand over the agreement, the Chief says, "Good! Why don't you two go and grab a coffee in the canteen and get to know each another a bit better? I need to finalize a few things with Robin here." And with this, my new buddy and I are thrust out of the office.

James Sabine sets off down the corridor at breakneck speed. I walk behind with an uncomfortable view of his tense, broad back clad in a tweed jacket. He strides along while I perform some sort of comical half-run in an effort to keep up. His legs seem to be twice as long as mine.

I arrive back at the canteen—my second visit in twenty-four hours. The inmates eye me suspiciously. James doesn't say a single word to me as we order our coffees; he won't even look at me. He gets his cup first and whooshes off to one of the tables and so I trot behind with mine. I timidly sit down opposite him, feeling like a little girl anxiously seeking for approval from a parent. He speaks without looking up.

"Well, you must be pleased with yourself. Managing to persuade Robin and the Chief this is a good idea."

I gulp. Golly, do we have to get straight into the boxing ring without gloves on? Can't we limber up a little first, with a few verbal stretching exercises? A bit of "the weather's been rather inclement lately"?

"Well, I realize this may be a bit of an inconvenience for you but . . ."

"A bit of an inconvenience? Having to wet-nurse some opportunistic reporter who's anxious to cut her teeth on me? No, no. It's not an inconvenience at all. IT'S A BLOODY MAJOR PISS-TAKE, THAT'S WHAT IT IS!" This last bit is shouted at about two million decibels and pretty much brings the canteen to a standstill. People stare and I slip down in my seat but James Sabine doesn't take his piercing green, serpent eyes from my red, cringing face. "Don't you think I have enough to do without having to hump you around with me as well?"

I bristle at this, especially at the use of the word "hump." It implies weight issues.

I try again. "But James . . ."

"It's Detective Sergeant Sabine to you," he growls.

"Detective Sergeant Sabine. It's a major PR opportunity. Imagine what it will do for the reputation of the local force."

"You mean our reputation will be gutter level, the same as the press', by the time you've finished with it?"

I suspect he doesn't like the press very much. I am tempted to ask him if he has had some sort of bad childhood experience with reporters. Perhaps one took his mint humbugs away from him or something. "No, I mean that it will create good PR. It will show people what wonderful work you do here."

"I am sure the criminals of Bristol will sleep safer in their beds knowing you will be on the scene." And he gets up with such force that his chair falls over backward, and then he strides off. Ignoring the chair, I get up and scurry after him because, to be honest, I'm getting annoyed now. If he thinks he can bully me, he can forget it. I have got my chance of a lifetime, one that might land me my dream career, and there is no way that he or anyone else is going to mess it up. Watch out James Sabine, you have a bona fide shadow for the next six weeks.

I follow him back into the office. As he wends his way through the maze of desks, I can see that the rest of his colleagues are finding all this extremely amusing. Every single one either grins or winks at him as he passes them by. The fact that he seems to be in a filthy mood delights them even more. I avoid eye contact with any of them, anxious not to exacerbate the situation. He sits down at his desk. The one opposite to him has been cleared, presumably for me, so I sit down there. I say, in a really low voice so the rest of the department can't hear, "Listen. I am really sorry you feel this way. I can assure you that I will do the best PR job I can."

He looks extremely cynical at this.

"Have you asked if someone else in the department can take me on?" I add hopefully.

"It was my first question."

"And what did they say?"

"What do you think? Why don't *you* ask if someone else will take you on?"

"Oh no. I only get one chance at this and if you're it, I'll have you."

"Well, don't expect an easy ride," he snarls.

I continue regardless. "We are stuck with each other for the next six weeks. If it would make you feel happier, why don't you lay down a few rules?"

We sit in silence for a few seconds as he considers this. Then he says slowly, "OK, rule one. You are not to interfere in any of my work. I do not want to hear a peep out of you. You are here to observe only."

"Understood." I make a zipping motion with my hand over my mouth. His eyes flicker.

Warming up, he starts to speak more quickly. "Rule number two. You consult me if you want to use any detail of my cases in your newspaper. Do you hear me? Any detail whatsoever. You could ruin an entire case by giving out information. And rule three"—he leans over his desk—"you will do the best PR job you have ever done, Ms. Colshannon."

"I fully intend to."

"Fine."

"Fine."

There is a pause. I add, "Good. Well, I think we understand each other. I am due to start tomorrow morning. What time do you come in?"

"Eight o'clock sharp."

"I will see you then, Detective Sergeant Sabine."

And with that I get up and a great cheer breaks out from the rest of the department. I can't help but smile and nod as I make my way through the throng. In fact, it almost completely restores my humor. I may never get on with James Sabine but I can tell that I'm going to like the rest of the department.

five

"So what is he like, this Detective Sergeant Sabine?"

I'm on the phone to Lizzie. I take another huge slug of my vodka and lemonade, sit cross-legged on the floor, lean my head back against the wall and settle down.

"What do you mean? I've told you what he's like. Mean, moody . . ."

"No. What does he look like?"

"Look like?"

"Yes Holly," says Lizzie patiently, "look like. Any warts? A squint? Buck teeth? You know, HIS APPEARANCE."

"Didn't you see him down at the hospital?"

"Well, yes," she admits, "but only the back of his head."

"Oh! Oh." I shrug to myself. "Well, I suppose he's quite average-looking. You know, boy-next-door." I use Robin's phrase.

"Boy-next-door? You mean he looks like Warren Mitchell? YUK! How gross! How . . ."

Lizzie and I have had much the same experience of boys-next-door. Not very talented. In fact, couldn't shake a bum cheek at a Levi's ad between them.

"No, Lizzie. Not literally. Not Warren Mitchell."

"Then who?"

"He's just nice-looking. Well, we know he's not NICE, but he's nice-looking. Green eyes. Dark blond hair. Tall. Well-built. Usual stuff, usual stuff."

Now it's not like me to describe a good-looking man and then say, "Usual stuff, usual stuff" afterward. But James Sabine really isn't making me very enthusiastic. You see, a man's personality matters a lot to me. He needs to be amusing without being too sarcastic. Detective Sergeant Sabine has certainly failed on that score as he is just plain sarcastic. He needs to be warm and friendly. Again, nil points. And kind. I like kindness best. And is it kind to be unpleasant to a girl on her first day on the job? NO, IT IS NOT.

"He sounds quite nice to me," says Lizzie dreamily.

"He isn't nice. He makes me feel about ten years old and he really doesn't want me around," I grumble.

"He must be quite fit, being a police officer."

"Where's Alastair tonight?" I say pointedly.

"In Scotland for some meeting."

"How is he?"

"I think he's fine. I haven't really seen him since the weekend."

Lizzie and I say our respective goodbyes and I put the phone down. I quickly turn my thoughts to weightier issues. What is a reporter on her new assignment shadowing a detective supposed to wear? What would Cagney and Lacey wear? No, too eighties. I think a touch of glamour may be needed. I put on some Aretha Franklin to inspire me, and clasping a new refill, I toddle through to my bedroom, fling open the doors of my wardrobe and survey the contents. Hmmm. I start emptying the clothes on to my bed in search of that elusive *je ne sais quoi*. Eventually I settle on a pair of black suede trousers, a little lilac jumper and a pair of high black boots. Which, to be honest, are the first items I took out.

". . . no, I am sure cream will be fine . . . chocolate ink? What's that? . . . Oh. OK, it sounds nice . . . no, it does. Look. I have to go . . . that reporter's here . . . what? Cream ink on chocolate? Are we talking about the same thing? I'm sure whatever you choose will be fine. I really have to go."

James Sabine has been on the phone since I arrived, the latest call presumably with his fiancée. Or at least I hope it is. It is a conversation I have unashamedly been trying to listen in on; it's enlightening to hear Detective Sergeant Sabine being pleasant for a change.

I have surprised myself this morning. With the assistance of a radio, two alarms and a wake-up call from the talking clock I have made it down to the police station for eight A.M. Rather like a kid at a new school, I have pilfered the contents of the generous stationery cupboard at the *Gazette* and armed myself with new notepads, pencils and several blank tapes for my Dictaphone. I have to say I wondered briefly whether to sew my name into my pants.

I have been putting my time to good use while James Sabine has been on the phone by making friends with the rest of the department. Or rather I have been made friends with. No effort has been required on my part. Various bods have just come up to me and introduced themselves. All rather jolly. And they seem to be really nice. Why I have got stuck with the Mr. Grumpy out of all the Mr. Men available I will never know.

I am happily swiveling in my swivel chair while James Sabine continues his phone conversation when a backside parks itself on my desk and a voice says, "Hi, I'm Callum. You must be Holly." He grins cheekily at me.

I grin back at him. Sometimes there is just something about people that makes you know you are going to like them. And I am going to like Callum.

"You know my name?" I say in surprise.

"The whole department has been talking about nothing else. It's caused quite a stir! The Chief and Robin have given us all a long lecture about this project." He looks extremely grave.

"What about him? I don't think they lectured him."

"Don't mind James." He gestures with his head toward James Sabine. "He's just being a grouchy bugger." I grin widely at this.

"It's because he's getting married next month," Callum says cheerfully and draws his finger across his throat, just as a ball of paper hits him squarely on the back of the head. "Which newspaper do you work for?"

"The *Gazette*."

Callum lowers his voice to an exaggerated whisper and leans toward me. "He doesn't really like reporters, you know."

I lean forward and whisper back, "I know. Any suggestions?"

"Get on the nearest plane with me to Greece?"

I eye James Sabine. "Tempting, but unfortunately not possible."

"Oh well, I'll ask you again in a week's time. You'll probably jump at the chance." He gets up and says, "Have a good day, Holly, see you later."

As soon as James puts the phone down he gets up.

"Come on, we have to go. There's been a drug theft at the local hospital."

Oooooh. My first piece of action. Detective Sergeant Sabine is already walking off as I scramble after him.

We descend into the bowels of the building. Well, I say "we." James Sabine is marching a good ten steps ahead of me and I'm scrabbling after him like a disabled spider. Pesky black boots. Just as I think we're going to the canteen again in some bizarre quirk of fate, we take a quick left and emerge into what is an underground car park. James marches over to a little booth, claims some keys off the man inside and then walks over to a discreet gray saloon car. He has already started the engine and fastened his seatbelt as I climb into the passenger side.

"You're going to have to move faster than that, Ms. Colshannon, if you don't want to miss anything. I will have no hesitation in leaving without you."

"I wasn't aware I was missing anything and it's Miss Colshannon. I am not ashamed to be single," I reply haughtily.

He raises his eyebrows and says, "Ah," in a tone that suggests my statement explains it all. I hunch my shoulders huffily, furious with myself for walking straight into that one. "May I suggest a more appropriate form of footwear?" he says, looking at my beautiful, to-die-for but admittedly high black boots.

"I will make a point of digging out my trainers as soon as I get through my door this evening," I say through gritted teeth.

The car emerges from the subterranean car park and into bright sunshine. I give Tristan a mournful look as we pass him in his space on the way out.

I look determinedly out of the window until it occurs to me that that's exactly what the marrow wants. So I get out my notebook, clear my throat pointedly, try to ensure my tone is at least civil and ask, "So, what do detectives do? I mean specifically."

"Anything, from rape to burglary to murder. Anything that needs detecting, as opposed to something uniform can take care of."

"Uniform?"

"Yeah, the boys in blue, Miss Colshannon. As opposed to this." He points down to his trousers. He is wearing a pair of beige chinos. My eyes rove up and take in the Ralph Lauren shirt and subtle tie. I quickly start writing his last comment down in my notepad lest he think I'm looking at him. "So, how long have you been in the police force, Detective Sergeant?"

"Nine years."

"Did you join from school?"

"University."

"Which one?"

"Durham." I stop scribbling and raise my eyebrows in surprise. He glances over at me. "Does that astonish you, Miss Colshannon? That I'm qualified? Or were you expecting me just to have a GCSE in woodwork?"

"Well, if you had, you might have been able to chisel that chip off your shoulder," I reply acidly. He's starting to rattle my cage.

"Touché," he murmurs. The rest of the journey is completed in silence.

As soon as we enter the doors of the hospital, the strong, familiar smell of disinfectant assaults us. I wrinkle my nose as cringe-making memories of the condom incident last week hit me. I look around me warily, hoping not to be recognized, and then give myself a shake as logic asserts itself. They must see hundreds of people here every day, so it's not likely they'll remember me. I follow James Sabine more confidently up to the front desk. He flashes his ID at the lady on reception.

"I'm here to investigate the thefts." The lady picks up a phone, speaks to someone briefly and then replaces the receiver.

"You'll need to speak to Dr. Kirkpatrick. He is in the Munroe wing, ask at the desk there." And with these words we are instantly dismissed as she turns her attention back to the magazine lying open in front of her.

I freeze. Dr. Kirkpatrick? DR. KIRKPATRICK? Oh no. This cannot be happening to me. James Sabine strides off at a break-neck pace, throwing doors open as he makes his way relentlessly toward the Munroe wing. I am lagging behind in an attempt to give my brain time to think. He shouts over his shoulder, "Keep up!"

On the way there I consider the various options open to me, including getting lost, catching chicken pox between the reception and the Munroe wing and various other extreme case scenarios. The problem with all of them is that I really need to be present at my first case, otherwise James Sabine will think he's got the better of me somehow.

Right. Only one thing I can do and that is brazen this out.

We reach the Munroe wing in Olympic record time and James Sabine asks for Dr. Kirkpatrick. The great man himself appears and there is much ceremonious hand-shaking as Detective Sergeant Sabine introduces himself. I surreptitiously scrape some hair over my face and wonder if I could squeeze between the bin and the vending machine. James Sabine then turns to me and says, "This is Miss Holly Colshannon. She is here for *observation only*." He says this to Dr. Kirkpatrick but the emphasis is really directed at me as a reminder of rule number one. As if I could forget. Dr. Kirkpatrick is staring at me.

"My word! There's a name I can't get away from! They should give you your own parking space!" Oh bum. This is going to be worse than I thought. Many curses upon his pedantic memory. I look through several strands of hair and smile weakly. Detective Sergeant Sabine has his eyebrows raised so high I think they're going to pop off the top of his head.

"Ha, ha! Hello again," I say in a pathetically weak voice.

"You were here last week, weren't you? Interesting, er, scenario." Now they are both staring at me.

"Yes, yes, I was," I say, maniacally twiddling my hair around my finger and going bright red. Goodness, do we have to spend so much time on the subject? Surely there are more important things to chat about? The Euro? Global warming? Third World debt?

"How's your friend? Is she OK now?"

"Yes, fine, thank you. Never better." For a rash moment I consider shouting, "Quick! Look over there!" and then making a run for it, but I uncomfortably hold my ground.

"You'll laugh about that in years to come!" Really? I think we'll probably smile awkwardly and change the subject. But I say in an unnaturally high voice, "Yes! I'm sure we will." Now James Sabine's mouth is almost open. To indicate my part in the conversation is over, I take out my notebook, open it up, lick my pencil (which I have never, ever done before) and wait. They still stare and finally the penny drops that I'm so terribly sorry, boys, but this particular freak show is now most definitely over. The detective manages to drag his eyes, which are out on stalks, away from me and turns back toward the fair physician. I think he's almost forgotten what we came for.

"Er, right," he says dazedly. "Er, where were we? So, Doctor. Could you tell us a bit more about the thefts?"

And we're off! At quite a pace too. It's James Sabine's turn to get a notepad out. Firstly the doctor shows us the cupboard where the drugs were taken from. We ascertain there is no sign of forced entry. James says, "I take it this cupboard is usually locked?"

"Absolutely. We're very strict about it. There are only four key-holders on this wing, myself included."

"What exactly was taken?"

The doctor reels off a list of ten ten-syllable drugs. Detective Sergeant Sabine does a better job than yours truly of getting them all down. He asks, "Do they have any street value?"

"Some of them, not all of them."

"Do you or does anyone else remember when the cupboard was last locked?"

"Well, all of the other key-holders were in there yesterday but we didn't discover the drugs were missing until first thing this morning."

"How often is the cupboard used? Say, on a busy day like yesterday?"

"About once every hour; sometimes more, sometimes less."

"Did you see anyone suspicious?"

"I didn't, but you'll have to ask the rest of the staff on the ward if they did."

"So, one of the key-holders could have accidentally left the cupboard unlocked and the thief just slipped in. Do you trust all your staff, Doctor?"

"Implicitly."

"So you don't think they took the drugs themselves or that the cupboard might have been left open deliberately?"

"Definitely not."

"I'll send uniform down to interview the key-holders and maybe have a general ask around the ward and the rest of the hospital too, to see if anyone has seen anything suspicious."

As I've stopped taking notes, it gives me time to observe the fine doctor. He's distractedly running his hand through his short dark hair. I find myself thinking that I wish it was my hair. I give myself a little shake; I am shocked at the lengths my pornographic imagination will go to. But he's nice, I think dreamily. Really nice. A voice breaks into my thoughts.

"Miss Colshannon? Hello?"

I'm jolted out of my rather delicious deliberations. I look at James Sabine. "Hmm?"

"We're leaving."

"Oh. Right." I hastily gather my bag and stand up, blushing guiltily. My poor blood seems to have had rather a lot of exercise recently.

"I'll see you out," says Dr. Kirkpatrick.

The two men make their way through the double doors and the doctor drops back to join me.

"So, you work with the police?"

"No, I'm a reporter actually. I am shadowing the detective here for a six-week diary for my paper."

"I haven't seen that before."

"No, it's a new thing—today's my first day."

"For which paper?"

"*Bristol Gazette*."

"I'll look out for it." We walk on in silence and my brain scouts desperately around for a topic of conversation. The seconds tick by. Eventually I say, "So, you're a doctor?" Nice one, Holly. Conversational hari-kiri.

"So they tell me." He smiles and his eyes go wrinkly. He must smile a lot. I search for another topic and gratefully seize on one I unearth from the back of my mind.

"Do you have to work long hours?"

"Yeah, I'm overworked and underpaid. Still, I get to meet nice people." His eyes twinkle at me and my heart misses a beat. In the midst of all this emotional turmoil I nearly trip over a wheelchair and several pairs of crutches someone has left at the side of the corridor.

When we reach the main entrance of the hospital, Dr. Kirkpatrick shakes Detective Sergeant Sabine's hand first and then mine. "It was nice to meet you, Holly. Again. I mean on a non-professional basis."

James Sabine and I walk toward the car.

"So last week wasn't just a one-off, I take it?" he asks.

"I'm in there more than most. I'm just accident-prone." I grin inanely, buoyed up by Dr. Kirkpatrick.

"Terrific," he mutters.

We zoom away from the hospital and I ask, "So, what do you think?"

"I'll send uniform down to question the staff. They might have been involved. And I want to see your copy before it goes into the paper. I don't want you cocking this inquiry up."

"You've already made that perfectly clear."

"Well, you know reporters. However often you say something, they always think they hear something else."

We stop for coffee en route to the police station. James Sabine goes into a café to get a takeaway, after grudgingly asking me if I would like one. I sit in the car and wait for him but the radio is talking to me. It keeps on talking to me. Is this like a sub-section of rule one (that's where I'm not allowed to talk to anyone)? On the other hand, he might be cross if we miss something.

It's still talking to me.

I tentatively press a button and say, "Hello?"

"Is that unit seventeen?" it says fuzzily.

"Er, maybe."

"You're the reporter, right?" There are big pauses between each reply.

"That's me!"

"Where's unit seventeen?"

"Er, gone for coffee."

"Tell unit seventeen there has been a code five at eleven Hanbury Road."

"Yep, will do, er, ten-four," I say, lapsing into TV crime-show speak.

My first radio call! I am so excited! James Sabine gets back into the car and hands me a steaming and welcome cup of coffee. I take it from him and say, "We've just had a call on the radio!"

"We have not had a call, *I* have had a call, and what are you doing answering the radio? What was rule number one again? Don't. Talk. To. Anyone. And what the hell were they doing talking to you over the radio? It's supposed to be classified!"

I think I will wait until he has had some caffeine before I say anything more. I sip my coffee and stare determinedly out of the window. I can feel him looking at me.

"Well? What did they want?" he asks impatiently. I quell my childish urge to ask what the magic word is.

"They said there was a code eleven at five Hanbury Road."

"A code eleven? Oh shit! Drop the coffee! Drop it! Out of the window!"

Our first call! Oh my God! We're on our way, the siren is blaring, we're ducking and diving in and out of traffic. Whoaaa! We just took out a traffic cone! This is fantastic! People are moving to one side as we . . . A tiny thought filters through my consciousness. Do you think that was . . . ? I flip my brain back to the ride

but the feeling of discomfort persists until the thought finally surfaces. It wasn't code eleven, was it? Do you think the number bit
is important? Do I tell him now? I say, in a really, really small
voice, quite hoping he won't hear me, "Er, Detective Sergeant
Sabine? It wasn't code eleven. It was code five."

"WHAT?!"

I'm in the queue at McDonald's to order some more coffee. He
was pretty annoyed. I might have to introduce him to the fruit
and veg swearing system. He practically had a whole guide dog
going there.

six

———

O ne of the smaller prerequisites of the arrangement between the Chief and my paper is that I keep Robin completely abreast of all the diary's developments. So with this in
mind, I drop by her office at lunchtime. We walk down the now-
familiar route to the canteen together to collect a sandwich.

"Can I have a tuna, no mayonnaise, on focaccia with rocket
leaves please?" she snaps out to the lady behind the counter, fixing
her with a stare that you could slice a ten-inch piece of steel with.
"What would you like, Holly?" Robin asks.

"Just a tuna sandwich, thanks. However it comes."

We sit down at one of the Formica tables and await our sandwiches. While we wait, Robin asks, "So, how has your first day
gone?"

"OK." I tell her about the radio incident and she laughs.

"It'll get better. He'll grow on you." Yeah, right. Like fungus.

I talk her through some of the ideas I've had for the diary.

"That sounds great, Holly! Just remember our part of the bar-
gain. Keep the good stuff rolling and we'll both be out of here before you can say . . ." She stops mid-flow and glances over at me,
aware she might have said too much. Just at that moment the canteen lady brings our sandwiches and so I pretend not to have
noticed.

The lady plonks two plates with identical squares of Mother's
Pride and tuna mayo in front of us. She goes off without a word.
Robin looks defeated in the face of such mutiny.

"Oh, to be back in London," she murmurs, looking down at her rocket-less, mayonnaised-to-within-an-inch-of-its-life, un-focaccia sandwich.

Again I have to wonder why she bothered leaving London if she is so anxious to go back there?

I walk back to the solace of my desk half an hour later. Callum waves as I wander past in a dream. I wave distractedly back. He's talking on the phone with his feet up on his desk and simultaneously eating a banana.

I settle down to write the introductory piece for the diary. I am desperately trying to think of an angle. Should it be serious and insightful? Or written with a touch of humor? What do people really want to read about? I chew my pencil thoughtfully and do a couple of spins in the chair just to get the old gray matter working.

People want to read about people. So this diary is going to be an absolutely honest account of my six weeks with James Sabine, right down to the sarcasm. As I know he's not particularly keen on the whole affair, I will change his name. To Jack. (Jack is one of my mother's cats at home. He is particularly vicious.) But you know what? I'm going to keep everything else the same. Warts, and in my opinion there are many, and all. The problem is going to be extracting enough personal details from Detective Sergeant Sabine for the readers to get to know him.

I stare thoughtfully ahead of me. Opposite, James Sabine is cradling the phone between his ear and his shoulder and simultaneously trying to get into a cellophane-wrapped sandwich. He pauses now and then to talk passionately and gesticulate with one hand. Eventually, frustrated by the sandwich manufacturer's determined efforts at preservation, he reaches into his drawer, flicks open a pen knife and viciously stabs the sandwich to death. I smile to myself and re-focus on the computer screen. The man is really in need of a holiday.

I work for a couple of hours on the introduction to the diary while Detective Sergeant Sabine slaves over paperwork and phone calls. At one point he gets up. Petrified he is trying to give me the slip, I ask, "Where are you going?"

He fixes me with a stare. I belatedly remember the fate of the sandwich and wince. "I'm going to the men's room. Would you like to come? Take some notes perhaps?"

"No, no. Thought you might be going out," I murmur with embarrassment. My blood tirelessly makes another trip skyward.

"Unfortunately, Miss Colshannon, as much as I dislike the fact, I have been told by our revered Chief that I am not allowed to go anywhere, except perhaps the bathroom, without you. So, believe me, when the time comes for me to go anywhere you will be the first to know."

"Glad to hear it," I mutter, staring at my computer screen.

"Why does he dislike me so much?" I ask Callum as he drops by my desk a few minutes later to ask if I want a cup of tea from the vending machine.

"Don't take it personally."

"I think it's meant personally."

"No, it's not. I told you before, he doesn't like reporters very much."

"Why?"

"The past always comes back to haunt us," he says mysteriously. "Sugar?"

The introduction to the diary reads:

Day by day. Blow by blow. You're right there on the front line with our correspondent, Holly Colshannon. The Real Dick Tracy's Diary. Starts Monday . . .

I stare thoughtfully at the words and, after tinkering a while longer, close down the application, attach it to an e-mail to Joe and send it over to the paper.

I have arranged to meet Lizzie and Ben after work at the Square Bar. So once James Sabine and I have exchanged curt goodbyes, Tristan and I make our way up Park Street and, after a quick scout around, negotiate a rather tight parking space.

The Square Bar is a chic little place set in the basement of a house in one of the old squares of Bristol. I like the old squares; they remind me of bygone times when the Regency gentlefolk raced their barouches and partook of the waters at Bath.

They filmed *The House of Elliot* in this very square. Yep, this very square. I know because I accidentally walked straight through the set one day. The cameras were rolling, children dressed in Edwardian clothes were playing with hoops, a carriage was waiting outside one of the houses and I didn't see any of it. I strolled straight through and the irate director yelled, "CUT," which did wake me quite suddenly out of my daydream.

I walk down the steps to the bar and peer in. Lizzie is thankfully already *in situ*, in possession of two bar stools and fighting off the throngs from her precious commodities.

I battle my way over to her, plant a kiss on her cheek, dump my bag at her feet and clamber awkwardly onto the bar stool. Sensing my need, she wordlessly passes me her drink and I take a couple of grateful gulps.

"How is the crime business?" she asks.

"Not good."

As a matter of priority, she gestures to the barman and orders another couple of drinks. She turns back to me. "I take it that things aren't much better with Morse?"

"Well, I don't think they could get much worse."

"What happened?"

I rant and rave about James Sabine's sarcasm, the radio incident, and then, working backward to this morning, tell her about being called to the hospital for a drug theft. "And you'll never guess who I met there?"

Lizzie grins, thoroughly enjoying the whole account of the day.

"The doctor from last week. Ha, ha!"

The smile from her face fades as I raise my eyebrows at her. "You're not serious?"

"Unfortunately, yes. He was the doctor we had to interview about the thefts. It was so embarrassing," I say, taking another sip of vodka and lemon.

"What was his name again?"

"Dr. Kirkpatrick."

"God. I thought you were going to say Teresa the Holy Cow!"

A voice interrupts us. "Hello Holly, hello Lizzie. My! What a surprise to find you two in a bar!"

It's Teresa the Holy Cow. Rhubarb.

We both say hello in very small voices because she's taken us aback a bit and probably overheard the Holy Cow thing as well.

"So, what have you two been up to?" she asks.

Lizzie replies acidly, "We're here celebrating *actually*. Holly has just got an exciting new assignment."

"How wonderful," says Teresa, her lips scarcely moving and, needless to say, certainly not smiling.

"Yes, it is."

"Doing what?"

"Breaking new ground, expanding horizons, ripping up blueprints, you know the sort of thing."

"Don't overdo it, Lizzie," I murmur out of the corner of my mouth. She is getting a bit heated on the subject, bless her.

"Yes. The newspaper is launching her new diary on Monday. You should look out for it," she continues.

I kick Lizzie sharply on the ankle because, frankly, this is more information than Teresa needs to know. And, as we have learned from bitter lessons in the past, the less information Teresa has the better. Lizzie winces but luckily Teresa doesn't notice as she turns to me.

"How brave of you, Holly, to do something so different. And in today's climate. I really hope it works for you." Yeah. Right.

"What are you doing here, Teresa?" I ask pointedly.

"I'm here with the Bible Society. We're also celebrating so we've come down for a quick spritzer before the meeting. We've just had two new members join. It's so gratifying when a person sees the error of their ways. Sees their superficial lifestyle for what it is. Full of boys, alcohol and soap operas. Pathetic really."

Just at this point Ben walks in, spots us at the bar and struggles across the crowded room. A grateful smile comes over my face. He has impeccable timing. He is looking, as usual, absolutely gorgeous. He smiles lazily as he smooths his floppy blond hair back with one hand. He gives Lizzie and me a quick kiss on the cheek and then turns to Teresa.

"I'm sorry, we haven't been introduced. I'm Ben." The thaw in Teresa is sick-making. She practically throws herself at his feet like a fawning puppy welcoming its owner home. A big smile comes over her frosty face and it is surprising to see how pretty she would be if only she did it more often. Ben always has this effect on people.

"Teresa. Teresa Fothersby. I am a friend of Holly and Lizzie's from school," she says, eagerly holding out her hand.

Lizzie takes another swig of her drink and womanfully murmurs under her breath, "She bloody well isn't."

"Can I get you a drink, Teresa? I was just getting one for myself."

"Thank you, Ben. That would be lovely."

After ascertaining whether Lizzie and I need refills, he sidles into a space a few feet away from us at the packed bar and Teresa follows him. Lizzie and I both raise our eyes at each other. I unashamedly watch their every move.

He's telling her something and she's laughing and has her hand on his arm. My top lip curls up in an unattractive snarl. What has happened to good old Christian values, eh Teresa? No sex before marriage and all that. I express this view to Lizzie.

"She's just showing us that she could do it if she wanted to," Lizzie says. "You know, telling us that she can get a man any time she chooses. Besides, she *is* wearing white ankle socks, for goodness sake!"

"Well, Ben isn't exactly fighting her off, is he? He's not swatting her arm as though it's a petulant wasp, IS HE?"

This has pissed me off, because not only does Teresa think she can get a man if she chooses to, she thinks she can get *my* man.

"Don't look at them! She knows you're looking over and she's playing up even more. Talk to me. So did Dr. Kirkpatrick recognize you?"

"Almost immediately," I say gloomily, dragging my eyes back to Lizzie. "He's so nice though. If it wasn't for Casanova over there I'd be seriously tempted to have some more accidents."

Ben rejoins us, carrying a pint.

"Are you both all right? That Teresa is a nice girl, isn't she?"

For a second I glare at him, then catch Lizzie's eye and smile. Men are so unperceptive, aren't they?

"Has she gone?"

"A couple of people she was meeting came in. Some sort of society thing. So how was your first day?"

I hesitate for a second and then say, "Fine," and smile at him. I might tell him later about James Sabine, but for the moment I've got my griping about the good policeman out of my system. Besides, I always find men singularly unhelpful when talking about such things. They always end up saying stuff like, "Do you want me to sort him out?"

Ben gets distracted by some work friends and goes over for a chat. Lizzie and I are left alone again.

"Are you all right?" I ask. "You seem a bit low." She's been a little subdued all evening. Her smile isn't quite reaching her eyes.

She bobs her head up and down without directly looking at me and sips her drink. "Yeah, fine."

"Are you sure?"

"Well, it's just that . . ." She shrugs a little.

"What?"

"I don't know. Alastair is a bit distracted and although I understand he has to work, I'm upset he wasn't around at the weekend after the hospital thing."

I reach over and pat her hand. "I'm sorry. I'm sure he would have been there if he could have been."

"And someone has just got engaged at work today. She seemed so happy. It sort of brought it home how distant Alastair and I have been lately. Sorry, I didn't mean to bring this up."

"It's OK." I look concernedly at her, wondering what to say.

"I'm worried he's gone off me and just doesn't know how to finish it, so he's hiding behind work. It was so wonderful at the start. I don't know how to get it back."

"I don't think he's hiding behind work. He probably genuinely is under pressure and it's making him distant." I'm not quite sure I believe this myself.

"Well, if he does want to finish it, I wish he would get on and do it."

"Poor darling. But I don't think you should just sit back and wait for it to happen. Why don't you be the proactive one?" I pat her hand again as she looks miserably into her drink.

"Yeah, you're probably right. I'll think about it. Aren't you and Ben going to that pizza place tonight?"

"We are. Why don't you come too?"

"That's kind of you but I'd be miserable company. Besides, you and Ben should spend time together. I'm going to have a hot bath and go to bed early."

"OK," I say, a bit loath to leave her. For a minute I'm tempted to tell Ben to cancel the restaurant. I look over at him. Probably feeling my look, he glances up himself and taps his watch. I nod and get up.

"Are you sure you'll be all right?" I ask Lizzie doubtfully.

"I'll be fine. Go on. You and Ben have a nice evening."

The three of us walk out into the relative quiet and cool of the evening and say our respective goodbyes. I give Lizzie a hug and tell her I'll speak to her tomorrow. She walks across the square to her car and Ben and I turn and walk, hand in hand, down to our restaurant.

seven

I arise somewhat groggily from my pit on Friday morning. From the mound of wet towels on the bathroom floor I conclude that Ben has already left for his early morning meeting.

I take care with my appearance as opposed to my usual method of grabbing the first thing to hand. This is a sort of psychological armor against the barbs of James Sabine.

I wend my way down to the police station, only stopping en route for a fruit smoothie in lieu of breakfast. This is a pathetic attempt on my part to feel better. After two days at the mercy of Detective Sergeant Sabine's tongue, I feel my self-esteem to be limping a bit. The emotional effect of having a fruit smoothie for breakfast makes me feel decidedly supermodel-esque.

I park in my usual spot at the station, successfully exit from Tristan and breathe in the early morning air. The sun bounces off the top few windows of the building and the air has a sweet, fresh tang.

"Morning!" I say brightly to Dave-the-grumpy-git-desk-sergeant. He at least makes eye contact and, with a curt nod, buzzes me through the security doors.

I pop my head around the door to the PR office and exchange morning pleasantries with Robin. Once up in the detectives' office, I make my way toward my desk. The room is half empty as some of the officers are on later shifts. Callum is already in state and greets me with a blaring, "Morning! How are you? You're looking downcast. Not the puckish young thing we've come to know over the last few days. Not been dreaming of the harsh Detective Sergeant Sabine have you?"

I grin at him, lean over his desk and whisper, "No, far, far worse than that. I dreamt I was being dragged by wild horses backward through bushes, while a Jamaican played Abba hits on his mouth organ *and* Detective Sergeant Sabine was giving me a verbal tongue-lashing."

He grins widely and murmurs, "Now there's a vivid image. It must have been getting noisy. You weren't in a bikini as well, by any chance? You know, in the dream?"

I straighten up. "No, definitely not. Dressed as a nun, if I remember correctly."

"Oh well. Can't have everything."

I smile to myself as I move on between the desks and arrive at my own. Callum reminds me of a rather boisterous Labrador and has the undoubted capacity to cheer me up. James Sabine is seated opposite. He is on the phone and gives me a nod as I sit down. The realization that I will have to deal with him today crashes my good humor as quickly as Callum has sparked it. I physically straighten up in my chair. I will have to be aloof and yet civil. Carry myself with aplomb.

I turn my thoughts to today's installment. I really hope there will be something juicy to write about, something to get my teeth into, as whatever happens today has to be written up for the first edition of The Real Dick Tracy's Diary and I have to file copy tonight. A dramatic raid perhaps, or a high-speed car chase at the very least. I suppose I could always kick off with the first day's local hospital drug thefts. I look across to the man himself, to the imaginary Jack—he has put the phone down and is shuffling some papers about and I wonder what he has planned for today. An arrest would start the first installment nicely.

"Are you arresting anyone today, Detective Sergeant Sabine? Anyone at all?" I inquire politely.

He fixes me with a stare. "Well, I don't know. I'll just have to check my diary. I could arrest you if you want." He gets up. "Come on, there's been a burglary in the Clifton area."

"Great!" I enthuse as I leap up.

"Miss Colshannon. I hate to be the one to tell you this, but burglaries aren't good things. Truly, they're not."

I try to assume an appropriate air of sympathy and concern.

"No, no, of course not," I murmur, picking up my bag and following him out of the room, trying to suppress the urge to execute gazelle-like leaps of joy.

Hurrah! A burglary. Never have I been so overjoyed at Bristol's soaring crime rate. Not a high-speed car chase perhaps but good enough. My mind is racing as we set off toward the car park. Let's hope it'll turn into a series. If it does, I could give them a name! Something catchy. I really hope he'll let me publish some interesting details. A thought occurs to me and I accelerate in an effort to catch him up.

"Er, Detective Sergeant Sabine!" I call.

"What?" he shouts back over his shoulder.

"Do you, like, er, say anything when you arrest someone?"

He stops suddenly. A little too suddenly. I cannon into the back of him like a cartoon character.

"Oooff. Sorry. You stopped."

He turns round and fixes me with those eyes.

"What do you mean, do I say anything? I read them their rights of course."

"No, I mean, do you say anything yourself to them? Anything at all?" I ask anxiously.

"Like what? Advice?"

"Well, yes, or anything else?"

"What exactly are you getting at?"

"I was just thinking that it would be really nice if you had a sort of, er, saying. Well, not you exactly, but the character in my diary . . ."

"A *what*?" This is said in a low voice that has the merest smidgen of danger lurking in it. Even I can see he's not too thrilled with the idea.

"You know, a saying. A catchphrase. Like Dirty Harry." He is looking hard at me but I valiantly soldier on, albeit in a distinctly smaller voice. " 'Go ahead, punk, make my day'?"

"You are absolutely unbelievable." He strides off again.

"That's the idea! Something like that. But I was thinking of something just a li-tt-le bit more threatening . . ." I shout after his disappearing back.

I arrive at the car park a few minutes after him, panting a little. I spot him in a far corner talking to a uniformed officer and frowning. He turns toward me as I approach.

"Do you have a car?"

"Yes, why?"

"No pool cars left, they were all scrambled this morning for an incident in town. Can we use yours?"

"Emm . . ." I hesitate. It's not that I mind going in my car, it's just that Tristan isn't renowned for his reliability and I haven't checked him for any compromising evidence. No girl wants to get caught with twenty empty crisp packets in her car.

"It's in your interest that we get there too. We either take yours or wait for a pool car to come back and I don't know when . . ."

That does the trick. I need to get to this burglary. Tristan will be fine, it's motorways that really upset him.

"No problem!" I say lightly. I lead the way to Tristan.

I try my best to climb elegantly into him. No easy feat. I get my bum in all right but quite a commotion with the rest of my limbs ensues. My right leg manages to get twisted around my left one, then sort of gets stuck underneath the bottom lip of the car and refuses to make the extra distance actually inside the vehicle.

"Won't be a minute!" I shout out, making a rather unattractive panting noise while frantically tugging on my errant leg.

"What did you say?" He comes round to my side of the car.

"I said that I won't be a minute."

I fervently wish he would return to the passenger side of the car where he belongs. I really do not need an audience. "What are you doing?" he asks dubiously, watching me.

"I am trying to get into the car," I reply haughtily, still tugging frantically.

"Really?" he says disbelievingly.

I grit my teeth and manage to squeeze a few words out. "Detective Sergeant Sabine. If you—" Just as I say this, I make an almighty effort to free the troublesome limb and suddenly—THWACK!—my knee hits me squarely between the eyes.

"Christ!" he exclaims, squatting beside me. "Are you OK?" His mouth twitches slightly.

I rub the spot and wonder how I could possibly have managed to hit myself in the face with another part of my body. "Yes, fine," I mutter mutinously.

"You, er, hit yourself in the face. With your *knee*." There is a definite emphasis on the word "knee" and it is accompanied by more face twitching.

More muttering. "I know. It's not terribly easy to get into this car, Detective. Why don't you try?"

He bounds around to the other side and simply hops in with the dexterity of an Olympic gymnast.

"Beginners' luck," I snap. Steady, Holly, steady. Was that acting "with aplomb"? Cool, even?

There is a pause while we both put our seat belts on. I would really like to give my head another rub but have no wish to bring attention to it.

"I can see why you're in Casualty so much," he remarks lightly.

I don't deign to reply.

"How is it now?" he asks, not trying very hard to disguise the fact that he is laughing.

"Fine, thank you," I manage to spit out. I truly hope it wasn't a hard enough blow to leave a bruise, which would only serve to give me and James Sabine a lasting reminder of this incident. I grasp the wheel in a rather hard, uncompromising, Tristan-don't-give-me-any-shit kind of way, put him in first gear and we whoosh off. For the first time since we got into the car I take a look around to see what state it's in.

"Gosh!" I say, looking down at his feet which are actually invisible among the piles of rubbish. Diet Coke cans, empty crisp packets and sweet wrappers seem to spill out of every corner. "Sorry, I haven't got round to cleaning it out." I bend over to try and unearth his shoes by sweeping all the rubbish to one side.

"S'OK. WATCH THAT . . . !" I look up hastily to find that the curb has rather unkindly leapt out at me. I swerve.

"It's fine. Honestly," he says tensely, sitting very taut in his seat. "You just drive."

I concentrate studiously on driving for the next minute. And breathing deeply. I knew that those many hours watching the Green Goddess from the comfort of my sofa would come in useful. In . . . out, in . . . out, in . . . out. See? Easy. Didn't need to take up Pilates to know how to do that. Eventually I regain enough control to ask, "Where are we going?" He duly gives me directions to an address near the Clifton Suspension Bridge.

As I negotiate a difficult one-way system, James Sabine looks around the car.

"Does this contraption break down very often?"

I visibly bristle. We're like two knights waging war and he's just spotted an almighty hole in my armor. I rise to the bait admirably.

"Tristan is not a contraption!"

"Tristan?" he repeats gravely, with just a hint of derision and a raised eyebrow.

Damn. I never tell strangers my car has a name. It's so naff. "He was called that when I bought him," I bluster.

"You *bought* this?"

"He happens to be an extremely valuable vintage car!" All right, only half of that is true. And it's not the valuable bit.

"They're only valuable if they actually work, Miss Colshannon," he says, picking up the RAC card from the dashboard where I leave it so it's always handy. He waves it at me to illustrate his point. Damn his little detecting skills.

I swiftly change the subject by snapping, "So, why are you being called out to this? Surely detectives don't normally investigate plain old burglaries?"

"The uniformed officer at the scene seems to think this one is a specialist. So he has called me in." He gets out a notebook from his jacket pocket and studies it. After a few minutes of silence, I try to fish for some personal details and ask, "So, how does your future wife feel about your job?"

"None of your business," he says without looking up.

"How about your family? Do they worry about you?"

"None of your business. Turn here." He points and we pull up to our address. I snap on the handbrake. "Will you always stay on active duty?"

He looks over at me. "Well . . ." he says hesitantly. I fish into my bag for my notepad. "The Chief said something interesting to me the other day." I poise my pen. Goody! A quote! "Do you want me to write it down for you?" he offers politely.

He takes the pad from me, writes a sentence and then gets out of the car, dropping the pad on the seat as he goes. It says: "CU-RIOSITY KILLED THE CRIME CORRESPONDENT."

I sigh to myself. This is going to be harder than I thought.

Minutes later we crunch up a path to the given address. It is an impressive Georgian house and I'm not surprised it's been burgled. If I were a burglar then this would be my first port of call. The path is carefully graveled and the lawn is attentively manicured. Not a blade of grass out of place. There are steps up to the smart navy door and on each step a topiary tree stands to attention. James Sabine pulls the bell. We wait for a few moments and then the door is answered by a butler. Both Detective Sergeant Sabine and I almost jump back off the step in surprise. I didn't know anyone had butlers anymore.

"Yeeesss?"

James Sabine flips up his ID. "I'm Detective Sergeant Sabine and this is Holly Colshannon. She is with me for observation *only*." Point taken. Again.

We follow the butler into the house and as James Sabine walks ahead of me I notice something rather colorful is stuck to his ass. I peer closer and my suspicions are confirmed. Yes, it is the wrapper of a strawberry-flavored chewy sweet and I think I can probably guess how it got there. I wince. Do I leave it for everyone to see? Or do I casually drop it into conversation? "By the way, Detective, a sweet wrapper seems to be attached to your behind . . ." Or do I even have a go at removing it myself? A fairly easy decision to make. Leave it there.

We are shown into a large, chintzy drawing room, complete with requisite grand piano. The tall windows, so typical of the Regency houses of Bristol, are draped with vast lengths of material. A uniformed officer is already sitting down, a notepad in one hand, cup and saucer in the other. He stands as we enter the room. Another man, sitting opposite him, also rises.

"Good morning, sir."

"Morning Matt." James Sabine turns to the stranger and out-stretches a hand.

"Good morning, sir. I'm Detective Sergeant James Sabine and this is Holly Colshannon. She is here for observation *only*." Blimey. How many times is he going to say it? Message received loud and clear.

"Sebastian Forquar-White. How do you do?" says the stranger in the plummiest voice I have ever heard. I mean, where do these people get their accents from? Really? He is dressed in a tweed suit. His slightly protruding stomach stretches the buttons of his waistcoat and his jowls flap around his paisley bow tie. He has an enormous, flamboyant, handlebar mustache.

James Sabine and he shake hands and then Sebastian turns to me and shakes mine as well. I murmur a gracious, "How do you do?" James glares at me.

"Really, the whole thing is most distressing. Most distressing indeed. Some of the items had been in the family for centuries. Do sit down. Would you like some tea?" Jowls flapping in agitation, Sebastian Forquar-Whatsit looks from Detective Sergeant Sabine to me.

"Yes, please."

"I'd love some!" I respond enthusiastically. James Sabine throws a death wish in my direction.

Sebastian Whatshisgob exits from the sitting room, loudly yelling, "Anton! More tea!" Anton presumably and hopefully is the butler. James Sabine immediately goes into a rugby-like hud-dle with Matt and starts talking in low, urgent tones. I switch seats, get out my notebook and put a serious ear to the ground (not literally) in an effort to overhear their conversation. I catch various words, including "time," "entry" and "interview," but nothing even vaguely resembling a sentence. They finally break apart and I jump in posthaste.

"What's so interesting about this burglary then?" I ask.

Detective Sergeant Sabine looks distractedly over at me. "It's just so . . ." I wait with bated breath and pen poised because this is going to be the opening episode of my diary and I really, really hope it's going to be good.

". . . organized."

Organized? *Organized?* He's making it sound like an outing of the Bristol Male Voice Choir. And I should hope they were organized; they're professional criminals, for pity's sake. This is hardly a scoop. I can see the headline now: THEY WERE OR-GANIZED! What does that mean? That they remembered to bring all their tools? I try not to sound disappointed as I look from one officer to the other.

"What do you mean? Organized?" But James Sabine is al-ready writing in his notepad and ignores me. Matt, probably feeling a smidgen of contrition for his superior officer's attitude, steps in.

He asks, "May I, sir?", looking at Detective Sergeant Sabine, who glances up and nods his consent before switching his atten-tion back to his notes. Matt turns to me.

"Truth be told that I've never seen anything like it. The bur-glar knew exactly how to disable the alarm system. And it was a really sophisticated one too, as you can imagine. He then knew the exact place to enter the house. The interior was scarcely dis-turbed; it was almost as though he understood precisely what he wanted to take and where to find it. And he only took the best stuff—bypassed the video and stereo and went straight for the jugular."

"And what was that?" I ask, on the edge of my seat.

"Antiques."

"Antiques?" I say disbelievingly.

Matt nods emphatically. "Antiques."

"Antiques?" I say again.

"For God's sake!" explodes James Sabine, his head whipping up from his notebook, "which syllable don't you get?" I glare at him and then return my gaze to Matt and raise my eyebrows encouragingly, unwilling to say the a-word again. Matt, thankfully, responds.

"Things like porcelain, silver, clocks and other knickknacks. All extremely valuable according to Mr. Forquar-White."

"So, the thief knew all about antiques?" I ask disbelievingly.

"It doesn't take a genius to come to that conclusion," James Sabine interjects wearily.

I am desperate to ask about the implications of this but am interrupted by Sebastian Forquar-White coming back into the room, followed by a loaded tea tray carried by Anton the butler.

"Sorry I was so long, had to take a phone call. The insurance people rang me back." He sits down on the opposite sofa. James Sabine, after thanking Anton for his cup of tea, turns to him. "When did you first notice anything was missing?"

"Anton, here, went into the dining room, where all of the collectibles are kept, to dust this morning. He immediately told me and I raised the alarm."

"When did you last see any of the missing items?" Detective Sergeant Sabine looks at Anton.

"Yesterday, sir."

"Were you woken in the night by anything?"

Both of them shake their heads.

"Is the alarm system always activated when you go to bed?"

"Always," growls Sebastian F-W.

"Have you seen anyone suspicious hanging around?"

"No."

"I'll dispatch uniform to question the neighbors, if that's all right with you, sir." Mr. Forquar-White nods his agreement to this. "Can we see the point of entry please?"

"Certainly, certainly," he responds. We all replace our empty tea cups on the tray and get up to follow him out of the room. Detective Sergeant Sabine goes first and Matt and I follow. After a few seconds, Matt taps James on the shoulder.

"Sir?"

"Yes Matt?"

"You seem to have something stuck to your, er, trousers."

Detective Sergeant Sabine puts out an exploratory hand and soon enough it emerges with the sweet wrapper. He places it in his pocket. I take an inordinate amount of interest in the hall furnishings.

"Thank you, Matt." His face is impassive and his steely eyes flicker toward me. We go through into an enormous kitchen and Sebastian Forquar-White opens up a door at the back of the room. It is a sort of larder.

"They got in here." He points to a really small window up in the corner. "The catch was forced. Bloody typical, you know, because the insurance company only told me last week to repair it. Always the way, isn't it?"

"Yes," says James Sabine thoughtfully, "yes, it is." He looks up at the window for a minute and then asks, "Has anything been touched while you waited for us?"

"No, no, nothing."

"Good. Matt, can you radio for the forensics officers to come down please, and get uniform on to the neighbors?"

Matt departs on his errand.

"Isn't that window quite small for anyone to get inside?" I ask.

"Well, maybe a small person got through it, Miss Colshannon," Detective Sergeant Sabine remarks acidly, not looking up from the notebook he's studying.

We go back into the kitchen and then out another door into the garden. Mr. Forquar-White gestures toward the burglar alarm which has been placed in a bucket of water. We go back to the sitting room and wait for the forensics team to arrive. James Sabine asks more questions. When forensics eventually turn up, he goes out to meet them. As an afterthought, he turns back to me. "Don't touch anything. And don't get in the way."

"Yes, sir," I reply, standing to attention and giving a mock salute. Possibly a tad cheeky, but really, he's winding me up like a clockwork toy.

The three forensics officers get changed into jumpsuits in the hallway and James Sabine briefs them on the burglary. I stand and watch, hoping for a chance to chat to one of them. I am banned from going into the dining room (I might contaminate the scene of the crime) so my chance doesn't come until lunchtime when they come clattering out having finished the job. I immediately dump the Marmite sandwich that Anton has kindly made me and leap on the nearest one. He is in his late fifties. Out of a thatch of thick gray hair peeps a pair of sparkling eyes. After the formal introductions (he is called Roger) I ask him if he has found anything.

"Sorry, love. Can't tell you that, only the officer in charge."

"Yes or no?" I ask pleadingly.

He grins at me. "Yes, but you'll have to ask him."

I look around and spot James Sabine speaking to an officer a few feet away.

"Detective Sergeant Sabine?" I call. He looks around.

"What?"

"Can Roger tell me about the forensic evidence?"

He hesitates for a second, probably weighing up the Chief's reaction if he refuses versus his own complete reluctance to tell me anything.

"OK. But if you print any of it, I'll wring your neck."

I turn back to Roger, beaming.

Roger begins, "Well, we found some fibers. They could pretty much be from anything—clothes, car seats, any sort of fabric really—and nigh on impossible to pin down to something particular. We also found a hair which can be submitted for DNA testing. Unfortunately that takes quite a long time to come back from the lab, but the positive thing is we can put the DNA information through the computer and if the culprit has a record then the computer will produce a name. Otherwise we can take the DNA from a suspect and link them to the scene. We also found a substance around the cabinet where the missing items were kept, but I don't know what it is. It may have been on the gloves that the burglar was using as it was also found around the window catch at the point of entry."

"How do you find all these things?"

"We run a sort of fluorescent light over the crime scene and various fibers, fluids and substances show up. This particular substance is peculiar because it is very localized."

"How do you mean?"

"Well, there isn't any anywhere else around the crime scene. Just on the window catch, the door handle into the dining room and on the cabinet itself. So the thief knew exactly where to go and exactly what he wanted to take. The other items in the cabinet haven't even been handled."

"And you don't know what this substance is?"

Roger sighs. "I've never seen it before."

I watch him as he clambers awkwardly out of his jumpsuit.

"So, you're the reporter, eh?" he inquires.

"That's right."

"How are you getting on?" He jerks his head toward James Sabine, who is in a conference with another officer a few meters away. I make a face and Roger laughs heartily. The other officers turn around and look at us.

Roger leans toward me and says in a whisper, "It'll get better, give it time."

"We've only got six weeks, Roger, not infinity."

After I have said goodbye to Roger and taken my empty plate back to Anton in the kitchen, I go in search of James Sabine. I find him in the sitting room, pursuing what sounds like a highly pressing and important phone call on his mobile about his ushers. I idly wonder what his wife-to-be is like and what sort of relationship they have.

"Are you ready to go?" he asks after ending his call. I nod and together we go through to say goodbye to Sebastian (him) and Anton (me).

"So," I say conversationally as we draw away from the house, "do you think you'll catch him?"

Detective Sabine looks wearily across at me. "This isn't *The Bill* you know. Cases are not solved in neat one-hour blocks. I know you'd like this all wrapped up within a few weeks so you can present your diary readers with a nice happy ending but I'm afraid real police work is simply not like that." Sigh.

Once back at the station, I deposit Tristan in a parking space and we walk toward the entrance together.

"James! Holly! Wait up!" We spin around. It's Callum.

"How's your day gone?" He looks from one to the other of us.

"Fine," we both say simultaneously. I suspect this is the standard answer for detectives as real answers may get more complicated than "fine."

"Coming out for a drink after work with us, Holly?" I sneak a look at Detective Sergeant Sabine. I don't think so.

"I don't think so. Have to file copy at the paper."

"Of course! The infamous diary! I have to say we are really looking forward to it. Especially Jamie here. Aren't you?"

"Jamie" shoots him a look which is very familiar to me.

Callum just laughs. "When's it out? Monday?"

I nod and smile and he bounds off again.

"See you then, Holly! Have a good weekend! See you later, James!" he shouts over his shoulder.

I work on the diary for what's left of the afternoon while James Sabine catches up on phone calls and paperwork, of which there seems to be an abundance. I knead and mold the diary into shape, creating what I hope is quite a good first installment from a factual point of view. I would like to bring the Jack character to life so readers can actually get to know him over the next few weeks (whether they can empathize with him may be another matter). He's not giving me an awful lot to work with but I do my best, and also work through the interesting parts of police procedure and focus on the actual crimes.

When I am finished, I attach the whole thing to an e-mail to Joe and send it across the ether. I breathe a sigh of relief. I have the weekend stretching ahead of me which is definitely going to be a police-free zone.

eight

———

"**D**arling. It's us. Let us in immediately. Your father is one of the walking wounded." My mother's voice has a certain presence, even over the intercom. Something to do with the dramatic training, I would imagine. This is a complete surprise to me—I thought they were in Cornwall. I feel a rush of pleasure and press the release key on the intercom before hurtling down the flight of stairs to greet them and help my father who has obviously met with an accident of some kind. This does not surprise me.

It is Saturday afternoon. I spent a very pleasurable Friday night celebrating the first installment of my diary with some of the other writers from the paper. This morning I went to the supermarket and this afternoon I was planning to lounge around before getting ready to see Ben this evening.

My mother is a flurry of dog, handbag and skirt. My father is hobbling but still seems pleased to see me.

"What on earth has happened?" I ask.

"Got any gin?" my mother says, obviously in dire need of a swift large one straight between the eyes.

"Er, yes. Dad, you're not supposed to be *carrying* those, you know," I say, pointing to a pair of crutches which he is carefully holding under one arm. "They're supposed to be carrying you."

"Can't get the hang of the bloody things. Give the old man a hand up the stairs?"

The two of us attempt to cart my father up to my flat—quite a feat. We are three abreast on the stairs, with my mother holding Morgan the Pekinese under one arm and practically holding my father up with the other. I have taken her handbag off her which, as always, is hopelessly flamboyant and makes me feel slightly like a drag queen, and I also have the crutches from my father which are doing quite a good job of propping me up. For every two steps we take forward, we sway a bit and then take one back. There is a persistent air of hysteria and my mother and I start to get a little giggly.

After we totter through the door of the flat, we drop my father onto the sofa and I go to prepare three large drinks. "So," I shout from the kitchen as I clink bottles and glasses together, "what are you doing up here?"

"It's a long and tedious story," says Dad. I hand their drinks over to them and they both take huge slugs. My mother frowns at my father.

"Darling, are you sure that you are supposed to be drinking this? Didn't the doctor give you some antibiotics?"

"Sod the doctor," he says defiantly, taking another huge gulp. They are both dressed smartly—my mother is wearing a typically swirly, flowery little number while my father is also running to form in a blazer and tie. They must have been to the hospital as the crutches have NHS emblazoned across them. My parents' friends seem to think this is some sort of trendy brand name from the States as there is quite a collection of memorabilia at home. The guest rooms even have NHS blankets, left over from when we were all involved in a flood and the rescue crews had to come and get us. My mother was carried out by a fireman, all the while telling him loudly he'd arrived thirty years too late.

I wait for the gins to deplete a little more before I re-start my inquiry.

"Well, it's perfectly simple really," my mother explains. "Your father and I were going to a retirement lunch in Bath. We just thought we would pop up, not disturb you as we're seeing you in a few weeks anyway, and then go back the same day."

"When are you seeing me?"

"I have told you, haven't I?" I shake my head. "Got a wedding here in a few weeks' time. Thought we might come up and stay a few nights before. Is that OK?"

"Fine. So whose retirement lunch was this today?"

"Alex's, darling. Alex Scott. You know, has that dreadful daughter. She's a Buddhist or something, dresses in a sari. Always chanting. Anyway, your father and I were early, so we thought we would stop by Weston-super-Mare and have a walk on the beach. We both take off our shoes and then your father goes and steps on some rock and gets it wedged in his heel. Very silly. But he said he was fine so we went to the lunch anyway. But the meal was perfectly ghastly and then they wanted me to sing some of my old numbers, so I stamped on your father's foot and had the perfect excuse to whisk him off to Casualty."

See? What did I tell you about this Casualty thing? Really, we all seem to spend most of our waking hours there. And such is the nature of my parents' relationship that my father doesn't seem at all upset she has stamped on his foot and she doesn't seem at all repentant.

"Your father made the most dreadful fuss down at the hospital. Thank goodness it's not our local because I don't know if we can ever be seen in there again."

"You didn't see a Dr. Kirkpatrick, did you?" It is my turn to look worried. I mean, I think it may be a bit soon to start meeting the parents.

"No, no. That wasn't his name, it was something quite ordinary. Can't remember. Anyway, the doctor said he was going to dig the stones out of your father's foot and that your father had to have a local anaesthetic which would feel just like a bee sting." They both start grinning wickedly at this point. "He put the needle in and Dad started writhing around, shouting, 'What sort of monster bloody bees sting you?'"

We all laugh. My father, normally very well-tempered and a perfect foil for my mother's more dramatic tendencies, seems to enjoy his momentary spot in the limelight.

"So, how are you, Holly?" he asks. "How's the crime business?"

"Oh, fine. Quite a change from features anyway."

"Who's this detective character you're supposed to be shadowing?"

"Detective Sergeant Sabine. Except I've called him Jack in the paper. After the cat. He's OK. Doesn't like me very much."

"We've arranged with the newsagent up the road to have the paper posted down to us each day. So, come on, tell us all."

I explain about the recent burglaries and then I go back and describe in full how I happened to get the job and all about Robin. I also tell them about James in more detail and how he seems to dislike me so much. They say they are sure he will like me more in time but I'm not convinced.

By now we are all nursing our second gin and tonics. I love spending time with my parents like this. They are really easy to be with. Great adult parents, if you see what I mean. All their eccentricities seemed so awful when I was a kid. You could absolutely guarantee that wherever they went some sort of drama would follow and I'm sure you understand that that is not the sort of attention you like when you're a child. I would drag my feet behind their considerable wake, painfully aware of the looks and glances I would be receiving. Parents' evenings, school plays, summer fêtes (which my mother usually opened due to her slight star status) were all the same. My mother, being an actress, would always "make an entrance" and then design a momentous exit, almost to a round of applause. Heinous crimes indeed when you are ten, but now they amuse me.

"How are the play rehearsals going?" I ask her.

"We're opening at the National in a few months' time." She frowns into her glass. "Always been terribly unlucky for me there since Mildred, my dresser, sliced the top of her finger off with the sword from the finale."

"Poor Mildred!"

She remarks breezily, "There's no theater without danger, darling." I'm not sure Mildred would feel completely the same way.

While she is saying this, Morgan the Pekinese seems to have come to life. He clambers purposefully off the sofa with the air of someone who knows exactly where he's going. My mother never travels anywhere without this little dog. Morgan now seems to be trying to form a deep and meaningful relationship with a chair leg. It's my turn to frown. I ask, "That dog isn't going to pee anywhere, is it?"

"Morgan is very sweet, if at times a little windy, but he never, ever pees in other people's houses." Hmm. "So, have you seen anything of that dreadful Teresa?" she continues.

It is quite strange—my mother seems to have taken a complete dislike to Teresa over recent years, bordering on obsessive hatred. She was always quite indifferent to her when we were young. Probably caught her wearing pink or some other such grisly crime that my irrational mother seems to think is a lynching offense. I shrug and say, "Now and again."

"Still religious? Ten Hail Marys for leaving the house without an umbrella?"

"Something like that."

"How is Lizzie? She still seeing that boyfriend? What's his name?"

"Alastair. Only just. It looks as though it might finish soon. She doesn't really get to see him very much as he's working all the time."

"Talking of boyfriends, when are we going to meet the mysterious Ben?"

Oh shit. I freeze as she says these words. I'd forgotten. He's coming over tonight and it is now, I look at my watch, bollocks, seven o'clock. This meeting may have arrived a little earlier than anticipated. Not that I am ashamed of my parents, don't get me wrong, it's just that I don't want Ben to feel I am forcing them on him. As though I am forcing him to make the next step in our relationship. I would definitely like him to meet my parents—five minutes before the wedding vows would be the best time. But it is a little unfair to surprise him with them now. I grit my teeth resolutely. They are going to have to go. I fly into action! There might still be time . . .

"You have to go!" I yelp.

Three pairs of puzzled eyes fix upon me.

"Ben's coming!"

"Well, isn't that a good thing, darling? We can meet him at last," says my mother, smoothing down her dress.

"No, no. It's a bad thing. A very bad thing. I'll explain some other time, but right now, You. Have. To. Go." I'm up on my feet and I've got my mother's bag over one arm and my father's crutches in my other hand. Then with my free hand I latch on like an octopus to my father's drink, which he is still trying to wrestle up to his mouth.

"Come on!" I am panting now with the sheer exertion of trying to evict three very unwilling bodies. "UP! UP!" I despair with my father and seize Morgan instead, who looks most reproachfully at me. Slinging him under one armpit, I help my mother heave my father up out of the chair and the three of us struggle to the door. Just as we reach it the intercom sounds. Bugger. We're just going to have to brazen this out. "BACK! BACK!" I yell, not caring now if my parents are finding my behavior a little strange, not to mention contrary. I dump all three of them back on the sofa under a pile of crutches and handbags, run to the intercom and pick it up. I deep breathe into it for a few seconds until I finally manage to wheeze, "Hello?"

"Holly? What on earth are you doing making dirty calls on your own intercom?" Ben's voice crackles down the line.

"I'm not, I've just, er, been, er . . . Anyway, do you want to come in?"

"Well, that would be nice."

"Oh, yes. Right." I press the front door release key and rush back into the sitting room.

"It's Ben. He's coming up. Act normal." Even I balk at this. "Well, as much as possible anyway."

nine

—————

I have always based my relationship with Ben on a "no commitment" scenario and I am absolutely positive it is the secret of my success because I have thus far succeeded where all of his past girlfriends have failed. It is the main reason I have been able to hang on to such a gorgeous specimen for so long. I always make sure I never appear too keen. I never ask when I am going to see him next or when he is going to call and I have found that being completely blasé about our relationship (although underneath I am a swirling sea of emotions) keeps him coming back. I know this unnatural state of affairs can't last for very long, but I was hoping it might last long enough for him to realize that I am absolutely, unequivocally, without a shadow of a doubt, the woman for him. Somehow, introducing my parents to him seems a major detour from this plan.

"Make sure you tell him you are here completely by accident," I hiss, and with this veiled threat I run through to the bedroom, hastily plaster some lipstick on, pass a comb through my bedraggled hair, try to take a few deep breaths—I seem to be having to do a lot of this lately—and then run back to open the front door just in time to greet Ben. He pecks me on the cheek and steps into the hallway. He is dressed in his blazer and club tie which all the team wear after a game. I can't help it. I go weak at the knees for him.

"Ben! Hi! How are you?" My voice is squeaky high. Ben views me suspiciously. Maybe a little over the top? I tone down my puckishness with a quick droop of the shoulders and drop my voice an octave. "How was the game?" I growl.

"We lost."

"Good. I mean, er, oh no! Look, Ben, my parents just happened to be passing and they've dropped in."

He stares intently at me. "Your parents?"

"Yes, my parents. My folks. My kin."

He pauses for a second and then seems to take it in his stride. "Right," he says blandly and marches through to the sitting room. I raise my eyebrows to myself. Maybe I *am* overreacting.

My mother leaps up as he enters and, being my mother, gives him a resounding smacker on each cheek. "Ben! How nice to meet you at last! We are sorry that it's such short notice but we did happen to be passing!" My father in the meantime has struggled to his feet and firmly shakes Ben's hand.

I gulp. I had forgotten, gazing at them anew as though through Ben's eyes, just how smart they look. It doesn't appear terribly accidental, does it? Why couldn't they have bloody well turned up wearing wellie boots or something? Do they have to look so "meeting the prospective son-in-law"-esque? I fume silently. Just remember, I tell myself, they *did* turn up accidentally. Repeat after me, Holly, they *did* turn up . . .

"HOLLY!" yells my father in my ear. I leap about a foot into the air.

"What? What?"

"I think Ben would like a drink," my father says in the voice he reserves for three-year-olds.

"Yes, yes. Right." I scoop up the empty glasses, trying not to drop them as my poor nerves literally fray at the ends, and rush into the kitchen to do refills, muttering madly to myself. I clatter ice into the four glasses and eye the gin bottle. Calm, calm. Happy thoughts. Think happy thoughts. Think gardens. Think water-falls. Think calm. I concentrate on splitting what was one unhappy piece of moldy old lemon into four bits and try to listen intently to the conversation next door. My mother is busy asking about Ben's rugby game. Thank God. Refills complete, I march back into the sitting room and hand them out.

"Darling, I have suggested that we all pop out for a bite to eat before your father and I head home." My mother smiles at me. I frown. I'm not sure two hours of my parents is going to safeguard any future with Ben, immediate or otherwise.

"Are you sure, Ben?" I say slowly. "Don't you have to meet the rest of your team?"

"Not until about ten, Holly, and it's only seven-fifteen now."

"Well, it's a Saturday night. I don't think we will get in anywhere."

"Don't worry!" breezes my mother. "I'll get us somewhere."

True to her word, half an hour later we are all seated around the best table that Melbourne's has to offer, complete with three bottles of wine (it's a bring-your-own). My mother immediately lights up a fag.

"Are you still smoking, Mother? You ought to stop—they'll kill you, you know."

"Either that or your father will, darling. I became so cranky last time I gave up that he nearly took to me with a machete. Frankly, I'd rather take my chances with the cigarettes, thank you. Do you smoke, Ben?"

"No, Mrs. Colshannon, I don't," he replies, a little stiffly. He's acting public school–like. I think he must be on his best behavior. The problem is that "public school" really doesn't go down very well with my parents. They are very big on ordinary schools.

I can feel my shoulders tensing up. They are sitting somewhere in the region of my eyebrows at the moment, giving me a distinct "Notre Dame" aura. The problem with anyone meeting my parents, or more specifically my mother, is that she tends to go into overdrive. She likes to test people to see if they can take her eccentric ways, and this is another reason why I have avoided staging a meeting between my parents and Ben. He just isn't ready for her. I am not concerned with what they think of him, I am simply petrified he'll think they are completely up the wall and then remember that I, as their daughter, have inherited their genes.

"So, Ben," says my father, "been watching the cricket?"

I never thought that I would say this, but thank the Lord for sports.

All in all it was a difficult evening. The conversation, although not stilted, was certainly not the most scintillating I have come across. But then I suppose all initial parent/boyfriend evenings are likely to be testing. I definitely think Ben thought my parents were rather unconventional and my parents probably thought Ben was a little stiff. But that's because they haven't got to know each other yet. I remember when my brother's girlfriend came to visit for the first time and my mother served her custard tart and salad for lunch, my mother thinking the custard tart was a quiche. Well, that's what she told us anyway. And my father nearly killed the girlfriend's little dog by accidentally dropping a rather large ashtray on its head. And now the girlfriend is like another sister to me. So you see, a bad start doesn't necessarily mean a bad ending.

After we waved my parents off down the M5, Ben went to meet his rugby pals for last orders and I went back to my flat. At about one in the morning his lithe, athletic body, smelling of smoke and beer, crept in beside me and I curled myself around him.

I wake with a great sense of excitement on Monday morning. Today is the day I'm going to see my diary in print! I scramble to clothe myself and then zoom around to the newsagent where I buy three copies of the paper. I rush back to my flat and, while eating my cereal, read the first installment of my diary. It's on page three of the paper, which is a really good place to be. It has a small picture of yours truly (fully clothed) and a huge heading. I peer anxiously at the picture, trying to remember when it was taken. I think it must have been last year when the paper was on a marketing splurge. I quickly scan the text but I am so familiar with my own words I can't tell whether it reads well or not. I ring Lizzie.

"Have you got it yet?" I say before she has a chance to speak.

A dopey voice replies, "Eh? Holly? Whatcha doing? What time is it?"

"It's er,—" I look at my watch. "—seven-thirty. You're not up yet, are you?"

"Well, I am now."

"Buy the paper and call me later."

Buggery broccoli. I put the phone down and look again at my watch. I'm a little early but I might as well go down to the police station and wait for crime to happen. What might today have in store for me, I wonder. A spot of arson perhaps? Maybe some fraud? Perhaps I could persuade Ben to set light to the rugby club? The roads are clear and I arrive in record time. Even Dave-the-grumpy-git-desk-sergeant isn't on duty yet. Instead I produce my ID to a complete stranger (who, may I say for the record, is decidedly too chirpy for this time in the morning and so on reflection I think I prefer Dave's economy with speech) and am buzzed through the security door.

Upstairs I meet the officers who are coming off the night shift. We exchange pleasantries and I ask them about the night's events. Gradually the rest of the office fills up and the night duty yawn and head off home.

Callum bounds in with his usual Labrador energy, waving a newspaper.

"Holly! It's great! Aren't you thrilled?"

"Yes, yes, I am," I say, trying not to look too pleased. He chucks it over to another colleague who asks to see it and then turns back to me.

"I can't believe it's called 'The Real Dick Tracy's Diary' though." His mouth twitches.

"Yeah, I know. Joe, my editor, thought of that."

"I don't think James is ever going to forgive you!"

I stare at him, aghast. "Why? How do you mean?"

"What, 'Dick'? Are you serious? He's not going to lose that little nickname for a long time to come." He grins.

I frown, puzzled at this. I'd never even thought of that . . . "People are going to call him 'Dick'?"

Just as I say that, a resounding chorus of "Morning Dick!" starts up from the other end of the room. I think Dick Tracy himself might just have arrived. I have no real wish to turn around. I know he's getting closer because I'm following Callum's eyes which are presumably tracking Dick's progress across the room. I bite my bottom lip.

"Good luck!" Callum murmurs, before straightening up and saying loudly, "Why, if it isn't the real Dick Tracy!" and bolting for the relative safety of his own desk. I wish fervently that I could also bolt for cover with Callum. Tucked up in his armpit or something.

James Sabine sits down opposite me.

"Morning," I whisper. His expression is very hard to read; unluckily the icy note in his voice is not.

"Couldn't you have come up with anything better than Dick?"

"It really wasn't me. It was my editor's idea," I say in a very small voice.

His green eyes lock on to mine. "Well, remind me to pass on my profuse thanks if I am ever fortunate enough to meet him. I am now going to be called Dick for the rest of my life."

"Sorry," I whisper.

"No, no, don't be sorry, Miss Colshannon. Because it is just another small incident in a catalog of unfortunate incidents that seem to have plagued me since your arrival here."

Bloody buggery beans. He really is quite annoyed. I feel thoroughly chastised and bite my lip uncertainly as he studies the mound of paperwork on his desk. Really, does he need to make me feel quite so uncomfortable? Couldn't he have said something nice about the rest of the diary? I catch Callum's eye. He gives me a wink and I grin back at him. James Sabine's head suddenly snaps up and he glares at me as though he can smell the happy juice. I wipe the smile off my face and study my notes.

His telephone rings. He quickly picks it up and snaps, "Hello?", then, "Yep, she's here. Unfortunately." He hands the receiver over to me, saying, "It's for you."

"Thanks." The temptation to add "Dick" is almost too much for me. Luckily the steely look in his eyes dissuades me.

"Hello?" I say into the mouthpiece.

"Holly, is that you?" It's Joe.

"It's me!"

"Have you seen the *Journal* this morning?"

"No," I say slowly. "I bought our paper to see the diary, but I didn't really look at the *Journal*."

"Get a copy as soon as you can," Joe says grimly. "We've been scooped."

ten

———

I replace the receiver and stare thoughtfully ahead for a second. James Sabine is absorbed in flipping through his pile of papers. "Back in a minute," I say. I pick up my purse from my bag and scurry out of the office. Five minutes later, I find myself in the little newsagent around the corner buying the *Journal*. I run back to the station and huff and puff my way up to the second floor and back to my desk. I quickly sit down and scour the headlines, then start to look for the story page by page. I don't have to look for very long. On page three the headline "CULTURED THIEF BAGS PRICELESS ANTIQUES" screams at me. I start to read.

Retired Colonel Sebastian Forkar-White was robbed of his family's finest antiques as he slept. The thief apparently forced a catch on a window and then stole into the house in the dead of night. "They must have a wonderful eye for detail," said a neighbor. "The Forkar-Whites only own the best." An inside source revealed the police are baffled and have no clues except for a strand of hair, which will be sent off for DNA analysis, and a mysterious substance found at the crime scene. First to the in-cident were Detective Sergeant James Sabine and a reporter from the Bristol Gazette *who is shadowing the detective for a supposedly exclusive six-week diary, but yet again your very own* Bristol Journal *brings you the full story. Continued on page seven.*

I take a long breath and stare unseeingly at the page in front of me. My brain is frantically turning over the facts. How on earth could someone have got hold of details like this?

"Er, Detective Sergeant Sabine?" He lifts his head and raises his eyebrows inquiringly.

"Have you seen this?" I ask, holding up the *Journal*.

"I prefer fact to fiction," he says, shifting his gaze back to his paperwork.

"Well, I think you should take a look at this." I hand the newspaper over and wait silently as he starts to read, watching as his face turns at first to disbelief and then to anger. His eyes lock on to mine.

"How the hell . . . ? THAT'S IT!" he roars. "I've had enough! You're responsible for this and I'm going to make sure the whole stupid diary thing stops now."

A week's worth of tension snaps inside me. You can almost hear it. "Stupid? STUPID?" I screech. Unfortunately screeching is a fair description. "The diary is not STUPID. Just because some of us don't have your high-handed, God-like approach to life doesn't mean all other careers are STUPID."

"Who's high-handed?" he shouts back.

"YOU'RE high-handed." I look around for Callum. My eyes alight on him sitting innocently at his desk watching us. "Isn't he high-handed, Callum?" I shout over.

Callum grins and nods. A few other people in the department are looking over with interest and they bob their heads around in a the-girl's-got-a-point sort of way.

"See?" I shoot back at James Sabine. "Callum says you're high-handed."

"Actually," interjects Callum as he wanders over, "I didn't *ex-actly* say James was high-handed. I was merely agreeing because sometimes he can be a little . . ."

"Keep *out* of this, Callum," thunders James Sabine.

"You have had it in for me from the start," I continue, unabashed. "You'll use any excuse just to get me off your back. You have been nothing but uncooperative, difficult and obstructive. What you don't realize though, Mr. Hot-Shot Detective, is that while you are swanning around playing superhero, other people's lives . . ." I pause for a second; is this a little melodramatic? Sod it. ". . . other people's lives and careers are being stamped underfoot, all because you can't put up with me following you around for a few weeks. Well, shame on you," I say, complete with some rather fancy finger-wagging. I sound as though I'm from a bad movie made prior to 1940.

I stop and slowly curl up my finger. Some scattered applause comes from our newly acquired pavement audience, which quickly disperses as James Sabine turns his glare on them.

"What *you* don't realize, Miss Colshannon," he says quietly, turning his gaze back to me, "is quite how annoying you are to have around. It's like being followed by a particularly persistent little mosquito who refuses to be swatted. We are so understaffed here that each of us carries the workload of three officers, and in addition to this I now have to deal with the extra work that you seem so adept at creating. Why don't you press people do something positive instead of slowing down the progress of all my cases?" He pauses. "I am going to have to report this leak to the Chief Inspector." He turns on his heel and strides off, intent on his mission.

I wince and stare ahead for a few minutes. So, Holly, how would you say that went? How exactly were you safeguarding your future there? The mosquito jibe has particularly struck home. I muse to myself for a while, wondering who was really in the right and who was in the wrong. It seems that maybe we both have a point. Obviously mine is bigger than his though. I sigh to myself and miserably pick up the phone to break the news to Joe

that the diary might be a little shorter than we first envisaged. I
dial his direct line extension.

"Hello?"

"Joe, it's Holly."

"Have you looked at it?"

"Yep. Detective Sergeant Sabine has just gone to report it to
the Chief Inspector."

"Shit."

"Yeah. They may chuck me out." This is understating the obvious a tad.

"Over my dead corpse," he growls. I don't think it is the moment to pedantically point out that (a) it might well be that way if
Detective Sergeant Sabine has anything to do with it and (b) "over
my dead corpse" isn't strictly speaking the correct expression. "Do
you know how the *Journal* could have got hold of this?"

"No, but I'll try and find out, if it will help. I'll speak to you
later." I replace the receiver, deep in thought.

Robin is my first port of call. She seems very distracted about
something initially until I tell her in full what has happened and
then her concentration seems to snap into focus. She is as appalled
as I am, and very concerned about the future of the diary. She
points out that the PR write-up has only been released today and
naturally doesn't contain the two important pieces of information
about the hair and the mysterious substance. I tell her about
James Sabine and our small disagreement. And she does exactly
what I had hoped she would. Robin gets on the phone to the
Chief to safeguard the future of her project. I smile to myself and
leave the room. I may be a little harder to get rid of than he
thinks.

I go back to my desk and stare at the article. James Sabine returns to his desk. I look up. "Well? Do I have to pack my bags?"

"Not yet. But don't get your hopes up," he snaps. The Sabine family motto is obviously not "forgive and forget." "The Chief just wants me to get to the bottom of it, for now."

"Him and me both," I murmur.

"What have you found out?"

"Nothing." I stare down at the article on my desk.

"Wonderful," he mutters sarcastically.

"I am trying," I snap.

"Extremely," he snaps back.

I ignore him and stare and stare at the text in front of me until something so obvious pops up that I cannot believe I didn't see it before.

"Detective Sergeant Sabine, how do you file the reports?" I say suddenly.

"How do you mean?"

"Do you have a file on each crime?"

"We write up the report on the computer and then file hard copies and additional documents in a paper file."

"Where's the paper file?"

"All working paper files are locked in my desk."

"How about the computer?"

"I don't think I could get it in the drawer," he says dryly.

"I mean, can anyone access the file on the computer?"

"Of course. Another officer may need the information on a case. You're not suggesting that someone here . . ."

"Can I see the computer file?"

He looks at me hesitantly and then shrugs. "I suppose so." He turns to the computer and after a few minutes pulls up the file. I walk around to his desk and look over his shoulder. He scrolls down.

"There!" I say, pointing at the screen.

"What?"

"There! You've spelled Sebastian Forquar-White's name with a 'k'."

"So?"

"The article did too. I checked the spelling of the name with Anton yesterday and it is spelled with a 'q'."

James Sabine doesn't say anything but sits looking at the screen. "That doesn't mean anything. Someone else could easily make the same mistake," he says after a minute.

"Perhaps. But could someone from the outside have hacked into this computer? Is the mainframe connected by modem to anything?"

"No. You have to actually be inside this department to get into the files."

"Can we see who last accessed the file?"

"I can't but the IT department probably could. I'll see what they can do." He gets up and leaves the room.

I wander back around to my desk and sit down heavily. My momentary elation is replaced by frustration. I look around the department, wondering, aside from the obvious suspect, if anyone in this office is taking handouts from the *Journal*.

My first foray into detecting seems to end here. Depressingly enough, there is nothing more I can do about it. I draft an e-mail to Joe saying that I'll be in later to discuss the situation. James Sabine returns after a while.

"Have you spoken to IT?"

"They're going to look into it."

He goes back to vetting his mound of papers. There must be something interesting there because he almost immediately picks up the phone, has a brief conversation while jotting down some notes, and then gets up. I look at him expectantly.

"Are we off?" I say hopefully.

"Well, I am."

What does that mean? Is he going to the loo or something? I hover uncertainly until he looks back over his shoulder and says, "Come on then, if you're coming."

I chase after him. There is a chorus of "Bye Dick!" and "Catch you later, Dick!" I fervently hope he didn't hear them.

Detective Sergeant Sabine accelerates our usual car up the ramp and out of the underground car park.

"Where are we going?" I ask.

"Uniform has been questioning some of the staff down at the hospital. For the drug theft. They didn't like the look of one of the nurses. I'm going to check him out."

"Him?"

James Sabine glances over at me. "He's a male nurse."

"Oh."

An awkward silence descends on us. Our past relationship is positively festooned with love hearts compared to the aftermath of our argument. I bite my lip and look out of the window. I suppose I really ought to apologize for the sake of the diary, but I can't quite bring myself to yet.

Finally, I grudgingly say through gritted teeth, "Look, I'm sorry if I appeared a little overwrought this morning. It hasn't exactly been an easy week." Well, it was *almost* an apology.

He replies, equally grudgingly, "That's OK. I'm sorry for calling you a mosquito. I mean, it's true, but I still shouldn't have said so." That was even less of an apology than mine. We both look as un-sorry as two people could ever appear and travel in silence to our destination.

My mind is on the impending questioning of a suspect as I catch up with James Sabine as he walks toward the suspect's house.

"Do you want me to say anything?" I ask.

"No. Say nothing."

"You don't want me to help at all?" I suggest, anxious to be involved.

"Help?"

"Well, you might want me to be the bad cop or something?"

He stops and faces me. "Bad cop?" he says wearily.

"Or good cop? I don't mind. Or—"

"Miss Colshannon. I appreciate your offer of help, but can I point out the fatal flaw here?" I arrange my face into a questioning look. "You are not a *police officer*. You see? Good cop," he continues slowly, pointing to himself as though explaining it all to a five-year-old and then, pointing to me, "No cop." He repeats the action again. "Bad cop, no cop. Do you get it? You're watching too much TV."

I resign myself to a non-speaking part and follow him as we climb a wrought iron staircase and ring the bell of flat three. No answer. We ring again. James Sabine turns to me.

"Remember, don't say anything." I shake my head vehemently as though the thought wouldn't have even crossed my mind. The door opens a crack. Detective Sabine holds up his ID and says, "Are you Kenneth Tanner?"

The shadowy figure nods his assertion to this question.

"I'm Detective Sergeant Sabine. I would like to ask you a few questions regarding a theft at the hospital where I believe you work?" The door opens slightly more at this point to reveal a man in his mid-twenties. He's wearing tracksuit bottoms and a sweatshirt and is looking decidedly the worse for wear.

"Yeah? What do you want to know?"

"May we come in?"

The man makes to open the door wider to allow us access, but instead slams it in our faces as we try to move inside. James Sabine, who obviously has more developed reactions than I, rams his shoulder against the door, but it's too late, the lock has already slipped into place. He takes a step backward and kicks the door, just above the handle, with his right leg. It swings wide open and crashes against the back wall.

"Stay here," he says to me as he runs inside.

Needless to say, I don't stay anywhere and peer in after him. I watch as he darts across the hallway and bobs his head around the door directly opposite. He then flings himself across the room and I catch up just in time to see him wrestling Kenneth Tanner away from an open window with a wrought iron fire escape outside it. Within about thirty seconds, James Sabine has got both the suspect's hands behind his back and is kneeling on them while feeling for his handcuffs. He produces them with a flourish like a magician and clicks them into place. I hear him reading Kenneth his rights.

"You do not have to say anything. But it may harm your defense . . ."

Blimey. It's not even lunchtime.

"Holly! Congratulations!" says Callum. "Your first arrest!"

"Yeah! Well done!" shouts another officer from his desk, and several others smile over at me.

I smile modestly back.

"Was it a difficult arrest?" asks Callum jokingly.

"Terribly."

James Sabine is standing behind me. Callum gestures toward him with his head. "Was Dick here much help?"

"Useless. Sat in the car." Callum and I grin at each other. Detective Sergeant Sabine raises his eyes to heaven and walks off, leaving us to it. I move toward my desk and come back to earth with a bump when I realize that the story of my first arrest is probably being leaked as we speak.

James Sabine makes a start on the baffling amount of paperwork that results from making an arrest (if it had been me, I think I would probably have let the suspect go) while I work on today's diary installment on my laptop. Now and again I look up and stare pensively ahead of me. Callum wanders over and throws a wad of paper onto James' desk.

"I was just down with forensics. Roger asked me to give you this."

"What is it?" I inquire.

"The report from the Forquar-White burglary." Detective Sergeant Sabine is already leafing through it.

"Have they got the DNA results from the hair?" I ask excitedly.

Detective Sergeant Sabine barely looks up but Callum replies, "It'll be weeks before that comes back from the labs, Holly. It won't be of high priority—"

I interrupt him. "Why?"

"Well, murder cases, rapes, that sort of thing, take higher priority than a burglary."

"They can't identify that peculiar substance," James Sabine murmurs to himself, his eyes still firmly glued to the report.

"Yeah," says Callum. "Roger mentioned it to me. He says he has no idea what it is."

"Are they going to try and find out?" I ask, aghast.

James Sabine's head snaps up. "They just haven't got the resources at the moment, Miss Colshannon. Lack of funding. There's something else you can write about."

The rest of the afternoon is taken up with interviewing Kenneth Tanner, which I'm not allowed to sit on. I fervently hope we won't be scooped again but realize with a sinking heart, as I watch James Sabine tapping the details into the computer, that it is unlikely it will stop here. At the end of the afternoon I pack up my stuff, say my goodbyes for the day and go over to the paper. Joe is waiting for me.

"Well?" he demands.

"Well what?"

"Did you find anything out about the *Journal*?"

"We found out that someone might have been reading Detective Sergeant Sabine's computer files, which basically means it could be practically anyone in the building with the possible exception of the canteen ladies. And maybe not even then. The IT department are trying to trace the culprit but not with a great deal of enthusiasm. How about you, did you find anything?"

"I called a few contacts, a couple of ex-employees of the *Journal*, to see if they could discover anything but all they said was that it was an inside source."

I sit down in the chair in front of Joe's desk. The man himself paces in front of me.

"Spike Troman is their crime correspondent, isn't he?" I ask. From what I've seen so far, Spike is a small weasel of a man whose name, unfortunately for him, does not belie his nature. There is nothing sharp about him.

"There's no way Spike could be doing this by himself. He would definitely need spoon-feeding."

"How long do you think he's had a contact at the station?" I ask.

"Well, they can't have just found him or her solely to ruin the diary. I mean, the diary was arranged so quickly that there simply wasn't time."

"But it was so blatant. Revealing the forensics stuff, I mean. They must know there's going to be an inquiry."

"Deliberate sabotage. The diary would have made them worried. I was hoping it would be such a success that people would permanently switch from the *Journal* to us. They probably thought it was worth taking a risk to try and show us up."

"What can we do?"

"Can you keep the details off the computer so they can't be leaked?"

"Detective Sergeant Sabine would never agree to that."

"Well, not very much then. Maybe with the IT department looking into it the informant might get freaked. Don't trust anyone there, Holly."

"No. I won't."

"Don't send your copy by e-mail; you'll have to come over to the paper every night and download it yourself. And Holly, can you try and do something different from the *Journal*?"

"Like what?"

"We haven't printed anything the *Journal* hasn't already known about so far. They're making us look like idiots. We're supposed to be the ones on the inside and yet they're still getting all the stories. You're going to have to try and get some interesting stuff out of this detective, things that the *Journal* couldn't possibly get hold of. Does he eat doughnuts? Are there any inside feuds in the office? Spice it up a bit! Give our readers something that the *Journal* can't. Details."

"Details," I repeat. I nod and walk distractedly out of his office and down toward Tristan. My hands close into tight little fists with fury at the *Journal* and the mole. They are ruining my one big chance. Who on earth is doing this? The only thing to gain would be money and even then the risks outweigh it. Unless . . . Unless an officer who doesn't like reporters very much is trying to get his newest sidekick thrown out? But would he really sabotage his own cases to do so?

eleven

Lizzie arrives for our Monday evening together in a state of very high excitement. Before I can even start on my weekend's events, she says, "I had the best day ever on Saturday. Guess what I did?"

"What?"

"I tried on wedding dresses!"

My God! Things have moved on quickly. I sit down suddenly in shock as she bustles through to the kitchen asking, "What have we got for munchies?"

"When? When did he ask you?" I shout after her. She pops her head back around the door.

"Who?"

"Alastair."

She comes out of the kitchen and plonks herself on the sofa. "He hasn't asked me, silly. It's just that I was passing this wedding shop at lunchtime and so I thought I would pop in for a little look. It was gorgeous, Holly." She stares dreamily off into space while I blink a few times and try to clear my fuzzy and confused brain.

As she starts with a description of one of the dresses she tried on, I am forced to interrupt her. "What happened? I mean, a couple of days ago you were wondering whether Alastair was trying to finish with you, and now you're getting married?"

"Well, I've been thinking about it a lot these last few days and something you said the other night came back to me." I really wish people wouldn't do this. I hate anyone quoting myself back to me probably because I change my mind so much. I ought to make all my friends sign an agreement stating that while I mean everything I say at the time, all quotes expire after a ten-minute period.

"What did I say?"

"You said I ought not to sit back and let this happen to me!"

"I said that?"

"Yep!"

"Well, I think I probably meant you shouldn't mope about," I say cautiously.

"You also said I should be proactive!"

"Did I?" I say slowly, playing for time. I frown to myself. I'm not completely sure I know what the word means.

"Yes, you did! So I'm being proactive!"

"How so?"

"Alastair and I are going to get married!"

"Does the groom know?"

Lizzie looks impatient and swivels herself around so she is fully facing me.

"What you said makes a lot of sense, Holly. I love Alastair, I truly do, and there is no way I am giving him up without a fight!"

"OK," I say slowly, "I understand that bit and that's good. But where does the white dress come in?"

"I'm going to make him marry me, Holly!" she says triumphantly. "That's the conclusion I have arrived at! Admittedly I may have got ahead of myself a bit with the wedding dresses, but I just couldn't resist it! Besides, it was good for me. Somehow it got me in the mood!"

"Did you pick out a bridesmaid dress for me?"

"Ha, ha. There is just no way I am going to let someone like Alastair escape. Good men are hard to come by." Fair point, I suppose.

"Well, how are you going to make him *marry* you? I hate to be the one to break it to you, but he does have to propose first. You can't go ahead and plan a wedding and then take him to it like a surprise birthday party."

A delicious image of two hundred wedding guests, all in hats, plus the vicar standing at the altar, shouting "SURPRISE!" at a bemused Alastair flashes before me for a second. Actually, it would be quite fun, wouldn't it?

"I have a cunning plan and I'm going to need your help."

I relent a little and relax my taut face. I have to say I am a bit curious anyway.

"Oh, all right. What is it?"

"LOCAL HOSPITAL IN DRUGS BUST" screams the *Journal*'s headline the next morning. I grind my teeth and walk back to the car where James Sabine is waiting for me. I clamber in and snap on my seat belt.

"It's happened again," I say indignantly and shove the newspaper over to him.

"Do they mention the suspect by name? We'll sue if they do . . ."

"Don't know, haven't read it." I look sulkily out of the window while he flicks in silence to the appropriate page and reads. "No, they don't. A good thing too." He hands the paper back to me, puts the car into gear and we whoosh off.

"Is there anything we can do?"

"Let IT sort it out."

Detective Sergeant Sabine and I, partners in the fight against crime, are on our way to interview someone about the Sebastian Forquar-White burglary. The other half of the magnificent duo isn't looking too thrilled though; his habitual expression is now accompanied by the rather irritating drumming of his fingers on the steering wheel as we sit at some particularly arduous traffic lights.

I get my notepad out of my bag. Right, down to business. Details.

"How would you describe your relationship with the rest of the department?"

"Good."

"Are there any competitions going on? You know, who can make the most arrests in the month?"

"Nope."

This is going well.

"Do you have lucky socks you wear in raids or anything?"

" 'Fraid not."

"Do you give your gun a name?"

At long last he looks over at me. "Miss Colshannon," he says patiently and I raise my eyebrows hopefully, "you would know if I had a gun."

"How would I know if you had a gun?"

"Because I would have *shot* you with it by now. Please stop these ridiculous questions." So much for personal details.

"Who are we going to interview?" I ask.

"Some of the staff at Sebastian Forquar-White's house; I want to go back over their statements."

"Something there that you don't like?"

"No, but it's got to be some sort of inside job because the burglar knew the layout of the house so well."

"Maybe they just got lucky."

"Maybe. There's a list down there, if you want to see, of the stuff that was taken." He gestures with his head toward my feet. I pick up a manila file, open it and pull out the top copy.

Absolute gobbledegook.

I'm sure there are quite a few people in the world that this list would actually mean something to. But I've never had a hotline to

The Antiques Roadshow. It's full of items such as "Ebonized Bracket Clock, c1780" and "Sèvres Vase, c1815." I frown at it for a second.

"How do you know that Sebastian Forquar-Whatshisgob isn't doing an insurance scam? That he hasn't just popped a few things, a few imitation knickknacks, down in the cellar to leave some empty spaces and reads *Antiques Today* on a regular basis? I mean, you would hardly know he has been burgled, you said so yourself. Sounds very suss to me."

He smiles a wry little smile.

"Well, it had crossed my mind," he admits, "but it's because you can't tell the burglar has even been there that I know he has."

I replay this remark a few times in my head, trying to make sense of it.

"How do you mean? Exactly?"

"Well, someone who attempts an insurance fraud always over-does the breaking and entering bit. Instead of a forced window catch on a very small window in the larder, you find positively tons of broken glass, ransacked drawers, several fake footprints and a note saying WE DID THE PLACE OVER, SORRY. LOVE, THE BURGLARS. The owners of the house will always say, 'Yes, Officer, we woke in the night to the sound of breaking glass and went downstairs in time to see two figures running across the lawn', not like Mr. Forquar, er, Thing saying 'Not a dicky bird disturbed me, best night's sleep I've had in ages.' "

There's a pause while I take all this in.

"Besides," he adds, "I checked with the insurance company. Every single thing on that list was a named item with them. So you see, he didn't fabricate anything."

"Well, it sounds a very expensive list."

"About seventy thousand pounds' worth."

I stare at him with my mouth open. "Seventy thousand pounds?"

"Yeah, makes your TV and video thief pale into insignificance a bit, doesn't it?"

"I shouldn't think the insurance company is very happy about that."

I jump in my seat as he leans irritably on the horn. "C'mon, c'mon," he mutters impatiently. I peer ahead; there seems to be a problem a few cars in front.

"Something's happened," I say rather needlessly.

He maneuvers the car to the side of the road, which affords me a great view of the increasingly tempestuous scene between two motorists ahead, snaps on the handbrake and turns off the engine.

"I'd better go and see. You stay here." He gets out of the car and strides off toward the two hapless motorists. I think there may have been some sort of accident. I fidget in my seat and peer anxiously out of the windscreen, trying to catch some of the action. Detective Sergeant Sabine always has this marvelous knack of making me feel like a grubby little six-year-old caught with my hand in the biscuit barrel. I settle down and turn my full attention to trying to lip-read the argument.

I jump as a mobile phone starts to ring. I locate it in the well between the two seats. I look at it warily, remembering what happened last time when I answered the radio. He was really peeved about that; I think I'll leave it.

It continues to ring.

I look ahead and try to ascertain whether the argument has moved toward some sort of finale. Quite a crowd has built up around them. I wonder whether I should just nip out and take the phone to him. Curiosity overtakes me a little—it might be his wife-to-be. I impulsively answer it.

"Hello?"

"Holly?" A male voice.

"Yep, it's me!"

"Where's Detective Sergeant Sabine?" It's the station.

I narrow my eyes and look at the scene ahead. "Er, he's a little tied up at the moment."

"Could you ask the detective to contact the station urgently as soon as he has untied himself?"

"Er, yes, OK."

I get out of the car, intent on my mission. The row seems to be really hotting up now and the good detective is standing right in the middle of it, attempting to keep the two men from slugging each other. I reach the outskirts of the group and try to push my way forward. The surrounding people seem to be surprisingly unyielding. Hmm. I shove a little harder and chuck a few "Excuse me"s in for good measure. Nothing. I'm getting annoyed now. A man in a flat cap swivels his head around and glares at me. "Look, love, we were here first. You can't just push your way to the front."

"POLICE BUSINESS, COMING THROUGH!" I roar.

This time a good few heads swivel round to clock the nutter.

"Give over, love," mutters flat-cap. "If you're police business then I'm Tom Jones."

There are titters from the crowd at this. Unable to face more humiliation, I give up and strop back to the car. Bugger. What now? I'm not going to attempt that mob again. I get into the passenger side and think. The messenger said it was urgent. How urgent is urgent? Drop-everything-because-if-you-don't-react-then-we're-all-going-to-die urgent or simply I've-left-the-oven-on urgent?

I peer anxiously out the window. The row doesn't seem to be abating.

I think I'll just flash the headlights. If he comes over, I can give him the message and absolve myself of all responsibility. If he ignores me then at least I can say I tried. Right. Yes. That's what I'll do and then no blame can be apportioned later.

I clamber over the handbrake and sit in the driver's seat. I peer and feel around for the headlight switch and in frustration start to push and pull all the levers. Suddenly, out of the relative quiet of rush hour Bristol, a police siren leaps into action.

Right next to my ear.

HOLY SHIT! I nearly leap out of my skin. I have a quick look around in case by some quirk of fate another police car has happened upon the scene and is parked on top of me making that God-awful noise. Then, seeing that there isn't, I accept the fact it is the unmarked police car in which I am sitting that is making the terrible racket. What the hell is an unmarked police car doing with a siren?

Shit, shit and shit. Like a woman possessed, I frantically start to pull and press everything I can to make the damn thing stop.

I think I may have got James Sabine's attention. And everyone else's as well. The crowd of people who were until a moment ago surrounding the two rowing men have all turned and are gawping at me with their mouths open. Pedestrians have stopped and are staring, people have come out of their houses and are staring and Detective Sergeant Sabine is striding toward me.

I increase my frenzied activity. The windscreen wipers come on and off. The headlights flash on and off. The radio turns on and off. James Sabine arrives at the car, throws open the door and reaches inside. The noise stops.

I close my eyes and bite my lip. I can feel him standing next to me. I can feel the waves of ill-will flowing out of his every pore.

"Did you want something, Miss Colshannon?" he says in a quiet voice. A dangerously quiet voice. "Were you perhaps trying to attract my attention?"

"Er yes. The station want you to call. Urgently," I say in a very small voice. Barely audible, in fact. I stare miserably down at my feet, wishing I could become something very tiny and slope away. Anything would do. Ant, earwig, whatever. Just as long as it was small and could disappear into crevices.

"Could you perhaps have walked over and told me that? Or were you, for some mysterious and invisible reason, unable to leave the car?"

"I did try but I couldn't get through. I meant to flash you." His eyebrows rise ever so slightly at this. "With the headlights," I hastily jump in. "Wrong lever."

"Right. Would you mind terribly if I just finished sorting this problem out?"

"No, no," I mumble as I hand his mobile over to him. He turns away. Was there . . . ? No, I must be mistaken. I thought, for the briefest of seconds, there was the ghost of a smile there. I watch as he strides back to the accident, dialing his mobile phone as he walks. I feel unaccountably sulky. I mean, how the hell was I supposed to know there was a siren in this car? I'm not Inspector Gadget. I pout to myself and clamber back over the handbrake, careful not to touch anything else in case I flip another all-important, it's-a-police-thing button. Like an ejector seat.

After a few minutes he gets back into the car and, without another word, executes a U-turn and squeezes out of our traffic jam into the free-flowing lane going the opposite way.

We sit in silence, as I am unwilling to increase his wrath any further by asking questions, until he says, "There's been another burglary. Uniform seems to think it's the same person."

"Really? Brilliant!" I enthuse. He gives me a look. I tone down my blatant elation and assume a more concerned air by tilting my head to one side, adopting my anxious face and examining the floor intently. He resumes his study of the road ahead.

We travel the rest of the journey in silence. No need for directions this time; he seems to know his way to the house. It is in the same area as the first burglary but I suppose there is nothing strange in that as it is quite a prosperous neighborhood. We draw up outside a large Regency house which looks very similar to the other burgled residence.

I leap out in a burst of enthusiasm and stride off along the pavement. My foot catches on something and with a loud shriek I stumble and rather inelegantly fall flat on my behind.

"God! Are you OK?" James Sabine comes around from his side of the car.

Flushed with embarrassment, I try to leap up in a sprightly way as though I was just investigating something very interesting on the pavement. "Yes, yes! Absolutely fine. Top hole, in fact. Seem to, er, have, er, tripped over something."

"You seem to spend an enormous proportion of your time doing battle with inert objects," he remarks dryly as we both peer at the pavement, eyes searching for that jutting paving stone or uneven surface. Nothing. Smooth as silk. For goodness sake, there must be something. I look suspiciously at the ground while furtively trying to rub my throbbing bum. And then I peer closer.

A fruit pastille sweet is stuck to one of the paving stones. Lemon flavor, by the look of it.

"What've you seen?"

"NOTHING. Let's go inside, shall we?"

He squints at the ground. "You tripped over a fruit gum?" He stares up at me and his voice is incredulous with disbelief.

"Well, it's stuck fast to the pavement," I mutter, giving the life-threatening sweet a small kick with my foot. "I think it's a fruit pastille anyway."

He raises his eyebrows at me. "I have a problem with my inner ear," I say defensively.

"Do you?"

"Well, maybe."

He gives a small shake of his head and then walks off toward the front door of the house, muttering to himself.

I eye the fruit pastille viciously. It is absolutely stuck fast to the pavement. The sun must have baked the damn thing on. I would like to vent my frustration on it but I have the feeling that if I enter into a bare-fist fight with my lemon friend I may come off worse. I trot after Detective Sergeant Sabine, swearing silently to myself. What is wrong with me? Could I just try and get through the rest of the day without anything else mortifying happening to me? Eh, Holly? Could you please try? More coordination is what's required. Please think about your limbs at all times, I instruct myself. One foot in front of the other. Left, right, left, right. See? Not so hard is it?

I catch up with James Sabine at the front door. It opens just as I get there. He flashes his ID to the person on the other side.

"Detective Sergeant Sabine. I believe you've had a burglary, Mrs. Stephens?"

"Do come in, Officer," says an old voice full of charm and serenity. As he murmurs his thanks and steps through the front door, I get my first view of the owner of the voice. She is an old lady. The sort of lady I would like as a grandmother, I decide within the same minute. She is dressed in a tweed skirt and a beige pullover. Her face, although creased with life, is carefully made up. She exudes tranquillity.

I step into the bright hallway and on to polished wood. My mind is taken away from thoughts of the old lady by the wary look James Sabine shoots me, presumably because of the extreme volatility of my balance and the smell of beeswax which indicates the floor is polished regularly.

"Could you attempt to try and stay upright?" he murmurs out of the side of his mouth.

"Could you stop mentioning it?" I murmur back.

We wait patiently as Mrs. Stephens very deliberately closes the front door and applies the door chain. She turns back to us.

"This is Holly Colshannon," says James, "she is here—"

"For observation only," I cockily finish for him, holding out my hand. The old lady smiles and delicately shakes it.

"How do you do?" she murmurs.

She then leads the way through to an elegant drawing room. A uniformed officer is already there and he gets up as we enter.

"Morning sir."

"Morning Matt."

"Would you like tea?" the old lady asks us. We all answer in the affirmative and, like a spooky *déjà vu* of the last post-burglary scene, she goes off to assemble the tea things while the two officers form a huddle. This time, though, I don't try to overhear their conversation. Firstly, they are speaking so quietly that I seriously doubt my ability to do so, and secondly, I don't really trust my capacity to make any coordinated movements right now. I would probably end up falling into their laps or something equally horrifying.

I spend my time looking around the room. A large grand-father clock reassuringly tick-tocks in the corner and dozens of photos are displayed on a grand piano. I get up and wander over to them. I identify the old lady in a few, along with various chil-dren whom I presume are grandchildren. While I am scruti-nizing them, the old lady comes back in bearing a large tray. James leaps up and takes the tray from her. When we are all holding delicate, rose-patterned china cups of tea, he starts his questioning.

"Do you live alone, Mrs. Stephens?"

"I am widowed, Detective. My husband died last year. My grandson lives with me at the moment. His father is in the Royal Navy and has just moved over to Italy. Andrew—that's my grandson—is taking his exams in the next few weeks and so he is staying with me until they are finished."

"We may need to speak to him. Would that be OK?" She nods.

"I understand the missing items were all taken from the din-ing room. When were you last in there?"

"Yesterday."

"So presumably the burglary took place last night. Did you hear anything at all?"

"Not a thing and I am a very light sleeper."

"Have you noticed anyone suspicious hanging about in the last few days?"

Mrs. Stephens thinks hard for a couple of seconds and then replies emphatically, "No."

"If it is OK with you, we may just send some officers round to talk to your neighbors." Mrs. Stephens nods her agreement and James Sabine looks across at Matt, who then glides silently out of the room.

"May we see where they got in?" James asks.

We replace our empty cups on the tray and she leads the way out of the room, back into the hallway and then into a dining room. It contains a huge table surrounded by eight large chairs. She points to a window over in the far corner.

"They got in there; took a pane of glass out of the window."

She then walks over to a huge glass display cabinet. It is almost empty. She stares at it forlornly.

"I kept meaning to have window locks fitted. They took everything of any real value. Still, they left me with a few pieces of porcelain that the children gave me. I'm grateful for that." The emotion in her voice is apparent. "They even took a clock that my husband gave me on our first wedding anniversary. It wasn't even working!" Her voice starts to break and a tear rolls down her cheek. We both unconsciously start forward, jolted by her distress.

Detective Sergeant Sabine says, with a surprising amount of gentleness in his voice, "I'm so sorry, Mrs. Stephens." There is a pause as he waits for her to regain some composure. After a few minutes he softly continues, "We're going to bring forensics experts in, Mrs. Stephens. Has anything been touched?"

She shakes her head slowly, and very gently he turns her around and leads her out of the room. Matt, the uniformed officer, rejoins me in the hall while James Sabine deposits Mrs. Stephens on a sofa in the drawing room. He comes back out to us and says to me, "Look, I know that you have notes to make, but would you mind sitting with her? Just for a bit?"

I nod my head and go into the drawing room. This is not at all pleasant. I can see why James Sabine was so uptight with me about burglaries. I mean, my first experience of them was with old Sebastian Forquar-Whathisgob, who, let's face it, was not a sympathetic character. But the crime against this old lady, whose every possession is a memory and something precious to her, feels like a huge violation. I sit down on the sofa next to her and put my professional skills to good use.

We talk gently for the next hour or so about her family—her late husband, her children and her grandchildren. She talks me through every photo present on that grand piano of hers. By the end of the hour she seems much better. Detective Sergeant Sabine has floated in and out, interrupting our session now and then with queries of his own. Finally he comes in and re-starts his questioning. Made redundant, I wander back out to the hallway and into the dining room. Roger is there. He looks up from his work.

"Don't come too close. You'll contaminate everything."

"Roger, you smooth talker, you," I say idly.

He grins. "How are you getting on?"

I hover in the doorway. "Oh, fine," I say uncertainly.

He looks up. "That bad, eh?"

I smile. "Yeah, that bad. I set off the car siren today and then fell over a sweet stuck to the pavement." Roger lets out a bellow of laughter. I grin and feel much better. Smiling to himself, he goes back to his work and I watch him for a few minutes.

"Sad, isn't it?"

"What?"

"An old lady being burgled like this."

He stops what he is doing and looks me straight in the eyes. "See a lot of sad things in our line of work, love."

"Yes, I suppose you do." I give a small half-smile. James Sabine comes up behind me.

"Come on, time to go. Did you find anything, Roger?"

Roger nods and says, "Some fibers. That peculiar substance we picked up on in the first burglary is on the handles of the cabinet too. Looks like the same person."

"Found it anywhere else in the house?"

"Nope, just in here. And nothing else has been touched but the handles of the cabinet."

"Any chance of you working out what that is?"

"Eventually, James. You know how it is."

Detective Sergeant Sabine sighs. "I know. See you soon."

Roger nods his affirmation and we both say goodbye to him.

We go through together to the drawing room. Mrs. Stephens is still sitting on the sofa, staring into space. James jolts her out of her reverie by saying, "Can we get you anything before we go?"

She gets up carefully and smiles at us. "No, thank you. I'll see you out."

We all walk together toward the door.

"It was nice to meet you," I say genuinely.

"You too. Thank you for our chat. I enjoyed it tremendously. Thank you for your kindness, Detective."

We start off down the path but I look over my shoulder halfway down and am surprised to see she is still there, patiently watching our retreating backs. She really is "seeing us out," a mode of behavior I am completely unfamiliar with. The only time I have been "seen out" before was to ensure that I actually left the premises.

* * *

James Sabine says, as we put on our seat belts, "Look, do you think we could drop this Detective Sergeant Sabine/Miss Colshannon thing? It's a ridiculous name anyway."

"I think that's a bit harsh. I mean, it isn't your fault your surname is unpronounceable."

"I meant Colshannon," he says tersely.

"We can use Christian names if you want," I continue.

"It wouldn't mean we're getting on though," he says grimly, putting the car into first gear.

"Don't worry, I didn't think for a second we were."

"If I had my way, you still wouldn't be here at all."

"You have made that fairly obvious," I say, my mind jolted back to the leaked stories to the *Journal*.

We are quiet in the car on the way back to the station. I think over my conversation with Mrs. Stephens and suddenly say, "Are these burglaries turning into a series?"

"I think they probably are."

We arrive back at the station. I leap out of the car first and wait at the front desk to be buzzed through the security door by Dave-the-grumpy-git-desk-sergeant. He doesn't look up. I sense a pattern may be emerging here. As soon as Detective Sab . . . sorry, James, steps through the doorway his head pops up. How does he do that? Does he have a system of reflecting mirrors down there or something?

"Morning sir!" Oh God. Is it still morning?

"Morning Dave. How are you?"

"Fine, thank you. Morning Holly," Dave says as he buzzes us through. I am so surprised that he actually knows my name that I can only manage an inane grin.

James and I troop up the stairs together. At the second floor he says, "I've got some stuff to do with another department so I'll see you later." I am summarily dismissed and make my way back to my desk. I call Joe.

"Joe, it's Holly."

"Have you seen this morning's?" I presume he is referring to this morning's edition of the *Journal*.

"Yep."

"Where are they getting it from?" He sounds desperate.

"Don't know, the IT department here is looking into it. I wouldn't hold your breath though." I don't think the IT department is going to be very forthcoming—they sound as though they have more important things to do.

"Look, Holly. You're going to have to give our readers something that the *Journal* can't. We've had the pollsters out today. The diary has had a rather lukewarm reception. The people who have read it like it, but it's not getting readers over to us. I think this scooping business is really stirring everything up. The *Journal* is blatantly poking fun at us and the diary. We need to get the readers to switch allegiance somehow."

"Right," I say slowly, "and how are we going to do that?"

"Well, you've got the private angle on this. The *Journal* can pilfer stories all they like, but you are actually in there with a real, live detective. You need to look to your laurel leaves. You're going to have to develop the detective more."

"OK," I say doubtfully. I don't like where this seems to be heading.

"How's your personal relationship with this Jack character?"

"James Sabine?"

"Yeah."

"Well . . ." Now, how can I put this? "We don't really have much of a personal relationship," I say carefully.

"Can you get one?" asks Joe impatiently. I am tempted to ask if Sainsbury's does them.

"I could try . . ." I say doubtfully.

"Holly! You are going to have to do better than TRY! I don't care what you have to do! Wine him and dine him! Bed him, for all I care! But get some sort of repartee going with him!"

"Have you met James Sabine?" I'm getting a little heated now. "Well, let me tell you, getting some sort of repartee going with him is like trying to get some sort of repartee going with HANNIBAL LECTER!" I am suddenly aware of someone standing in close proximity to me and I glance up to find James Sabine staring straight back down at me. I don't know how long he has been there, but probably long enough. "Who is my cousin and a very nice man . . ." I murmur into the mouthpiece while simultaneously going puce. James picks up something from his desk and then walks off again. I close my eyes and swear silently to myself as Joe continues to rant down the phone into my ear.

After replacing the receiver and carefully weighing up the odds, I think the pressure would come off me and my "personal relationship" with James Sabine if the leaks to the *Journal* stopped. With this great deduction in mind, I trot up to the IT department, situated on the top floor of the building, intent on some no-holds-barred, unashamed begging tactics. IT department is probably a bit of an exaggeration. "Group" might be a more accurate description, or even "huddle." I spot a lady in a corner and make my way over to her.

"Er, hello?" I say in a bid to attract her attention.

Her head shoots back in shock, her eyes wide with surprise.

"Sorry, did I scare you?"

"Er, no. Not at all. Are you lost?"

"I'm looking for the IT department."

"You've found it!" she says, beaming at me. "How can I help?"

"Well, I know Detective Sergeant Sabine has already reported it, but I've come to see if you've made any progress with tracing the leaks to the *Journal* newspaper?"

She looks absolutely dumbfounded at this. But then these academic sorts are always lost in some other world, aren't they? They're a bit vague because their minds are on higher planes than us mere mortals. I smile understandingly and lean a little closer. I say slowly and clearly, with the emphasis on my pronunciation, "The leaks to the *Journal* newspaper are from Detective Sergeant Sabine's computer. You are supposed to be tracking them."

"I don't know what you're talking about, love. Nobody's reported anything here."

I step back in surprise. "Nobody's reported anything?"

It's her turn to speak clearly and slowly; in fact, seeing my baffled face, she probably feels words are too much for me and resorts to shaking her head very slowly.

"Well, might it have been reported to someone else?"

She points behind my head to a large white board. "If it's not up on the board, it's not a problem," she recites in a mantra-type fashion. "There's no way if he had reported it that it wouldn't be up there. It's what we all work from." She shrugs. "Maybe he forgot."

After restoring communication and officially reporting the leak, I wander slowly back down the stairs, frowning to myself. Why did James Sabine not report this? My mind runs over the various possibilities and keeps returning to the same conclusion. Unfortunately, there can only be two reasons for it. Either he wants the leaks to continue in an effort to get me chucked off this job or there is no leak to be traced as it has come directly from him. Either way it confirms the fact he wants me out, a fact he hasn't been disguising anyway. I clench my hands. He is deliberately ruining my career just because he can't put up with a reporter for a few weeks.

Muttering furiously to myself, I slowly walk toward Robin's office. I need to talk to someone and I feel I can trust her as she wants this diary to work as much as I do, for whatever personal reasons of her own. What I would really like to do right now is have it out with Detective Sabine, but I know that since there is no direct proof against him it would probably result in me being thrown out of here. My options are really quite limited and I hope that Robin may have a solution. I stride into her office.

"Robin, have you got a . . ." I stand rooted to the spot and the hairs instinctively go up on the back of my neck. You know how, if you interrupt two lovers having a row, or a very intimate conversation between two people, there is a certain atmosphere of intensity and high emotion? Well, I've just walked in on such an atmosphere. I feel my arrival has sent shock waves around the room. Emotions are running high in here. James Sabine holds Robin in his arms. He looks crossly at me.

I say, quickly, "I'll come back," and turn and walk out of the room.

twelve

———

Ben comes over for the evening but I am so distracted that I either ignore his questions altogether, laugh in the wrong places during his account of the day or come out with peculiar responses like "would you prefer sausages with that?" He finally gives up on me and watches *A Question of Sport*, but not before tipping his dirty kit into the washing machine and then asking me how to run the cycle through.

I toss and turn all night, listening to Ben's rhythmic breathing beside me. Questions run through my head. Are Robin and James having an affair? Is that why Robin wants to leave Bristol so badly, because James Sabine is getting married?

James Sabine just doesn't seem the sort to be having an affair though. Maybe it was one of those poor-sods-just-can't-help-themselves things. But Robin has only been there a few months. I suppose these things can develop quite quickly and she is so glamorous. In which case, why is he still getting married?

Whatever is going on between those two still leaves the problem that I can't trust Robin now she is sharing pillow talk with James. I don't know who else to turn to regarding these leaks. Now that I have officially told the IT department about them, they can be traced. In fact, I think suddenly, if I subtly let James Sabine know that I have been up to the IT department to alert them to the leaks, he may feel obliged to stop as they won't be able to find anyone getting into his computer but him.

Even with some sort of plan in place, sleep still eludes me.

Eventually I drop off into a restless doze, my dreams punctuated with images of James, Robin and computers.

I get up early and, after kissing a sleepy Ben goodbye, leave for the police station. I am already at my desk and working on my laptop by the time James Sabine arrives. We eye each other warily. My hackles are up. The last time I saw him he was with Robin and I had just learned he was shopping me to the *Journal*. He is the first to speak.

"Look, I know what it must have seemed like yesterday—"

"I don't think it's any of my business," I say. I really don't want to have this conversation and so stare stubbornly at my laptop screen.

"It's just that . . . I would appreciate it if you didn't tell anyone."

"Sure," I snap.

So there is definitely something going on then. If there is just an innocent explanation, surely this would be a great opportunity to tell me? We work in silence for a few minutes more, then I say casually, "By the way, I went up to the IT department yesterday to see if they've managed to trace the leaks."

I think he suddenly looks wary. "And what did they say?"

"They said they haven't been able to yet."

In the true spirit of nosiness, I drop in to see Robin later in the morning. She is looking a little subdued, but still exudes glamour. Looking at her beautiful and troubled face I decide that James could be excused for falling for such a gorgeous woman, even though she is as hard as nails and it *really* isn't any of my business. Besides, I don't know the full story and it's easy to make quick judgments about people. Before I can even open my mouth, she says, "I'm sorry about yesterday. I was going to come and find you today to apologize."

"No need. It's nothing to do with me, Robin."

"So did he tell you . . . ?"

"We sort of discussed it," I admit cagily.

"I feel so guilty."

"Well, the wedding is quite soon, I suppose."

"That's going to be awkward." There is a small pause and then she continues, "You don't know the whole story."

"You could always tell me."

"I will. Soon, I promise." I don't push her any further but just nod. She adds, "What did you want to see me about yesterday?"

"Hmm?"

"When you interrupted us yesterday, what did you want?"

I hesitate for a second, thinking about my own, pressing problem of the scooping, and then shake my head. "Nothing. It was nothing."

This week James surpasses himself with his bad temper. The sign of a guilty conscience. His ability to make me feel uncomfortable is without rival but it seems he doesn't limit his bad humor to me. I have caught him rowing not only with Callum (and I ask you, who but the worst tempered person in the world could row with Callum?) but also a mild mannered, non-assuming bloke called Bill, who has always been polite and courteous to me.

As bizarre as this may sound, my days have actually fallen into some sort of pattern. I arrive down at the station by around eight A.M. and exchange friendly banter with Callum, spend the rest of the day running around with James, exchanging non-friendly banter, and then write up my diary in the early evening. It's been tough doing police work by day and then, when everyone else is packing up to go home, having to head off to the paper to write my obligatory two thousand words every evening. Particularly hard when all you want to write is "Nothing much happened today but we nearly ran over a pigeon." Not that there have been very many boring days, but James has had a few leads to follow up from cases that were before my arrival on the team. So those are things I can't write about.

My life has also been made much easier by the fact that the leaks to the *Bristol Journal* have stopped! My cunning ruse to tell James Sabine about my trip to the IT department obviously worked. When I went to tell Joe, he gave a huge sigh of relief and became conciliatory, and I uttered a huge sigh of relief at the fact I don't have to try and develop a better relationship with James Sabine.

"Have you tried explaining to Detective Sergeant Sabine how important it is for us to try and stay ahead of the *Journal*?" Joe inquired.

"Yep."

"And what did he say?"

"I think he said he couldn't give a shit."

"Ah." He paced around the room for a minute and then said, "We need to try and safeguard our position against the *Journal* a little better, Holly. This whole scooping business could start up again at any time. The numbers aren't showing any increase in our circulation. We've got to somehow make people sit up and take notice."

"How about some advertising?" I asked.

"Yeah, I've briefed the publicity department today. They're going to try and get some mentions on local radio shows and local TV. We've put aside a small advertising budget as well. Back of buses, that sort of thing." Terrific. I've always wanted to be on the back of a bus. I could imagine the comments back at the station.

He paced for a while longer. Then he turned suddenly and gripped my shoulder hard. Oh-oh. He'd finally lost it. I tried to look over my other shoulder to locate the emergency exit in case he started to foam at the mouth but he had me in too firm a grip. "I've got it!" he announced to me. I looked nervously at him. Was I supposed to break into a spirited rendition of *The Rain in Spain*?

"A photographer!"

Joe wants me to try and persuade James to have a photographer along with us. He thinks the addition of photos will boost the ratings dramatically and that photos will provide their own story (which is just as well as Detective Sergeant Sabine doesn't seem to be telling me anything). How I am supposed to persuade the good detective it's a winning idea, I simply do not know. I am going to wait for inspiration to strike me.

Since Roger has officially linked the two burglaries (Mr. Forquar-White and Mrs. Stephens) by formally matching the mysterious substance from the first burglary to the second, the pressure has been stepped up to catch the thief. Roger still doesn't know what the substance is and so we are waiting on the result of the DNA from the hair in the high hope that it can just be run through the computer to cough up the name of the guilty party. According to the insurance company, the thief made off with approximately fifty thousand pounds' worth of goods from the second burglary. You have to have a grudging respect for that. Since the burglaries have practically turned into a series, I have tagged the thief with the nickname The Fox on account of the stealthy fashion of the crimes.

Arduous questioning of anyone and everyone connected with the two households has not brought anything fresh to light. James Sabine is still doggedly pursuing the line that the thefts could only have been committed by someone who has actually been inside both houses. I, on the other hand, am despairing of the crimes ever being solved.

Joe, particularly since the intervention of the *Journal*, has been taking a special interest in the welfare of the diary. He is on my case about catching The Fox. Not for the sake of public safety, oh no, but because he doesn't want me writing about a crime that will remain unsolved. And not only does he want it solved but he wants it done before James' wedding. However, I have devised a cunning plan in the eventuality of it remaining unsolved. I am going to frame Steve from the paper's accounts department for it. He's always getting my PAYE wrong. *Et voilà!* Everyone is a winner. (Apart from Steve, that is. Ho hum. It will be a sharp lesson for him not to play fast and loose with someone else's tax code.)

I have unfortunately also missed out on meeting up with some of the detectives for drinks after work. Callum always asks me if I would like to come, or if I could meet them all after I have filed copy, but I haven't been able to yet. I'm getting on really well with the rest of the department—everyone is friendly and pleasant and I am well looked after. Callum brings me endless cups of coffee and pointedly doesn't bring James any since their stand-up row at the beginning of the week. Don't ask me what the row was about as I only got back for the tail end of it. But Callum has been wonderfully sweet and cheerful with me. It's amazing the difference that one person can bring to your day.

Even though Robin and I have drunk coffee together a few times this week, things are still a little awkward between us and she hasn't volunteered any further information about her relationship with James. Perhaps she feels she can't trust me yet, especially since I am a member of a profession where the word *trust* doesn't really exist. I have spotted the two of them together once or twice, talking earnestly. I catch her occasionally looking sadly into space when she thinks I'm not looking and my heart feels for her.

Since the whole Robin/James affair came to light I have to say my interest has been piqued. Every time James speaks to his bride-to-be, I am ashamed to say I listen intently. He is exceptionally nice to her as well (considering what he is like with everyone else, I would imagine it's the guilt talking). Oh, and I found out what she's called! Fleur! What sort of girlie name is that?! (I mustn't pre-judge people. I mustn't pre-judge people.) The unfortunate thing is, once my lurid imagination gets going it's hard to stop it. I spend my time wondering what she looks like and what they do together at weekends. But the more I overhear their conversations, the more I feel sorry for her. Does she have any idea about Robin? I am hoping we'll bump into her over the next few weeks. I'll just have to make sure I don't blab the truth in some misdirected "doing the right thing" idea. Not something we journalists are stricken with very often.

Talking of weddings, I think Lizzie is finally losing the plot. One particular evening she popped round for a chat on the way back from work. She dropped the bags she was carrying and chucked herself on to the sofa with a, "God! What a day! I'm knackered!" I went through to the kitchen to forage for supplies and when I returned, bearing a bottle of wine and two glasses, she was poring over a magazine.

"Which do you like best, Hol, orange blossom or jasmine?" she asked dreamily, looking off into the distance. I was just about to offer my very distinct views on the subject when a thought occurred to me.

"What. Are. You. Reading?"

She held the magazine up for me to see. *Brides* magazine. Hmm.

"Isn't this perhaps a little premature?"

"Don't be cross! I saw them in the newsagent, couldn't resist. Here, you have one." She chucked another magazine over.

"How is the groom-to-be?" I asked, snuggling down with my legs crossed under me on the sofa.

Lizzie's face clouded over. "Oh, a bit distant. But that's going to change soon. How's Ben?"

"Oh, fine, I think. The only time we seem to meet each other is either in bed or the hallway."

Out of curiosity, I did have a little leaf through the mag. And then another one, and before you could say, "I do," I was well into the subject and Lizzie and I were comparing the virtues of a winter wedding against a summer one and what our bridesmaids would wear. Altogether a completely addictive subject. I can see perfectly well why some women get obsessive about it. It was midnight before Lizzie finally got up to leave but I was still completely absorbed in an article entitled "Real Life Proposals."

"Holly?"

I barely lifted my head. "Hmm?"

"I'm going now."

"Just let me finish this."

"Keep it. I'll pick it up next time."

"When do you want me to start phase one of this plan you've concocted?"

"How about next weekend?"

"Fine."

"I'll call you when it's time."

"No problem. See you."

"Bye!"

I finished reading the article and, deep in thought, went through to brush my teeth. Apparently all I have to do is get Ben, a mountain, a sunset and a bottle of champagne in the same place at the same time and plaster a surprised expression on my face. How hard can it be?

thirteen

———

I think the whole world is wedding-obsessed at the moment. Even my mother! I answer the phone to her before I leave for work. That is my first mistake of the day, answering the damn thing.

"Hello?"

"Daaaarlingg!"

"Hi! How are you?"

"I'm fine, but the question is, how are you?"

"I'm fine," I reply doubtfully. Is there a reason I shouldn't be? An urgent operation that perhaps has slipped my mind? I clutch my vital organs for reassurance. My mother doesn't enlarge on her mysterious comment and sweeps on regardless.

"Now, darling. Do you remember I told you about that wedding? The one we're coming to?"

"Er, yes." Er, no.

"I was just ringing to check if it's still all right to stay in your box room."

This is an accurate but scathing description of my spare room. "Fine. Whose wedding is it? Am I invited?"

"No, you're not. It's Miles' daughter's; do you remember him? Dreadful old letch. One of my play's backers."

"No, I don't remember. When is it?"

"In about three weeks' time. We've been invited to some drinks party with them the weekend before as well. A sort of pre-wedding thing, but I don't think we're going to bother with that."

"Fine."

"Talking of weddings, you're not thinking about eloping, are you?"

My mind reels at the sudden subject change. "Er, no."

"Good. I saw a hat recently that I want to wear at your wedding so I just thought I'd make sure before I bought it."

"But I'm not getting married," I say slowly.

"Never?"

"Well, maybe not never, but not in the foreseeable future," I bluster.

"Well, darling, don't hold out forever."

"I'll bear it in mind." I am too tired to argue. She has probably been watching daytime television again and they've done a report on weddings. My mother absolutely loves to be aboard a bandwagon, regardless of its destination.

"How's your detective?"

"James Sabine?"

"Now, that name's familiar . . ." she says thoughtfully.

"That's because you've heard me say it a million times," I reply patiently. "You know him as Jack."

"Ah yes! Jack! We're getting acquainted with him quite well from the paper. Have you caught The Fox yet?"

"We haven't got any leads."

"The suspense is killing me. I do hope it lasts. How is Jack?"

"Bad-tempered."

"Good!" she says vaguely. "Darling, I have to go. One of your brothers has just arrived with a sheep in his car."

"See you soon."

I smile to myself. My family always amuse me. Especially with a distance of a few hundred miles between us.

"So, James, how would you feel about having a photographer along with us?"

I frown at myself in the mirror. Maybe that's a little too straight. Maybe I should sugarcoat the request a little. It's the start of my third week as crime correspondent.

"My editor feels you shouldn't hide your light under a bushel any longer. He wants your gorgeous good looks captured on film."

Too creepy-crawly. The door to the Ladies bangs open and two giggling WPCs barge in. I busily wash my hands at the basin and listen to their careless chatter as they shout to each other across the partitions. The problem with James Sabine is that he can cut through any sugar-coating with those piercing, I-can-see-straight-through-your-soul green eyes. I give an involuntary shiver.

I press the button on the hand dryer and hot air whooshes out to supposedly dry my wet hands. I shake them impatiently. I really wish I didn't have to ask James for this, but I popped into the paper on my way in today and Joe caught me. I dropped the mouse from my laptop into the loo last night (don't ask, just don't ask) and so had to make an unscheduled pit stop at the paper to beg and plead with the IT department to give me another one (it was my second this month so I was ready to use some good, old-fashioned bribery). Luckily the offices were half empty as the full day shift hadn't started yet. I was just tiptoeing over to see Andrew, the IT head of department, whose bald patch I had espied over the top of one of the computers, when Joe roared behind me, "HOLLY!" I jumped and then turned around in what I hope was a jaunty fashion.

"Joe! Morning! How are you?"

"Fine. You were on your way to see me, I take it?"

"Of course." If you have to lie, I always say do it blatantly. I had actually been studiously avoiding seeing Joe ever since he'd told me he wanted to get a photographer out with James and me. Not that I didn't want a photographer with us—obviously it would be marvelous for the diary—it's just I had yet to actually ask James. I was waiting a li-tt-le bit longer until he'd become more used to me. I sighed and forlornly followed Joe into his office. I suppose it had been just a matter of time.

Joe sat down at his desk, leaned forward and linked his fingers together. He fixed me with a stare. I wriggled uncomfortably and trained my gaze on a spot just above his head.

"So, have you asked him yet?"

"I'm just about to. This very morning." I gave what I hoped was a sanguine and winning smile.

"Well, seeing that you are so confident, I'll book Vince to join you at lunchtime." My cocksure smile drooped a little.

"Vince?" I said doubtfully.

"He's the best that we have, Holly. You should be honored."

"Ohh, I am, I am," I replied, nodding frantically. Vince? VINCE? Now, don't get me wrong. I love Vince, I worship the ground that Vince walks on . . . in his elfin boots with chains around them. You see . . . how can I put it? I'll give it to you straight (or not as the case may be). Vince is gay. Very gay.

If you want a chat about the latest fashions, then Vince is your man. If you want to talk over any problems with your love life, then you reach for Vince's mobile number. If you want the best photographer on the paper, then you get Vince on the job. But James and Vince? I wasn't sure they were going to get on.

"Holly, are you listening to me?"

"Hmm?" I said, dragging my thoughts back into the room.

"Do you want the diary to do well? A photographer is just what we need to send the whole thing through the roof."

"Great!" I meant it. I suddenly felt excited. He'd put it all into perspective for me. The success of the diary was the most important thing. What was I? A woman or a shirt button? What did I care what James Sabine thought? As long as the diary did well, then that was all that mattered. You see, Holly, I told myself, you

and James Sabine will part company in a few weeks' time, but the
work you are doing now will dictate your career for many years
to come. Right. So, get down to the police station and tell him
about the photographer.

"And I have some more good news for you."

"What?" Can I stand any more good news?

"The local BBC TV station wants to do an interview with
you!"

"Fantastic! When?"

"End of the week. You know where the studios are?"

"Whiteladies Road?"

He nodded. "Be there on Friday at seven."

And that is why I now find myself in the Ladies loos at the police
station, drying my hands under a hot air dryer in a rather mania-
cal fashion, trying to think of the best way to ask James Sabine
about the photographer. Stop flapping about, just go and ask, I
tell myself firmly.

I march resolutely through to the office. I stride past the buzzing hives of desks and up to James, who is sitting filling in the
never-ending forms.

"James," I state purposefully.

"Holly," he states back, without looking up.

"Photographer. He won't get in the way. What do you say?"

Now he looks up and stares at me for a second, looking as surprised as if I had said, "You and me. Stationery cupboard. Five
minutes' time."

"Will he be as much trouble as you?"

What's a girl supposed to say to that? "No."

"Well, considering there is a wide gap between 'no trouble'
and 'as much trouble as you', can I ask if he will be quite a lot less
trouble than you?"

"Lot, lot less. Lot, lot, lot less."

"Fine," he sighs wearily, as though he were Canute up to his waist in water.

I sit down suddenly at my desk opposite him. "Really?" I say in surprise.

"Check with the Chief first. No photos of suspects," he replies, turning back to his forms.

"OK!" I grin at him. That was much easier than I had antici-pated. "What are we doing this morning?"

"Going back to see Mrs. Stephens from the second burglary. I just want to ask her some more questions."

We get up and start walking down toward the car pool.

"Can I call the photographer and get him to meet us there?"

"I suppose."

We arrive at Mrs. Stephens' house to find Vince already parked outside. In fact, I spotted his car from the end of the road—he drives a souped-up VW Beetle, painted lilac. James pulls our no-nonsense gray Vauxhall into the curb. I jump out and run round to meet Vince who, as soon as he sees me, gets out. He is dressed in distressed tie-dye jeans teamed with his habitual elfin boots with chains around them and an itty-bitty coral mohair sweater. He has spiky black hair which is plastered with so much gel that he must have the entirety of Bristol's hairdressers begging for his custom. He flings his arms wide open.

"Ducks! How lovely to see you! How are you? Cooped up with all those handsome police officers all day; it must be driving you mad! We're all desperately jealous!"

I grin widely and hug him. James has got out of the car and is walking toward us. His face is a picture. He is trying to maintain a normal expression and yet, at the same time, trying to stop his mouth from hitting the ground.

In the meantime, Vince and I have disentangled ourselves and stand waiting patiently for his arrival. He seems to be taking an inordinately long time to cover the two hundred yards between us.

"Who. Is. This. Gorgeous. Man?" murmurs Vince under his breath. "You lucky, lucky thing."

"Hands off. He's engaged," I murmur back.

James has regained some composure by the time he reaches us and I make the necessary introductions.

"Vince, this is Detective Sergeant James Sabine. James, this is Vince, our photographer," I gaily announce as though I am a hostess on a game show. James manfully thrusts out his hand.

"Hello Vince, nice to meet you."

"Pleasure is all mine," Vince coos as he shakes hands.

I smother a grin. "Shall we go?"

"Just need to get my gear out of the boot. You two go ahead, I'll catch up." Vince minces over to the rear end of the lilac love machine (as he calls it) and throws open the boot.

James and I walk toward Mrs. Stephens' house.

"You could have warned me," he whispers.

"What about?" I ask innocently. He glares at me. "Well, you might not have agreed if you'd known you'd have Vince fluttering his eyelids at you all day."

"Holly, contrary to your opinion of me, I am not completely prehistoric. I have no objections to gay men. Mind the fruit pastille." He points to the ground.

We turn through the front gate and on to Mrs. Stephens' pathway. Almost immediately James breaks into a run toward the house and yells, "STOP! POLICE!"

I follow his line of vision and spot a figure in dark clothing leaping from the ground floor window and disappearing around the side of the house.

"Vince!" I yell. "Come on!" and I run up the path after James and our suspect, dropping my bag onto the lawn on the way. From the sound of pounding feet behind me, Vince is not far behind.

I run around the side of the house, through an open wooden gate and into the back garden. I slow down momentarily to look for them and then spot James, agile as a cat, diving through a gate in the corner. Vince has taken advantage of my transient lull, overtaken me and is belting after them. "I really—pant—must buy—pant—a sports bra," I gasp to myself as my breasts and I jig along together, unfortunately not in sync. I didn't have this particular little scenario in mind while dressing this morning and thus I am wearing a tight-ish, straight, long gray skirt and a pair of strappy heels.

I dive out on to the small narrow road that runs along the back of all the properties and spot everyone about one hundred yards ahead of me. They actually haven't got too much of a distance on me. What I plan to do, if I ever catch up with any of them, I simply do not know. Yell "TAG" perhaps and run in the opposite direction. A stitch decides to assail me at this rather inconvenient moment. I clutch my side and slow down to a bit of a limp. I think I'm going to be sick. Just need . . . a . . . bit . . . more . . . oxygen. I pause for a moment and then make a concerted sprint toward them. The youth in dark clothing makes a leap for a wall at the end of the road. James leaps after him and, in a sort of vertical rugby tackle, grabs hold of one of his legs. Vince starts snapping away just as I arrive at the scene. James seems to have gained control of the situation but as I arrive next to him, the youth gives an almighty kick out with the captured limb. James doesn't let go of his iron grip but his arm involuntarily jerks back and his elbow hits me—SMACK!—in the eye.

I fall back slightly, my hand clasped over my eye. Shit. That hurt.

"Holly!" James' head swivels round over his broad shoulder

while he continues to grapple with the young man. He turns his full attention back to the youth, and in one swift movement gives the leg a hefty tug. The boy falls to the ground and James niftily spins him over and cuffs him. He leaves him on the road and runs over to me.

"Are you OK? Here, let me see. Will you stop that?!" he snaps at Vince, whose shutters simply have not stopped whirring.

"Sorry," says Vince sheepishly and walks over to me.

James is trying to remove my hand from my eye. I think my eye will fall out if I take my hand away. James wins.

"What the hell were you doing practically in my armpit?"

"It hurts."

"I can see it hurts. Skin's not broken though."

I squint through my good eye at the youth on the ground. Right now, I feel like giving him a good kick in the . . .

"Sorry," says James, shrugging. Obviously all in a day's work for him.

"S'OK," I mumble, still viciously glaring at the prostrate fig-ure. James gets him up and we all walk back toward the house. Vince has resumed snapping away and my hand has resumed its position over my eye. An old lady is walking up the road toward us and had my sense of humor not deserted me I might have laughed. She looks absolutely horrified and steers a very large berth around us. We must look a very motley crew. One sulky, handcuffed youth. One dusty detective. One gay photographer and one blond weirdo doing a good impersonation of Pudsy the Bear. Terrific. This is a day to look back on with fond memories.

We walk into Mrs. Stephens' back garden.

"I live here," says the youth sulkily, his eyes firmly fixed on the ground. We all stop in surprise and huddle around the saturnine juvenile.

"You what?" says James.

"I live here."

"Then why were you climbing out of the window?" James asks. Good question, well put.

"Yes. Why were you climbing out of the window?" I echo fiercely, my hand still firmly clasped over my throbbing eye.

"Grandma doesn't know that I'm home," he mumbles. Grandma? GRANDMA?

"Let's go in and talk to her, shall we?" James says lightly. The group walk on, leaving me gnashing my teeth like Mutley behind them. I've got a black eye because he didn't want to tell Grandma he's home?

James knocks loudly on the back door and after a few minutes Mrs. Stephens appears. From the surprise on her face I can tell our suspect really is her grandson. They all go inside, and then James pops his head back out. "Holly? Are you coming?"

I trail my bitter body into the house and follow them down the back corridor and into the sitting room I was in a few days earlier. James takes the cuffs off the youth and we all sit down in a very civilized manner, in a strange contrast to the frenzied behavior of a few minutes ago.

"Andrew, what are you doing? What's happened?" asks Mrs. Stephens, her gentle face panic-stricken at the scene before her.

James interjects. "Mrs. Stephens, I saw him climbing out of a window. Naturally, I assumed he was a burglar. I yelled 'Stop, police' but he made a run for it. That normally tends to indicate that the person in question doesn't wish to be caught. I'm sorry."

She clasps her hand up to her mouth and looks genuinely distressed. "*I'm* sorry, Detective. For putting you to all this trouble." I clasp my hand back up to my face in a pathetic attempt for the spotlight. Nothing. Everyone ignores me.

Mrs. Stephens turns to the boy. "Andrew, why aren't you at school?"

"Didn't feel like going," he mutters sulkily at his shoes. Well, sunshine, we all feel like not doing things occasionally, I think to myself savagely. In fact, I feel like it every day at the moment.

"Why?" she asks gently.

"Dunno." Absolutely riveting stuff.

James gets up. "Well, as this seems to be a purely domestic dispute, we'll be on our way, Mrs. Stephens. We did want to ask you a few questions, but I'll come back another time when you're less busy. Don't worry about seeing us out," he adds as she makes a move to get up.

Vince and I similarly get up and shuffle over toward the door. I resist the urge to give Andrew a swift kick as I pass him.

Once outside, I pick my bag up from where I dropped it during the chase and we stand around, strangely subdued. Vince says, "That was a bit strange, wasn't it?"

"Not really. Just a case of mistaken identity." James shrugs.

"Is that it for today?" Vince asks.

"Yeah, I think so. In a pictorial sense anyway. Holly isn't up to much else, are you?" says James with a grin, obviously finding it a little more amusing than I do. Oh sure, chortle away, laughing boy.

"I don't know how you do this every day, Detective Sergeant. I think I'm getting a migraine," says Vince, clasping his hand to his forehead and wandering off toward his car.

James guides me into the passenger seat of our car as though I am a suspect being taken in for questioning, and then walks around to his side. I tentatively unclasp my hand from my eye and blink slowly. The throbbing sensation has gone and now I am left with just a dull ache. We set off back to the station but stop after a few minutes at a small corner shop. James leaps out without saying anything. I immediately whisk down the passenger sunshield in order to survey the damage to my face in the mirror. Not as much swelling as I would like, but still I think it's going to be a shiner.

James comes back and, without saying anything, chucks a bag of frozen peas and a bar of chocolate onto my lap. In spite of myself I smile, and we wordlessly drive off.

Back at the station, Dave-the-grumpy-git-desk-sergeant doesn't say anything at all at the sight of me with a bag of peas stuck to my eye. I grin mindlessly at him. He raises his eyebrows.

"Everything all right, sir?" he says to James.

"Yes Dave. I, er, hit Holly in the eye. Accidentally, of course."

"Of course, sir. Accidentally," he murmurs, managing to intimate that he wouldn't have blamed James at all if he had just socked me in a non-accidental and rather deliberate fashion.

We reach the office and Callum bounces over as soon as he sees us. James and Callum are back on talking terms.

"Latest fashion accessory, Hol?" he asks doubtfully as soon as he clocks the peas.

"James punched me in the eye." A look of horror comes over Callum's face as he stares at James.

"I did not. Well, I did, but it was an accident." James looks round at me. "Would you not use the verb 'punched'? It sounds deliberate."

"How can a verb sound deliberate?"

"Just don't use it," he snaps and walks off.

I grin. I am now starting to enjoy this enormously and appreciate the pure potential of the situation—I could milk it for weeks! Callum and I work our way toward our desks and it takes an inordinately long time.

Rest of the department (horrified): "Holly, what happened?"

Me (gleeful): "James smacked me in the eye!"

James (crossly, from by the coffee machine): "Accidentally!"

Callum (disparagingly): "That's what *he* says."

Rest of the department (wickedly): "Well, that's not very Dick Tracy–like, is it?"

After Callum has brought me a cup of hot sweet tea, I give myself up to the fact that I'm not going to get anything else done today and settle back to read the forensics reports from Mrs. Stephens' burglary. Basically, they still don't know what the mysterious substance is that keeps being found at the scene of the crime. As I know that the forensics department is hopelessly overstretched and we are way down on their list of priorities, reading between the lines I sense that unless the solution presents itself on a plate we are unlikely to ever know what this substance is. Opposite me, James gets on with some reports.

Partly due to lack of other material and partly because I think it will make a good story (especially with Vince's photos), I write up today's escapade on my laptop for the diary, as well as the latest update on The Fox.

James gets off the phone.

"That was Mrs. Stephens. She was calling to apologize for this morning."

"Hmph."

"She's sorted it all out with Andrew. Apparently he's been missing his parents. Anyway, he's agreed to go back to school and she says he seems a lot better after their chat together."

"Hmph."

"She asked how your eye was."

"What did you say?"

"I said it was bad. Very bad."

"Good." He smiles and goes back to his work.

Toward the end of the afternoon, after I have been down to see Robin to show off my black eye and generally been fed doughnuts and cosseted by everyone, I head off to the paper and once there go straight to Joe's office.

"That's going to be a beauty," he says as I waltz in after the habitual "COME!"

"Got smacked in the eye." I turn to examine it in the mirror hanging on the back of his door. Blimey. The bruise is already starting to come out. My eye is slightly closed and surrounded by purple and yellow tissue.

"I know. Seen the photos," he says, pointing down at his desk. I look at the colored spreads in front of him and he reads my diary installment while I pick the best ones out. I'm careful not to include Andrew in any of them. We then agree the photo choice between us and include a couple of great action shots of James' elbow making contact with my face. That done, we both lean back in our chairs and Joe links his hands behind his head.

"Had any more problems from the *Journal*?"

I shake my head slowly. Joe chuckles to himself. "They couldn't scoop us on this one anyway! One of *their* journalists wasn't bashed in the eye during a chase!" he says triumphantly. "I think we've got them licked! You go home now, Holly."

I smile and nod thankfully. I am actually feeling a little tired. Must be all the excitement.

"Get that boyfriend of yours to look after you." Some hope, but I suddenly remember that he's due to be coming round tonight as Lizzie can't make our usual Monday night ice cream fest. It's not like me to ever forget Ben is coming round. I am normally soaking in three feet of soapy, scented water and frenziedly brandishing my razor by now. I suppose a lot has been going on today.

"And don't forget that TV thing on Friday."

I stare at him in horror. I had actually forgotten all about it.

"I can't go on TV with this." I point at my half-closed eye.

"Sure you can. Bruising will be down by then. Besides, it will be great publicity. It will show just how genuine the diary is. Go on, go home," he says, waving his arms in a shooing motion. "Some of us have got work to do."

I can't be bothered to argue and besides, the end of the week feels like years away. I make my way home and immediately start running a hot bath. Not for Ben particularly, just for me. I lie in it and let the comforting warmth of the scented water seep into my bones. The phone rings just as I am getting out. I quickly wrap my toweling robe around me and run to answer it.

"Hello?"

"Darling! How are you?" It's my mother. I settle myself down cross-legged on the floor.

"I'm fine except for the fact I've got myself a black eye."

"How careless. How did you manage that?"

"Well, James . . . I mean Jack . . ." and I give her the whole story.

"Darling, how absolutely thrilling! It sounds as though you're having a *fabulous* time!"

"Well, maybe not fabulous. I mean, it did hurt at the time," I say doubtfully. "Anyway, you'll see it all in the diary. We've got pictures too now! Oh, and I have a TV interview on Friday with the local TV station! Do you get it down there?"

"No, I don't think we do. How wonderful! You'll have to make sure you record it for us!"

"I will, I promise."

"Do as my director tells me. Enunciate clearly, remember your vowels and sit up straight."

"Thanks for the advice," I remark dryly.

"I always pass on good advice. I've got no other use for it. Shit MacGregor, darling! Have to fly! The cat's on fire!"

I raise my eyes heavenward, replace the receiver and go and get dressed.

* * *

Ben arrives twenty minutes later. I open the door to him and he recoils at the sight of my swollen face.

"What the hell have you done?"

"Accidentally got hit in the face."

"Well, I can't take you out looking like that. People will think I did it." He troops into the sitting room and plonks himself on the sofa. "Did it hurt?"

"A bit."

"Get them all the time in rugby," he says with an attitude lacking in the relevant sympathy.

"How was your day?" I ask.

"Really good. Do you remember that bloke I told you about? From accounts? Well, he came up to me today . . ."

After half an hour I decide I'm a little bored of staring at him adoringly and admiring his teeth.

"Aren't you going to ask me how it happened?"

He stops mid-flow, surprised at my interjection. "Of course I am, babe. I didn't think you wanted to talk about it."

And so I relate my story again.

"You'll read all about it tomorrow anyway, so you'll just have to skip over that bit."

He stares at me. "Read about it?" he asks doubtfully.

"Yes. In the diary," I say patiently.

"Of course, of course! The diary. Could you try and plug the game on Saturday?"

"It might be a little difficult as it's about the police. But I'll try."

I get up and go through to make some omelettes for supper. I busy myself getting eggs, milk and cheese out of the fridge. "Do you want cheese or herbs or both, Ben?" I shout.

No answer.

I walk through to the sitting room. Ben is standing over the magazine rack, staring down with the strangest expression on his face.

"What's wrong?"

His head jolts up. "Eh?"

"Cheese or herbs?"

"I, er, just remembered. I can't stay. Got a team meeting."

"Tonight?"

"Er, yes. On, er, team strategy."

"Do you have to go?"

"Yes, very important. Can't miss it, in fact."

I raise my eyebrows in surprise and then shrug. "OK," I say and walk with him to the door. I open it and lean on the frame.

"Well, might I see you later in the week?"

"Er, yes, probably. I mean, definitely!"

I lean forward to kiss his mouth. He moves, probably to kiss me, and so I end up planting a square one on his ear.

"You moved!" I say embarrassedly.

"Yes! Sorry! See you soon! Bye!" he says and sprints out into the hall and down the stairs. I close the door and stare at the white paintwork for a minute, biting my lip. How strange. He was behaving a little oddly. Almost as though . . . I wander back into the sitting room, sit down on the sofa and stare into space. I didn't even get a chance to tell him about my TV interview.

My face suddenly gets very hot and I involuntarily clench my hands into fists. He didn't have a rugby meeting. He wanted to leave, to get away. I remember where he was standing when I came into the sitting room. I get up and walk over to the magazine rack and stare down. A beautiful girl dressed in pure white and clutching a bouquet of flowers stares straight back at me. A bride. It's one of Lizzie's bridal magazines.

fourteen

I glare at the magazine, my thoughts racing. What had Ben been thinking? That I was plotting to marry him? Or I was a closet wedding freak? I walk back over to the sofa and sink into its cushions, wishing the whole thing would just swallow me up instead. Oh God, he must have thought this was a rerun of *Fatal Attraction*. He is probably sitting in the nearest pub right now, nursing a large brandy and telling a sympathetic barman all about his lucky escape. A groan unwittingly escapes my lips and I cover my face with my hands and then wince as one of my fingers catches my sore eye.

I'll just call and explain, that's what I'll do. I sit up eagerly. I'll ring him and explain that the magazines are Lizzie's. I sink back into the soft cushions and wonder despondently to myself if he'll believe me. Lizzie's not even engaged, and this little escapade has come hot on the heels of my parents arriving dressed up to the nines and eager to greet the prospective son-in-law. So what if that wasn't how it really happened? The point is that it doesn't look that way. And now this.

Surely he's got to believe me. It's the truth, for heaven's sake! A nagging little voice at the back of my head asks, why should he be so averse to the idea of marriage anyway? And why to you? Would he still run a mile if Cindy Crawford said, "How's about it, big boy; you and me, Gretna Green?" Or is it just the idea of matrimony that panics him, whoever it's with? Do I really want to be with a man who bolts at the sight of a wedding magazine?

I don't know. All I do know is I can't bear to let it finish this way. I can't bear to let him think I have been running around covertly plotting to have him "for better, for worse." And what would you do, whispers the little voice, if it did finish? Would you collapse in a heap on the floor, or would you secretly, in your heart of hearts, be just a little relieved? No more Saturday nights in, waiting for him to turn up. No more fascinating discussions about Jonny Wilkinson.

I shake my head resolutely. Am I mad? I don't want this to finish. Girls would kill to go out with that boy. Those shoulders, those eyes, those golden looks. No, no. I set my teeth determinedly. "You can butt out, girls," I say to an imaginary group of circling harpies. "He's mine and I'm going to keep him that way. Jonny Wilkinson or no bloody Jonny Wilkinson."

I walk resolutely over to the telephone and dial his number. He probably won't be home yet but I'm too anxious to care. No answer. I replace the receiver and pace my flat nervously for the next ten minutes. I go back and try again; still no answer. I put the television on in an effort to take my mind off things, but my thoughts keep straying back anyway. Just tell him straight, I say to myself. He has to believe you because it's the truth.

All in all, I must dial his number at least ten times. Each time the phone just rings and rings. Where is he? Where the hell is he? At midnight I give up and go to bed. I pull the duvet up to my chin and then lie on my side in the fetal position, praying for sleep. Willing for its gentle oblivion. Finally I think I must doze off, because I am awakened by a persistently shrill noise. I blink my eyes blearily and turn off my alarm clock, but still the noise persists. I focus at the hour on the clock. It isn't even time for the alarm to go off. I suddenly realize it's the front door buzzer and I leap up and run through to the hall. It must be Ben! He must have realized he'd made a mistake and come round on his way to

work. He couldn't bear for the day to pass without apologizing! I
lift the receiver of the entry phone.

"Hello?" I say eagerly.

"Holly?"

"Yes?"

"It's James."

"James?"

"Buzz me up."

I duly do as I am told. I can hear him coming up the stairs as
I run back into my bedroom. I hastily wrap my dressing gown
around me and then run back into the hall just in time to open
the door.

"James? What are you doing here?"

"There's been another burglary. This time someone was hurt.
Are you, er, OK? I mean, apart from the eye thing," he says, peering at me.

I put a hand up to my face. "Er, yes, fine. I think. I'll just go and
get dressed. I'll be two seconds. Help yourself to a cup of tea if
you want." I point the way through to the sitting room and the
kitchen.

"Thanks."

I go back to the bedroom and peer in the mirror. I recoil instantly. Well, I can see why he might be concerned. My black eye
has almost completely closed up and is surrounded by a tapes-
try of glorious Technicolor. My other eye is looking as bad, full
of sleep and puffed up. My hair has its parting halfway down
my head, hovering a fraction above my left ear, and I am looking pasty and tired. Nothing half a day with the Clarins range
wouldn't fix but unfortunately I have no time for that now.

"How did you know where I lived?" I yell through to the
kitchen.

"Robin!" he yells back. Of course, Robin. Is he still seeing her,

do you think? Or is it just old-fashioned little moi who thinks
he ought to break it off *before* his wedding? "Do you want tea?"
he adds.

"Yes, please!"

I have no time for a shower and so I hastily throw on some
black combats and a black polo-neck sweater instead of my habitual pencil skirt and little top. With my black eye I might as
well look as *Reservoir Dogs* as I possibly can. I perform damage
limitation on my face and hair as far as possible and then walk
through to the kitchen in my bare feet in search of some suitable
shoes. James hands me a mug of tea.

"I could only find some of that disgusting Earl Grey stuff."

"That's all I drink."

"Oh."

We sip our tea and lean against the countertops. "How's the
eye?" he asks.

"OK, thanks. Doesn't look too attractive though. Has the person been hurt badly? In the burglary?"

"I don't know. He's in the hospital. The night shift took the
call but they thought it might be the same thief so they called me
early. The Chief wants these burglaries to be my priority now.
Sorry to wake you, but I thought you wouldn't want to miss it."

"Thanks."

I collect some things together and then we walk down to the
car and head off toward the hospital.

"You're very quiet. Are you sure you're OK? You haven't got
concussion or anything?" he asks.

For a second I'm tempted to pour all my troubles out, to tell
him about Ben and how he thinks I'm plotting to marry him. But
I don't think James will be able to cope with such sensational rev-
elations. He might even think I'm lying about the magazines
being Lizzie's etc., so I decide to keep my mouth shut. Like the
wide-mouthed frog.

"No, no," I murmur out of the corner of my tightly shut mouth. Besides, James has his own wedding issues right now. He's getting married in a few weeks' time and poor Robin must be devastated.

En route, James calls the station to request that the forensics officers go to the address of the latest burglary.

As he turns the mobile off, I ask, "Do you think it's The Fox again?"

"The Fox?"

"That's what I call him in the diary. The same person who did Mrs. Stephens and Mr. Forquar-White?"

"Oh, well, I don't know. But hopefully Roger might find something. At the very least that peculiar substance so we can link all the burglaries."

We travel in silence, each musing on our own private thoughts until we reach the hospital car park. We come to a standstill. James pulls up the handbrake.

"Holly?"

I look inquiringly at him and raise my eyebrows.

"Would you mind wearing your sunglasses? People are going to think I've hit you or something."

"But you have," I say, intentionally missing the point.

"But not deliberately."

"Are you sure it wasn't?"

"Just put the damn sunglasses on."

Once in the hospital we ask to see Mr. Williams and then set off down the labyrinth of corridors in the direction we are told. Mr. Williams looks to be asleep when we reach him. For an awful moment I actually wonder whether he's dead. Two ladies who are sitting on either side of him rise as we approach. The older woman, I discover, is Mrs. Williams. She is tearful and distressed, constantly wringing a white handkerchief she has in her hands.

We go through the normal rigmarole of IDs and introductions. James suggests tea in the canteen which is a few doors down from the ward. Mrs. Williams leaves instructions with the younger lady, who I think from the resemblance is her daughter, and accompanies us down the corridor.

While James and Mrs. Williams sit down at one of the Formica tables, I trot up to the counter and buy three teas. Suitably equipped with a tray I head back toward them, anxious not to miss anything. James is sitting next to the lady on the same side of the table and has his arm around her. Her head is down and she is silently weeping. He looks up as I place the tray gently down and smiles at me.

"Thanks, Holly. Here, Mrs. Williams, have some tea. You'll feel better. Is there anyone I can call who could look after you?"

She snuffles into her handkerchief and accepts the proffered cup of tea.

"That's my daughter in there. She's staying for a few days. Thank you anyway."

"I've sent some forensics officers to your house, if that's OK? I'm told that your neighbor is there." She nods and James continues. "When is your husband expected to be released from the hospital?"

"They're keeping him in for observation. Maybe tomorrow, they said."

"In that case, we will need to interview him today. It really is important to get his statement as soon as possible. Mrs. Williams, I know this is difficult for you but I also need a list of everything that has been taken. Could you send it over to my office this afternoon please?" She nods. James writes down his fax number for her and then goes on to ask her a few more questions, but it is clear the poor lady really isn't up to talking very much.

* * *

We go back to the main ward. Mr. Williams still has his eyes closed. The young lady excuses herself and leaves us to it. James says loudly, "Mr. Williams?" The man opens his eyes hazily. He's probably around retirement age—just like my father, really. I don't like the thought of this frail old man being hit over the head. He has a large bandage on his forehead and his left eye is black. It's horrible to see old flesh torn and bruised.

James Sabine makes the appropriate introductions while Mr. Williams sits up and takes sips of water from a glass at the side of his bed. James then says, "Can you take us through the events of last night please, Mr. Williams?"

"I'll try, it's a bit hazy, like," he responds. "I woke up at about three in the morning because I'd heard a noise. It wasn't a loud noise but I'm a very light sleeper, see? On account of my prostate. Need to widdle in the night a good few times, you see? Anyway, I looked over at the clock and saw the time and then listened for more noise. I didn't hear anything but I just had this feeling something wasn't right, so I got up and went downstairs to check. I suppose that after reading about The Fox I'd been feeling nervous. Not that I'd mention anything to Marjorie—that's my wife—but I was feeling a bit on edge. You see, Marjorie inherited the house from her mum, along with pretty much everything in it, and we do have loads of little precious knickknacks; well, that's what the insurance man told us anyway. She won't get rid of the house, oh no. She says it would be a step toward the nursing home. She says—"

"Mr. Williams?" says James gently. "You were telling us about last night?"

"Oh! Yes, sorry. Anyway, I went downstairs and went into every room and turned the light on. He was in the dining room. I suppose he must have been hiding behind the door because just as I turned around to come out I remember a whoosh of air and a terrible pain in my head and then nothing. I came to in here.

Marjorie says it was about six this morning when she found me and called the ambulance immediately."

"So you didn't see the suspect at all?"

Mr. Williams shakes his head. "Sorry."

James sighs. "Well, thanks, Mr. Williams, for your help. I promise that we're doing all we can to find the culprit."

I spontaneously lean across and pat Mr. Williams' hand. He looks over at me and smiles. "What's up with you, love?" he says, gesturing to the sunglasses.

I take them off. "Snap!"

"How did you do that?"

"He smacked me in the face." Mr. Williams looks over at James, aghast and just a little confused.

"Accidentally," says James patiently and probably getting on for the hundredth time.

I wait in the corridor while James tries to find out exactly when Mr. Williams will be released.

"Hello! Fancy seeing you here!" says a friendly voice behind me. I spin round.

"Dr. Kirkpatrick!" I am tempted to add he is a sight for sore eyes because he is just that. His dark hair flops sexily down and his lazy smile almost meets his eyes.

"I suppose it's not such a surprise considering your past record of self-mutilation."

"One tries one's best," I say, grinning delightedly at his flirtatious tone.

"What are you here for this time?"

"Official business."

"Are you sure?" he says, pointing at the sunglasses.

"Ah. Well." I take them off and display my vibrant eye. "Wasn't me though."

"Official business?"

"Yep, Detective Sergeant Sabine accidentally hit me." Dr. Kirkpatrick leads me to some chairs and sits me down. He stands over me and peers closer at my eye. I think I'm about to pass out.

"Hmm, looks OK. I've been following your diary, you know," he says, still peering.

"Have you?" Unfortunately this comes out as a rather high-pitched squeak.

"Yes." He releases me. "It's developed quite a little cult following."

"You can read all about this in today's episode," I say lightly.

He grins at me. "I will."

"Holly!" James makes me jump and Dr. Kirkpatrick stands up. They shake hands in a manful, hearty fashion.

"Just looking at Holly's eye. Quite a bash you gave her!"

"It wasn't deliberate," James says, practically through clenched teeth. He glares at me in an if-you-tell-anyone-else . . . kind of way. I quickly put my sunglasses back on. My jolly banter with Dr. Kirkpatrick culminates in a pledge to injure myself again soon. Unfortunately, he isn't aware of just what an easy promise that is to make.

On the way back out to the car I buy the *Bristol Gazette* from the hospital shop. Today is the first day that the photos appear. In the car I quickly turn to the diary pages.

"What's that?" asks James.

"Vince's pictures of yesterday."

"How do they look?" he asks, trying to glance at them as we go along.

"Good. There's a great one of your elbow making contact with my head." I hold it up for him to see.

"Shit! I bet that hurt!" he says, looking across.

"It did rather."

"I think you really must have something wrong with your inner ear."

"Why do you say that?" I retort huffily.

"Nobody can be that uncoordinated. Do I really look like that?"

"Yes, you do," I snap. James's mobile rings shrilly, interrupting us before the row escalates.

I close the newspaper and stare out of the window. James barks down the phone as I try frantically to catch one of my running thoughts. Ben, The Fox, Mr. Williams, Dr. Kirkpatrick. They all go round and round in my head without slowing down. I feel as though I'm on a rollercoaster ride and I'm not allowed to get off.

It's still only mid-morning by the time we get back to the station. The desk sergeant is his normal cheery and charming self, completely ignoring yours truly while asking after James' health. We walk into the offices upstairs and are stopped continually en route to our desks by officers asking me how my eye is and telling James off for doing it. I keep shooting glances at James, wondering just how long his temper is going to hold out under this barrage. It seems to be weathering it tolerably well. Callum is not around but he has bought me a pirate's black eye-patch as a joke and has left it on my desk with a note.

I am determined to sort out this wedding-magazine-thing with Ben as soon as I possibly can. I find the opportunity when James is seated at his desk. I slip out to the corridor and dial Ben's direct line work number into my mobile.

He answers.

"Ben, it's me."

"Oh, hi," he says awkwardly.

"Ben, I know why you rushed off last night and I'm just calling to explain . . ."

And I go on to tell him all about Lizzie's marriage fetish and how she left the magazines at my house.

"... and I have no interest whatsoever in marrying you. I haven't thought about it at all. Not that I might not want to marry you at some point in the future or ..."

"I believe you, Holly. I'm sorry for getting the wrong end of the stick."

"Oh, OK." I breathe out in relief and let my shoulders go—I hadn't noticed they were tense but they seem to visibly sag. "Right." I can't think of anything else to say and because my playing-it-cool method has been shot to bits I think it may be wise to finish the conversation as quickly as I can.

"Well! Glad we sorted that out then! Have to go, see you soon." We say our respective goodbyes and hang up. I'm just about to make my way back to my desk when my mobile rings. I look at the number and answer it.

"Hi Lizzie. How's it going?"

"I know you don't like to be disturbed at work, but I had to call and say how fabulous the pictures are!" Her voice ends in a high-pitched squeal of excitement.

I smile, genuinely pleased. "Oh, thanks."

"So how are you?"

"OK, I suppose," I say wearily.

"What's up?" So I tell her about Ben finding the magazines and leaping to the wrong conclusion.

"I'm so sorry," Lizzie says forlornly.

"I think we've patched things up now."

"No, I'm sorry because they're my magazines."

"The thought had occurred to me," I say a trifle pointedly. "Don't worry about it. Look, I've got to go. See you tonight?" She agrees and I return to my desk.

A while later, I am tapping away on my laptop in preparation for this evening's diary edition and wearing my eye-patch from Callum to annoy James. Vince has been dispatched to the hospital to take some pictures of Mr. Williams. James is on the phone to the DNA lab. I am halfheartedly listening in, but start to listen intently as a few snippets reach my ears.

"God, I'm really sorry. No, we had absolutely no idea. Of course Roger wouldn't have known . . . I didn't see it myself. Yeah, I do know how much all this costs. Yeah. Thanks again. Bye."

"What's up?" I ask as soon as he puts the receiver down, my one eye wide with excitement.

"The hair we sent away for DNA testing turns out to be a cat hair."

"A cat hair?"

"A cat hair."

We look at each other doubtfully for a second, then both of us start to smile.

"They were furious," he says. "Accused me of wasting time and resources."

"You would think Roger would know the difference between a cat hair and a human one."

"You would, wouldn't you?"

"It brings a whole new meaning to the phrase, 'cat burglar.'"

"You're not going to print this, are you?"

I smile. "Our secret. What color was the hair, by the way?"

"Ginger."

"Pity you can't run it through the computer. Known felons who own a ginger tom."

He grins, but then slowly his smile fades. "Damn, it was our one strong lead. I spoke to Roger earlier today. That peculiar substance was only on the *one* door handle in the third burglary. Someone has got into all those houses previously to case them. How did they do it? Who would you let into your house?" He uncaps a pen and reaches for a notepad to make a list.

I rack my brains. "Er, gas and electricity people, telephone too.

How about builders? Piano tuners?" He raises an eyebrow at this one but humors me by writing them all down. ". . . salesmen, finance people perhaps, about pensions or something. Accountants. Erm, can't think of any more."

We look at each other for a while, he adds a couple of his own ideas and then recaps the pen. "We need the common link among all the houses. Come on." He gets up.

"Where are we going?"

"Back to the beginning."

"Could we put the siren on this time?"

"NO."

fifteen

⎯⎯⎯⎯⎯

Firstly we visit the homes of Mrs. Stephens and Mr. Williams. We write down the names of anyone they can remember who has visited their house in the last two months. Plumbers, delivery men—anyone and everyone. We then emerge forty-five minutes later from Sebastian Forquar-White's house. We have cross-referenced the lists and exhausted every possibility of a link between the three houses. We've drawn a complete blank.

I follow James down the path and out on to the road. He leans against the car and distractedly runs his hand through his hair.

"Are you sure the burglar would have been in these houses before he robbed them?" I ask, exhausted with the list-making.

He looks up at the grand house before him. "They have all said the thief knew exactly where to find everything and how to disable the alarm systems. The thief would have known these houses have good security systems in them. It would have been too risky just to wing it. None of the neighbors claim to have seen or heard anything at all. Whoever it was *must* have had prior knowledge of the houses. Besides all of that, the substance we can't identify is only in the rooms where goods were removed and even then very sparingly. The thief must have known exactly where everything was. We're just missing whatever the link is."

We drive back to the station and, since it is toward the end of the day, park in the above-ground car park. We pull into the entrance and sweep into a parking space. I am just wondering what the next step is, as we walk together toward the reception, when I notice a girl coming toward us.

A singularly beautiful girl.

Her hips sway gently as she carefully places one long-limbed leg in front of the other. She walks with a grace and an elegance that would not look out of place on the catwalk. Her hair is a cropped, shiny black mass and her makeup has a chic nonchalance I could never hope to achieve. It seems James has also noticed her presence. She comes straight up to him and plants a kiss squarely on his lips. This must be Fleur. I can see why Robin wants to leave Bristol now. She's got more than a little competition on her hands.

"Hello darling! I thought that we could travel home together." She turns to me and extends a hand.

"Hello! You must be Holly! I have heard so much about you!" I daren't look at James at this point because we both know it can't have been anything good. "I'm Fleur, James' fiancée."

I shake her hand and say hello. She comes and walks between us, linking her hand through James' arm.

"So, have you two had a good day? Or has it been all blood and guts?" she asks chattily.

"No, it's been fine. How was yours?" James says.

"Oh, the usual." The usual what? I think. The usual fashion shoot? The usual PR for celebrities? Her glamorous presence seems to make me feel strangely shy.

We reach the entrance and James says, "I just need to pop up and collect some things. I'll be two secs."

"Don't worry! I'll stay here and have a nice chat to Holly."

In actual fact I need to collect my stuff as well and shoot my little ass over to the paper, but let's just say I am inquisitive. All right then, nosy.

She plonks herself down on the steps and smiles up at me. I join her on the steps.

"So, how are you finding it?" she inquires sweetly.

"Oh, fine thanks," I say a little warily, because although she seems very nice and I am sure she is very nice, I know whatever I say will go straight back to James. She politely doesn't mention the shades I am sporting and I wonder if she realizes I am wearing them because her future husband has given me a beauty of a shiner. I opt for a swift change of subject.

"Congratulations! I hear you two are getting married."

She smiles, a little mistily. "Yes, we are. In three weeks' time. It will be bliss! We're going to the Maldives for our honeymoon! Imagine! Two weeks away from work! I can hardly wait!"

"What do you do?"

"Didn't he tell you? Well, that's how we met. It was last year. I work as the administrator for a bereavement charity. His brother was killed."

Oh. My. God. "I'm sorry, I didn't know."

"He was killed in a sailing accident, no one's fault. So tragic. James was devastated. He came to us for counseling." Golly, not only does she look like a ministering angel, she is one as well. A picture flashes before my eyes of a grieving James, slowly brought through the mourning process by this beautiful woman and falling in love on the way. I inwardly gulp. This is way out of my league. I feel like a big cheese plant next to her stunning orchid. A skilled conversationalist, she leads the way out of our slight pause by asking, "Have you met Callum?"

"Yes, yes, I have."

"He's nice, isn't he? He's going to be our best man." I didn't know that.

"I didn't know that." I raise my eyebrows in surprise and suddenly wonder if the row they had last week was about Robin.

James appears at the top of the steps. "Come on, Fleur. Stop telling Holly our deep, dark secrets." He looks at me intently as if to warn me off from telling Fleur a couple of his deep, dark secrets.

We both scramble up. Fleur turns to me. "It was really nice to meet you at last, Holly. We must go out for a drink sometime, just us girls."

"I would like that," I say truthfully.

"Take care of him, won't you?"

"I will. Bye Fleur, bye James."

I decide to walk the three flights of stairs up to the paper as a little exercise wouldn't go amiss. I bang open the emergency exit doors that lead into our offices and then make my way to Joe's office.

I knock and wait for the habitual "COME!" Upon hearing it, I walk in and, seeing that Joe is on the phone, make myself comfortable and await his attention, my thoughts still full of James and his brother.

Joe puts down the receiver.

"Blimey, Holly! It's turned into a blinder, hasn't it?"

I look at him, absolutely mystified. What are we talking about? The diary? The Fox's latest job? What?

"All the colors of the rainbow." Still I stare at him. What is this? Some sort of new code language nobody has bothered sending me a memo about?

"Your eye, Holly. Your eye," Joe says patiently.

"Oh!" My hand flies up to touch it. I had completely forgotten I'd taken my sunglasses off. I get up and examine it in the mirror on his door. Even I wince at the sight of it. Damn, I should have been making more of it. What is the point of having an injury if you don't exploit it to its full advantage?

I immediately adopt an injured animal air and go back and sit down.

"All in the line of duty, Joe, all in the line of duty," I murmur faintly.

"How's it going?"

"It's still a bit sore," I say pathetically.

"Not your eye, the diary. How's it going?"

"Oh!" I adopt a more businesslike air. "Another burglary today."

"Another one? The Fox again?"

" 'Fraid so. Unfortunately a bloke got hurt too."

"Really?"

"Yeah, he interrupted the burglary. Got walloped over the head. The Chief wants us to make it our main priority from now on. Vince went down to the hospital to take some photos of the victim. Probably still developing them."

"Will these burglaries be solved before the diary finishes?"

"Maybe!" I say brightly. Well, maybe they will and maybe they won't. There's a pause as he mulls this over.

"Had the opinion pollsters out today as it was the first day with photos."

"How did it go?"

"Brilliant. People are loving it! Circulation is up. Don't forget the TV interview; we started trailing it today. I want you to really play up the live aspect. You know, fly on the, er, door, that sort of thing. Basically, do the PR blurb that you did to trail the diary."

"Yeah, I will." I get up to go.

He frowns, looking at me. "I hope your black eye will still be there by then. Is there anything you can do to prolong the bruising? Syrup of figs or anything?"

"A little self-flagellation perhaps? Would you like me to take to my head with a frying pan?" I'm not sure that I like this attitude. Clonked yourself around the head? Oh, terrific stuff! Could you see your way to managing a broken limb next time?

I gather up my bag and make my way to the door. Just as I am about to leave, Joe calls out, "How's Buntam?"

"Hmm?"

"Buntam, your cousin. How is he?"

"Er, Buntam's fine," I reply, blinking a little.

"I didn't see him playing last weekend."

My mouth opens and shuts a few times and I blink some more. Normally I would be prepared for this sort of eventuality but the diary has been all-consuming. I wonder briefly what sort of miraculous story-telling my mouth is going to come out with.

"Did I say he is fine? I meant he's fine after his accident." I nod gravely.

"Accident?"

"Runaway golf buggy on the sixth hole. Very nasty. Hit and run too. Looks like dear old Buntam will be out of the game for a few months." Bravo mouth! A fine effort!

"Hit and run? In a golf buggy?" There is a note of incredulity in Joe's voice that makes my brain pause for a second. Unfortunately it doesn't seem to slow my over-ambitious mouth up at all.

"It was one of those new speedy American ones. Nobody got his license plate." Do the damn things have license plates?

Joe shakes his head and tuts to himself for a while, then mutters, "License plate?"

"Well, the new ones have to have them. Because they go so fast." Even I inwardly wince at this. My problem is too much embroidery. Why couldn't I just leave it at a simple accident? Oh no, I had to bring in golf buggies too. But the important thing is to leave and quickly before any more awkward questions come up. "Anyway! Got to go! A friend is expecting me!"

"Give Buntam my regards!" shouts Joe after my disappearing back.

*   *   *

It's about eight o'clock when I reach home. As soon as I put my handbag down, Lizzie arrives.

"How was your day?" she asks.

I frown. "Interesting. How was the wonderful world of computers?"

"Tedious."

"Did you read the diary today?" I ask, noticing the paper poking out of her bag.

"God, yes! I read it every morning. Honestly, I look forward to it." I walk over to the fridge and open the door. I am greeted by a very mopey-looking lettuce and some out-of-date yogurts.

"Do you mind if we go to Sainsbury's?"

"Not at all."

Lizzie and I meander our way down to the supermarket in her car and on the way she insists I tell her why my day was interesting. So I talk about Mr. Williams and the hospital (which she will read about tomorrow in the paper) and then about meeting Fleur (which she won't read about tomorrow in the paper).

She sits up suddenly. "You mean he's got a fiancée?" wails Lizzie.

I glance over at her impatiently. "You knew he had a fiancée."

"I thought she might be made up or something. For the diary."

"Er, no. Why would we make that up?"

"I don't know. Extra publicity or something."

"Lizzie, I thought you were trying to get Alastair to marry you."

"I am," she says sulkily, staring out of the windscreen. "It's not rocky or anything is it?" she carries on hopefully.

I shake my head firmly. "Rock of Gibraltar, I'm afraid. She's absolutely gorgeous and inordinately nice to boot," I add pointedly. "Why are you so interested anyway?"

"Come on, Holly," she says, wide-eyed with the obviousness of it.

"What?"

She nearly chokes in the effort to tell me exactly what. "He. Is. Ab-so-lute-ly. Gorgeous."

I shrug. I mean, I know he's good-looking. And tall. And broad.

"The girls in the office are in a right tizzy about him."

"Well, they wouldn't think he was quite so gorgeous if they'd had the sort of start I've had with him," I say, leaning to one side as she narrowly avoids a kid who is insisting on roller-blading in the gutter.

"He can't be that bad! He looked really concerned about your eye in the diary!"

"I would hope he did! It was his bloody fault!" I say indignantly, swiftly changing the subject. The conversation is making me feel distinctly uncomfortable. "I sorted everything out with Ben."

"Oh, good."

"Well, I hope he believed me."

"I'm sure he did. If you like, I'll call him and tell him the magazines were mine."

"No. Thanks anyway. He might think I'd put you up to it or something. Least said, soonest mended. I'm sure it'll be fine. Will you take the magazines back with you though and get them out of my flat?"

Lizzie pulls a face. "Alastair might see them then and think the same as Ben."

"Lizzie," I say with a warning note in my voice. I mean, if she hadn't brought the bloody things around in the first place then I wouldn't be in this mess with Ben.

"OK," she says sulkily.

We toddle about Sainsbury's, popping various bits and pieces into the basket. Lizzie and I are busy contemplating the pros and cons of sugar-free baked beans compared to good old Heinz when a voice from behind us says, "Hello!"

Lizzie and I look at each other, tins in our hands. It's Teresa. Oh, un-yippee and un-hooray. My hand involuntarily tightens around my can and Lizzie's knuckles are looking a shade on the white side themselves. We plaster a smile on our faces and turn round.

"Hello Teresa. How are you?"

"Fine. My goodness, fancy seeing you two here. I would have thought you'd be out clubbing or something." She laughs an innocent-sounding tinkle. Now you may think this is a very in-nocuous comment, but coming from the lips of Teresa it has a different slant on it. The kind of slant that implies we are two trollops with a drink problem. It's all I can do not to club her over the head with the can of baked beans.

"I would imagine you are doing the same thing that we are doing here, Teresa. No prayer meetings to go to?" says Lizzie pointedly.

"Just come back from one." She smiles smugly, completely oblivious of the sarcasm.

"Have you been reading Holly's diary in the paper?"

"No, I don't read the tabloids. Full of smut." Right, now I'm going to clock her one. "But I do know Fleur. I believe she is the fiancée of the officer you are shadowing, Holly?"

Will we ever be free of this girl? Ever? Why couldn't we have met someone nice in the supermarket? The Beverley Sisters per-haps? How on earth does she know Fleur?

"How do you know Fleur?" I ask in surprise.

"My prayer group does some Bible work down at the bereave-ment charity where she works. Such a nice girl. She is so sweet. And kind." And what are we, the twin sisters of Genghis Khan? "We were just chatting the other day and she mentioned her fi-ancé was being shadowed by a reporter. And of course I knew that was you, Holly, although I have never read your diary." I think she has mentioned that before.

"We would love to stay and talk, Teresa, but we do have to get back," I snarl. We all smile a little stiffly. Teresa goes to walk away and then hesitates. "I would just like to say, Holly, that your Ben was nice." There is a peculiar, smug expression on her face. It flashes there for a moment and then it is gone. She adds, "Bye," and walks off.

"God!" I fume as we walk toward the car, "what has she got to be so bloody self-righteous about! And don't you think it was a funny thing to say at the end about Ben?"

"Oh, don't let the annoying cow get to you. She's got it into her head that any ordinary person needs to be rescued from themselves and she's probably thinking you need to be pitied just because you have a normal, functional relationship."

After we have consumed a bottle of wine, half a quiche Lorraine, two French fancies and a sherbet dip each, we seethe and bitch about Teresa to our heart's content. Then Lizzie takes her leave, pleading an early morning meeting.

After she has left, I wander around the flat, strangely restless. I pick things up and put them down again. I mindlessly puff the cushions on the sofa. I wipe the work surfaces in the kitchen and then I go through and phone Ben.

"Hi! It's me."

"Hi!"

"Just called to see how you are."

"I'm fine. Do you want me to come round?"

"Yes please."

Long after Ben has gone to sleep, I lie awake. My head is full of Fleur and James. To distract myself, I turn to thoughts of the burglaries. Who would Mr. Williams have let into his house? If he had seen the person who assaulted him, would he have recognized his attacker?

sixteen

This being my first-ever visit to a television studio, I have to admit to feeling just a little apprehensive. I am greeted at the reception desk by an over-bright, shan't-keep-you-a-minute peroxide blonde. While I sit patiently in the reception area for someone to collect me, I look at the photos all around me of the studio's stars. Some I recognize, most I do not. This is unsurprising as I am not an avid viewer of local television. I have never been on television before, if you don't count the time my school class were given a slot on the local news for creating an Easter garden. I was the only child not to have a plant in the garden. We all had to bring one from home and my mother dug up what she thought was a lily-of-the-valley, while waxing lyrical about what a gorgeous flower it was and how beautiful it smelt. Unfortunately, she was actually digging up wild garlic. My plant and I stank the classroom out and we were both banned from the Easter garden. The crew who filmed our two-minute slot thought it would be amusing to bung me in at the end with my wilting garlic plant. Not quite so amusing to an eleven-year-old who cried for a week afterward, and it took almost two terms for me to shake off the nickname "Humming Holly, the greatest-known antidote to vampires."

A girl wearing an outfit consisting of black leggings and a bobbly, sloppy jumper, complete with customized Union Jack Dr. Martens, comes out of a door to one side of the reception. Her hair is colored bright orange, her ears are pierced three times each side and her nose is pierced as well.

"Holly Colshannon?" Her plummy accent is in complete contrast to her appearance; she sounds as though she was taught to speak with several toffees in her mouth. But then this is the BBC. Queen's English and all that.

"That's me!"

"Follow me."

We twist and turn through a maze of corridors. We don't talk at all as there is only enough room for us to walk behind each other. We finally come to a stop in front of a door and the girl knocks politely and goes in. I follow. The room is small and completely lit by artificial light from overhead strips. There is a large barber's chair facing a wall of mirrors and the man who is sitting in it leaps to his feet. He has several tissues tucked into his collar, and a woman, who I presume is some sort of makeup artist, appears next to him.

"Hello!" he exclaims jovially. "Jolly nice to meet you!"

"Hello! I'm Holly." He pumps away at my proffered hand as though he's aiming to produce something from me. Maybe he's expecting water to start gushing from my mouth.

"Super to meet you, Holly! Simply super! I'm Giles, *Southwest Tonight*'s host. How are you today?"

"Er, fine, thank you. How are you?" I ask politely.

"Very well, very well. I suppose it's been a big week for you!"

"Er, yes. It's all happened so quickly, quite a surprise really!"

"Oh no! Surely not? You must have been preparing for this for a long time."

"Well, no, not really. I was covering pet funerals before this."

"Not your own?"

"Er, no. Other people's."

"Tragic, tragic." He observes a couple of seconds' silence for the deceased pets while staring solemnly at his shoes. I stare at them too. He looks back up, respects paid. "So, where are the little critters?"

"Sorry?"

"Where are they?" He beams at me. I frown.

"Well, most of them are in Bristol Cemetery. They have a special section there."

"No, I mean the live ones. Didn't you bring them?"

This man is completely off his rocker.

The girl with orange hair tugs at Giles' sweater.

"This is Holly Colshannon, Giles." She speaks slowly, as though spelling it out to a five-year-old. I'm hanging on to her every syllable. "She's from the *Bristol Gazette*. She's doing the diary with the police detective." Giles' eyes clear and light dawns.

"Sorry, thought you were the lady with the prize-winning ferrets. She's on tonight as well." Orange head, standing just behind his elbow, raises her eyes to the ceiling. I grin.

"Er, no. No ferrets, prize-winning or otherwise, I'm afraid."

"Oh, right. Well, I wondered where the black eye had come from. Thought you might have had a run-in with one of the judges or something," he chuckles. "How's the newspaper business then?"

"Er, fine." I am saved from having to go through this very arduous conversation once more by the makeup lady, who huffily says, "Look, Giles, I'm not going to get time to do your eyes unless we start now."

I am whisked away to a sort of waiting room by orange head (whose name turns out to be Rosemary). "I am soooo sorry. He doesn't normally mix the guests up. Can't think why he did it this time. You'll be on in twenty minutes. A sound man will come and rig you up with a microphone."

"Do I look like someone who raises ferrets?" I ask jokingly.

"Well . . ." She leaves me in the waiting room. I stare after her. That's a bit rich coming from someone with flags on their feet.

In due course a sound man with the rather appropriate name of Mike (Mike's-my-name-and-miking's-my-game) turns up. It seems he has one intention and one intention only and that is to get as familiar with my body as is feasibly possible within the space of two minutes. He keeps up a steady patter throughout. "All right love? Just going to slip this down there . . . Oops! No need to look like that love, you're in expert hands here . . . Had Su Pollard in last week. Now there's a one. She says, 'Mike, go one inch further and you'll know me better than my gynecologist!'" He roars with laughter at this. "There you are, love. Any slippage, just shout."

Rosemary comes into the room clasping a clipboard to her chest. She walks over to me. "Ready?"

"I think so." I get up and follow her out of the room.

"Rosemary? Can you tell me what sort of questions Giles is going to ask?"

"Oh, nothing to worry about. He's just going to ask you some general things. Remember to talk to him, not the camera."

She puts her finger to her lips to indicate we are about to enter a live studio and sweeps me inside. Before I know it, I'm stepping over cables on my way to a squashy sofa where Giles is sitting in state and talking to the camera. I'm forcibly taken by the arm and plonked next to him. Butterflies start up in my stomach. I listen to his patter.

"As I am sure most of you have been 'reading all about it', our next guest needs no introduction to the residents of Bristol. She is Holly Colshannon and she works for the *Bristol Gazette*, where she has been writing a day-by-day account of her adventures with the Bristol Constabulary and one officer in particular, Detective Sergeant Jack Swithen."

He turns to me. "So, Holly, tell us about life on the force." And we are off, and fairly speedily too. I don't know if Giles wants to spend more time on the prize-winning ferrets but we gallop through my "fly on the wall" stuff and fairly canter through the details about The Fox until we come to one of his last questions. I wriggle uncomfortably in my seat. The microphone case that Mike has fixed to the back of my skirt has come a little askew and is busy trying to work its way down the back of my legs. Much like the human version was doing earlier. I reach for a glass of water someone has thoughtfully placed on the table in front of me and try to disguise the fact that I seem to have ants in my pants.

"Right, Holly," Giles says, fixing me with what I suppose must be his winning smile, "for those people out there who haven't had the chance to read your diary, tell us how you got that black eye. Were you pursuing the famous Fox when it happened?"

I don't actually manage to answer the question. As I am leaning forward to replace the glass of water on to the table, my hand catches my microphone wire. The half-full glass is jerked forward as my hand comes to a sudden stop due to the restraint. The water is thrown in a perfect parabola and lands neatly in Giles' lap. Simultaneously, my microphone case, suitably loosened now, flings itself on to the floor like a child having a tantrum and lands with a loud clatter in the pool of water. Giles has leaped up the instant the water has infiltrated his boxers and is standing there staring at me with an open mouth. I stare back at him, frozen with horror to the spot. Then, all of a sudden, the studio seems to come to life. Two people run on to the set, one armed with a tea towel who starts feverishly mopping at Giles' crotch area and another who tries to pick up my abandoned microphone casing. The fact that it is lying in a pool of water doesn't seem to disturb him but unfortunately the rules of physics conspire against him. He gets an electric shock, which he receives with a loud "SHIT!" before dropping the mike back into its pool of water. Amid all the chaos, I am gazing intently at Giles. He is the anchorman of the show and I am willing him to lead us out of the wilderness. He seems, however, to be having some problems controlling himself. His mouth is twitching suspiciously and he appears to be in danger of snorting. I daren't look at him any more but instead I breathe deeply, stare down at the floor and fight for some control. I bite down hard on the inside of my cheeks and try to suppress the wave of giggles that is coming up my throat. Giles doesn't seem to be faring any better. With a loud snort from him, I can't control myself any longer and we both collapse. I clutch myself and sink down on the sofa, tears pouring down my face. Slowly the laughter subsides amid furious hand signals from the floor manager behind the camera. I wipe my eyes. "I'm so, so sorry," I whisper. Giles grins at me with the camaraderie of a shared moment and turns back to the camera.

"Golly! Well, thank you, Holly, for coming in. Don't forget to read all about Holly's adventures in the *Bristol Gazette*. Our next guest . . ."

The telephone rings for the third consecutive time just as I am walking away from it. I pause and look down at my feet for a second in the vain hope it might stop ringing. I curse BT forever inventing the Ring Back request and then despondently turn round and drag my weary feet once more into the hall.

"Hello?"

"How was it?" It's my mother.

"Terrible," I groan.

"Why?"

"You didn't see it?"

"I told you, we don't have it in our area." A good positive point there, I think, grasping at this last comment. Humiliating oneself on local television isn't quite as bad as doing it on national television. Fewer viewers.

"I threw water over the host, electrocuted a technician and then laughed about it. All on live TV." My rather cavalier attitude to the catastrophic television interview has vanished after a phone call from Joe, who told me just how awful the whole thing had looked and generally gave me a good dressing-down. The only way I could get him off the phone was to promise I would be slitting my wrists as soon as I replaced the receiver, if not before. That was the first phone call.

"How marvelous, darling!" My mother laughs her tinkling little laugh. I idly wonder where I inherited my great Father Christmas guffaw from. "People will definitely remember you now! Just think, you could be on one of those *It'll Be Alright on the Night* deliberate mistake things!"

"Gosh. Do you really think so?" I say mutinously.

"Absolutely!" says my mother, not catching the edge to my voice. "I can't wait to see a copy!"

"I am personally trying to ensure that every single copy will be burned on a giant bonfire."

"I'm sure it wasn't that bad."

"No, really. It was."

There's a pause and I can almost hear her scraping around for something good to say. I would normally pitch in and try and help out at this point but (a) I can't think of anything and (b) I'm interested to see if she can.

Longer pause. The wheels are frantically turning. There must be something she can think of.

"At least it was only local television and not national. I mean, no one watches local TV, for goodness sake!"

I drag my feet back into the kitchen to fix myself another drink. I have run out of tonic and don't want to trail round to the corner shop to buy some more in case I am pointed to and laughed at by the local children. I am drinking vodka and water. It has a kind of desperate feel to it.

Grasping my glass close to my heart, I stagger back through to the sitting room and flop onto the sofa. I reach for the remote control and will the cathode rays to brainwash me into oblivion. Avoiding any channels that might invoke disturbing images of Giles and *Southwest Tonight*, I turn to Channel Four and their Friday night comedy fest.

My second phone call (the one before my mother) was from Lizzie. Had she called before Joe, I might have been a little more responsive and indeed amused to hear her snorts of jocularity.

"Oh! Oh! Holly! That was priceless!" Pause as she struggled for control. I shifted uncomfortably. She was finding this a little too funny. "His face when you threw the water over him! Oh! It was a picture!" She was doing a passably good impression of a drain.

"I didn't throw it, Lizzie, it was an accident."

"And then when the technician swore out loud! It was just hysterical!"

"Well, I wish Joe thought so," I said dully.

Lizzie eventually calmed down and we got around to talking about Alastair. The long and the short of it is, they are at last spending the whole day together tomorrow and she wants me to put parts A and B of OPERATION ALTAR, which is her rather elaborate plan to force Alastair to marry her, into play. I did rather gloomily inquire as to what was wrong with the old-fashioned method of getting pregnant, to which she tartly replied that they would have to be sleeping together now and then for that to happen. In order to get her off the phone so I could return to my depressive state, I agreed.

Thinking is too much of an effort.

In the morning I lie in bed for a while, contemplating the day ahead, before remembering my rash promise to Lizzie. I groan softly to myself. Damn. Why couldn't I have resisted the very considerable charms of my vodka and water and tried to talk her out of her ridiculous plan?

I faff about in my dressing gown for the next hour or so, drinking tea and opening post and basking in the joy of a whole weekend stretching before me. Ben is coming over tonight after the obligatory rugby game and bonding and then we'll spend the day together tomorrow. Normally the very thought of this should have me squealing for joy on the one hand and reaching for the polish and clean bed sheets on the other. I should be chilling wine, scrubbing the place clean and artfully chucking fresh flowers about like a woman possessed. But not today because I really can't be arsed. I frown to myself, deep in this particular line of thought. What does this mean? Am I going off him? No—I can't expect to remain in the "honeymoon" phase forever; besides, with recent events I don't want to be seen to be too keen. Right, absolutely. Don't want to seem too keen. Conscience appeased, I get dressed and wander into Clifton village to execute Part A of OPERATION ALTAR.

The lady at the flower shop says she can deliver the flowers later today and I hand over the name and address. The lady looks at me highly dubiously, probably imagining me in some sort of lesbian sex triangle. I mutter goodbye, wildly hoping I will never have the occasion to send flowers again. Why can't Lizzie send Lizzie flowers you might ask? Yes. Quite.

To sum OPERATION ALTAR up, the plan is to drive Alastair (or "POB" as I think of him nowadays, standing for "poor old bastard," or "poor old beetroot" according to the vegetable system) into a frenzy of jealousy, culminating in him realizing that he cannot live without Lizzie, throwing himself at her feet and immediately proposing marriage. Well, that's her version anyway. I'm not actually sure this will run completely to plan. But then I do have a very reliable past record of being completely and utterly wrong.

As soon as I arrive home, I decide to get part B over and done with and dial the number of Lizzie's mobile. What I do in the name of friendship. She answers after four rings.

"Lizzie? It's me."

"How nice to hear from you! How on earth did you get my number?" Her voice and tone are distinctly flirtatious. It is a peculiar sensation, being flirted to by your best friend. I have obviously called at exactly the right time and she and Alastair are together.

"Is Alastair there?"

"Oh, I'm not doing anything. What are you doing?"

"Nothing much, just sent your blasted flowers."

"Yes! I would love to!"

"This is absolutely ridiculous, you know! Pretending that I am a man!"

"See you then. Bye!" This is said in low, sultry tones that should be reserved for four-poster beds, champagne and the like. The woman means business.

"Call me later. Bye."

I stare at the receiver for a second in disbelief. I mean, she actually did it. She actually pretended another man was calling her. I sigh. As long as she knows what she's doing, and I'm in no position to judge with my past history in the relationship department. I go back to my sofa with no intention of moving from it for quite a while.

seventeen

It's Monday morning and I am on my way to the police station. Tristan is behaving himself and even my black eye has reduced sufficiently for me to be able to remove the sunglasses that have become such an essential fashion accessory. Now I just look like I have black circles under my eyes. Well, one eye anyway. Nothing that half a tube of concealer couldn't fix. I had quite a nice weekend but to be honest I'm glad it's over. Ben and I were a little strained with each other, as though treading on egg shells, but I think that's only to be expected for a while until recent events have blown over and we get back to some sort of normality.

It is a beautiful day and even the hustle and bustle of the city seems peaceful as I wend my way through the traffic. I park Tristan, snap on the handbrake and gather up my bag and laptop.

As I bounce up the steps to the front desk, James appears in the doorway.

"Turn around!"

I stop on one of the steps and stare at him. "Why? What's happened?"

He looks resigned, pissed off and furious all at the same time. "Another burglary."

I remain fixed to my step. "Not another one? The Fox again?"

"Probably. It's an antiques shop." He marches past me and leaves me standing with my mouth open.

"Come on, we'll go this way to the car pool. Caught your TV

interview by the way," he shouts back over his shoulder. I catch a flash of a smile but I am more intent on the burglary. I determinedly chuck my bags over my shoulder and set off at a trot after him.

"That's a bit blatant, isn't it? An antiques shop," I say breathlessly.

"Yeah, it is. The owner has just called us. It must have happened sometime over the weekend. Here, let me take that," he says, holding out his hand for my bulky laptop case.

"Oh. Thanks."

"Forensics are meeting us down there. Thank God that no one was hurt this time."

"Maybe he got scared after slogging Mr. Williams and decided an empty shop would be easier."

"Maybe."

"Blimey, this is the fourth one in as many weeks."

"Yeah, that's what I'm worried about."

"How do you mean?"

"Well, when burglaries are this intensive, it usually means the burglar intends to do just a few of them. Then they'll suddenly stop and we'll never hear from him again."

We reach our usual discreet gray car.

"I'll drive," says James, heading for the driver's side.

Once inside, he shoves a piece of paper in my hands.

"Directions." We set off out of the underground car park.

As we swing up the ramp to the outside world, I reach into my bag for my mobile. "Just going to call Vince; he can meet us there."

"Fine."

I duly hand over the address details to Vince (ignoring Vince's pleas of "Put him on, put him on!") and then settle into my seat and snap on my seat belt.

"So, what did you get up to at the weekend?" he asks.

"Oh, usual stuff," I say, privately adding to myself, You know, sending fake flowers, pretending to be someone else in order for your best friend to trap her boyfriend into marriage. Usual stuff. "How about you?" I ask.

"The wedding. There seems to be loads to do." The mention of the wedding seems to have a curiously dampening effect on both of us but I haven't time to even contemplate why as James is looking impatiently over at me. "Right, where now?" he asks as we reach the end of the main one-way system.

Oh, buggery broccoli. Directions. I look nervously at the piece of paper in my hands. I'm not very good at directions. I don't know my left from my right, and since Detective Sergeant Sabine is doing such a spectacularly good job of making me feel utterly useless and generally a pain in the tubes, I daren't admit it to him.

"Erm, er, we want Richmond Road, in Clifton," I say cagily. He obligingly heads toward the area of Clifton and gives me a few minutes to try and decipher both his handwriting and the actual directions. To distinguish left from right, I covertly hold both my hands up and make an "L" shape with my thumb and first finger. Only one hand shows an actual "L," you see. L for left.

"Where now?"

"Er, just looking." Right, mustn't get flustered. Need to concentrate. The roads flash by and then I spot the one I'm looking for.

"TURN!" I shout.

"Which way?"

"Er, er, left. No, no, RIGHT." Too late. We've missed it.

"Could you possibly tell me a little earlier? Like before we've actually passed the turning?"

"It would help if we were traveling slightly more slowly," I say emphatically. We both glare ahead of us. Really, the man is absolutely intolerable. We do a highly illegal U-turn in the middle of the street and head back.

"Left or right, which was it?"

"Right," I say confidently—but then we've turned around, haven't we?

"No! Left! I mean left!" He screeches to a halt and pulls in by the side of the road.

"You. Are. Driving. Me. Mad! Which is it? And what are you doing with your hands?"

There is a pregnant pause while I consider various lies to explain the situation. The problem is I can't think of a good enough one. I look at my hands, hoping they might give me an answer. They are being particularly uncommunicative. Truth is my final option.

"I don't know my left from my right," I say in a small voice. I'm really not having a very good day so far. There's silence in the car. I await the firing squad, but to my surprise it doesn't materialize.

"Here, shove over. You drive and I'll do the directions."

He gets out of the car and goes around to the passenger side while I climb over the handbrake into the driver's seat.

"Are you dyslexic?" he asks as we both re-attach our seat belts and I adjust the seat for my shorter legs.

"No!" I reply hotly. " I just don't know my left from my right."

"That's not dyslexia?"

"No, it's not."

I start the engine and wait for instructions. He studies the directions for a second. We smoothly arrive at our destination within ten minutes or so and not once does he use the words "left" or "right." He just constantly points with his hands and says "Turn here." I have to say I'm nicely surprised. In fact, James Sabine appears almost human for a minute.

We pull up outside a quaint little shop in the depths of Clifton Village, an opulent part of Bristol. The shop is just how I would have imagined The Olde Curiosity Shop to be. There is a silence

as we get our stuff together. We look at each other, not really sure
what to say. His mobile rings shrilly, interrupting our awkwardness, and he answers it.

"Hello? Hi, yeah, quite busy . . . Don't worry, I remembered.
Where does he live again? Is he going to ask how many times I go
to church? No problem . . . see you there around eight. Bye!"
The future wife, I presume. I, in the meantime, have picked up
my handbag and fiddled around with a few things, trying not to
look as though I am eavesdropping on his conversation. Our moment of awkwardness over, he reverts to his usual efficient self.

"Ready?" he asks as he slips his mobile back into his pocket. I
lock the car up and together we walk toward the address. Vince's
customized lilac Beetle pulls up behind us.

"Coo-eee!" He waves at us out of the window. James groans.
Vince gets out and minces toward us. Today he is wearing white
jeans and a turquoise T-shirt with the emblem "Shag-tastic
Baby!" on it. A beret sits perkily on top of his spiky hair and the
whole ensemble is completed with, yep, you've guessed it, elfin
boots with chains around them. I can't help it. I love him. He
kisses me on both cheeks.

"Darling! Saw you on the telly. You made my night when you
emptied that glass of water over Giles! The beast dumped me
last month!" He doesn't pause for breath as he turns toward
James. "Good morning, Detective Sergeant! You're looking very
summery!"

"Thank you, Vince." James smiles awkwardly and I look at
him. He is dressed in an open-necked blue shirt, sleeves folded up
to show tanned forearms, and a pair of faded corduroys. Quite a
contrast to our photographer.

"Vince," James continues, "would you mind terribly putting a
jumper on or something? It's just that it's supposed to be a police
inquiry and I don't think . . ." He looks pointedly at the phrase
"Shag-tastic Baby!"

"Detective Sergeant Sabine, of course I will. I understand what you're saying but don't you worry, I'll just *blend* into the background." Vince makes sweeping motions with his hands to indicate his blending abilities. "You won't know I'm there."

James looks enormously doubtful.

As Vince turns around to go back to his car, we catch a glimpse of the phrase "Do you feel horny?" emblazoned on his back. James and I just look at each other.

An old-fashioned bell rings as we enter the shop. James has to bend his head to get through the doorway. The musty smell of age welcomes us. Furniture of every shape and size visually greets us. The shop is lit by a dingy half-light as the windows are too small to let an acceptable amount of light in. At the sound of the bell, a man appears out of nowhere to receive us. He is small and dressed from head to toe in tweed (including a matching waistcoat). He has a little mustache and round glasses. James flips open his ID.

"I am Detective Sergeant Sabine and this is—"

"Holly Colshannon." I step forward eagerly. "I'm here for observation only."

He duly shakes both our hands rather limply. "I'm Mr. Rolfe, the owner of the shop."

"Can you show us where the burglar got in?"

"Certainly." We move with him through to the back of the shop. "I arrived, as usual, at about eight o'clock this morning. I rarely use the back door, just occasionally for putting the rubbish out, but it was soon apparent to me that some items were missing and so I came through here to find out where the intruder might have got in." He gestures toward a glass-paned door which has a pane broken and a lock that looks as though it has been forced.

"Do you have an alarm at all, Mr. Rolfe?"

"Yes, I do. I think it's been disabled in some way. It wasn't working when I put the code in this morning, but I thought there might have been an electricity cut or something. The actual alarm seems to have been placed in a bucket of water outside." He starts to move outside, presumably to show us the water-logged alarm, but James puts an arm out to stop him.

"I'd rather our forensics team had a look first, Mr. Rolfe. They're on their way down. While we're waiting, could you make out a list of what's missing please?"

We walk back through to the main room. I spy Vince taking some shots of the shop outside.

"I've been doing that while I've been waiting for you," Mr. Rolfe says as he bustles to a desk, produces a sheet of paper and hands it to James.

James fleetingly looks down at the list. "How would you rate the value of the items taken?"

Mr. Rolfe clears his throat. "Well, I would say that whoever has taken these things has a remarkably good eye for quality. For instance, they took the Lalique vase and yet left this little trinket box." He points to the item on a table. "Reproduction. Relatively worthless."

He looks up as the bell on the front door rings. Roger and his team enter, and amid all the introductions Vince slips in too. He mouths, "I'm blending in."

James hands the list over to me as he leads the team through to the back of the shop.

"Is all this going to be in that diary, then?" Mr. Rolfe asks me.

"Er, yeah. If that's OK?"

"Out tomorrow?"

"Should be."

Vince takes a couple of shots of me as I frown and study the list. He then gives up on an unresponsive subject and follows the others through to the back of the shop.

I continue to study the list. There's something here that I'm not happy about. I just can't put my finger on it. The thought had flit-

ted through my head but then the noise of Vince's camera dis-
turbed me and I lost it. I frown even more, trying to remember.
My eyes read down the list again and then stop on one item.

EIGHTEENTH-CENTURY ACT OF PARLIAMENT
CLOCK.

Light chinks through my brain. Wasn't there a clock on Sebastian Forquar-White's list? And didn't Mrs. Stephens say that the
burglar even took a clock her late husband had given to her
which wasn't working properly? I can't remember if there was
one on the Williams' list.

I walk through to the rear.

"James?" He spins around and I beckon him over.

"Have you noticed there is always a clock on the list of stolen
items?" I say to him in a low voice.

"Yeah, I have."

"So doesn't that help a bit?"

"I don't know," he sighs. "You see, all the items taken have to
be small enough for the burglar to carry, so it could just be a coincidence. It's not like we're going to find too many Louis XVIII
sideboards on there."

He turns around and goes back to where the work is progress-
ing. I shrug to myself. Oh well, I suppose I should stop playing
detective and let the real ones get on with their job. I sigh, get out
my notebook and take notes as everyone goes about their work.
Someone has put tape all around the affected area of the entry
point and Roger is there, dressed in a white plastic jumpsuit (the
forensics team's habitual uniform), endeavoring to lift some
fingerprints from the door frame. Someone else is examining the
floor and James is talking to Mr. Rolfe over to one side. Vince is
standing on the outskirts of all of that with his camera click-
ing away.

When James has asked all his questions, he starts to make the
appropriate leaving noises. I make wild jolting head gestures at

Vince to indicate that we are going. Mr. Rolfe takes off his glasses and tiredly rubs his eyes, saying as he does so, "The insurance company may want to talk to you. Is it OK to give them your number?"

James nods his acquiescence, Vince joins us and all three of us leave together, the bell on the door ringing joyfully as we go.

As James and I head back through the city traffic, I chew on my lip thoughtfully. Something else is bothering me now. Something that someone has just mentioned. What is it? I suddenly sit bolt upright in my seat with a gasp. James instinctively brakes.

"What? What?"

"Insurance!"

"Oh." He breathes a sigh of relief. "I thought I'd run over something." He settles back down into his seat. "What about it?"

"Maybe that's the link. Maybe that's how the burglar knew where to get in and out of the houses so easily and just what to take. If all the details were listed with an insurance company, they wouldn't have to get into the house to case it. All the information would be on file."

James stares at the car in front for a few seconds.

I continue. "Didn't you say that everything stolen from Sebastian Forquar-White's house was a named item with the insurance company?"

"Yes, it was. And I remember him saying that his insurance company had requested he have the catch fixed on the small window where the burglar got in. I remember thinking how ironic it was to be burgled straight after that." His brow creases thoughtfully.

"Do you know which insurance company the other victims use? Mrs. Stephens, the Williamses and Mr. Rolfe?"

"No. But we can call as soon as we get back."

"Would an insurance company actually look around a property though? I mean, I've never met anyone from the company who insure my home. I arranged it all over the phone."

"Somebody would look around a property that's of a considerable size, especially if they have a number of expensive items which need to be named. They would have to check that they actually exist. Good idea, Holly." I raise my eyebrows in surprise. Goodness, that was close to an actual compliment.

We travel in silence for the rest of the journey. I feel just a little excited. I mean, what if I'm right? What if it is something to do with the insurance company? We drive into the underground car park and then make our way up toward reception.

"Morning Dave!" says James to Dave-the-grumpy-git-desk-sergeant. Dave looks up and greets him with a smile.

"Morning sir! I've got a few things for you!" He bends down and fishes underneath the desk, then produces some gaudy, hand-written envelopes.

"What on earth . . . ?"

Dave leans forward conspiratorially and loudly whispers, "Fan mail, sir, if I'm not mistaken. Strong smell of perfume." James stares at him and a large grin spreads across my face which I instantly wipe off as James turns toward me. I look at him concernedly as though I haven't heard.

"This is your fault," he says through a pursed mouth. I can't help it. The grin starts across my face again.

"James, I can't help it if women write to you. That's nothing to do with me."

"Hmph." He turns back to Dave. "You haven't, er, told . . ."

"Our little secret, sir."

"Right. Good. Thanks."

We sweep through the security doors. Dave doesn't glance at me but he smiles down at his desk without looking up.

We climb the stairs to the second floor in silence.

"So," I say eventually, "fan mail, eh?"

"If you dare mention this to anyone, anyone at all, I'll . . ."

"You'll what?"

"You'll see. It won't be pleasant."

We enter the offices and a chorus goes up as we pass by the desks. "Oh James, we love you soooo . . ." says one high-pitched voice. "Dick, you're my hero!" says a second. Another officer called John falls into a mock swoon in front of us and we have to step over him.

"You know, James," I say as this continues all the way to our desks, "I think they might have found out somehow."

Callum is grinning at us and leaning back in his chair. He saunters over as soon as we both sit down. James opens the bottom drawer of his desk and quickly tosses the offending envelopes in. Callum perches on the end of my desk.

"What's a guy supposed to do?" he asks.

"How do you mean?" I ask suspiciously.

"Well, I don't know what to do first. I mean, should I take the piss out of you"—he points at me—"for the TV interview? Or you"—he points at James—"for the fan mail?"

He shrugs and we all laugh. Robin walks into our little group and immediately the atmosphere changes as though she has turned off the sunshine. The tension she brings with her is even more unbearable due to the contrast of a few seconds earlier.

"Am I missing anything?" she says lightly but her face belies something else.

"Nothing at all," Callum says, matching her tone, but their eyes lock in mutual distaste. Callum seems to be taking James and Robin's affair very personally, but then I suppose he should feel some sort of immediate responsibility as he is James' best man. Every time Callum and Robin meet there is a distinct air of hostility. "But then you never miss a trick, do you, Robin?" he snaps now.

"And what is that supposed to mean?" Robin snaps back.

"You know what it means. You know exactly . . ."

"What can we do for you, Robin?" James hastily jumps in.

"I need a word with Holly."

"Sure," I say, quickly getting up, and together we wander toward the door. Callum and James watch us all the way and then James turns to Callum and talks intently to him.

"I just wondered how you were getting on," asks Robin. "Anything to report?"

I shrug. "Nothing really. We may have a lead on The Fox burglaries."

"You and James are getting on a lot better I see."

"Yeah." I bob my head around in agreement.

"Good," she says shortly, without meeting my eye, and takes her leave.

I go back to my desk with the distinct impression that she was checking up on James and me. Her manner was unfriendly.

"OK," says James, turning back to me. "You call Mrs. Stephens and Mr. Williams. Ask them who their insurance company is, who their contact there is and when they last came and viewed the house. I'll do the other two. Mr. Williams came out of the hospital yesterday so he should be there."

I get on with the calls; I'm surprised and a little honored that James has asked for my help on this. Ten minutes later I put the phone down. James looks at me expectantly.

"Mr. Williams uses Royal Sun Alliance but Mrs. Stephens says she uses a local company, Elephant Insurance Company. I've got both the contacts there."

"Who is the contact at Elephant?"

"A Mr. Makin."

"Sebastian Forquar-White uses the same company and has the same contact."

We look at each other for a minute. "What about the shop—Mr. Rolfe?"

"He uses a different company. But then the burglar could always have cased the shop himself, couldn't he? He only needed to browse for a bit to note the items of value and then take a short walk down the alley at the back to look at the alarm. He could have said he was lost if anyone saw him."

"But what about Mr. Williams? How could he have possibly found out about his house?"

We stare at each other again, both of us deep in thought.

"Call him again," James says suddenly. "Ask him if he has ever used any other insurance companies before Royal Sun Alliance. Or even if he has had quotes from other companies."

I re-dial the number for Mr. Williams.

"Hello?"

"Mr. Williams? It's Holly Colshannon. I'm sorry to disturb you again, but can you tell me if you've ever been with a different insurance company?"

"No, love. Always the same one."

"Well then, have you ever had quotes from any other companies?"

"I always get quotes from other companies!" He sounds shocked. "Don't want no one thinking they can pull a fast one over me just because I'm an old feller! I always take the cheapest quote. It just happens it's always my usual insurance firm."

"And did the other companies come and look around the house as well?"

"Oh yes. Don't do things by halves. I didn't want them quoting for something and then changing their quote once they'd seen the house. Oh no."

I hold my breath. "Can you tell me who the other companies were?"

"Not off the top of my head, no. But I've kept the quotes somewhere—do you want me to look them up?"

"Yes, please. Could you call me back?"

I replace the receiver and impatiently drum my fingers on the desk. After a few minutes I get us both a drink from the vending machine in the corner. James and I sip our coffee and look thoughtfully at each other. I realize belatedly that it's a bit strange to be staring at each other like this and hastily look away. James' phone rings.

"Hello? Is that Mr. Williams? You can give them to me . . . Yep . . . Yep . . . Thank you. Bye."

He looks over at me.

"Well?" I say impatiently.

"One quote from a Mr. Makin at Elephant Insurance Company."

eighteen

"Blimey," I breathe. I didn't believe there really would be a link.

"Don't get too excited, Holly. It may just be pure coincidence. They are a local company and they may specialize in large houses or antiques or both. We'll just go down and see them. I'll call our Mr. Makin."

Ten minutes later, he replaces the receiver. "Mr. Makin left this morning to go to a conference for a few days, but I've made an appointment for Thursday morning."

"But you didn't say you were from the police."

James rolls his eyes. "If he is involved, and that's only an 'if,' do you think it would be a good idea to give him warning that we're on to him?"

"Er, yes. Maybe you're right."

James goes out to follow up some old cases and doesn't return for the rest of the afternoon, so when I have finished my latest diary installment I leave a note on his desk saying I will see him tomorrow and go to the paper to file copy. I spy Joe over a sea of heads and computers and wave enthusiastically at him in a pathetic effort to win some favor after my disaster of a TV interview. He seems to have forgotten all about it as he trots over, smiling happily at me. Really, the man's mood changes are frightening.

"Holly! Filing copy?" When I nod he adds, "Great! Keep up the good work!"

I frown to myself; what's happened to "bloody disgrace" and "absolute shambles"? But I have no time to prevaricate as I need to get somewhere tonight. Fleur called over the weekend and asked if I would like to meet up for a drink. Naturally, I readily agreed. I am really quite curious to get to know her better but I have no idea why she would want to go out with me for a drink. Maybe there is a distinct lack of female company at the counseling charity where she works. We're meeting at a watering hole on Whiteladies Road at six so I need to get a shift on. I've arranged to see Lizzie for our usual Monday night fest afterward.

I hastily download my copy into the main computer, shout to various appropriate bods that I have done so and then scarper to the door. I emerge into bright sunshine a few minutes later. Tristan is beautifully behaved all the way to Park Street, but then starts to splutter and slow down. "Oh please, Tristan. Not here, not now. I'm going to be late," I cry. I bang my hands on the steering wheel in frustration and then in desperation promise him a service which seems to give him a relatively new lease on life. With one large, final splutter he hums into motion again. We arrive intact on Whiteladies Road a few minutes later and I look in vain for a parking spot. They are a rarefied luxury in this part of the city at the best of times. I spot one next to a Porsche a few minutes later, apologize to Tristan for parking him next to such a smart car, hope they have something in common and march into the bar. Only two minutes late.

Fleur is already sitting at the bar, chatting away to the barman. I'm a little disheveled so I straighten my top, run my fingers through my hair and put my shoulders back. Fleur is looking exquisite I notice as I negotiate the furniture to get to her. She looks as though she has just stepped out of the shower. Her long legs are crossed and she is wearing a little shift dress with a jacket to match. She shakes her head now and then as she laughs at something the barman has told her and the light glints off her glossy, black bob. I slip onto the bar stool next to her.

"Fleur! Hi! Sorry I'm late."

She turns to face me. "Holly! You're not really late; besides, I've been well entertained!" She smiles at the barman. He asks me, "What will you have?"

"Vodka and, er, ginger ale please," I say, plunging into unknown territory for vodka drinkers.

"So, how was your day?" she asks.

"Good." I wonder how much I can tell her. I mean, I know James and she are going to be married but he might not tell her details of cases.

"How's the Fox case going?"

"We may have a lead." Surely that would be OK?

"Really?"

"Yeah. Anyway, how was your day?"

"Oh, fine." Scintillating stuff. My initial enthusiasm waning, I suddenly wonder how successful this is going to be. We probably don't have much in common. Apart from James Sabine, that is. Seizing on that very topic, I say, "James disappeared off this afternoon, I haven't seen him since lunchtime."

Fascinating, Holly. Absolutely fascinating. We fall into a slight pause as the barman serves me my drink and Fleur insists it's put on the bar tab.

"So, how's the wedding going?" From my very small experience of weddings I know this is always a captivating topic to all brides.

She tells me a bit about the bridesmaids and the church and then goes on to say, "I'm so sorry, this must be really boring for you."

"No, not at all."

"I'm just looking forward to the honeymoon so we can be

alone for a while. James has been working hard lately and I've been sorting out the details for the wedding."

I nod sympathetically and wonder fleetingly if some of James' time has been spent with Robin.

"I've been meaning to ask you, actually. There is a Mr. and Mrs. Colshannon on the guest list. They're not any relation to you, are they? They're friends of my father."

I frown suspiciously. It's quite an unusual name, as I've said before.

"Do you know what their first names are?"

"Em, can't remember. I think one of them is a herb or something . . ."

"Sorrel."

"Yes! That's it!"

"That's my mother," I say despondently. They just can't resist it, can they? They just can't help muscling in . . . Fleur is staring at me wide-eyed.

"Your parents are coming to my wedding! That's amazing, isn't it? What's your father's name?"

"Patrick."

"My father was a financial backer with the theater for a while, that's how he knows your mother. In fact, I think I might have met them once at a party. I remember her . . ." she says excitedly. And she regales me with tales of how amusing they are and how glamorous they are. I mean, I have no objections to basking in their reflected glory for a while, but really, this is too much. As Fleur talks on, I marvel at how they have managed to get themselves invited to James' wedding. Curious, isn't it? To think that James Sabine will be meeting my parents. I wonder what he'll think of them? I am jolted out of my reverie by a strangely loud silence. Was I supposed to laugh back then? I give a little goodwill chortle. Fleur laughs again.

"Really, it was frightfully funny! You must come, you know!"

I look mystified. "Where?"

"Why, to the wedding of course!" I stare at her, suddenly jolted. It might be bizarre to see James getting married. I realize I'm going to have to say something to this generous, if a little misplaced, offer.

"Oh lovely! But you don't need any latecomers now!"

"Nonsense, the more the merrier! I'm sure James would like you there as well!" I'm sure he wouldn't actually. There's nothing much else I can say but . . .

"Gosh, well, thanks!"

"And you will come to the hen bash, won't you?"

To be honest, I can't think of anything worse. Hen dos are the worst invention ever. I quite like them if they are for really good friends, where you can get companionably drunk together and put the world to rights. But a room full of estrogen-charged screaming strangers—I give an involuntary shiver. The problem is, I can't think of a good enough excuse to get out of it and Fleur's eyes are fixed hopefully upon me. "Great!"

"It's next Monday."

"So soon?"

"Yes—we're getting married two weeks on Saturday you know."

"Gosh, are you? It only seems like yesterday I started with James at the station! That means I've got less than three weeks left on the diary!" I stare down into my drink. I am actually truly surprised by this; the weeks seem to have raced by.

"Teresa's coming to the hen do as well."

"Teresa? Teresa the—Fothersby, Teresa?"

"Yes, she says she knows you!"

"You could say that," I say darkly.

"I know her from work. It's been terribly difficult with all the invites for them. I couldn't invite one without offending someone

else, so Daddy told me to just invite the lot! He said it was easier!"
Clever old Daddy.

We order some more drinks. I seem to have become surprisingly thirsty. Tristan may have to be collected in the morning. I'm sure he'll understand it was an emergency.

So much information seems to have been tipped into my brain over the last half hour that I'm in danger of drowning in it. I blink hastily and try to concentrate. Right. Another topic of conversation is called for.

"So, are you and James planning a big family?" I know this isn't going to get me the gold medal in the conversational Olympics, but it's the best I can do, all right?

"Heavens, no!" She sits up straight on her bar stool. I blink in surprise. In my little daydreams of married life I have always imagined children. Children, Agas, chickens. That sort of thing. Maybe a little conventional, I grant you, and in my case perhaps destined for another lifetime, but still infinitely comforting.

"I couldn't possibly do that to my figure!" she continues. I look down at my figure and sharply draw in my stomach. "Think of all the stretch marks, Holly! Piles! A flabby stomach!" She shivers to herself. I have a sympathetic shiver as well to keep her company. "No, I couldn't have that!" I lean eagerly forward on my stool to hear her alternative. If there is some other miraculous way that we can have the little blighters without physically giving birth to them then I'm all for it! Science can do marvelous things nowadays.

"So how will you do it then?"

"Well, we don't want any! We're perfectly happy with life as it is! No point in ruining it!"

"Oh." I raise my eyebrows in a vacant, stupid kind of way. And we move on to talk of other things.

Tongues loosened by the vast array of drinks that follow, we have a surprisingly good time. Fleur asks me about Ben and although I don't know her well enough to share the rough patch we have been going through lately, I do tell her everything else. In usual female style we talk about a huge range of subjects but I couldn't actually tell you what exactly. At half past eight, much to the disgust of the barman (he was doing a roaring trade), I glance at my watch and realize I am going to be late for Lizzie. I heave myself up from my now rather comfortable bar stool.

"Fleur, I have to go, someone's coming over."

"Yes, I'd better be off too. James will be wondering where I've got to."

We say our goodbyes at the entrance and arrange where to meet on Monday for the hen do. I turn down her offer to share a cab as my flat is only about ten minutes' walk away and I could do with the fresh air. I leave her manfully trying to hail a taxi as I head off toward Clifton, Lizzie and home.

I wander through the leafy avenues, not making any particular effort at all to get there quickly for Lizzie. I am now spectacularly late but I'm working on the premise that a few minutes either way aren't going to kill her. As I walk and mindlessly pick leaves off hedges, I think about my parents coming to James' wedding. It really is astonishing that they are invited, and now I think about it, I distinctly remember my mother saying they were coming down to a wedding soon and would be staying for a few days.

I turn the corner into my road and spy a very sulky-looking Lizzie sitting on the steps to my flat. I start walking a little faster. I wonder how she has fared with Alastair after my phone call.

"Hello!" I call.

Lizzie has her head cupped in one hand and is busy picking at her toenails with the other hand. She looks up as she hears my voice.

"Where have you been?"

"In the pub! Hic!" I grin at her and she smiles good-humoredly back. "With work?" she queries.

"No, with Fleur. She's James' fiancée."

"Good time?" Lizzie asks as I fish my key out of my bag and let us into the building.

"Yeah, but I managed to get myself invited to her hen do."

"Bad luck."

"It was a bit." We start up the stairs to the flat. "What's up?" I ask. She's not as lively as usual, her eyes aren't quite meeting mine and she doesn't seem as interested in Fleur as I thought she would be. She shrugs. "Alastair?" I press as I slot another key into the door of my inner sanctum and she nods.

I wait until we are settled down and then say, "Didn't it go well on Saturday?"

"Not quite to plan."

"What happened?"

"Well, nothing really. That's the problem. I received the flowers in the afternoon after your phone call and I was expecting him to either go into a rage of jealousy and demand an explanation or fall on his bended knee and declare undying love. A big finale, whatever. But neither of those happened; he just seemed to go into his shell. He didn't ask who was on the phone, he didn't ask who sent the flowers, he just seemed to distance himself from me. And it got worse as the day went on. I had this big speech planned about how I just didn't see him any more because of his work." She is very close to tears, so I go into the kitchen and rip off a piece of kitchen towel. "Go on," I say, sitting down next to her on the sofa and handing her it.

"I tried talking to him, Holly, really I did. I asked him what was wrong, was he OK, did he want to talk about anything, but he just withdrew further. It was horrible." The tears are starting to fall now and once they start they come thick and fast. Any vague sense of inebriation is lost as the world comes sharply into focus for me.

"I even started jabbering that the flowers were from my mother, but I could tell he didn't believe me. So we went to bed and I thought maybe everything would be better in the morning, but it wasn't. It seemed there were miles between us even though we were only a few feet apart. In the morning he just left without saying anything. I've been so stupid."

"Why didn't you call me?" I ask, taking her hand.

"Well, I knew Ben was here and, to be honest, I was a bit ashamed. I was so convinced he would come round; not that he would ask me straightaway but that he would at least give a show of feelings." I put my arm around her and let her cry for a bit, and then, just as she is reaching the catchy-breath stage, I reach over and pick up her wine for her. She takes a few shaky gulps. At times like these we could both do with being smokers.

"Do you know what the worst thing is, Hol?"

"What?"

"The feeling of hurt in his eyes. Not anger or love, but pain. He did show me how he felt, didn't he?" I nod. "And now I've lost him."

"That's not true! You don't know that. What happened at work today?"

"He didn't speak to me all day. That's what has really convinced me. And it's not been one of those impossibly busy days full of meetings; I've walked past his office several times just to give him the opportunity of talking to me and he hasn't."

I let Lizzie talk and talk. Then, when she quietens down, I tell her what's been happening with James and the diary. There is such an air of intimacy that I talk more than I normally do and tell her all about our day. Conversations that we've had, things that have happened. She laughs a little and I think she finds the conversation generally soothing. Lizzie stays the night on the sofa, not wanting to face the solitude of her own place. By the time we get to bed it is past two in the morning and we have drunk our way through two bottles of wine.

As I slip into Morpheus' arms, albeit with a drunken stumble, I remember that on Thursday we are seeing Mr. Makin and my dreams are full of police cars, clocks and James Sabine.

nineteen

⌇

I seem to have spent the last day or so running between the station, the paper and Lizzie. The situation between her and Alastair seems to have rapidly deteriorated. On Tuesday afternoon she went to his office in a last attempt to try and explain but apparently he wasn't interested in hearing anything. He just told her it was over and practically slammed the door in her face. I offered to call and tell him I sent the flowers and made the phone call but Lizzie seemed to think it would be useless, he wouldn't believe me. I even tried to find the Visa receipt for the flowers until I belatedly realized I had paid in cash. All I could do in the end was be there for Lizzie. I have ensured we have a proper supply of tissues, wine and ice cream at all times and she has now taken up permanent occupation of my sofa. I have canceled all social activities, which means I haven't seen Ben since Sunday. But that's fine—I don't mind doing it at all because what else are friends for?

The diary has been hectic as usual. James and I have spent our days going back over various statements from the burglaries, dealing with forensics and sorting out some of his cases from before I became the crime correspondent. James has been enormously annoyed with me as the latest line of people questioned in relation to the burglaries have all asked if they are going to be in the paper. I wouldn't normally get involved in these interviews and most of the time I have simply gone along for the ride—even though I'm sure he'd rather have someone else along with him, I think James likes the company.

I also dropped by the paper to see Amy in the publicity department and ask how the recent opinion polls have been.

"Brilliant!" she exclaimed in answer to my question.

"Really?"

"Yep. I think the photos have made all the difference. And we all seem to be getting to know Detective Sergeant Sabine a lot better!" she added, giving me a wink and a nudge in the ribs.

"Amy! He's getting married in a few weeks' time," I replied defensively.

"I know," she sighed, "we're all a bit disappointed."

"So, the opinion polls have gone well, have they?" I repeated, anxious to get her off this particular subject.

"Yes. A couple of people commented that they didn't like the skirt you were wearing on Tuesday though." She referred to a clipboard of notes.

I frown. "Which one was that?"

"The beige one with the huge poppies on it."

"I like that one!" I exclaimed.

"And someone said she thought you ought to get your hair cut. She thought the detective might like you better if you got your hair cut."

"What's wrong with my hair? I don't want the detective to like me better anyway!" I replied hotly, a slow blush coming up from my toes.

"And . . ."

"What about him? What have they said about him?"

"Well, some of them have asked for his phone number. Quite a few have asked if he's married, but of course, as you know, Joe doesn't want his wedding mentioned."

"I'm beginning to see why," I said darkly.

"And a couple have asked whether there's going to be a happy ending."

"Very happy," I snapped. "He and I are going to part company for good."

James' fan mail has increased. He now receives on average two or three letters per day which Dave-the-desk-sergeant hands over every morning with barely concealed glee. The envelopes join the growing pile of other envelopes in the bottom of one of his drawers, and he has to put up with at least one member of the department pretending to fall into a dead faint every time they see him. Callum says he has set up a fan club for him and goes around wearing badges saying "I heart (picture of) James Sabine" and "Dick Tracy for President." Copies of the badges have even fallen into Vince's fair hands and he gleefully turns up every morning with one on his hat and one on his left or right nipple, depending on how he's feeling. James initially greeted all this hilarity with annoyance, then more annoyance, and finally resignation. He keeps asking them to take the badges off, which both of them duly do but immediately whip them back out and on again as soon as his back is turned.

"So what do you think of your fan mail, Detective?" Vince asked yesterday.

"I haven't really read it."

Vince pouted. "I spent ages writing that letter. Took me hours."

"Vince, please don't tell me you've been adding to these damn things?"

Vince winked at me, grinned and walked off, waving as he went.

Thursday morning dawns. I shower and dress quickly and, after waking Lizzie with a cup of tea, slip out into the fresh morning air. Today is the day we will interview the mysterious Mr. Makin and I am anxious to get on with it. I walk into the station a few minutes after eight. Dave-the-grumpy-git-desk-sergeant has turned into Dave-the-not-quite-so-grumpy-desk-sergeant. Although we haven't quite reached the pinnacle of an actual conversation yet, we do now smile at each other. Yep, that's right. It's not a beaming, can't-stretch-my-face-any-further smile but it is a smile nonetheless. After being admitted to the inner sanctum by old smiler himself, I bound up the two flights of stairs and into the office.

I hail various officers as I work my way through the maze of desks, ending up at my own, now very familiar, working space. The equally familiar sight of James Sabine with a telephone attached to one ear greets me. We smile at each other as I plonk my laptop and bag on top of the desk and then I bustle off to complete our morning ritual by getting two cups of coffee from the vending machine. By the time I have returned, bearing two steaming plastic cups of caffeine, James is off the phone and writing notes. "So!" I say, sitting down, leaning back and sipping from my cup. "Mr. Makin!"

"Yep!" says James, mirroring my movements. "Mr. Makin." We stare at each other thoughtfully for a second.

"Do you really think he may be the link between the four burglaries?"

"The more I think about it, the more I believe he might be. Maybe our Mr. Makin is feeding someone with information. The someone who is actually carrying out all these burglaries. From Mr. Makin they would find out the exact layout of the house, the exact value of any costly items on the insurance schedule and also what alarm system the house has in place. They wouldn't need to gain access to the property to case it because Mr. Makin would have done it for them." He looks into space for a few seconds and then his eyes seem to snap into focus. "Come on, we'd better get going. We're supposed to be meeting him at nine."

We quickly finish our coffee and I wait while James gathers some papers together. I have nothing to pack up since I hadn't quite got around to unpacking anything.

We arrive at Mr. Makin's offices just before nine. As James reverses into a parking bay, he places an arm behind my seat and peers over his shoulder into the space behind. I sharply breathe in the sweet tang of his aftershave. This and the sensation of almost having his arm around me is not altogether unpleasant. I have no time to even contemplate why as his voice breaks into my consciousness.

"Come on, Colshannon! Stop staring at the dashboard, I promise it will still be there when you get back." And with that he is out of the car and impatiently waiting to lock it. I gather up my bag, get out of the car and together we walk toward Mr. Makin's building.

Elephant Insurance Company is situated on the second floor of a well-kept building. A somewhat overweight, middle-aged secretary is halfheartedly stabbing at a typewriter as we walk into the reception area. She looks up swiftly as we enter. James introduces himself, still without mentioning the rather significant fact that he is from the police, and tells her we have an appointment with Mr. Makin. She purses her pink-frosted lips together, murmurs something about not keeping us waiting, at which we all look faintly disbelieving, and then disappears. James and I sit down on a couple of chairs placed against the wall.

"Don't say anything in there."

"I never say anything," I whisper indignantly.

"I think 'never' might be a bit of an exaggeration," he mutters.

We sit in silence for a second. I take in the slightly faded floral wallpaper, the old desk the secretary was sitting behind and the rather ancient typewriter that should have been retired and replaced by a computer system long ago. There is a slight air of refined shabbiness and the distinct impression that the offices, along with Elephant Insurance Company, have seen better days.

I glance over at James. He is quietly surveying the scene before him. This morning, I would guess in anticipation of this interview, he is wearing a smart blue shirt and tie coupled with faded beige chinos. His boyish, short-haired good looks are somewhat at odds with the room.

He looks over at me under the intensity of my glance and smiles. "What's up?"

I quickly look back to the floor. "Nothing. Bit nervous, I think."

I mentally give myself a shake. Good Lord, for a moment there I was almost lusting after him. Try not to make a complete tit of yourself, please, I tell myself firmly. He's getting married to Fleur in a matter of weeks, Robin is doing a passably good impression of *The French Lieutenant's Woman* and now even you are starting to hum "Another One Bites The Dust." Get a grip. He barely tolerates me, let alone likes me.

The pink-frosted secretary comes back and tells us Mr. Makin will see us now. As we get up to follow her through to another office, James asks if Mr. Makin owns the company and the secretary answers in the affirmative. The room we are shown into is a complete contrast to the reception. A bejeweled chandelier hangs from an ornate ceiling and thick-sashed drapes hang at the windows. A gentleman, whom I presume is Mr. Makin, rises from a fine antique desk where a laptop lies open and moves toward us holding out his hand. He smiles jovially.

"Morning, morning! How do you do?"

I would place him in his late fifties. His gray hair is thinning, terrible bags hang from his brown eyes and he has a ruddy complexion that to my mind speaks of too much alcohol. There is a faint smell of cigar smoke in the air. He is wearing a three-piece, dark, pin-striped suit with a perky red handkerchief poking out of his top pocket.

After shaking hands, James flips open his ID. "I am Detective Sergeant James Sabine and this is Holly Colshannon." He waits for a reaction and apparently not in vain. A look of horror comes over Mr. Makin's face and his mouth drops open.

"It's not my wife, is it?" I don't think this was the reaction that James was hoping for and certainly not the one I was expecting. Without me even being aware of it, I think I had all but sentenced Mr. Makin.

"No, Mr. Makin," James says quickly. "We're here about a business matter. We've made an appointment."

Mr. Makin lets out a stream of air and stares at the ground for a second. He fishes the red handkerchief out of his pocket and mops his forehead.

"Thank goodness. I thought you were about to tell me my wife had been in an accident or something."

"I'm sorry to have alarmed you, sir," replies James. I think we've got the wrong guy—I was naively expecting him to hold out his hands to be cuffed and say, "It's a fair cop, guv'nor."

Instead Mr. Makin does none of that. He strides over to the door and pulls it open. His secretary almost falls in. He ignores her apparent over-enthusiasm and says calmly from his elevated position, "Ah! Miss Rennie. Could you kindly get us some coffee?"

She quickly nods and disappears off on her mission. He returns behind his desk and looks from one to the other of us.

"Now, I'm afraid I only have half an hour as I have to go out to an appointment later. So how can I help?"

"Damn. Damn and bugger," says James furiously once we are out on the pavement and striding toward the car. We both get in.

"He didn't seem very guilty."

"No, he didn't."

James sits behind the steering wheel and stares into space. I don't like to say anything just in case he's about to solve the whole case. You know, like when Miss Marple is talking about knitting and then suddenly, *voilà!*, she knows who the murderer is! The minutes tick by and I start to worry that maybe he's thinking about how to achieve that ribbed effect on his latest sweater.

"Er, James?"

"Hmm?"

"Anything wrong?"

"Something," he murmurs. I leave him to his contemplation of the moss stitch for a little longer. After a few more minutes I can bear it no longer. "What? What's wrong?"

He shifts in his seat and turns his body toward me. "Nothing's wrong. Nothing at all on the face of it. There's just something . . . Did you notice all the clocks?" he says suddenly.

"The clocks?"

"Yeah." He looks at me intently.

"Well, there were a couple . . ."

"There were five in his office alone."

"Were there? Maybe he's late a lot."

James looks at me impatiently and sighs.

"Sorry," I say. "Well? What do you want to do?" I add after a bit longer. I'm getting a little impatient of this sponsored silence stuff.

"I want to see where he goes on his appointment."

"Fine. So, er, what does that entail?"

"Sitting here and watching where he goes."

"I knew that."

James starts the car and drives off, just in case the secretary is watching us from the window. We go once around the block and then park further up the street where we can't be seen from the windows of the office but we can see who comes out of the door.

"How do you know there isn't a back door?"

"I counted the number of doors in each room," he explains patiently with a glimmer of a smile. "It's something I learned at detecting school."

"So could you call this a sort of stakeout?" I ask excitedly.

"If it makes you happy. The term 'stakeout' imparts a sort of glamour though. And I don't think you could describe a ten-minute session sitting in a Vauxhall as glamorous."

"We could be here for hours though!"

An hour and a half later I have called the paper, called Lizzie, called Vince and made a start on today's diary installment on my laptop (and if we sit here much longer, boy am I going to be pushed for subject matter). James also has called his office, Fleur and his office again. Once the mobiles have fallen silent for a couple of minutes, I say, "Do you want some coffee? I can go and see if I can find some."

"That would be great."

"Do you want something to eat as well?"

"I'm starving. Didn't have a chance to have breakfast this morning."

"What do you want?"

"Surprise me." He gets out his wallet and shoves a ten-pound note toward me. "Hurry up, because I'll have to go without you if Makin leaves, and don't walk past his offices."

"I may not have been to detecting school, but I am not stupid," I say haughtily. I wander off down the road and find a little corner shop about three hundred yards away. After loading myself up with goodies, I make my way back to the car.

"No coffee," I say as I drop my purchases into the foot well, "but I do have . . . a banana milkshake!" I triumphantly produce it from my carrier bag.

"Thanks." He takes it from me and shakes it vigorously in the manner of someone completely au fait with banana milkshakes, his eyes still trained on Mr. Makin's front door. "Got any crisps?"

I chuck a packet of salt and vinegar and another one of cheesy puffs at him. "No Monster Munch?" he asks, aghast.

"You are not going to stink out our stakeout with Monster Munch."

I curl my feet up under me and we munch in silence.

"Fleur tells me your folks are coming to the wedding."

"Yeah, sorry about that. They always seem to turn up where you least expect it."

"I'll look forward to . . ." James never finishes his sentence because a figure suddenly looms up outside my window, waving some black hardware around. I almost literally jump out of my skin and in a reflex action grasp my handbag to me (you can always count on me in a crisis). James leaps out of the car, runs around to my side and before I know it has thrust the figure into the back of the car. The figure is giggling to itself and wearing a particularly fetching pair of leather trousers and a pink shirt.

Vince leans between the two front seats. "What's going on?" he whispers theatrically.

"Vince!" I say hotly, smacking him with my handbag, "you complete parsnip. You scared me. We're on a stakeout."

"How exciting! Can I be on it too?"

James gets back in the driver's side. "Vince, what the hell are you doing? We're trying to keep a low profile."

"I can keep a low profile," Vince says indignantly.

"No, you bloody can't. The only profiles you know are loud and conspicuous."

"Oooh, you cad."

"How did you know where we were?"

"Holly called half an hour ago and happened to mention it."

"I didn't mean for you to come down. Anyway, where did you get your leather trousers from?" I interject, more weightier matters pressing on my mind.

"Do you like them? There's this little shop on the Bath Road and . . ."

"Holly! Vince!" says James heatedly. We both look at him in surprise. "Do you mind?"

"He *is* a cad, isn't he?" I say to Vince.

"I should say so. Can I have a crisp?"

Once James has forcibly ejected Vince from the car and forbidden him to come back, we continue with the important business of watching the offices.

"Flapjack?" I proffer.

"Thanks."

I fight with the wrapper and remark, "Flapjacks always remind me of my childhood. My mother used to give them to us after school. She can't cook to save her life though; used to take us half an hour to clean our teeth afterward."

"Do you have any brothers and sisters?" he asks without taking his eyes from Mr. Makin's building.

"Yeah, I've got three brothers and one sister."

"Blimey. Your mother probably gave them to you to shut you all up."

"Meal times did get a bit noisy."

James takes a bite of his flapjack, his eyes still firmly fixed on his quarry. "Tell me about them."

So I tell him a bit about my childhood, and how we used to move around with my mother's career because she insisted on having us with her when she was on tour. I tell him what fun we all used to have as we moved from town to town and how the rest of the actors and actresses in the tour group became our surrogate aunts and uncles. I explain how my father was a consultant, so his posts only lasted for a year or two before we moved on, which suited my parents' wanderlust perfectly. But I also mention how miserable it was to keep on moving from one school to another, constantly leaving friends behind and having to make new ones. I tell him how we finally settled permanently in Cornwall when my father retired and I was able to go to the same school for a number of years. In turn, I ask him about his childhood. He tells me about an existence that is completely alien to me, generally due to the fact that it all took place in one spot. We laugh at his tales of woe concerning an unrequited crush on the barmaid at the local pub and he even tells me a little about Rob, his brother who was killed last year.

"I suppose you see a lot of horrible stuff?" I say randomly.

"Yeah, I suppose I do."

"So why do you do it? Why did you want to join the police force?" I ask, suddenly curious.

He glances over at me, probably suspicious of my question and my motive for asking it. After a second, his face relaxes and he says, "I've always wanted to join the police force."

"Why?"

"Something happened when I was a kid."

"Tell me?"

He hesitates for a second. "Well, I grew up in Gloucestershire. My folks had a farm in a village where absolutely nothing ever, ever happened. In fact, Rob and I used to daily berate the fact that nothing ever happened. Imagine it—two spotty, hormonal teenagers moping around, chucking themselves on to the sofa like the archetypal Kevin, griping about how bored they were. Not that we didn't have plenty to do; there is always loads to be done on a farm. But then one day this little girl from the village just vanished, just disappeared. The manhunt was enormous; everyone turned out and we searched with the police day and night for about twelve days until they called the search off. Then the people from the village searched by themselves for another five days until one by one we all went home. But we all grieved for this little girl and the community was never the same again. This village, where nothing ever happened, had been violated. The parents of the little girl were so traumatized and harassed that they moved away. I just felt so helpless throughout the whole thing. There was nothing I could possibly do to alleviate any of the pain. So I joined the force as soon as I could, thinking I might perhaps be able to help somebody in the future." He shrugs and looks a little embarrassed.

"You said the parents of the little girl were harassed?"

"Yeah. By the press." He glances over to me. "They camped on their doorstep, waiting to catch their pain on camera and in words. It was horrible."

"So that's why you don't like the press very much."

"Correct."

"Did they ever find out what happened to the little girl?"

"Yeah, they found her body a month later. Raped and strangled."

We sit in silence for a few seconds and now, at last, I can understand why he hated this diary idea so much and why he was so antagonistic toward me. And I don't blame him at all.

"So, have you ever regretted your decision? To go into the police force?"

"Never. I love it," he says with a warmth that surprises me. "I like the fact that I meet people, you know, normal people, and although we can't solve every single case, it's really satisfying when we do."

"You said your folks *had* a farm. What do they do now?"

"They sold it last year and retired early."

There are a dozen more questions I would like to ask him. But not for the diary, for me. I would like to know. But I don't want to look as though I am being the delving reporter, the "I'm your

best friend so bare your soul to me and then you'll see our intimate conversation splashed all over the news tomorrow" type. So
instead we fall into a companionable silence and both stare ahead,
lost in our own thoughts. My head is full of images of his childhood and I wish I could see pictures of him back then.

A thought occurs to me and I feel that with our newly found
air of intimacy I can ask him this. "You know that scooping business by the *Journal*?"

"Yeah?"

"Was it anything to do with you?"

James frowns and glances over at me. "No, why do you think
that?"

"I went up to the IT department."

"I know you did. You told me," he says patiently.

"Well, they said no one had been up to report the incident."

"I reported it. Why wouldn't I? I reported it to, er, what's his
name, Paul. I reported it to Paul. Who did you see?"

"A woman."

"Well, there you are. Bloody IT department, they've always
got their minds on other things."

"But the scooping suddenly stopped after that."

"That was me. I found out who it was."

"You found out who it was?" I say, sitting up suddenly.

He glances over at me. "Yeah."

"Well, who was it?" I ask impatiently.

"You know Bill?"

"Bill? Nice Bill? Meek, butter-wouldn't-melt-in-his-mouth
Bill?" I say disbelievingly.

"I found him at my terminal one evening, when I came back to
the office to collect some files. He said he was just looking something up. So a couple of nights later, I took a case we had just
started that day, the drugs arrest one, off the main computer and
put it on a floppy disk. When you were scooped the next morning,

I knew someone had accessed that disk to get the information because it wasn't on the mainframe computer. So I confronted Bill and he confessed."

"Why didn't you tell me?"

"I didn't want you to make trouble for Bill. He's got a lot of problems at the moment, financial ones. And it wasn't as if he was doing something awful. It was just unethical."

"Well, it was pretty awful for me!" I reply hotly.

"It must have been. I seem to remember your editor reacted by asking you to try and get on with me a bit better. And you told him it was like trying to get on with Hannibal Lecter," he observes dryly.

I feel myself going a little pink. I start fiddling with the hem of my skirt. "Well, it's not as though you were terribly easy to get on with when we first met."

"Yeah, I know." There's a small silence and then he says, "But *Hannibal Lecter*?"

I grin. To change the subject I say, "Actually, I remember you having a row with Bill now!"

"Yeah, I did."

"I thought you were just being bad-tempered!"

"OK, enough of the bad temper/Hannibal Lecter thing."

We fall into a convivial silence, staring at Mr. Makin's door. With his eyes still fixed there, James says, "Did Robin tell you what is going on?"

I jump uncomfortably at the subject matter. "What? With you two?" I ask awkwardly.

"Yes."

"Sort of."

"It's over. That's why she's so upset."

"So, there's nothing going on?"

"No." There's a pause until he adds, "It really wasn't . . ." and then stops abruptly and leans forward. I follow his line of vision and spot Mr. Makin carrying a briefcase and about to get into a car. James starts the engine and we both click our seat belts on. I glance at my watch. We had been here for more than three and a half hours.

We travel in silence, distanced a few cars behind Mr. Makin. The office buildings start to drop away as we move into residential areas and it becomes more difficult to maintain an unsuspicious distance behind him as the traffic becomes sparser. About a quarter of an hour later we have traveled right into the suburbs of Bristol.

"He's not going home," James says suddenly as Mr. Makin takes a right turn.

"How do you know where he lives?" I ask.

"Looked it up on the computer yesterday."

Mr. Makin takes a swift left, followed by another one, and we follow him. He finally comes to a standstill outside a semi-detached house and we pull into the curb about five cars away from him. We watch as he climbs out of the car and walks up the path to the semi.

"What number is that?" I whisper.

"Why are you whispering?"

James reads the number of the house we are parked in front of and then counts down to the house Mr. Makin has disappeared into. "Number sixteen." He then peers around, looking for the name of the road. "Maple Tree Drive," he says, getting out a notebook and writing it down.

"James!" I nudge him and point to something ahead of me.

A large ginger cat pads up the semi's pathway and disappears through a cat flap.

"The cat hair," I breathe.

We turn around and head back toward the station. Once we have collected more fan mail from Dave-the-not-quite-so-grumpy-desk-sergeant ("I'm surprised we haven't had more for you after your recent TV interview, Holly," he says, which raises a smile from James and a, "Ha, ha. Very droll," from me), we make our way up to the offices. James sits down at his desk and, after briefly leafing through his messages, logs on to the computer to check out the address of Mr. Makin's rendezvous. I lean against his desk, watching the computer screen. We wait for a few minutes as we access the appropriate records and then James types in the address to check if the resident has a police record. We wait again. The computer bumps and grinds and then finally coughs up something. NO KNOWN RECORD.

James leans back in his chair and links his hands behind his head, absentmindedly staring into space.

"We should have waited for the cat to come out of the cat flap again and then wrestled it to the ground for one of its hairs. We could have sent it off for DNA testing to see if it matched the one Roger found," I comment.

"The ridiculousness of that idea aside, it would take weeks for the results to come back from the lab."

"Well, could we just go up and knock on the door?"

"They could refuse us access without a warrant and then move all the stuff out if it's there."

"What if he's just visiting his sister or something? Loads of people have ginger cats. Are you sure Mr. Makin is anything to do with this? I mean, you could arrest my Aunt Annie. She owns clocks and a ginger tabby."

"It's just a hunch."

"A detecting thing?" I ask sarcastically. Please don't do the hunch thing. I was in the room when we spoke to Mr. Makin and he seemed innocent to me. Journalists have hunches too.

"It's not just some clocks and a ginger cat. It all makes sense." He frowns to himself. "I'll get uniform to ask some questions. Also put surveillance on the house before we get a warrant. I need permission from the Chief." And with that he disappears off in the direction of the Chief Inspector's office.

I really ought to be getting on with the diary, but instead I stare pensively into space, my mind full of the events of the last hour or so. I wander over to see Callum for a chat while I impatiently wait for James to return.

"So . . ." I sit on his desk and pick up his paperweight. "You and Robin not getting on?" I ask ultra-casually. OK, it isn't the most innocuous of beginnings, but the eternal triangle of Robin, James and Fleur seems to be playing on my mind a lot lately. And it's not very often that Callum and I are alone together nowadays.

"I should say not. Has James told you then?"

I nod and fiddle some more with the paperweight. "Are you pissed off with James as well?"

"Of course I am! He wants to invite Robin to the wedding. Can you imagine how awkward that will be? I've told him no way, but he's not listening. He seems to think that Robin needs protecting." He sighs and leans back in his chair. "You'll be well out of it by then though; the diary will have finished. What are you going to do after all of this, Hol?"

I shrug. "Go back to features, I guess. I hope I might get some better pieces to cover as a result of the diary."

"I'm sure you will. It's been a great success!"

I see out of the corner of my eye that James is back. I sling a hasty, "See you later," at Callum and run back over to our desks.

"Well?"

"The Chief has grudgingly agreed to put the house under surveillance for a few days."

I write up my diary for that day. It is relatively thoughtful (for me anyway). It begins:

I got to know Detective Sergeant Jack Swithen a little better today.
We talked a bit about his childhood and where he grew up. He told me
a story about a little girl . . .

On Friday morning, James comes striding in. "Dawn raid on Tuesday. I've got five other officers and until then to arrange it."

My eyes open wide. I mean, how much can one journalist take? A stakeout and now a dawn raid! "How fantastic!" I exclaim, clapping my hands together. "So the surveillance was a success?"

"A lot of things were going bump in the night, apparently. Also, uniform has been talking to a few people and I got some of the other detectives to talk to their contacts in that area as well. Too much nighttime activity has been going on at that place."

"So what time are we leaving on Tuesday?"

"You're not coming."

The smile slowly fades from my face. "What do you mean, I'm not coming?"

"I mean that you're not coming."

"Why not? Is it dangerous?"

"Not dangerous, just unpredictable. You might get hurt, especially with your overwhelming talent to be in the wrong spot at the wrong time." He turns his attention back to the papers on his desk.

"You can't do this to me. This is my whole career."

"I'm not talking about your career, I'm talking about you."

"What if I stay in the car and don't come in until it's safe?"

He hesitates. "You wouldn't move until I came to get you?"

"I promise."

He sighs resignedly. "OK then."

"Vince too?"

"Don't push your luck, Holly," he says, returning his attention to his papers.

* * *

We spend the afternoon in court as Kenneth Tanner, the hospital drug thief, is due to appear. James and I mooch about drinking endless cups of coffee, doing the crossword in the paper and reading out each other's horoscopes (he's a Scorpio and I'm a Virgo). It is a complete waste of time being there and James isn't even called to the witness stand in the end. Vince takes some photos of us standing in front of the courthouse though and even a couple of us larking about on the steps until I fall down them, needless to say nearly breaking both of our respective necks.

At the end of an unexciting afternoon, I gather my things together and go over to the paper to file copy. These burglaries and the solving of them (if this is the solving of them) could dramatically increase the diary's ratings. Sometimes journalism really is about being in the right place at the right time. I smile to myself as I wind up my laptop leads and wonder if I'll be given a new post after this or whether Joe will send me back to covering pet funerals.

I burst through the front door of my flat. "Lizzie? Are you home?" I shout from the hallway as I tear off my coat, getting my hands stuck en route. A lethargic rustling greets me from the vicinity of the sofa. She must have found the custard cream hiding place. I walk through into the sitting room and her mournful face stares at me from the darkest depths of the couch. I wrinkle my nose sympathetically. "How are you feeling? How was work today, any progress yet? Alastair still ignoring you?"

She valiantly stuffs another custard cream into her already full mouth and shakes her head. "I even wore my sexiest two-piece," she says, spitting crumbs at me. "Nothing. Not a flicker, not a glance, not a word."

"Oh," I say dejectedly.

The clichés are starting to sound a little tired so we have agreed I can stop using them now. Please don't think Lizzie is wallowing in self-pity (although a wallow is good for us all from time to time)—she isn't. It's just a reaction to the strain of carrying on as normal in the office. Lizzie would rather poke herself in the eye than let people watch her cry. So at work she holds her head high and looks as though she hasn't a care in the world. When she gets home she collapses in a crumpled heap, exhausted by all that play-acting.

To take her mind off things, I tell her about the exciting developments in the Fox case.

"To think we might even be able to put a name and a face to The Fox by next week!" I say excitedly.

"What time is a 'dawn raid'?"

"I think James said about six A.M."

"Aren't you supposed to be on that hen do the night before?"

I stare at her. I'd forgotten all about the damn thing. "I have to go. I promised Fleur I would."

"Why are you looking at me like that?"

"I really think it's high time you came out for an evening," I say seriously.

"You. Must. Be. Mad. I'd be slitting my wrists by midnight!"

"Awww, come on! It could be fun!"

"Fun? FUN? Running around with veils and L-plates? I'll stay at home with some French Fancies and Ant 'n' Dec, thanks all the same."

"I'm sure Fleur won't mind. I could just give her a call."

"NO; unequivocally, positively, unconditionally NO."

twenty

———

Lizzie and I stroll through the entrance to Henry Africa's Hothouse approximately ten minutes late. I spot Fleur sitting at the bar, surrounded by an odd assortment of friends. I can easily recognize the girls she must work with at the bereavement charity. They are huddled in a small group to the left of her, some sporting spectacles, others with haircuts so uninspiring that if I had been Nicky Clarke the scissors would have been whirring by now. One is even wearing a kilt (no, it isn't by Versace and no, it isn't twenty inches above her knee).

The other group are much easier on the eye but also much more terrifying. They probably are wearing Versace and their hair really is cut by Nicky Clarke. I would imagine these are Fleur's friends from home. I suspect Daddy has a private income. I can't really see James Sabine getting on with any of them. (I must not judge by appearances, I must not judge by appearances.)

I can feel Lizzie's eyes boring into the back of my neck as I lead the way toward them. I wince slightly to myself—Monday night telly was looking infinitely more appealing. In fact, I had nearly been persuaded to stay in tonight, but not by Lizzie. Ben had come round after his rugby training, just as Robbie Williams and I were getting ready. Well, he was singing and I was getting ready.

"Do you have to go tonight?" he pouted, lying on the bed in his dirty rugby gear. "I thought you could scrub my back in the bath and then we could perhaps go out to your favorite restaurant?"

He raked his blond locks off his forehead and I smiled indul-
gently at his bribery attempts.

"I promised I would go; besides, it will be good for Lizzie to
get out," I said, scraping my mascara wand around in the tube in
a desperate attempt to try to prize some out.

He scowled. "How long is she staying for? Surely it doesn't
take this long to get over that Alastair? What does he do for a living again?"

"Computers."

"Poofy profession."

I sighed. "Ben, just because he doesn't run around in the mud,
put his head between other men's legs and then take a bath with
them, doesn't mean he's a poof."

"It does in my book."

"Darling, come round tomorrow evening and I will scrub your
back all night if you want." I snapped my compact shut and sat on
the bed with him.

"You look too gorgeous tonight to be wasted on a bunch of
girls," he said, putting his arms around me. I have to say I was
pleased with the results myself. I had decided, after the hectic
time I'd been having with Lizzie, the police station and the diary,
to take my time getting ready this evening. I'd had a bath, shaved
and plucked myself to within an inch of becoming a Christmas
turkey, put on a a face pack, which I'd worn until my face cracked,
and even dried my hair properly. I was wearing a tailored gray
skirt which split either side up to my thighs (Ben had bought me
it for Christmas, although I suspect his mother *really* bought it as
he never seems to recognize it), a little beaded lilac top and a pair
of the finest earrings Butler and Wilson had to offer. I kept tugging down the lilac top until Lizzie pointed out it was supposed
to be showing my midriff.

"Well, I have to say I'm not looking forward to tonight," I
sighed.

"See? Stay in with me then."

"Even Teresa the Holy Cow is going to be there to make my evening complete."

"Teresa the Holy Cow?"

"Yes, you know. You met her a few weeks ago. In the Square Bar."

He fiddled with the corner of my duvet cover. "Oh yes, I remember," he said vaguely. He looked back up at me. "Come round to my place tomorrow and then we can be by ourselves for a bit."

"I can't leave Lizzie right now."

"OK. I'll come around here tomorrow," he said sulkily.

I dropped a kiss on the top of his head. "Thank you."

We say our greetings to Fleur, who is sitting resplendent on a bar stool in the middle of the group. No veils or L-plates for her; she is wearing a pair of pink hipsters that I might just have been able to get one tree trunk of a leg into, and a snazzy little top which shows off her slim, brown midriff. I desperately breathe in and hope comparisons are not made. She greets us with huge "MOI"s directed at either side of our faces and Lizzie, smiling tightly, thanks her for the indirect invite. Fleur then introduces us to the rest of the group. I remember the name of the first friend she introduces, who apparently is the bridesmaid. She is standing next to Fleur and is flicking her hair as though her life depends upon it. She is called Susie and gives me a thin-lipped smile while looking fixedly over my shoulder. I could have stabbed her and she would never have been able to pick me out of an identity parade, which may be worth bearing in mind for later. I promptly forget the names of everyone else and smile inanely throughout the rest of the intros.

"We have a float and a bar tab, so get yourselves a drink," says Fleur. We duly hand over twenty quid each for the float and then turn our attention to the baffling array of cocktails.

"Don't let me drink too much this evening," I whisper to Lizzie. "I have a police raid in the morning."

"Don't worry. I'll drink your share."

We watch the barman make up two Long Island Iced Teas and, just as we lean against the bar with the aforementioned items in hand, we spot Teresa the Holy Cow planting a "MOI" near Fleur's cheek. Lizzie turns back to the barman.

"We'll have two more of those, please."

Teresa comes over to the bar under similar instructions to order a drink. "Hello Teresa," Lizzie and I dutifully mutter.

"Hello Holly, hello Lizzie. Fleur said you'd be here, Holly, but she didn't mention you'd be coming, Lizzie." Damn, tripped up at the first hurdle.

"Funny. Holly didn't mention you'd be coming either," Lizzie said, glaring at me.

"Didn't I?" I say weakly.

"So what *are* you doing here, Lizzie?" Teresa asks. Lizzie and I glance at each other and I start wildly fishing around in my brain for excuses. Lizzie is too quick for me.

"I'm looking after Holly in case she gets too drunk."

I glare at Lizzie.

"I'm sure that doesn't happen *very* often," says Teresa with a smirk.

"No Bible meetings tonight, Teresa?" I ask savagely.

"No, I left early. It's important to support a friend as she joins in the holy union of matrimony."

"I'm sure the barman here is going to do just as good a job."

She ignores the jibe, orders a white wine spritzer and then goes over to join the rest of the charity group.

I angrily suck up the remainder of my drink through my straw, recklessly abandon the glass and move on to my next one.

"Why didn't you tell me she was coming?" hisses Lizzie.

"Because then you wouldn't have come."

"Too bloody right."

We go upstairs to the restaurant to eat and I thankfully find my-self sitting miles away from Teresa. I have a very earnest girl called Charlotte sitting on one side of me and Lizzie on the other. After Teresa insists that we all say grace, I turn to Charlotte and ask her, "So what do you do at the charity?"

"I'm one of the counselors there," she says softly. She is a plain girl with straight dark blond hair. She has the sort of manner that makes me want to lie on the floor and pour out all my troubles.

"Do you know James Sabine?" I ask.

"I wasn't his counselor, Judith over there was." She points across the table to a gentle-looking girl. "But I saw him a couple of times in reception. You're the reporter who's doing the diary with him, aren't you?"

"Yes, I am."

"I recognize you from the paper."

I smile at this, not quite knowing what to say in response, and continue with my probing. "Fleur's so nice, isn't she?" Please say something like "Oh no, she's wanted for heinous crimes in four countries."

"Yes, she's so lovely to everyone." Damn.

"So, how long ago did James and Fleur meet?"

"About a year and a half."

"Did they hit it off straightaway?"

"Well, I don't know about him, but Fleur talked of nothing else! Of course, he was devastated about his brother so it was a number of months before they started going out together."

"Oh, right," I say nonchalantly. It's quite hard to appear noncha-lant when you're dying to say, "Spill your guts! Tell me everything!"

She continues, "And now look where we all are! About to cele-brate their wedding! A perfect happy ending. Wonderful!"

"Yes. Marvelous isn't it? Has Fleur worked at the charity long?"

"A couple of years. Just between you and me . . ." She drops her voice to a whisper (ahhh, heavenly words to a reporter's ears) ". . . I don't think Fleur really needs to work."

"So why does she?"

"I think she enjoys helping people." Bloody hell, the girl is all sugar and spice.

"I'm sure she does it just to help out," I reply sweetly.

"I shouldn't be telling you all this, you being a reporter. It's probably the drink."

I look longingly at my own empty glass, hail a passing waiter and order two more cocktails. "Don't worry, I write about the po-lice and James, not Fleur and James."

For the next course, Fleur thinks it would be a good idea if we all move around the table one place so "we can get to know each other better." Alternate people get up to move and I sit down on the other side of Lizzie and find myself next to Susie, the best friend. I might have to revert to the stabbing idea. I smile warmly. "Hi!"

She condescends to focus on me. I promise myself that after five minutes' effort I can spend the rest of the evening talking to Lizzie.

"So, you're the bridesmaid?" Well, it's a start. She flicks her hair and nods.

I try again. "What's your dress like?"

At last! Some semblance of enthusiasm. "It's a cross-bias cut with a mermaid train."

"Sounds beautiful!" I say, without the slightest clue of what it might look like. "Have you met the groom?"

She pulls a small face. "He's very . . . bright, isn't he?"

I bet she has been on the wrong end of James Sabine's sarcastic tongue on a few occasions. I try not to smirk and concentrate instead on looking at my napkin.

"He's a policeman, isn't he?"

"A detective, actually."

"Same thing."

No, I think to myself, it's not the same thing at all but I decide to let it pass. She, unfortunately, doesn't.

She lowers her voice to a whisper. "Not the best profession in the world, is it?"

Well, lovey, it's the only profession that stops me from reaching over for that butter knife and plunging it into your skinny, white thigh, I think to myself, but I concentrate on nodding instead. I could imagine what James would say (apart from "well done") if I knifed his bridesmaid a week and a half before his wedding.

A few hours on, I am decidedly pissed. Lizzie and I have degenerated to speaking between ourselves and the last few weeks have made me forget what a good time we actually have together when we're out.

"Lizzie," I hiss, "you said you weren't going to let me drink."

Lizzie tries to prize the glass out of my hand. "S'too late now," I say, hanging on to it for dear life.

She shrugs and gives up. "What are you going to do tomorrow morning?"

"I'll be all right."

"What time is James picking you up for this raid thing?"

"Half five."

"Blimey!"

"It'll be fine. We just won't go to bed!" I clink my glass to hers and hoover down yet another Long Island Iced Tea. "How are you feeling?" I ask sympathetically.

"Fine, fine." Lizzie nods her head dementedly. I watch it anxiously to check it's not going to fall off. "Sod Alastair!"

"Sod him!" I agree. "Fleur!" I exclaim as she, swaying gently, crouches down beside us. "How's the hen? Having a good time?"

"Great, are you two all right?" she asks.

"We couldn't be better!"

"You and James are working tomorrow, aren't you?"

"Shhhh," I say clumsily, putting my finger to my lips. "Don't tell him about this. He won't let me come." I look around me; everything is a little blurry and I wonder if I might need to start wearing glasses. I make a mental note to book an optician's appointment.

"Where'sh Teresa?"

"She got a call on her mobile and went off. Obviously a red-hot lover!"

"Nahh. One of the choir boys hash drunk the altar wine."

"We need to pep everyone up a bit. People are fading fast." I briefly look around at the surrounding hen-sters. I have to agree the party has quietened down a tad.

"I know a game!" I say enthusiastically.

"Holly, what the hell is going on?" James says angrily.

I open one eye. I was just resting them for a minute, you understand. The light is a little bright. That's the problem with the NHS today. They insist on using those awful, glaring overhead strips. I'm going to instantly pen a terse note to the government on the very same subject just as soon as they let me out of here.

"James!" I say delightedly, with one eye squinting at him, "what are you doing here? Have you hurt your toe too?"

"No, I haven't. I am here because Fleur called to tell me she may be a little late home because she had to take you to the hospital," he says angrily. I take a better look at him; his short hair is tousled and his clothes obviously hastily dragged on. He doesn't seem too amused at having been pulled out of bed.

I frown gravely at this. "You're not cross, are you?"

"I'm not cross."

"You seem cross."

"That's because I'm bloody *FURIOUS*!" Those green eyes practically pin me to my pillow with the force of their gaze. My hangover is starting to kick in and now I know what it feels like to be faced with an angry Godzilla. I wonder if the alcohol is having hallucinogenic effects on me and close my eyes again, fervently hoping he is just an apparition dreamed up by my over-fertile imagination. I coax an eye open after a second to check if he is still there. Unfortunately he is.

In a dramatic change of subject, I say, "James, this is my best friend, Lizzie." It's very hard to make the appropriate introductions when you're lying on a hospital stretcher. Not to mention managing to speak in whole sentences, complete with the appropriate nouns and verbs.

James relaxes minutely and shakes Lizzie's hand. He mutters, "Hi, Lizzie, how are you?"

"Nice to meet you, James," Lizzie says wearily—all in all it has been quite a night. "I was just about to get some tea for us; would you like some?"

"That would be great." Lizzie wanders off, intent on her mission, and James then turns his very unwelcome attention back to yours truly.

"You are aware that we are supposed to be involved in a raid in"—he consults his watch—"approximately three hours' time?" His face swims in and out of focus. I blink hastily to try and clear the fog that is threatening to envelop my brain.

"Just let them get the bottle off and I'll be as right as rain and raring to go!"

"You're not coming!" he roars.

"Then why are you here?" I ask, frowning, clearly not under-standing the obvious.

"Because my errant fiancée," and he points to Fleur, who is lying across three chairs fast asleep, "didn't tell me what was wrong with you on the telephone, she just hung up. For all I knew you could have been in a car accident."

"Oh." I hang my head in shame, deeply sorry it wasn't something more serious than a drinking game gone slightly askew.

"So what did happen?" he asks pointing at the wine bottle that is hanging off the end of one of my toes.

"Well, we were playing this game I know. You all have to per-form a little trick, or perhaps make up a poem, or maybe even a . . ." I glance over at his seething face. "Yes, well, anyway. Hav-ing introduced the game, I felt I ought to kick it off myself." I look for a glimmer of understanding and sympathy but funnily enough there isn't any forthcoming. "So I decided to do some-thing my brothers used to do with empty bottles. It was always really impressive when they did it." I look miserably at my swollen foot. "The problem is, I think they used to do it with plas-tic bottles. I should have telephoned one of them and asked them!" I end excitedly, flushed with the success of remembering how exactly the evening had gone wrong.

"And you thought you would try it with a bottle of . . ." He looks down at my foot. "Merlot?"

"Well, we drank it first," I hastily assure him, concerned he might think I'd wasted it.

"That much is obvious," he says dryly.

"The problem was, the more we tried to pull it off, the more my toe started to swell up. It's stuck," I explain.

"I can see it's *stuck*." He spits the last word out. "Right, well, if you will excuse me, I'm going to go back to sleep for another cou-ple of hours and then I have to go to work."

"But you're not going without me!"

"Holly." This is said in a dangerously quiet voice and, hangover aside, I think I prefer the burst eardrum version. "Even if I wanted to take you with me, which I can assure you I don't, how on earth do you think I'm going to get you there with a bottle on your toe?"

"But James! I've got to come with you!"

"I'm not taking you anywhere with that on your toe."

"Joe will fire me if I don't go!"

"Then let him fire you. Since you got given this assignment four weeks ago, trouble has followed me wherever I have gone. You are famine, pestilence and plague all rolled into one."

"Hasn't it been a bit more fun than usual though?" I ask in a very small voice.

"Fun? FUN? If you think fun is . . ."

My bottom lip starts to wobble precariously and it seems the more I try to concentrate on not letting it wobble, the more it wants to do so. Tears fill my eyes—I am not normally given to emotional outbursts and I think this lapse may have something to do with the gallon of booze I have poured down my throat this evening. Whatever biting comment is on the tip of his tongue stays there. I don't think he can cope with the screaming heebie-jeebies from me at three in the morning. He looks down at his feet for a minute and then says in a softer voice, "I'm going to take Fleur home. If they have got the bottle off by the time I get back then you can come with me."

"Thank you," I whisper, bottom lip still a-wobbling.

He turns away and gently wakes up a sleepy Fleur. He leads her by the hand out of the room, but turns back suddenly at the door.

"Holly?"

I turn my face toward him. "Yeah?"

"You're right. It has been more fun than usual."

I smile at him, but he has already gone, taking his future wife with him.

twenty-one

I sit in the car, trying to forget that my head thumps, my stomach would really like to be somewhere else and my mouth feels like the bottom of a budgie's cage. Oh, and my swollen toe throbs too. All my own doing, of course, but I am not remorseful enough to feel anything but heartily sorry for myself. Thirty minutes ago, six burly officers surrounded sixteen Maple Tree Drive and James and Callum knocked politely at the door before uttering the chilling phrase, "OPEN UP, POLICE." They were duly let in by a sleepy woman, whom James dashed straight past, while Callum shut the door, and that's the last I've seen of them. After some hasty radio communication, the other four officers who were positioned around the house went in through the front door. What on earth are they all doing in there? Making paper dollies?

The valiant hospital staff eventually managed to prize the bottle off my toe by applying cold compresses to my foot for over an hour to bring the swelling down. I was then carted off for an X-ray, but luckily nothing was broken. A singularly unamused James Sabine returned from dropping Fleur home and took me to an all-night café where he bullied me into eating toast and drinking coffee. All of which I was convinced would reappear within a few minutes. Thankfully, for my sake, none of it did. We then drove through the beautiful breaking dawn to meet up with the other officers, one of whom was Callum, who looked at my green face, then at James' expression, and very wisely kept his mouth shut.

* * *

Finally James appears in the doorway of the house. He looks forlorn and my heart sinks. I watch as he walks slowly down the pathway and then wordlessly gets into the car beside me.

"What happened?" I ask anxiously. "Did you find any of the stolen antiques?"

He shakes his head. I instinctively put out a hand to touch his knee. "Oh James, I am so sorry."

He shrugs a little and then says, "Don't be, because we did find a computer database with the details of all three houses on it and an invoice for a rented garage on the other side of town." He looks at me sideways and relaxes his face into a smile.

I let out a squeal of joy and then heartily wish I hadn't as the adrenaline whooshes about my already highly stressed nervous system.

"So we've caught The Fox? We've finally caught him?"

"It's not a him. It's a her."

"It's a woman?" I say incredulously, my mouth hanging open.

"I think our Mr. Makin has been feeding the information to her and she has been performing the burglaries."

"But I thought it was a man."

"No, we presumed it was a man."

"All by herself, no one else?"

He nods. "I think so; we'll have to wait to interview her. Her uncle lives with her too and you'll never guess what . . ."

"What?"

"He repairs clocks in his spare time. There's a whole room in the house dedicated to it. From the look on his face I don't think he knew anything about the burglaries, but we have to bring him in for questioning."

"What about Mr. Makin?"

"I've dispatched uniform to pick him up."

I smile excitedly at him, but as we gaze at each other the smile slowly fades from my face. I shift awkwardly in my seat. Is this a romantic moment or is my overburdened and very confused body chemistry playing tricks on me? We stare intensely at each other for what seems a very long time. The tension of the situation seems to have gripped us. My breath feels as though it's coming out in gasps now, and in fact I fear I am panting rather unattractively. James keeps those beautiful green eyes fixed on me.

"Holly," he says quietly, without moving his eyes from my face, "do you . . ." A knock on the driver's side window makes us both jump. Callum gestures to James and, without another word, James gets out and together they make their way back into the house. What was he about to say? Do I what? Tango? Wear an anorak? Eat peanut butter? (No, no, yes.)

While I wait, I try not to think about what might or might not just have happened between the two of us. You're tired, I tell myself, tired and probably still a little drunk. You're imagining stuff that just isn't there. I think about the woman they're about to take in for questioning and I have to say I feel a grudging respect for her. She nearly got away with hundreds of thousands of pounds' worth of goods. I wonder about the uncle and hope he is going to be OK. Too soft, that's my problem. There is no way I could be a police officer. I would worry too much about people. I have to sternly remind myself of Mrs. Stephens' sad face when all her memories had been stolen and Mr. Williams' bandaged head when we visited him in the hospital. People can't go around doing that. I get out my notebook and frantically scribble an account of the last few hours for the diary.

When all the officers finally troop out of the house, they are holding a woman by her arms, the same woman who answered the front door. She is wearing an old pair of jeans and a jumper. They are also more gently escorting an older man. Only the woman is wearing handcuffs. I watch as one of the officers guides them into an unmarked police car and then slams the doors shut. The remainder of the men are all holding things in big plastic bags and, after depositing them in the boot of our car, they all disperse.

James chats to a couple of the other officers and then walks toward our car. I hastily look down and continue to write in my notebook. He gets in, clicks on his seat belt and we follow the other cars down the road. He asks, "Are you coming down to the station? Or do you want me to drop you home?"

"Are you doing the interviews?"

"Yeah, we can only hold them a short while before we have to charge them, so we need to do all the interviews today. You won't be able to sit in on them though."

"That's OK. I'll come to the station if that's all right and write up the diary."

"Sure."

The woman's name is Christine Stedman. James interviews her and her uncle for hours. Now and again they have a break to discuss the situation with their solicitor, who was dragged from his bed in the early hours of this morning. On one such break, James wanders back into the office to get a coffee from the vending machine. I'm tapping away on my laptop, getting today's story written up. I look up as he comes over and flops down in the chair opposite.

"How are you feeling?" he asks.

"Fine!"

He eyes me suspiciously. "You don't, do you?"

"No, I feel terrible."

"How's the foot?"

I glance at the makeshift sandal the hospital made me out of an old flip-flop. "A bit sore. How are you feeling?"

"Tired."

"Ah," I say, looking down at my laptop. I would have nothing to do with that, of course. "Charged them with anything yet?"

"Nope."

I wait impatiently for further developments in the case. My deadline for the next edition of the paper is looming and although I can't publish specific details of the case if they are charged, I would like to tell my readers that an arrest has been made.

Finally James comes back into the office.

"What's happened?" I ask anxiously.

"She confessed—going for full cooperation with a view to a reduced sentence. So she has been charged but we've released the uncle."

I hastily attach the now completed version of the diary to an e-mail and send it over to the paper. I've managed to hit the deadline. I lean back in my chair. "Well done! Are you pleased?"

"Relieved, more like. At least the Chief will be happy."

"So what happens now?"

"She's taking us down to the lock-up tomorrow. Apparently most of the stuff is there."

"So Mrs. Stephens will get her things back?"

"I hope so."

"Did she do all the jobs herself? No accomplices?"

"Nope, she did them all on her own. Mr. Makin delivered his records of insurance to her for a fee, including details on those houses he had quoted for but didn't get the contract. We also interviewed Mr. Makin and it seems he is retiring next month and wanted a little money to retire on. The business hasn't been doing too well recently so he thought he would sell his database. He may get off though as according to his solicitor he had no idea what the records were being used for."

"What do you think?"

"I think he knew but he didn't want to know, if you see what I mean." I nod. "Apparently the shop was the last burglary she'd planned to do. They were just going to load up a van and move out of the area. She'd told her uncle she wanted to move to Lincolnshire to be near her brother."

"So the database told her how to get into the houses and exactly what to take?"

"The database contained details of the type of alarm each house used and any weaknesses the house had. For instance, when Mr. Makin told Mr. Forquar-White to get a lock on that small window at the back of the house, he recorded the fact on the database. So she used that information when she broke into the house."

"I remember thinking the window was a bit small for a man to fit through."

"The database also had a complete list plus description of all items worth more than three thousand pounds and specified in which room the item was kept."

"How did she recognize them though? I wouldn't recognize an antique if it smacked me in the face."

"And it probably would, knowing your difficulties in staying upright. She was brought up in the business. Her uncle owned an antiques business before he retired. An interest he and our Mr. Makin share. In fact, ironically enough, Mr. Makin used to insure the uncle's shop. That's how they knew each other."

"Gosh, she must have bashed poor old Mr. Williams over the head too."

"Yep. That will increase her sentence considerably."

"Did she just case Mr. Rolfe's shop by going into it and looking around?"

"That's right. We're bringing Mr. Rolfe down to see if he can identify her."

I sit back in my chair, digesting all this information. A thought suddenly occurs to me.

"What about that substance Roger kept finding at the scene of the crime? What was that?"

"I'm not sure, but I think it might be some sort of specialist cleaning agent the uncle uses to clean his clocks. She was wearing a pair of his old gloves. Roger will confirm that tomorrow."

"The cat hair Roger found must have got on to her clothing. So she always took a clock for her uncle, did she?" James nods. "Did he know what she was doing?"

"I don't think so. He thought she worked nights."

We partake in minor celebrations with Callum, who insists we all go out for a drink around the corner at the Rod and Duck. Once there, James tells him all about my eventful night in the hospital while I cringe in the corner with embarrassment. I'm sure James is madly exaggerating and it wasn't as bad as he is making out. Callum roars with laughter. Pleading tiredness (I am absolutely exhausted), I pop back to the station to collect my stuff and to see how Robin is. She is looking very low at the moment but seems pleased for James and the rest of the team at today's arrest.

After an ecstatic reception from Joe down at the paper, who is absolutely elated we have such a thrilling finale to the last couple of weeks of the diary, I make my weary way home and, once there, flop straight down on the sofa. Lizzie comes out from the kitchen.

"Well? What happened? Did you catch him?"

"Her."

"What?"

"Her. We caught her. The Fox is a woman."

"Really? Blimey. Aren't you happy? I mean, surely this will guarantee the diary's success! You should be delirious!"

"Yeah," I mutter. What the hell is wrong with me? Lizzie's right—I should be punching the air with victory salutes by now but instead I feel strangely empty. I go through to my bedroom, where I drop on my bed and, instead of lying awake pondering today's events, fall immediately asleep and stay like that all the way through to morning.

I awake with a start and stare panic-stricken around me. My racing heart gradually slows as I recognize my surroundings. Let's face it, my scene changes are so quick nowadays that my poor body doesn't know where it will be waking up next. I slowly sit up and glance at the clock—it's still early. Someone has kindly undressed me. I am lying underneath the duvet in my bra and knickers. I clutch my aching head and wander through to the kitchen to make some tea. Grasping a very welcome cup of Tetley's finest (the tea bags, not the ale), I go back to my bedroom and sit down at the dressing table to survey the damage. I peer at the stranger in the mirror. Do you think it would be too rude for me to suggest to her that she should get every pot of moisturizer she owns and slap it on? As I reach across to pick a pot, I notice a note. I smile. It's from Ben.

> Came round as promised to find you out for the count. Don't worry, understand from Lizzie you had eventful night. Will hold you to the back-scrubbing though.
>   Love, B.
>   PS Nice knickers

I promise myself I will make it up to him and slap some moisturizer on my poor, ill-treated skin. It acts as though it has been living in the Gobi desert and sucks up the moisture. After a shower, I shrug myself into a pair of hipster trousers and locate the flip-flop for my injured foot under the bed. I shudder to myself; I have no wish to know where the desperate hospital staff found that and wonder fleetingly whether I should be disinfecting it. Oh well, it's a little late now. I pull on a red polo neck and tie my hair back. Feeling marginally fresher, I gather my things, leave a note for Lizzie and clamber into Tristan. We initially perform a series of bunny hops down the road as I struggle to dislodge my flip-flop which has got stuck underneath one of the pedals.

I find Dave-the-not-quite-so-grumpy-desk-sergeant at his usual post. He looks up as I flash my ID at him and smiles. "Congratulations! I hear you and your detective made an arrest yesterday."

"Gosh, thanks!" I say in surprise, and he buzzes me through the security door.

I find I can walk surprisingly well on my injured foot. All the swelling seems to have gone down now, but it's still pretty bruised. I walk fairly normally up to the second floor and just as I am plugging in my laptop, James strides in to clapping and congratulations from the rest of the department, an honor always displayed to an arresting officer. He looks better than yesterday.

"Morning!" he says. "How are you feeling?"

"Better; did you get some sleep?"

"Yeah, I went straight to bed when I got in."

"When are we visiting the lock-up?"

"Christine's solicitor said he would arrive at nine. We'll wait for him and then all go down together."

We have a cup of coffee while we wait and talk about the events of the last couple of days. A phone call alerts us to the fact that Christine's solicitor has arrived and together we make our way down to the car pool. James pulls our Vauxhall around to the front of the building and I call Vince and tell him to meet us at the lock-up and give him the address. We watch as Matt, our usual uniformed officer, brings out the handcuffed Christine and guides her inside a patrol car. Another uniformed officer and a gentleman who I presume is her solicitor get into the car also.

Our little convoy sets off across town. As James and I chat idly about nothing in particular and laugh about silly things, I can feel the tension of the last few days melting away from him. I realize he must have been under a huge amount of pressure from the Chief to solve this case and I'm really happy, not just for him but in a selfish way for the diary as well.

After about twenty minutes of traveling out toward the Avon-mouth side of Bristol, which is toward the Bristol Channel, we pull into a narrow alleyway which is lined on either side with garages. Never having had any particular need to be out this way before, I am surprised at how rural our position is. Lush green pastures, dotted with hamlets and speckled with lonely houses, lie before us at the other end of the alleyway. We sluggishly bump our way along until, about halfway down, we grind to a halt in front of one particular garage.

We all get out and slowly assemble in front of it.

"This it?" James asks Christine. She nods sullenly. He takes out a huge bunch of keys from his pocket.

"This is a set of keys we found at your house; do you recognize them?" She nods again.

"Do you want to tell me which one fits the garage?" She shrugs, so James steps forward and starts trying them one by one in the huge padlock on the door. We all fidget restlessly. A chill wind whistles down this alleyway, probably straight off the Bristol Channel by the feel of it, and I nestle my neck down into my polo neck and shiver.

"Why can't we just break in?" I whisper to Matt who is standing next to me.

"If it's not the property of the person who has been charged with the crime then the police department has to pay for it. She hired it and we're short on funds," he whispers back. The solicitor glares at us. After about ten minutes of trying all the keys, of which there must be about fifty, James turns back to Christine. He has a very familiar, impatient look on his face. I try to transfer the thought "Tell him. Tell him now, before he loses his temper" to Christine.

"Christine, you are supposed to be cooperating with us. Please could you tell me which is the correct key?" She glances over to her solicitor who nods slightly at her. She turns back to James. "It's that one," she says, helpfully nodding toward the entire key ring.

"Which one? This one?"

"No. *That* one." She gesticulates with her head.

"Which one?" His voice is sharp. I have pushed past James Sabine's temper threshold enough times to know exactly where it is. We've just reached it. "Matt, uncuff her," he snaps. Matt hesitates for a millisecond and then steps forward and swiftly undoes her cuffs. Christine moves as if to look at the keys but then, with one seamless action, barges through the gap between her hapless solicitor (who is going to have trouble explaining this in court) and Matt. She belts down the alleyway, the opposite way to which we came in, toward the fields and pastures. James has the quickest reaction. "Oh shit," he says and hares after her. Matt and the other officer follow, leaving me and the extremely unfit solicitor to bring up the rear.

I ignore the pain in my foot as I run along the alleyway, for once not hampered by tight skirts or high heels. As I reach the end of it, I realize the chill breeze must indeed be coming directly off the Bristol Channel as the lush pastures before us run down to the unmistakable glint of silver water. I spot Vince's souped-up lilac Beetle bumping toward us from the right. In fact, Christine must have nearly passed him before she veered off to her left and into the fields.

"Come on!" I yell at Vince. All credit to him, he leaps out and, after having secured a small camera which must have been sitting on the passenger seat ready for an emergency such as this, pelts after the figures. We all reach the second fence at about the same time; Vince and I, benefiting from everyone's experiences at the first one, manage to gain some valuable seconds. As I run up, I notice the second fence is much higher than the first. It's too high to jump over. James must have had exactly the same thought as me because, while still running hard, he makes a powerful leap directly on top of the barbed wire fence in order to bring it down.

It's my last memory of that day. A loud crack rips through the air. Alien sounds and sensations assault my mind and body. A sharp pain expands in my head and after that there is only darkness.

twenty-two

Voices drift in and out of my consciousness. I hazily open my eyes to find several other pairs staring straight back at me. I hastily close mine again and hope the other eyes will go away. I wait a few seconds and slightly open my left one to check the situation. Nope, they're all still there. I don't really want to rouse myself yet, everything feels like such an effort, but the thought of all those people scrutinizing me is too much. I look slowly from face to face. Mother, Dad and James. James? JAMES? What the hell is he doing in my bedroom? I sit bolt upright and gather the covers to my chin, my heart racing in my ears.

"Holly, it's all right. It's OK," says my mother as though she is trying to soothe a frightened horse. She's going to start stroking my nose any minute.

I look frantically around and realize that I'm not in my bedroom at all. "Where am I?"

"In the hospital, darling. You've had a bit of a knock on the head."

"What time is it? How long have I been asleep?"

My father looks at his watch. "It's about nine in the morning. You've been out for about twenty-three hours."

Upon being told that I've been asleep for twenty-three hours, I frown and surreptitiously sneak a hand to the top of my head to smooth down my hair. I always look my absolute worst on waking. No one, *no one* looks more horrendous than I. I rub my eyes and then run a finger underneath them in a bid to remove the mascara that I know will be lodged there. While I subconsciously run through my beauty routine, or rather my not-feeling-quite-so-ugly routine on one hand, my other hand has a quick float about underneath the covers and confirms my worst suspicions. I am absolutely stark naked apart from one of those very flimsy hospital paper gowns which I am fairly sure doesn't meet around the back. Hang on, what am I doing? WHAT DO I THINK I AM DOING? I have just had a brush with death and I am fussing about what I look like. I am absolutely sure the appearance police will let you off this once, Holly. Absolutely sure. I cast an apprehensive, frowning look at James. He smiles at me. Just how much has he seen?

"How are you feeling?" he asks.

"OK," I say doubtfully, because to be honest I am a little doubtful about that. I try to cast my memory back and hazy images start to come through. We were chasing someone. I was keeping a very safe distance from James, not wanting a repeat performance of my black eye. Then we came to a fence. James went up and over it, and as he did so I remember a loud crack and then darkness. Complete blackness.

"What happened?" I say. James looks a little sheepish.

"It was an accident."

"What was?"

"Do you remember chasing Christine?" I nod. "Well, we had to get over a barbed wire fence, so I jumped on top of it, thinking my weight would push it down. Unfortunately, the farmer must have nailed it to a dead tree nearby, and as my weight pulled down the fence, the tree just snapped. And, er, landed on your head . . . It was quite a large tree, but luckily relatively light . . . On account of it being dead . . ." he trails off.

There is a long pause as I absorb this information.

"Did you catch her? Christine?"

"Er, yeah. Matt caught up with her. I stayed with you. I thought I'd killed you."

"I was trying to keep at least three meters between us because of the black eye scenario. And you said *I* was the apocalypse. That's twice that you've injured me now," I say lightly. He grins and I catch myself thinking that that must be what Fleur fell for. His smile. That grin must be fatal when deployed properly.

"Oh well, better luck next time, eh?"

James casts a hesitant glance over at my parents. I had forgotten they were there and they are looking fairly concerned. They must think he's some sort of maniac.

"We're just kidding; when did you get here?" I say to them.

"Last night. When James called us, we came as quickly as we could," my father says.

My mother interrupts. "We came quicker than that. I ran around the house throwing anything I could get my hands on into a suitcase, despite which your father has a complete lack of underwear and Morgan has no dog biscuits." I look over at my father, alarmed by his underwear situation.

"I've had to go commando, darling." James smothers a smile. My father picks up some ridiculous phrases from my brothers and I simply do not wish to know how that one came up in conversation. "We were all here last night but they wouldn't let us see you. We waited for ages until they told us you were fine and that there was no point in staying."

"Where is Morgan?" I ask.

"Sitting in the car, probably chewing the gear stick as we speak. He's hungry."

James says, "I think I'll just get one of the nurses and tell them you're awake."

My mother watches him walk out.

"THAT is your detective?" she whispers theatrically, her eyebrows racing up and down like demented caterpillars. Her nostrils flare slightly. She can smell drama at fifty paces. Twenty, if she's standing downwind.

"He's not *my* detective."

"I thought he didn't like you?"

"Well, we're getting on a bit better than we used to."

"You certainly are. He telephoned us last night in a terrible state. Poor love, he's been really worried, beetling all over the place for you." OK, hang on. How come I'm the one in the gown and the bed and we're talking about poor old James? Poor old James, the assaulter of innocent reporters.

"Well, he was probably *worried* he'd killed or at least maimed me," I hiss vehemently. "Didn't want a lawsuit hanging over him on his honeymoon. He's getting married in a week's time."

"I *know*," she says in a gossipy voice, oblivious of my tone. "Imagine Miles' little girl getting someone like that. Well, well. A small world, isn't it?"

I frown. "What do you mean? Someone like that?"

"Well, it's just that they are so different, darling. But they say opposites attract, don't they? He's been charming; quite, quite charming. Took us to our hotel last night and then brought us down here to the hospital and still receiving police calls on his mobile all the while. How he has found the time to worry about us I just do not know."

"Probably trying to stop you suing him," I say in my Eeyore voice, crossing my arms and huffing down into my pillows.

"The way you described him I thought he was going to be a monster. Mind you, what you've written about him this last week or so, the whole village has been . . ."

I interrupt hastily. "So, have you told anyone else I'm here? Lizzie? Ben?" Not that I want people to worry, you understand, but a potentially dramatic situation such as this shouldn't be wasted.

"Well, I called Lizzie last night, but I'm afraid I didn't know how to get hold of Ben so I asked Lizzie to contact him. I'll call her in a sec and tell her you're awake."

James walks back in carrying three cups on a tray.

"The nurse is sending the doctor down to have a look at you. A cup of coffee, Sorrel? Patrick?"

Sorrel and Patrick? SORREL AND PATRICK? My word, someone has got his feet firmly under the table. I haven't heard them called that for absolutely years. In my small circle of friends they're known as Mr. and Mrs. C, and their friends all "darling" each other to death. I had almost forgotten those were their names.

"Thank you, James. How sweet of you."

My mother sits herself down in one of the chairs and gets out a packet of cigarettes.

"Did you get me a coffee?" I ask James a little pathetically.

James frowns. "No. The doctor's coming to see you in a minute. I don't think you should be drinking coffee." Oh no, silly old moi. I eye my mother's cigarette packet. No coffee, because the caffeine would be bad for you, as opposed to being suffocated by someone else's smoke fumes.

"Do you think I can smoke in here, darlings?" asks my mother to the general ensemble. James shrugs and looks up. "Can't see any detectors." What has happened to the pedantic, sarcastic detective? Not to mention law-abiding?

"No, I don't bloody think you can smoke in here," I bluster.

"Oh, don't be so stuffy, darling. Honestly, we poor smokers are in the minority now. We're pushed out to the very fringes of society. Not welcome anywhere." She lights up and pats the chair next to her. "So, James, come and tell me all about how you managed to meet Miles' little girl. I was absolutely amazed when Holly told me that you were the groom. Have you met Miles? A frightful old fart, isn't he?"

Oh fine. That's just fine. Don't mind me. I've just regained consciousness, that's all. Nothing at all to concern yourselves with. I'll just lie here and wait until you finish your little chat.

And so it is in this convivial ambience that Dr. Kirkpatrick finds us a quarter of an hour later. One slightly smoky room, one sulky patient, one charming police officer (who, I might add, is being so bloody charming my mother will probably think I've been making the stories up about him) and two laughing parents. I perk up a little when he enters the room because (a) it is Dr. Kirkpatrick and he's gorgeous and (b) the attention is back on me, albeit for a brief and probably short-lived while. That is, of course, if the three musketeers over there can break off from their fascinating conversation. Hats off to James Sabine, as my family's ability to talk about nothing for hours on end is legendary. And it takes someone of a fairly deep character to understand and keep up with the superficiality. My mother starts to frantically spray perfume lest her smoking is detected.

He is gorgeous. Dr. Kirkpatrick, that is. His dark hair, freshly washed, flops suggestively down over his face.

He grins at me. "Back again, Holly?"

"I can't keep away," I murmur. He takes my wrist and concentrates intently. He "hmm's" a bit to himself and then walks around to the front of the bed and picks up my chart. He scribbles a few notes.

"Well, can't see any long-term damage. But I would like to keep you in until about teatime for observation. Can't be too careful with concussion cases." I look over to the three of them to ensure that they are carefully heeding his words.

He also turns to the corner group. "Can one of . . . oh, hello Detective! How are you?" He shakes hands with James. "Keeping well?" He's bloody buggery fine, I feel like shouting. I'm the wounded one, over here in the bed. The one he almost clubbed to death.

Dr. Kirkpatrick continues: "Can one of you take Holly home? Around about teatime?" They all nod their agreement and the doctor turns back to me.

"I'll be back on my rounds after lunch, Holly, to check on you." A brief smile and he's gone. James gets up.

"I'm going to go and get some work done," he says.

A thought occurs to me. Butterflies of panic suddenly start up in my stomach.

"What happened with the diary? Did Vince let the paper know?"

"Of course. In fact, I helped Joe write it last night. Well, supplied the information anyway. And don't worry; I'll do the same at the end of today. To be honest though, there won't be much to report. I'll be interviewing Christine and then I'll have to start preparing the case against her. So it's paperwork for the most part."

"James, dear," says my mother, "would you mind calling Lizzie on the way out? Here's the number. Only mobile phones aren't allowed in here." Oh right. As opposed to smoking, which is of course perfectly legit. My mother's interpretation of the rules never ceases to amaze me.

He takes the number from her. "I'll come back at lunchtime."

"Call Joe too!" I shout after his disappearing back. He raises his hand in acknowledgment.

We all sit in companionable silence for a few minutes.

"Dad? Could you do me a favor? Could you see if you could get a copy of the paper? I'd like to read the diary." My father duly disappears on his errand and I take the opportunity of a room relatively empty of people to make a run for the loo. I wrap the flimsy gown around my backside, scurry into the bathroom and then return to settle again on my pillows.

"Well," says my mother, "what a nice bloke that James is. I have to say I like him excessively."

There is another few minutes' pause. I am starting to feel distinctly uncomfortable as I can see the way my mother's mind is working. The cogs are turning and she's thinking "What on earth is this very attractive young man doing racing around most of Bristol all in aid of my daughter? And shouldn't I, as the mother of the aforementioned daughter, and indeed a wedding guest at his impending nuptials, be inquiring a little deeper into this?"

"So, do you like him, darling?"

I stare intently down at the sheets and wonder whether the hospital has its own laundry.

"He's OK," I say noncommittally.

Pause.

"The whole village is reading the diary, darling. We've taken to photocopying it and putting it up on the notice board! They're all huge fans! You'll be opening the church fête soon! Mrs. Murdoch thinks you must like him a lot." She tacks this neatly on to the end.

"For goodness sake! He's getting married in a week's time!" I explode. "You are invited to his wedding; for that matter, so am I! His fiancée, Fleur, the daughter of your friend Miles, is a really nice girl. And what about Ben? Do you like Ben?"

"Of course we do, darling. Of course we do." She pauses. "Although . . ."

"Although what?" I snap, starting to get well and truly rattled now. My God! I've just been bonked on the head, out cold for practically days on end and she breezes in here with a quick "Feeling better now, darling?" and then it's gloves on. Never mind my blood pressure. Never mind the doctor's "Can't be too careful with concussion cases."

"He went to public school, didn't he?" she murmurs.

"So? SO?"

"Well, it's just that I find public school boys, generally speaking, to be a little . . . There is the odd exception, of course . . ."

"A. Little. What?"

She looks me straight in the eye. "Emotionally retarded."

I gulp. "Emotionally retarded?" I can't believe the front of the woman. This is the lady who regularly tries to change TV channels with a calculator and hides Christmas presents in the freezer.

"Yes, emotionally retarded. Their parents chuck them off to boarding school when they're about five and it's all 'No tears, stiff upper lip, little man, your grandfather shot tigers in India.' Then they all have fags; God knows what that means but let's face it, darling, the word has highly dubious connotations. And before you know it they're all grown up, know the school song by heart, have their old school ties but are unable to form a proper emotional relationship with anyone."

She has obviously been reading *Tom Brown's Schooldays*.

"Well, that's not Ben," I say staunchly, but a slight seed of doubt sows itself in my mind, which I daresay is her intention.

"That's OK then," she says swiftly. She lights up another cigarette and lies back in the chair puffing smoke rings into the air and watching them float away. Now I'm feeling cross.

"So, do you like him? Ben?" I persist.

"Hmm?" she says, as though we finished discussing the subject ages ago. "Of course we do, darling. Just as long as you know he'll make the commitment. Just as long as you're happy."

She's very smart, my mother. Many just dismiss her as an empty-headed actress. It's all a carefully constructed front. She says those words with just the right degree of indifference. Of nonchalance. And even despite knowing it's all an act, it still has the desired effect on me. I start to doubt. Bravo, Sorrel Colshannon. A fine performance.

But you know what? I really don't want to think about this. I really, really don't. For some reason I'm feeling a little emotional and I'm having a hard time holding back the tears. It must be the shock setting in. And my life is complicated enough right now. I don't want to think about love because, frankly, there are more important things. I'm sitting in a hospital with concussion, my career has taken a big upturn with the diary, my best friend has just finished with her boyfriend and I also have . . .

"TV interview. Tomorrow at seven. Your detective called; I came straight down." Joe waltzes into the room.

"I'm feeling better, Joe, thanks for asking. How are you?" I say crossly.

"Fine thanks." He turns to my mother and proffers a hand. "Joseph Heesman. Nice to meet you. You must be Holly's famous mother."

"And you must be her notorious editor. Your reputation precedes you."

"All bad, I hope?"

"Appalling."

"What's up with her?" He gestures his head in my general direction.

"Cranky. Knock on the head."

He addresses himself to me. "You'll be all right for tomorrow, won't you? Right as a shower?"

"I don't know . . . one always has to be careful with concussion."

"Come on, Holly! They've been on the phone all morning after the latest installment." He winks at my mother.

"Why 'after the latest installment'? What did you write?"

"Had all the makings of a high-class thriller. A criminal on the run. The good guys chase the bad one. Boy knocks girl out. For the second time as well! Not a traditional ending, admittedly. And the photos are knockout! Sorry, no pun intended. I've saved some of them for the interview."

"Who's the TV interview with?"

"The same guy as before, just at the local station. But don't look at a Trojan horse's mouth. I have to say, the whole thing has generated a lot of interest. We've had people calling all morning to see how you are. Quite a little cult following you've got going."

This, as blatant flattery always does, cheers me up.

"Really?"

"Yep, really."

At this point my father comes back in and hands the newspaper over.

"Sorry it took so long. It's a bloody warren in here."

I turn to my page quickly while my father and Joe make their introductions with lots of manful handshaking.

"Blimey Joe!" I say. "No wonder it's caused some fuss!" He's looking very pleased with himself and so he might. It starts:

I am writing this in lieu of our normal correspondent, Holly Colshannon, as she lies unconscious in a hospital bed as a result of today's dramatic developments . . .

"Photos are good too, aren't they? Vince is chuffed to bits with them. But he only had time to develop the first half of the film so we thought we would save the other half for the TV interview. He'll be coming down later, if that's OK? Take a few of you for tonight's edition."

"Fine," I say, grinning stupidly, still looking down at the article. The photos are excellent. There are a few of all of us (except Christine) running in a straggly group, looking like rejects from the *Keystone Cops*, and then a couple of the back of Christine haring off into the distance with us running after her. I finish reading the article and hand the paper over to my parents for them to see.

Joe stands up. "Well, I'll be off. As long as you'll be all right for tomorrow. Everyone sends their best wishes from the paper, by the way. Should have brought you some flowers, shouldn't I?"

"Yes. You should have."

"I'll write tonight's edition again, so don't worry about that. Well done, Holly. Great stuff," he says, as though I am not only personally responsible for being knocked out but also for engineering the whole thing as well. "Are you being let out today?"

"Yeah, teatime."

"Good, good. Every cloud has a bit of a coat, hasn't it? See you tomorrow, look after yourself tonight." And with this he says goodbye to my parents and makes his exit.

I'm starting to feel tired. My mother, noticing my droopy eyes, says, "Why don't you have a nap, darling? We'll go and get some tea in the canteen."

I really am feeling sleepy now. A little nap. Maybe just for a minute.

I wake up with a start. My heart is racing. I was being chased . . .

"Holly? It's OK. You're all right." People leaning over me come into focus. I gulp mouthfuls of air and gradually my heartbeat subsides. Lizzie is here, I notice, and my parents have returned.

"How long was I asleep?"

"About an hour. Lizzie arrived just after you nodded off," says my mother.

"Hello! How are you feeling?" Lizzie's sympathetic face hovers over me.

"Oh, fine. Why aren't you at work?"

"Your detective called me and said you were awake. My whole office has been talking about nothing else since the paper this morning. Talk about drama! So I went through to Alastair and told him what had happened and he let me come immediately. You should do this more often, Hol!"

"So people keep telling me," I say grimly. I lie back on my beloved pillows for a while.

Lizzie natters inanely about this and that and I let her mindless chatter wash over me while I slowly wake up.

"Have you called Ben?"

"I spoke to him last night and this morning. He's coming over in his lunch break."

"Good!" I exclaim enthusiastically, looking at my mother out of the corner of my eye. See? He does care. "Have things improved at all with Alastair?"

Lizzie shakes her head slightly. "No," she says shortly.

We sit in silence for a second. Lizzie obviously isn't up to going into the whole Alastair debacle with my parents present.

"Have you seen the paper? I brought it down with me," she says.

"Yeah, I've seen it, thanks."

"So, IS there anything going on, Hol?"

"What do you mean?"

"Well, you know. Between you and the detective. There is no other topic of conversation in the office!"

"There. Is. Nothing. Going. On. Between. Us," I say angrily. "You out of everybody must know that, Lizzie. Did you put her up to this?" I direct my last comment at my mother who is idly looking at her nails. My father has bought the *Guardian* and is rather sensibly hiding behind it.

My mother looks offended. "Of course I didn't, darling. It's not just me who thinks it. I was talking to the lady in the canteen and she said . . ."

I gape at her while she is saying all this, speechless for a second.

"You talked to the lady in the canteen?"

"Well, not exactly. We got chatting and I said I was visiting my daughter and that you were a reporter, and then she said were you *the* reporter, and I rather proudly said yes you were. And then she said that she and the rest of the staff read the diary every day, to which I said thank you very much, although I'm not quite sure why I was thanking her. By the way, she said she wasn't quite sure about one of the skirts you were wearing the other day. The others thought . . ." My father lowers the newspaper, makes eye contact with me, sighs theatrically and then re-erects the paper.

"Get to the point," I say, sensing one of my mother's diversionary tangents.

"All right, darling, don't get your gown in a twist, I'm just relating what was said. I can't help it if . . ."

"GET TO THE SODDING POINT!"

"Well, then she asked if there was any chance you and the detective would get together."

Lizzie interjects. "I've got ten pounds on it in my office pool since this morning. But, Holly, I don't want that to influence you in any—"

"You have an office pool? On what?"

"On you and James, of course."

"HE. IS. GETTING. MARRIED. IN. A. WEEK'S. TIME."

"Who's getting married?" asks a voice from the doorway.

"You are," I say in a very weak voice, staring in horror at James. "Hooray! Lizzie was, er, just asking, er, when the wedding is," I add, carefully avoiding further eye contact with him while surreptitiously trying to glare at my mother and Lizzie. No mean feat, I can tell you. I'm practically cross-eyed with the effort. "How's work? Got Christine all tied up?" I continue quickly before he can cross-examine me. I wonder if it's at all possible that I could regain unconsciousness and start this day again.

"Yes, all done." He pauses. "The boys had a whip-round and got you these." From behind his back he brings out a huge bunch of lilies.

"Oh, how gorgeous!" I breathe joyously, smelling the powerful, heady scent of the flowers. I can almost feel the nudges passing between my mother and Lizzie. I pick out the card nestling between the stems. It reads: "SORRY DICK KEEPS GIVING

YOU BLACK EYES. LOOK FORWARD TO HAVING YOU
BACK SOON."

"How nice of them," I say pointedly. "Please say thanks to
them, won't you?"

"And I got you these." He pulls out his other arm and presents
me with a big bunch of freesias. I am so delighted that for a second I am caught off my guard.

"My favorites!"

"I know, I remember you mentioning them," he says quietly.
For a second I feel perilously close to tears. "Robin is with me!"
James says brightly. "She's parking the car." My grief is quickly
replaced by annoyance.

"Great!" I say, putting my hand to my forehead. I wonder if
I'm menopausal? A little premature perhaps but it would explain
the mood swings and the hot flushes.

Dr. Kirkpatrick comes in. He smiles generally around.

"Everyone still here?" Unfortunately. Yes.

"Is it lunchtime already?"

"It certainly is. So, how are you feeling, Holly? Any better?"
he asks, moving around the bed and doing the usual checks.

"I'm fine." He wraps a black swathe around my arm to check
my blood pressure and we wait while it electronically cali-
brates. Robin comes into the room and I wave from the solace of
my bed.

"How are you feeling?" she asks. I bob my head about in an
"OK" mode. She stares a little at the fair doctor, which doesn't
surprise me at all. He's very stare-able. Easy on the eye, as they
say. He smiles at her. She smiles back. He smiles some more. The
electronic monitor is beeping. Hello? Hello? Remember me? The
patient? I pointedly clear my throat.

"Hmmm? Oh yes, sorry, Holly." He turns his attention back to
my blood pressure. "You're fine. Give yourself a few hours before
you leave. Now, do you need any painkillers?"

I look darkly around the roomful of people. That depends on what context he means . . . "Not for my head," I murmur.

"If I don't see you before you go, try to take it easy over the next couple of days and I have no doubt that I'll see you soon."

He smiles at Robin. "Nice to meet you," he says to her, before turning on his heel and leaving.

Robin stares after him. "Blimey Holly! You get all the luck!" Yes. Don't I just? She looks back at me. "He's divine!"

I smile. "He is, isn't he? And you should see him when . . ."

"All right, all right, I don't think you and Robin need to drool quite so blatantly over the doctor. Besides, we can't stay long, we need to get back. Holly, your boyfriend is here," snaps James and gestures his head toward the door, obviously jealous that Robin likes the beautiful doctor. He does lead a complicated life. I look over to where Ben's handsome silhouette is framed in the doorway.

"Ben!" I exclaim as he comes in, covering the distance between the doorway and the bed in three easy strides.

"Lizzie called last night, I've been so worried! I didn't come down though as she said there was no point." He bends over and kisses me. "How are you feeling?"

"Fine. Absolutely fine." I make the appropriate introductions and Ben duly shakes everyone's hand. He then sits on the end of the bed.

"So how did it happen?"

I give lengthy explanations about the tree and now and again gesture to James, who is leaning against the far wall and still looking fairly bad-tempered. I am greatly relieved that Ben has put in an appearance. This may sway his critics a little.

"So how long are you in for?"

"They're letting me out today, thank God!"

He frowns. "I've got a training session later but your folks could bring you home, couldn't they?"

"Sure, no problem."

A nurse bustles in. She has a kindly, motherly face that is creased with life, and bright red hair peeps out from underneath her cap like flames framing her face. She gives a cheerful "All right?" to everyone as a greeting. "Bit crowded in here, isn't it? Why don't you all go off and get a cup of tea and let the patient have her lunch in peace? Come back in half an hour." Glory hallelujah! Hurray for the health service! James, Robin and Ben all make their goodbyes while my parents and Lizzie head off toward the canteen.

"Are you all right, love? All those people are likely to give you a headache!"

I smile and lie back on my pillows gratefully. The nurse bustles around, straightening my covers and picking up a stray pillow which has fallen on the floor.

"You're the reporter, aren't you? The Dick Tracy girl?"

"Yes. Yes, I am."

"I was on yesterday when they brought you in. That detective of yours was in a right state." I involuntarily stiffen under the covers. Here we go. This woman is obviously a mole planted by my mother. "He was barely registering anything at all. After we got you settled in, I said to him, I said, 'Jack! You look just like your photos!' and he stared at me as if I were mad!"

I relax a little. Of course James would look at her as though she were mad. He wasn't in a "right state"; he had just forgotten that his stage name was Jack.

"So which one is your boyfriend?" she continues chattily.

At last, someone who sees sense. Someone who understands that just because I write about a person doesn't mean we're engrossed in a passionate affair.

I grin at her, pleased at her question. "The really tall blond one. He's a rugby player for Bristol."

"Is he? He looks lovely."

"Yes, yes, he is," I say staunchly.

"You must love him an awful lot."

"Yes, I . . ." I stop suddenly and frown. "Why do you say that?"

She looks over at me. "Because you were calling out all night for him. Ooh yes, all through the night. Getting yourself in a right little state, you were. I sat with you for a while until you quietened down but an hour later you started up again."

"I'm sorry," I say contritely.

"No problem, love. It's what I'm here for; besides, it did my heart good to hear it."

I really wish Lizzie and my mother could be here to witness all this. It would prove there is nothing in that silly notion of theirs . . . A nasty little thought occurs to me. I firmly squash it but a second later it comes wriggling back. My palms become sweaty and I just don't know how to ask this lady what I need to know.

"Was I using his name or his nickname?" I say lightly. "Just so I can tease him later."

"His name, love. Definitely his name." There is a pause. "James doesn't sound like much of a nickname, now does it?"

twenty-three

I stare down at the lunch tray she has left me, trying to grab hold of one of the thoughts that are rushing through my mind. James. I was saying James' name. So what? He had just knocked me on the head; *obviously* I was thinking about him. Right. Yes, that must be it. I mean, he must have been one of the last people I saw before I was knocked out. It is only natural I was calling his name. It was probably in a "James, you complete git" sort of way.

I pick up my fork determinedly and look at the potato salad. It is on one of those little plastic trays that you have your meal out of on airplanes. I prod the ham. But what was it the nurse said? "It warmed my heart" or something. I gulp. She also mentioned how much I must love him. I drop my plastic fork, fall back on to my pillows and feel a slow blush coming right up from my toes. Oh turnips. What if he had been there, at my bedside, at that point? What if he had heard me?

And how *do* I feel about him? Really feel? I think intently for a second about the past few weeks together. Of his face, his eyes, his smile. And then I think about his wedding, and of Fleur. And I know. The force of it hits me squarely between the eyes. I can't bear to even *think* about his wedding. I know that I love him.

My bottom lip starts to tremble a little. How on earth could this have happened? Another awful thought occurs to me. My God, it must be *so* obvious. My bottom lip is starting a lively new dance step now. Everyone, EVERYONE has picked up on the fact that something might be going on between us. My mother, Lizzie, Mrs. Murdoch from the village—even the hospital canteen lady. And how? BECAUSE I WROTE ABOUT IT, THAT'S HOW. Not him, me. Not his testimony to how he feels about me but mine to him. And simply because my feelings were transparently there, down in black and white for all to see, people have naturally presumed he may be romantically inclined that way too. Because I have gleefully related over the last couple of weeks the instances when we have been able to have a conversation without snarling at each other, which let's face it has been quite a progression, people have presumed there is "something going on." How embarrassing.

How I wish there was.

I clamp my hand over my mouth. How could I think that? How could I? When Fleur has been so nice to me?

The blood is burning my face now and tears fill my eyes. I feel like disappearing under my bed covers and not coming out until, ooh, shall we say Christmas? Do you think the hospital would notice if they lost a patient? Surely it happens all the time? I look wildly round the room; where is the oxygen kept? Better still, where's that gas they give expectant mothers?

Seeing the room is sadly empty of mind-numbing drugs, I resort to chewing my fingernails instead, which is something I haven't done for a good ten years. I concentrate on not crying because I know that once I start I won't be able to stop. I try to think of non-passionate things. The Euro. The local by-elections. But my mind drags itself back to James Sabine.

My diaries must have practically been love letters for people to jump to these conclusions. Everyone is laughing at me. They must all be saying "There goes that reporter, the one with the thumping great crush on the detective who is getting married in a week's time." And although that alone is awful enough to contemplate, there is also James. James, who is getting married *in a week's time.* To Fleur. I repeat those words again, trying to get them firmly lodged into my consciousness. And it becomes obvious to me that I have been deliberately avoiding thinking about his wedding. In a slow, tortuous fashion I play a video to myself of their wedding day—of Fleur walking down the aisle, looking beautiful in cream lace, James waiting for her at the altar—and I force myself to look at it. I'm going to lose him. Lose him as soon as I have found him.

Now I really am going to cry. A lone tear rolls down my cheek. That's fine, I tell myself. Just limit it to that. No hysterical weeping.

Maybe this isn't love, I think hopefully. Maybe this is just some sort of crush, an infatuation. Let's face it, he's a good-looking bloke and I have been practically locked up with him for the last few weeks. Don't they say kidnapped girls sometimes fall in love with their kidnappers? Don't they? Well, maybe it's something like that. Absolutely, that must be it . . .

Whatever it is, there is one thing for sure. He doesn't feel the same way about me. Definitely not. He is marrying someone else. Next week. Someone who is beautiful and kind and altogether way out of my league. Not to mention the fact that he is possibly having an affair with someone equally beautiful and way out of my league. Outmaneuvered on two counts.

Everyone is going to be back in a minute. And it will be very obvious to my mother and my best friend that something is up. Quickly, think about something else. Ben. Complete mushy peas. Good choice, Holly, good choice. OK, let's think about Ben. Why not? An infinitely less painful subject than James. No tears needed there. I purse my lips together, intent on thinking. Come on, Holly. Think about Ben. Nothing. I frown and push my head down into my neck. Think. How hard can thinking be? A minute ago I couldn't breathe for all the thoughts rushing about, but now they seem to have staged a mutiny. I wait for a minute and then give up. There's nothing there for him. Oh, I can picture him all right, and I can even agree he is tremendously good-looking in a detached sort of way, but nothing else. I can't remember why I ever thought I might want to marry him. How could I have thought he was the real thing? I didn't love him, the real him. I loved his looks, his position on the rugby team, the hordes of girls running after him, but take all of that away and there isn't much left. And I thought he was the main event when he was clearly just the warm-up act. This new realization is another blow to my fast-disappearing morale. I sink further down into my bed and close my eyes, hoping the whole thing will just go away. I've been backing the wrong horse.

Well, Ben is obviously going to have to go. The lily-livered coward in me raises her weak little head. "But then you'll be left alone," she whispers. "James will be married in a week, will bugger off to the Maldives and you'll be left by yourself." I can see her point of view. I even prod it around for a bit. Rather to my surprise though, I can honestly say that I would rather be left alone than pretend with Ben. Besides, Lizzie will be around and I have a close, loving circle of family and friends. Speaking of which, where is my loving circle of family and friends? I frown and look at my watch. It's been a good hour since they departed for the canteen. Why aren't they, as I speak, huddled around my sick bed, mopping my fevered brow? Being loving and supportive?

A shriek echoes from the corridor. My frayed nerves are almost at the end of their tether. I sit bolt upright in bed. Probably some poor patient in the throes of kidney stones. It happens again. This time I recognize the voice.

My mother appears in the doorway, tears of laughter pouring down her face. My loving circle has returned. Lizzie follows her in, also in the throes of hysterics, with my father bringing up the rear and frantically rubbing his arm.

"Oh darling! It's been the funniest thing! Your father got stuck in the lift doors!" My mother sits down in the chair, weak with laughter. "The doors were closing on some hapless patient on one of those trolleys and your father, in what was a thoroughly over-dramatic fashion, threw himself in front of them. I was desperately trying to open them by pressing the 'open door' button but the damn things kept opening up and then slamming closed again on your father! It turns out that I was pressing the 'close door' symbol instead!"

My father glares at her. "It must have been so confusing."

"I wasn't wearing my glasses."

"That may just explain it."

"Anyway, how are you, Holly? How are you feeling?" says Lizzie.

"Oh, great. I'm absolutely fine now," say I, not feeling fine at all. How can so much change so quickly? Since they left this room an hour ago I feel as though I have been on some sort of emotional rollercoaster, and I have the nastiest suspicion the ride isn't over yet. I am prevented from any further contemplation by the arrival of Vince.

"Ooh, ducks, are you all right?" he says from the doorway. He minces in and my mother's eyes light up. She can recognize a fellow thespian from about one hundred paces.

"What a palaver! It's all been just too, too thrilling! And the pictures! Well, I tell you, love, it's the Pulitzer prize for me. Make no mistake about it." He turns to my parents. "You must be Holly's parents. You are the spitting image of each other," he says to my mother. Then he turns to my father, who extends a hearty hand. Vince sort of limply strokes it, saying "And you! Well, you . . ."

"Vince! This is my best friend Lizzie!" I exclaim, before he says anything too outrageous to my father. Not that my father is a homophobe, you understand, it's just that gay men make him nervous. Very nervous. I'm-just-going-to-stand-with-my-back-to-the-wall nervous.

"Nice to meet you, Lizzie." Vince turns back to me. "How are you feeling, love? It was a hell of a knock! THWACK! Straight on the head! Of course, as soon as it happened, James came haring back over the fence. I almost wished it was me." He gives an involuntary little shiver and stares off into the distance in his own private daydream. I really wouldn't like to venture what it involved. I am in my own little fantasy world as well and am quite enjoying hearing about how James came running over to me. "Go on," I urge, "what happened then?"

"Ooh, it was so manly! Very Rhett Butler. He just stopped chasing that woman and left the other officer to catch her. I, of course, started taking photos of you. Sorry about that. He pulled the tree off you and was shouting, 'Holly! Holly!' The photos are fantastic! And the light was just right! I didn't need a filter or anything; I managed—"

"Vince?"

"Sorry. Anyway, as I was saying, he was getting really panic-stricken and was trying to feel for a pulse. Then, when he found one, ooh! The relief on his face was obvious!" I know looks are passing between my mother and Lizzie but I simply do not care. I am leaning forward avidly, anxious for more. "He was kneeling next to you and then he sat back on his heels and just closed his eyes, murmuring to himself. It was wonderful! I nearly cried!"

"What was he murmuring?" I ask lightly and with an attempt at nonchalance.

"Hmm? Oh, I don't know. Couldn't hear." A little voice inside me says, "Maybe he does care about you." Maybe he does. Maybe . . . But then wouldn't I be quite relieved to learn I hadn't killed someone? Wouldn't I be quite reassured to find a pulse on the person I'd just brained with a dead tree? Wouldn't I be quite thankful to know I wouldn't be standing in the dock pleading "Not guilty"?

My thoughts continue to occupy me as Vince arranges me in various poses. Needless to say, he is quite happy with the moroseness of my expression. No acting called for there. He swiftly snaps a few shots and then, with a bright "Toodle-doo!," heads off back to the paper.

I pull myself together. "Well, I'd better get dressed, then we can be toodle-doo-ing off too!" I say brightly. I awkwardly gather my gown around me, anxious not to bare my essentials. My father takes to staring out of the window and my mother gathers my things and carries them for me into the bathroom. I quickly throw on yesterday's clothes and emerge just in time to hear a phone ring. I look to see where the noise is coming from and notice there has been a phone sitting next to my bed the entire time I have been here and I hadn't even spotted it.

We all look at each other. I gingerly pick it up.

"Hello?"

"Hello? Is that Holly?"

"Yes?"

"Holly, it's Fleur!"

"Fleur!" I say slightly hysterically to the rest of the room. "Fleur! Fleur! It's Fleur!" A cold hand of panic grips me. Is she calling to warn me off? To say, listen old thing, I know my husband-to-be is most fearfully attractive, but would you mind not making such obvious baby eyes at him?

"Fleur! How are you? Keeping well?"

She sounds slightly puzzled. "Er, I'm fine thanks, Holly. I was really calling to ask how *you* are?"

"Me? I'm just fine. Absolutely tip-top hole. I couldn't be better!"

"Gosh, that's good. I have to say I was really concerned when James told me. He said there was a number I could call you on."

"No cause for concern! I'm fine! Just on my way home, in fact."

"Oh, is James taking you?"

"James? JAMES?" I say with such a hysterical tone of surprise in my voice that she might as well have said Prince Charles. "No, no. My family are here to collect me."

"Great! Well, I *am* glad you are feeling better."

"Me too! Thank you for calling! I'm sure I will see you soon!"

"Well, you know we're hosting this drinks party on Saturday, don't you? The one your parents are invited to? I thought you might like to come too. You know, introduce them to everyone. I have to say I am looking forward to meeting them again."

"Gosh, well, thanks," I say, willing to agree to anything to get her off the phone at this particular moment of complete emotional confusion. "Saturday! See you then! Bye!"

I replace the receiver feeling slightly sick. Crappy cabbages. Saturday. Maybe I could have a relapse by then; it happens in these cases, doesn't it? Not feeling well on Tuesday, dead by Saturday? I could possibly get out of going to the wedding that way too. But maybe it would be good for me to go to the wedding. What do the Americans call it? Closure. That's why we have funerals. A sort of finality is needed. Her phone call is a fresh assault on my senses. James gave her my number and she was nice enough to call.

"That was Fleur! She called to see how I was; nice of her, wasn't it? She says she's looking forward to meeting you at the drinks party on Saturday. She invited me too." I inwardly gulp and busy myself with gathering my things together. I am absolutely amazed no one can see how I am feeling. How can they not notice this huge shadow of emotion hanging over me? This huge pulsating cloud of mixed feelings that is threatening to envelop me.

The red-haired nurse pops her head around the door. "Are you off then?"

"Yes, we are."

She comes fully into the room. "Are you the parents? I was just telling Holly earlier how troubled she was during the night. She was . . ."

"COME ON THEN!" I roar. This is one story I could do without them hearing. "We don't want to overburden the NHS, do we?" I gabble as I hustle them all toward the door. "Poor old NHS, they are absolutely bursting at the seams! They don't need us clogging up the system, do they? Probably need the bed for a liver transplant or something. Off we go!"

And with this I whisk them all out of the room and into the rabbit warren of corridors, all painted with gaudily colored countryside scenes in a transparently obvious effort to try and disguise the fact that we are in a hospital. My mother amuses herself by reading all the ward names out to us as we go along. I feel decidedly ill with all the adrenaline whooshing about inside me.

Morgan the Pekinese is waiting for us in the car and for once I am pitifully glad to see him. He is something familiar and loves me unconditionally. Not as much as he loves my mother, admittedly. This he makes very obvious as once he has greeted me with a wagging tail and a few licks he then goes on to blatantly fawn over my mother.

Once at home, I flop on to the sofa. I'm not terribly impressed with this love thing so far. Not impressed at all. Where is Cupid, the music, the *A Room With a View*–esque cornfields? I've been misled, that's all I can say, because to be honest the whole experience is painful. Actually physically painful. A dull ache seems to have taken up permanent residence in my body.

"Can we get you anything, darling?" says my mother, hovering in front of me. "Anything at all?" She puts Morgan down on the sofa. He immediately climbs on to my lap and lies down with a contented sigh. Normally Morgan and I share a tempestuous relationship but today he seems to sense my need for comfort. Peculiar how animals can do that.

I shake my head wearily. "No, I'm fine." Then I frown—she's got that floaty, "I'm just off" feel about her. "Are you going anywhere? Are you going home?" I sit up suddenly, aghast at the thought.

"No, no, darling. We may as well stay here now and get some more stuff sent up. I'll just tell my director that I'm taking another week off to look after you. No point in going back before the wedding next Saturday. Only if it's OK with you though?"

"Yes. I would like you to stay." She seems to relax at this and sits down opposite me. "Where's Dad?" I ask as she lights up a cigarette.

"He's gone to Sainsbury's. Your fridge resembles the *Marie Celeste*."

Lizzie comes out from the kitchen with a large tray. "Tea!" she says brightly.

There is a huge pregnant pause as Lizzie slowly and deliberately pours the tea out. She sloshes it into the cups. More silence. The air seems to pulsate with unspoken words; it's charged with emotion.

"ALL RIGHT! I GIVE UP!" I yell.

My mother looks at me. "So you admit it?" she breathes.

"Yes, I admit it."

"We knew it! Didn't we, Lizzie? We knew it! I wish they had this category on *Countdown*! I'd clean them out."

"He doesn't love me though, that's the problem," I say in a small voice.

"How do you know?"

"I would imagine his marriage to another woman would be a small clue."

They concede the point with a nod of their heads.

"But that was before he met you," Lizzie points out.

"And he is still getting married." We all pause for a minute, each occupied with our own thoughts. I fiddle with Morgan's ears. "There's also somebody at work he might be involved with."

"Was that before you too?"

I nod.

"Well, that's something, isn't it? Is it still going on?"

"I'm not sure."

"What's Fleur really like?" asks my mother.

I look straight at her. "Beautiful, kind and works in a bereavement charity." She reels a bit at that. I think she was hoping I would say "Spotty, mean and works part-time in an abattoir." I then go on to tell them how James' brother was killed in an accident and how he met Fleur. "He once said she saved him. So, you see, it's hopeless. Absolutely hopeless. What's her father like?"

"Miles? Oh, like practically every theater backer I know. Adores being associated with the famous. Likes to drop names over the dinner table. They're all budding actors at heart; they thrive on being around the success of a first night, the smell of the grease paint, that sort of thing. Of course, when he wasn't chasing me around my dressing room, he could be a terrible old stick in the mud. Kicked up a huge fuss if the director went a penny over the budget." She shrugs. "But then that was his job and, more to the point, his money. I wouldn't say we were ever good friends."

"Are you sure James doesn't feel something, Holly?" Lizzie says anxiously. "I mean, with what you've been writing, it just sounds like you both . . ."

"That's the point, Liz. *I've* been writing it and, although I may not have realized it before now, it was my slanted viewpoint. Sure, we get on well, but that doesn't mean he loves me. I love him. My writing is just wishful thinking. God, I feel such an idiot. Has the diary been that obvious?"

"No!" protests Lizzie, seeing my expression. "Take my office, as impersonal readers. We were all interested at first and read it every day. But once the photos started appearing, that's when it really got exciting. He just looked so gorgeous and you're not exactly bad-looking yourself. And then, after some more personal details about James started coming through, and the whole black eye incident, well, everyone began jumping to conclusions. I am sure the photos the paper put in were designed to make us think just that. There was a lovely one last week where you two were laughing, and then they had a nice one of you . . ." She trails off as she sees my face. "Anyway, before you know it, the whole office is talking about nothing else. Your whole diary is being analyzed. It's like being back when *Pride and Prejudice* was on the telly, do you remember? God! We were so excited! You're just like Elizabeth and Darcy!"

"Except Darcy actually got married to Elizabeth," I point out.

"Ah. Yes. Maybe not exactly then."

"No, Lizzie, it's not the same at all, IS IT?" My voice rises dangerously at the end. "Because I don't remember Elizabeth having to watch Darcy marry Miss bloody Havisham? Do you? DO YOU? I think the Beeb may have had a few letters of complaint if that had happened, don't you?"

"Dickens, darling," says my mother.

"PEOPLE LIKE HAPPY ENDINGS!" I roar.

"No, I mean it was Dickens. Miss Havisham is from *Great Expectations*."

"Bugger Miss Havisham!" I move Morgan off my lap and get up.

"Where are you going?"

"Out," I say, tempted to add, "and I may be some time" in an Oates-esque fashion.

They both look panic-stricken. "What are you going to do?"

"Chuck myself off Clifton Suspension Bridge. Do a bungee jump without the elastic." They both squeal in horror. "No, I'm not. I'm going to finish with Ben."

"Thank God for that!" says my mother as I stride out of the door. I knew she didn't like him.

I set off round to Ben's. My blood is really up now and I am mad. Hopping mad. I couldn't even tell you what about. But I do know it is a good time to finish with Ben while I am like this. Before apathy seizes me and I end up going out with him for the next ten years. I didn't say marry him, you'll notice. No. I know now he would never have married me. In fact, I'm quite sure that if you just put another tall, blond girl in my place, who laughs at all his jokes and assumes a horizontal position once in a while, he might never even notice I've gone.

I am suddenly aware of what I am so mad about. My previous thoughts-embargo on Ben seems to have been lifted and now they positively flood in. When was the last time he did something for me? Just for me? When have I ever told him any of my worries, for fear of being branded a needy, insecure person? When did we last share a joke together as opposed to him telling me one? That's why we've been going out for so long, because I'm such a pushover. In fact, pushover is completely the wrong word. There's no pushing involved whatsoever; I go over completely of my own volition.

I thought I was being smart. Playing the game. Play it cool and eventually he'll come round, isn't that what I told myself? But it wasn't smart at all because I fitted rather neatly into his life. Slotted in perfectly between his sport, work and social life. Imagine a girlfriend who never complains at the training sessions and the rugby games, never asks for anything back from the relationship. God, how stupid I am, I fume to myself. Just because outwardly he is so good-looking, so charming, so perfect, I thought he was the man for me. I thought I ought to be in love with him.

My footsteps slow as I realize he said he was going to be at a training session tonight. Right, I'll just sit on his steps and wait until he gets back. He couldn't even make time to bring me back from the hospital, could he? Couldn't possibly skip a training session, even for his concussed girlfriend. Ex-girlfriend, I tell myself grimly.

I turn the corner into his road and see that waiting outside won't be necessary as there, sitting outside his flat, is his car. He must be back from training.

I bound up the steps, all traces of yesterday's accident wiped away. I am a woman on a mission. I impatiently ring the bell. No answer. I frown and peer round into the window. The curtains are closed but light is shining out through a chink. I lean on the bell in sheer frustration. The door opens a crack and Ben's face peers out.

"Holly! What are you doing here?"

"Ben, we need to talk."

"What? Now? This really isn't a good time, I've just come out of the shower." He opens the door a little further and I see he has a towel wrapped around his waist.

"Fine. We can do this out here then. But I don't think you'll want that, will you? I think SHOUTING might be involved."

He grabs my arm, pulls me inside and then gives me a nudge in the direction of the sitting room.

"What the hell is wrong with you? What is this about? Why can't it wait until tomorrow?" There's something not right. Something in his demeanor. His arrogant, just-don't-care attitude, which used to be so attractive to me, isn't there. He's worried about something. We walk into the sitting room. My antennae are up and I cast a suspicious look around me. Nothing. Everything looks exactly the same. But there is something wrong with his appearance. And then it strikes me. For someone who has just come out of the shower, his hair is surprisingly dry.

"Good training session?"

He looks wary. "Fine, thanks. What do you want to talk about?"

"This and that. It just seems ages since I've seen you," I say, playing for time.

He stares at me. "I saw you at lunchtime, Holly, at the hospital? Do you remember? How bad was that knock to the head?"

"Of course I remember! I just meant it has been a long time since we've actually talked. You know, had a conversation. How about some tea? I'll make it!"

He jumps up. "No, you stay here, I'll make it. Can't have you racing about when you've had a knock to your head, can we? You stay right there." He steams like a maniac through to the kitchen. Right, now I'm downright suspicious. Something is definitely up. I prowl about the room, looking for clues. Something on one of the side tables next to the sofa glints in the light and catches my eye. I walk over to it and look down.

It's a small gold crucifix.

twenty-four

I pick up the gold chain and cross up and let it dangle from my hand in front of me. I stare at the necklace, unmoving for a second, disbelieving its significance. But there's no denying it; in fact, I have no wish to deny it. I have been looking at this necklace on and off for the last twelve years. I know exactly who it belongs to.

I look up as Ben clatters through the doorway in double-quick time carrying two mugs of tea, the white towel wrapped around his waist somewhat at odds with the domesticity.

"Here we are! Just what the doctor ordered . . ." His words trail off as he slows to a stop in front of me and stares. He knows the game is up just from the look on my face, let alone the fact I seem to be holding a piece of jewelry which doesn't belong to me. I gallantly ignore the fact that all that lies between his todger and a scalding cup of tea is a flimsy bit of towel and, before he can even open his mouth, slip past him into the hall and up the stairs. I stealthily make my way across the top landing and then throw open his bedroom door. My suspicions are instantly confirmed. For lying there, underneath the duvet, as cool as the proverbial cucumber, is Teresa the Holy Cow. Or Not So Holy Cow.

She seems to be expecting me. She is neither shocked nor distressed; in fact, her face shows no semblance of feelings whatsoever. Her eyes coolly meet mine and she looks squarely into them. I am not being as cool as the proverbial cucumber—my mouth is doing a good impression of catching flies. Although I knew damn

well who the little gold crucifix belonged to, it is still a surprise to
see the aforementioned owner languishing on a set of pillows that
I myself have spent a great deal of time languishing on in the past.
I set my mouth firmly. In a way, you see, this makes things so
much easier. I gather my thoughts rapidly together.

"I believe this may belong to you," I say, waving the necklace in
front of her. She looks at me steadily.

"Yes it does and I would appreciate it back."

"Take it," I say and, slinging it on to the bed, turn on my heels
and walk back down the stairs. I feel alarmingly calm. I stroll into
the sitting room where Ben has put the two mugs down on a side
table and is staring at them and anxiously biting his lip. I nonchalantly toss myself into an armchair.

"So! How long have you and the singing nun been going on
for?"

"It was nothing. It was only a few times," he mutters, still staring down at the mugs. Well, I'm sure that I can multiply "a few
times" by at least ten.

"How long?"

"A few weeks."

"When did you two . . ." Ahhh. Light dawns. They met each
other in the Square Bar that night when I was celebrating the
diary thing. "Surely not since you met in the Square Bar?"

For the first time he actually manages to look at me.

"No. Not since then. She was very keen though. Made me take
her number."

"How long after that did you start to see her?"

"Not until you started trying to push me into a commitment,"
he says sulkily.

"I tried to push you into a commitment?" I ask incredulously.
Does he know what the word commitment actually means? Or
does he still think making a date for next week qualifies?

His head snaps up as he thinks he might have happened upon some moral high ground. "Well, first you bring your parents up to meet me with some cock-and-bull story about how they just *happened* to be in the area. Then I actually find wedding magazines in your flat! I mean, do you think I'm stupid? Do you honestly think I believed you when you said they belonged to Lizzie? She's not even engaged! What is a boy supposed to do when you plot and scheme to try and get me to marry you?"

OK, you know how I just told you how calm I feel? Well, scrub it from the records because now I am angry. Furious, even. I briefly let my blood come to a rolling boil before it slows back down to a simmer.

"They *were* Lizzie's," I say furiously.

"Oh, come on, Holly! You don't expect me to believe that, do you? Why would Lizzie keep wedding magazines in your flat?"

A nasty little thought occurs to me. "Did you call Teresa on the night of the hen do? Are you who she slipped away early to see?"

He stares down at the carpet. He doesn't need to answer, it's written all over his face.

"Would you believe the fact that I was coming round here to finish with you?"

"Finish with *me*?" he echoes, disbelief plastered all over his face.

"Yes, finish with you because we are finished. Over. Kaput."

"You're just trying to save face."

"Oh, am I? How come I'm not more upset then? How come I'm not prostrate on the floor wailing over the fact I've found you in bed with another woman? How come I'm not slitting my wrists with despair because I'll never get you down the aisle? I'll tell you why. It's because I. Couldn't. Give. A. Shit."

He stares at me open-mouthed. You know what the awful thing is? I don't think anyone has ever done this to him before. I carry on before he can stop me.

"And as hard as it is for a catch like you to believe any girl would not wish to trap you into matrimony, I'm afraid you are just going to have to believe me. My parents did turn up accidentally and those magazines were Lizzie's. I would not want to marry you if you were the last sperm-producing male on earth. I think you are egotistical, selfish and unamusing. Besides which"—I jerk my head up to the ceiling—"you are obviously spreading your sexual favors around like . . . like . . ." I search in my vocabulary for a suitably cutting *Blackadder*-esque line, ". . . like MARMA-LADE!" Oh well. Can't have everything. He stares at me, aghast. Taking advantage of this momentary lull in conversation, I go to walk out and then turn back.

"Just two more things; firstly, I *hate* that restaurant you insist is my favorite." He stares at me and does the very familiar gesture of pushing his hair from his eyes. "And secondly, get your hair cut. I prefer short hair nowadays, preferably accompanied by green eyes."

I leave him to try and make some sense out of my words and stalk out of the flat, slamming the front door on my way out.

I march down the steps and self-righteously stride toward home. After a few minutes a voice behind me starts calling my name.

"Holly! Holly! Wait!"

I turn around to find Teresa running toward me. What the hell does she want? I stand where I am and wait for her to catch up.

"What do you want?" I ask as she reaches the spot where I'm standing.

She has the good grace to look a little sheepish. "Just to explain."

I shrug; to be honest I'm a little curious. "I'm listening." I turn and start walking slowly, but then I jump in before she can say a word. "I mean, what's all this hypocritical stuff? No sex before marriage and all that?"

It's her turn to shrug. "Look, Holly. You and I have never got on particularly well. Have you ever wondered why?" She lifts her chin defiantly.

It is on the tip of my tongue to say "Because you're a miserable cow?" but instead I say nothing and let her continue.

"You and Lizzie were always so popular at school, so sure of yourselves. I really hated you both for it. You had boyfriends, could do what you wanted, it was all so effortless for you."

"Teresa, that was twelve years ago," I say impatiently. "There's not much we did at school that counts for anything now."

"I know, but I just wanted to prove I was attractive to men too. That I could have your man. So I gave Ben my number that night in the Square Bar. It was just a stupid test to see if he would call and he did. But then your diary seemed to be going so well. I didn't see why you should have it all, so I decided to sleep with him to show you, you couldn't."

I sigh deeply. "Believe me, Teresa, I don't have it all." We walk in silence for a few seconds.

"Was that the first time you'd slept with anyone?"

"No."

Blimey. "Why all the pretense, Teresa? Why all the 'Jesus wants me for a sunbeam' stuff? Why not invest in some Maybelline eyeliner and join the party with the rest of us?"

"With *my* parents?" She gives a bitter small laugh.

"Yes. Well." I think of my carefree, unconventional parents and suddenly I can't really be bothered to feel angry with Teresa. I don't even think I can be bothered to hate her any more.

"You're welcome to him. I was going to finish with him tonight anyway," I say staunchly. I might not be bothered with her any more, but I still have some pride.

"Yeah, I heard. From upstairs. Well, I'll be going. See you around." She crosses the road and walks off. I shake my head after her in wonderment. It just goes to show you never actually truly know anybody. Even yourself.

* * *

I come home to find Lizzie and my mother still up. I know they have been waiting for me to see what has happened—a small clue to this great deduction would be my mother's first question as I walk through the door.

"What happened?"

I wearily tell her and Lizzie all about it, but I am so washed out with emotion that I can't drum up anything but the barest facts. Lizzie is suitably shocked. In fact, she is more like shell-shocked. Actually my mother isn't reacting as I thought she would. She doesn't seem surprised at all. Lizzie just sits there with her mouth wide open, saying, "Teresa? Teresa?"

"Yes. Teresa."

"Teresa the Holy Cow, Teresa?"

"Yes."

"Bloody hell." And then, "Bloody hell." And then, "Bloody buggery hell."

My mother sits silently throughout. "Aren't you shocked? Aren't you surprised?" I ask her.

She calmly studies her fingernails and then smooths down her dress. She is carefully avoiding eye contact. "Why aren't you surprised?" I demand.

She hesitantly looks up at me. "Darling, now promise me you won't get upset. This was a long time ago." Too late, I am upset.

"What was?"

"It wasn't much, but do you remember Matt?"

"Yes, of course I remember Matt." He was one of my first boyfriends.

"Well, I saw them once in town. Teresa and Matt. Kissing."

"So?"

"You were seeing him at the time. I've always hated the little tart ever since. I didn't say anything and luckily you stopped seeing Matt a while later. I never knew if you found out or not."

"So that was her little game, was it?" I almost breathe fire out of my nostrils.

"I take it you didn't know then?" my mother asks weakly.

"Try and steal all Holly's boyfriends. Oh yes! What fun sport! Well, I would like to see her try with James Sabine," I say heatedly.

"Er . . . James Sabine isn't your boyfriend," Lizzie points out unhelpfully.

"Thank you."

"Right. Yes. Sorry."

"You're not devastated though are you, darling?" my mother asks with an air of concern.

My shoulders sag suddenly. I'm too tired to go through the pretense of being upset about something that happened more than ten years ago and I was going to finish with Ben tonight anyway. I shake my head wearily. "It's been quite a day. I'm going to bed." I kiss them both and trail my careworn body into the bedroom.

I must have been really tired, or maybe the concussion was still wearing off, because despite my tumultuous emotions I sleep straight through to daybreak and then wake up with a start, wondering where I am. I have a heavy feeling of foreboding hanging over me and I realize something bad must have happened to me yesterday. Slowly the events come flooding back. I groan slightly. I'm in love with James. He's getting married to Fleur. Ben's sleeping with Teresa. Right. Terrific. Things couldn't be better.

I wonder if I could slope off into the country for a bit. Find myself a nice little remote cottage somewhere and quietly go to pot. But then I remember I will see James today and my heart lightens just a little.

I get up and make myself a cup of tea. I study my reflection briefly in the mirror before returning to bed to nurse my cup. I'm looking a little bit sorry for myself, but the only lasting marks from the past few days are two faint black eyes. To be honest, I think most people would now be shocked if I turned up without a black eye in some shape or form. They probably wouldn't recognize me, I think gloomily.

I have no wish to lie in bed and contemplate my past, present or future, so as soon as I have finished my tea, I quickly shower and slip out of the house before my parents wake. I head down to the police station where I intend to collect my e-mails and catch up on the diary.

There are a few officers from the night shift still there, yawning wearily, but they pat my arm or my shoulder and tell me they are pleased to have me back. I arrive at my desk and spend the next half an hour or so catching up on what I have missed. I lean back in my chair and look at my watch. It's half past seven. The day shift will be arriving soon. I go to the Ladies and patch up my makeup, trying to cover the bruises under my eyes. I am feeling inexplicably jumpy at the thought of seeing James. My stomach is churning and I feel quite sick with the tension. "Get a grip," I tell myself, "it's just another ordinary day on the job. What are you expecting? For him to run through the door with his arms open wide?" I shakily apply a line of eyeliner. It would be nice if I knew he cared just a little about me. You know, as a friend.

I walk back to my desk and try to concentrate on the screen of my laptop in front of me. I focus on the words but they don't register, and instead I look anxiously up at the door every few minutes. A hand suddenly clasps my shoulder.

"Holly!" I leap about ten feet into the air. "How are you? How are you feeling? I wanted to come down to the hospital but James wouldn't let me!"

I look round, clutching my hand to my chest. "Callum! You surprised me! I'm fine. Why wouldn't James let you come down to the hospital?"

"Said there were too many people down there. You don't look too bad, apart from the black eyes of course."

"Er, thanks." He takes up residence on my desk next to the laptop. One by one, the day shift arrive on duty and come over to say hello. I smile and thank them for their flowers. A familiar voice filters through the small crowd.

"WHO PUT THE PICTURE OF FRED FLINTSTONE INTO MY SECURITY PASS? Dave wouldn't let me in the building on the grounds that I didn't look anything like my photo. Which I suppose is something to be thankful for."

James grins wryly at them all. Much sniggering and back-slapping from the rest of the department accompanies this state-ment, another stark reminder his wedding will soon be upon us. James sits down opposite me.

"Morning Holly! How are you feeling?"

"Fine, thanks. How are you?"

"Good. I never thought I'd say this, but it's nice to have you back." He grins widely at me and my stomach does a triple som-ersault. He gets on with emptying his in-tray and I get on with the all-important task of sneaking looks at him over the cover of my laptop. I feel as though I am almost seeing him for the first time, or at least through new eyes. I watch him opening some post, shouting over to one of his colleagues, talking on the phone. I try to file images of him away in my memory so I can take them out and look at them when all this is over. He jolts me out of my thoughts.

"Are you coming tomorrow? To the drinks thing? Fleur said she invited you."

"Yeah, the parents are too, I'm afraid."

"I liked them. Thought they were great."

"Oh. Thanks."

"What are you doing tonight?"

"TV interview. Why?"

"Another one? Thought you might want to come out for a drink with the rest of the department. Some other time perhaps."

Damn and blast the BBC.

Despite, or indeed because of, James Sabine's presence, it is quite an unpleasant day all in all. I read undue meaning into his every word or expression. It is hard to stop staring at him and whenever Fleur phones up to talk to him it feels like someone has punched me in the stomach. I wonder how anyone has the stamina to keep up this love thing on any sort of permanent basis without a regular subscription to a health spa. I dramatically yo-yo between wanting to drop to my knees, clasp his feet and tell him everything and the more realistic position of saying nothing because he is getting married to a beautiful and kind girl one week from tomorrow, whom he did, freely and without coercion, ask to marry him. The whole thing makes me a little damp under the armpits and determined to invest in a new deodorant. The rest of the afternoon I spend dabbling in bizarre fantasies of what might have happened with my life if I had been assigned to anyone else in the room but James Sabine. Also, a more delicious but macabre fantasy of what might have happened if James' brother Rob hadn't died and James hadn't ever met Fleur, thus leaving the way clear and decidedly uncluttered for yours truly. But that's the ironic thing, I belatedly realize; the only reason I was assigned to James Sabine was because he was getting married.

I pop over to the paper to file copy. For some peculiar reason, Joe is absolutely insistent that he come to the BBC with me for the TV interview this evening. I am in the middle of a lovely conversation with Valerie from accounts about how I should look after myself after such a nasty accident, and am just about to suggest that she could take up residence chez moi, take on a mumsy capacity and perhaps see her way to preparing a few scooby snacks, when Joe leaps on me (not literally, figuratively) and insists he will accompany me. I point out I will have to go back home to change first, but he says, "No matter, I will come and pick you up at six." I shrug to myself because, to be honest, life is just one big surprise to me nowadays, and then I wend my way home to get changed. So here I am at home, drinking the sloe gin that my mother had the foresight to pack, with Lizzie and the aforementioned relative trying frantically to decide what I should wear on *Southwest Tonight*.

Lizzie and Mother, bless them, are trying to be terribly cheerful and upbeat for me. But I wish they would stop. It's quite depressing and it's having the very opposite effect to the one they intend. Fortunately the sloe gin is hitting the mark quite nicely.

We finally settle on a beautiful, feminine, pale blue dress which clings in all the right places and is embroidered throughout with little white daisies. I stare unseeingly ahead of me as my mother dresses my hair and wonder if I'll ever be happy again.

My parents and Lizzie opt to stay at home to watch the interview from the comfort of the sofa, and as we don't know how to preset the video someone has to do it manually anyway. Joe and I walk into the reception area of the TV studios just after six P.M. In an exact replica of my last visit, the "Shan't-keep-you-a-moment" secretary signs us in and then Rosemary, the aspiring punk, collects us and wordlessly deposits us in the hospitality suite. I wearily sit down on a chair against the wall.

"Do you know what you're going to say?" asks Joe.

"I don't know what I'm going to be asked."

"Right. Well, try and plug the fact we're the leading regional paper and also mention we're at the cutting edge of journalism."

I look at him. Cutting edge? What cutting edge would that be? Joe seems agitated, I suddenly notice. He nervously licks his lips. "Oh, and they might show some photos of that chase;

Vince had the other half of the film developed. So be ready to talk about it."

I frown at him; what the hell has he got to be worried about? I have no time to prevaricate as Giles, the host of *Southwest Tonight*, bounds in.

He enthusiastically shakes our hands. "Holly! Hi!" I introduce Joe to him. "Joe! Nice to put a face to the voice!" I frown to myself—I suppose they must have talked over the phone to arrange this. Although I thought researchers did stuff like that?

Giles turns back to me. "We've removed all glasses of water from the set so we can avoid a repeat incident of last time! Ha, ha!" I smile at the memory. It feels like a lifetime ago. "After you're miked up, someone will bring you down." He says good-bye and we wait for the sound man.

Down on the set, I am deposited once more on the squishy sofa while Giles talks directly to the camera.

"Our next guest is Holly Colshannon, the journalist who has been writing a hugely popular daily column in our local news-paper, the *Bristol Gazette*, called 'The Real Dick Tracy's Diary.' " He turns to me. "Welcome back to the program, Holly."

I smile. "Thank you."

"I have to say, I'm a big admirer. Just for the benefit of the view-ers who haven't read your diary, could you tell us a bit about it?"

"Sure," I say in a voice that doesn't quite sound as though it comes from me. "I have been assigned to shadow a detective sergeant at the Bristol Constabulary—"

"That's Jack Swithen," interrupts Giles.

"That's right, and every day I shadow Jack on real cases and crimes and then write up my diary."

"It's been fascinating so far—you've reported a number of bur-glaries, thefts and goodness knows what else! But your most re-cent development has been the case of The Fox, hasn't it?"

"Yes. We've been investigating a series of burglaries and, after a dramatic dawn raid on a property, the police made an arrest a few days ago."

"I understand you ended up in hospital though."

"The suspect we apprehended . . ." It is disturbing how easily I can lapse into this police speak so I modify it. ". . . made a bit of a run for it. We all gave chase and unfortunately I was knocked out in the process."

"Can you attribute the success of the diary completely to the officer, Jack?"

I shift in my seat. I'm not quite sure what he's getting at. "Em, well. Jack Swithen has a great deal to do with it. I mean, people have gradually got to know him over the last few weeks. I think he stands for the values we all would like to see in our police officers. It was difficult, at first, to get any personal details out of him for the diary readers to actually be able to relate to him."

"Did your relationship with him at the time have anything to do with that?" I think I'm starting to see where this is heading now.

"We didn't perhaps see eye to eye at first . . ."

"And now?"

"We are getting on better."

"We have a few pictures." Giles gestures to a monitor to the right of me and up on the screen flashes a photo. A peculiarly intimate photo of me lying on the ground with quite an impressively sized tree next to me (no wonder I had a headache). James is bending over me. I feel a bit funny and try to compose my features. And then another picture appears of James apparently yelling for an ambulance. And yet another with his hands on my head. I'm starting to feel a little hot. I nervously fidget with my necklace.

"I have to say, Holly, since we've been trailing this interview, we have had quite a few faxes and e-mails asking if anything is going on between you and the detective? Would you like to confirm or deny the rumor?"

My eyes briefly flicker toward Joe. Undoubtedly he set this up. I say, in a strange voice, "Ha ha! Of course there's nothing going on! He's actually getting married in a week's time!" Leave it there, leave it there, I try to communicate to Giles.

Far from leaving it, he says, "IS he, indeed?" Giles' eyes light up. "That's not actually mentioned in the diary, is it? Then he's looking very worried for a man who's getting married in a week's time!" This is a bloody hatchet job.

"He thought he'd killed me! He should look worried, he didn't want my editor suing him!" Attack suitably deflected. Giles' eyes flicker briefly toward Joe but he stops it there.

"Well, thank you, Holly. You've certainly given us all some food for thought and I'm sure people will be following developments in 'The Real Dick Tracy's Diary' more avidly than ever!"

"Did you have to deny it so vehemently?" whispers Joe on the way back through the maze of corridors to the car.

"You did that, didn't you? You set me up!" Joe at least has the good grace to look sheepish. "Not content with blood and guts, you had to chuck a bit of sex in there too for good measure, didn't you? The journalist shagging the detective! Oh yes! That'll get the circulation up, won't it? Is that what you were talking to Giles about on the phone? Didn't bother telling me, oh no!"

"We needed it to look genuine. I don't know what you're getting so upset about, it will help your career too. You're going to have to learn there's more to good journalism than just good writing."

"Well, if that's what it involves, I don't want to know," I whisper viciously.

"There was absolutely no need to tell everyone James is getting

married next week. You could at least have let them wonder. Besides, people really have been asking so we just thought we would
bring it up on air, that's all."

"That would have nothing at all to do with your choice of pictures, would it? It hasn't escaped my notice you've been putting
more and more intimate shots in lately."

"Maybe there have been more and more to choose from lately.
What on earth is your problem? There isn't actually something
going on is there?" he breathes excitedly.

"No. There. Isn't," I say adamantly and unfortunately truthfully as well.

twenty-five

———

"Don't make me go!" I wail.

"Holly, you have to go," says my mother emphatically. "People will have seen that TV interview and think there is no smoke without fire."

"Bloody Giles," I mutter furiously.

"You not showing up will really get tongues wagging."

"Bloody Joe."

"If not for you, then do it for James."

"Bloody James," I mutter.

"Holly. Don't mutter."

We are standing in my bedroom the day after the TV interview, having a scene that is reminiscent of ones we used to have more than a decade ago. The only difference being the wallpaper doesn't have pictures of Duran Duran and George Michael on it any more. (Yes, I know they're not particularly *cool*.)

"Why would it matter to James if I'm there or not?" The drinks party at Fleur's parents' house is this evening. I would rather slit my wrists than face all those people who think that either James and I are having an affair or that I have a thumping great crush on the fair detective. Ever since the TV interview I have developed various murderous intentions toward Giles and Joe in turn.

"Because he has to cope with people wondering whether it's true or not as well, you know. It can't be very pleasant for him. He is the innocent party in all of this."

"What are you implying? That I've done this deliberately?" I say hysterically. All the toys are coming out of the cot.

"Don't be silly." She sits down on the bed and pats the space next to her. I sulkily go and sit beside her. She takes my hand and says gently, "You know, darling, this may seem very painful right now but bad times enable your character to grow."

"I've got character coming out of my sodding ears," I mutter into the floor but nothing is stopping my mother as she warms to her theme. She stands up and waltzes into the middle of the room, turning to face me with a flourish.

"But you'll find your experiences will help you grow inside." I feel a flutter of recognition. "Until, like a butterfly—"

I interrupt hastily. "Isn't that a speech from one of your plays?"

She stops, hands in midair. "Hmm?"

"Isn't this from one of your plays?"

"Is it, darling? I thought it sounded vaguely familiar. So easy to slip back into them." She comes back down to earth and sits beside me again. "Anyway, you're going to go into that party looking beautiful and as though you haven't a care in the world. People will soon forget all about this silly rumor. They probably didn't even see the interview."

I absorb all of this and then say, "Still, I can't dress up and look beautiful, they'll just think I'm some sort of hussy!"

"Would you rather dress down and let people think you've developed a huge great schoolgirl crush on him? Better a hussy than a fool."

I hesitate for less than a second. "You're right. Where are the heated rollers?"

Lizzie arrives a quarter of an hour later, looking fabulous in a red dress. Twenty curlers dot my head. I am intently trying to shape my eyebrows in the mirror (a little sarcastic voice in my head says, "Oh yes! That's sure to bring him round, your *eyebrows*") while listening to M-People in an attempt to empower me. I swivel round as Lizzie comes in.

"Lizzie! You look gorgeous! Where are you going?"

"With you! I'm going to deflect attention from you by being the scarlet woman!" She giggles and does a little twirl for me.

"But you're not invited."

My mother bustles in. "I called Miles and asked if I could bring her; I said she was our cousin staying for a few days."

"Can you do that?"

"Darling, it's just a drinks party, not a sit-down dinner, so they won't be trying to decide how to get another portion out of the tarte tatin. Besides, we thought you might need the moral support." She winks at Lizzie, who giggles.

I shrug and turn back to my eyebrows. Lizzie sits on the bed while my mother bustles off again.

"I couldn't believe it when Giles started asking you if you and James were carrying on! I thought you were going to pass out!" she says.

"Joe put him up to it," I say grimly.

"Two people from my office called me up to ask if I was watching!"

"I just hope James and Fleur didn't catch it."

"Are they likely to have done?"

"Well, James was supposed to have been having a drink with some of the other officers but I don't know what Fleur will think if she saw it."

Lizzie shrugs. "I wouldn't worry. She is marrying him next week. If she doesn't trust him by now . . ."

"How are you feeling?" I ask Lizzie after a minute, suddenly aware I'm not the only person with problems.

She smiles. "Better, I think. It's good to have something to take my mind off it."

"I aim to please."

* * *

The four of us and a sulky Pekinese clamber into my father's enormous Range Rover. No mean feat in a pair of three-inch heels, I can tell you. We are all looking incredibly smart; my mother is wearing an elegant knitted wool suit and my father is in the obligatory blazer and tie. I would much rather we were going somewhere else. Out to dinner in a peaceful country pub perhaps. I indulge this daydream as we drive into the country-side surrounding Bristol—anything to keep my mind off horrific fantasies about the drinks party. My parents argue about the map reading and my mother ferrets about in the front in a desperate attempt to unearth the invite, which apparently has a map on the back of it. The car is a mound of papers and I'm surprised my father can see out of the windscreen to drive as the dashboard is literally piled high with debris. This is all part of my mother's unique filing system. They got bored of dashing around the countryside trying to find parties, winding down windows to ask locals vague questions because they'd forgotten the map, the invitation or both, when they'd much rather be chatting and drinking their host's booze. So now my mother keeps all the invites in the car and just has difficulty finding the damn things.

We locate the venue at long last, swing into a driveway and speak into an intercom at the gates. We wait as the pair of huge iron contraptions swing open. A beautiful, tree-lined driveway stretches before us. "James is marrying into this?" I ask incredulously. "What does Fleur's father do again? I thought you said he was a theater backer?"

"He is, darling. It takes a lot of money to be a theater backer—his main career is something to do with finance." My mother dismisses the many acres in front of her with the vague phrase "something to do with finance."

I sink into my father's upholstery with a sigh. How on earth did I ever think I could compete with this? My sharp-eyed pater notices my reaction in his mirror.

"Gilded cages and all that, Holly. Shouldn't think it's as much fun as it looks."

Well, even half the amount of fun it looks would be enough for me.

The driveway soon gives way to a glorious old Georgian house. Dad parks the car next to an assortment of BMWs, Audis and Alfa Romeos. My heart is in my mouth and my immediate reaction is to make a bolt across the fields but my mother takes tight control of my hand. "You look gorgeous," she whispers into my ear and gives my hand a conciliatory squeeze. In the end we chose a sophisticated black dress with slits up the front and back, cleverly backed with a brilliant purple lining which glints through the material. It is, as Lizzie wryly remarked, the pulling dress I wore before I met Ben.

I look up in wonder at the house. It is built from mellow Cotswold stone and has large Georgian windows. A Virginia creeper spreads across half of the house and the huge front door, painted in red, stands out proudly against it.

We are greeted by a discreet waiter who takes our coats and then shows us through to the drawing room. The buzz and hum of voices gets closer as we walk across the vast hallway until it reaches a crescendo as the waiter throws open the door. We walk in and are immediately greeted by a gentleman whom I presume is Miles, Fleur's father.

"Miles! How fabulous to see you! How are you?" my mother confirms.

"You look wonderful, Sorrel! Patrick, how nice to see you again," he says as he turns toward my father. My father shakes his hand rather stiffly. He has never been a big fan of any of my mother's financial backers, shrewdly suspecting their motives for getting involved with the theater. My mother turns to me. "This is my daughter, Holly."

"You need no introduction, Holly! I have heard so much about you!" He finishes this sentence with a great guffaw and I truly wish I could be anywhere else but here. Maybe it was the way he said it, or the laugh afterward, but he is making me feel very uncomfortable.

My mother hastily shoves Lizzie in front of him. "This is our cousin, Lizzie, who's with us for a few days."

While this introduction is going on, I glance around the room at the array of people chatting in groups, clasping glasses as waiters circulate with canapés. I spot James and Fleur talking to an elderly couple and Callum in a group next to them. Callum spies me looking over and excuses himself from his group. James, noticing Callum's movement, looks up and follows his gaze to me. My heart misses a beat and we smile at each other.

Callum wrestles through the throng, twisting his body this way and that to reach me. He finally arrives at my side and grimaces slightly. Due to the social situation, he plants a kiss on my cheek. I smile and squeeze his arm, genuinely pleased to see a friendly face.

"How's it going?" I ask.

He fiddles with his collar. He is looking very smart in a gray suit with a pristine white shirt. The Donald Duck tie ruins the effect a bit.

"It's all a bit of an effort for us simple coppers," he whispers.

"Feeling the strain?"

"What I do in the name of friendship! You look gorgeous, by the way!"

"Thank you. So did you have a good time last night?" I ask conversationally as he grabs two glasses from a passing waiter and hands one to me.

"Last night?"

"Yeah, you went for a drink with the rest of the department." I notice James out of the corner of my eye saying hello to my parents and Lizzie.

"Oh, *that*. Yes, it was fine," he shrugs.

"Stayed out all night, did you?"

"No, no."

"S'pect you all needed to relieve the tension from the week," I prompt, fishing madly.

"You want to know if any of us saw the TV interview, don't you?"

"Did you?" I gasp.

"No, my flatmate spotted you and recorded it for me. He missed the first five minutes though. So I caught the video but no one else saw it."

"Thank God," I say fervently. I glance over again to James and my parents. They seem to be sharing a joke and laughing raucously.

"It wasn't that bad," says Callum, grabbing a canapé from a tray as it whizzes past.

Be careful, I warn myself. I try to shrug nonchalantly. "No, just a bit embarrassing the way Giles stitched me up."

"My flatmate is a real fan of the diary. He says that he didn't like the skirt you were wearing the other day. The beige one with the—"

"Poppies on it," I finish wearily. "He's not the only one. I will be burning it as soon as I get home. So have you written your best man speech yet?"

"Haven't even started! I'm a bit nervous about what to say in front of all this lot. I have a feeling coppers aren't really their thing. James seems to fit in OK though." He lowers his voice to a whisper. "Have you met that girl Susie? Now she's a—"

"You called me Jack after one of your cats?" whispers an amused voice in my ear.

I jump as James sidles into our conversation. "I suppose my mother told you?" I grin.

"You suppose right."

"You should count yourself lucky—the other one is called Jasper."

"Well in that case, thank you for calling me Jack. Not tempted to show us all the bottle trick with your toes yet?" he asks, eyeing my glass of champagne.

"Maybe later."

He smiles. Callum makes the excuse that none of the canapés seem to be heading our way and wanders off in search of nourishment. James and I are left alone. I examine the carpet intently. Is it Persian or Siamese? Or am I thinking of cats again? Never having been in a social situation with James, I feel awkward and gauche suddenly. What on earth do we talk about?

I clear my throat and ask, "Are you feeling nervous yet?"

"What of? You?"

"No, the wedding."

"Oh, the wedding." He shrugs. "No, not yet. Are you coming? You can make free and loose with my father-in-law's booze."

"If you want me to. Come, that is."

"I would like you to come."

We look at each other for a second and I think I detect some sadness in his expression but it could be wishful thinking on my part. If only we had some more time together, but from my brief experience of James Sabine, I know this wedding will go ahead. He is a man who keeps his promises.

We glance over sharply at my mother as her shrill laughter peals out and I smile.

"She's wonderful," he says.

"Thank you."

"What's with the expression, 'Shit MacGregor'?"

I sigh, emotional crisis avoided. "Don't, whatever you do, ask her to tell you."

"Why?"

"Because it rather predictably involves a Scotsman, a rowing boat and it's not funny when you've heard it for the hundredth time."

James laughs and Fleur miraculously appears at his elbow.

"Holly, can I borrow him for a minute?"

"He's all yours," I reply truthfully.

"Darling, there's someone I want you to meet . . ." she says as she leads him away. I wander over to my parents' group, picking up a fresh glass of champagne on the way. I stand politely on the outskirts, trying to pick up the conversation, when a figure by the door catches my attention. I frown to myself. He's very familiar. It's like seeing your postman in the supermarket—you can't place them when they're out of context. He starts to look aggressively around and then relaxes minutely as he spots his prey. He strides over to the subject of his gaze and just at that moment I recognize who it is.

It's Alastair.

I take a step toward him but it's too late. He's punched James Sabine squarely in the face. "Bloody hell," says my father.

twenty-six

J ames goes down like a sack of potatoes and a collective gasp
goes up. A strange hush then falls around the room. Everyone stands motionless, stunned. It is like that statue game we used
to play as kids. Callum and Lizzie are the first on the scene. I can't
hear what Callum is saying to Alastair but his body language indicates that it's along the lines of, "You're completely loopy but I'm
going to speak calmly in case you've got a gun." He looks enormously relieved when Lizzie, after checking James is OK, spins
around to confront Alastair.

"What the hell are you doing?" she shrieks, doing a good impression of a banshee which goes down particularly well with the
room's acoustics. For a moment I think she might stop and ask
whether we can hear her at the back, to which I would give a
hearty thumbs-up. I inwardly wince and hope no one remembers
I brought her.

At this point James gets back to his feet and a morbid little
group presses forward, myself among them, to see how much
blood there is. I have a more personal interest than just plain old
curiosity. Enter Fleur from stage left. She pushes through the
crowd and throws herself on him. "James, darling, are you all
right? How many fingers am I holding up?"

"Fleur, don't be ridiculous," he snaps, "I'm fine." I suppress a
smile.

Alastair must have caught his nose. I make this lightning

deduction from the blood pouring from it. Fleur pulls a handkerchief out from somewhere and hands it to him. I almost have to stand on my hands to stop myself from playing the ministering angel and flinging myself into the middle of the intimate group.

Although Alastair's actions must have made sense to him at some point, he is looking very confused now. All eyes swivel to him; he has center stage and looks as though he doesn't know quite what to do with it. Lizzie stands before him, drawn up to her full five feet four and a half inches, hands clenched into tight little fists, and I have a shrewd suspicion she is quite enjoying all this. The red dress was absolutely the right choice of outfit.

"Have you been drinking? What do you think you are doing?" she repeats.

"I . . . I . . ." Cue some goldfish impressions until inspiration obviously dawns. "Well, what are *you* doing?" he asks triumphantly.

Lizzie's turn to do the goldfish thing. A sarcastic voice interrupts. "I take it you two know each other?"

Lizzie turns to the voice. "Yes, we do. I'm so sorry, James. I don't know why—"

"I thought he was called Jack?" Alastair demands.

I wince as this verbal body blow ricochets off James and hits me directly. *Please* don't say this is anything to do with the diary. James' eyes look over in my general direction.

"Well, yes, he is. In the diary." Lizzie throws a sympathetic glance my way. I look over to my mother, who makes an "isn't this exciting" face at me. Any minute now she is going to start passing round the chocolates.

"Shall we all go and talk about this?" James says in a quiet voice. The crowd leans forward, trying to catch his words. He gently hustles Lizzie, Alastair, Callum and Fleur toward the door, like a shepherd herding sheep. He then looks back, jerks his head at me and I sheepishly follow like a good little baa-lamb.

As we all exit the room, with me bringing up the rear, the hum of conversation resumes, louder than ever. Our somber little group moves across the hall and into another room directly opposite the one we have just exited. It, too, is a beautiful room. A huge stone fireplace, laid with paper, wood and coal but remaining unlit, takes up most of one wall. The other walls are full of books and a huge antique mahogany desk sits grandly below a bay window. I sink into the welcoming softness of one of the chintzy sofas in front of the fireplace.

"Fleur," says James, "go back to the party. I'm fine, really."

She puts her head to one side in concern and I feel like giving her a good kick up the . . . It's amazing how quickly your feelings can change toward a person when you know they're about to marry the love of your life next Saturday.

"And you, Callum. It's not a police matter." I raise my eyebrows at this. Maybe they get lunatics throwing punches at them all the time? Callum and Fleur quietly leave the room.

Alastair draws himself up to his full height. James, by contrast, ignores him and flops down on the sofa opposite me. Alastair turns to Lizzie. "How long has this been going on for, eh? I'm no fool. The flowers, the phone calls. Holly introduced you to him, didn't she? DIDN'T SHE?" I don't know what he's talking about but I'm taking it personally.

"Alastair. I don't know what you're talking about," Lizzie cries. "The first time I met this man was with Holly in a hospital a few nights ago."

"Which time was that?" I ask James from the sofa.

"The bottle on the toe incident," he says from the other sofa.

"Oh." The whole conversation is above us in both a metaphorical and physical sense.

"Who are you having an affair with?" demands Alastair.

"No one. Am I, Holly?"

"Not unless you count me. She's practically moved into my flat," I reply.

"I thought you were staying with him." He points in a dramatic, accusing fashion at James but luckily James is too busy checking his blood situation to notice.

"No," Lizzie explains patiently, "I've been at Holly's. How do you know I haven't been at home?"

It's Alastair's turn to look a little sheepish and examine the fine stitchwork on the rug in front of him. "I've rung and I might have popped by a couple of times."

"Checking up on me?"

His head snaps round. "Maybe you need checking up on."

"Well, I'm surprised you could spare the time away from your precious *work*," Lizzie spits out.

"I am trying to get a promotion, and did it ever cross your mind why?" Alastair is practically shouting now.

From the relative safety of the sofa, James asks wearily, "Do Holly and I need to be here any more?"

Lizzie glances down. "No, I think we need to work this out by ourselves. I'm sorry about your nose."

Alastair adds, "Er, so am I. I thought that . . ."

James waves his explanation aside and says, "That's OK," but in a voice that clearly indicates it's not. We heave ourselves up from our respective sofas and wander out into the hall.

"Do you want to get some ice for that?" I ask as the blood still trickles. "I think it might stop the bleeding." James nods and leads the way across the hall, down a set of stairs and through a door. Inside a large, airy kitchen five people are working, crudités and smoked salmon pinwheels almost literally coming out of their ears. The kitchen has an old-fashioned Aga in one corner and I could probably fit my entire flat inside this one room.

James slumps down at a large oak table surrounded by chairs in the middle of the room. I bustle over to one of the people and ask for some ice. Call me a sad female (in fact, I might call myself that later), but I get a great deal of pleasure from doing this one simple thing for James. What is it with us women? Couldn't they have beaten this nurturing instinct out of us at birth or some-thing? I find a tea towel, wrap the ice up in it and place it over his nose. "Thanks," comes the muffled response. We sit in silence for a few minutes, until he asks, "Was she having an affair?"

"No!" I reply emphatically.

"Then why was she getting flowers and phone calls?" Damn, I should have known his sharp little detective ears would pick that up.

"Was she?" I ask innocently.

"He said she was. This is nothing to do with you is it, Holly?"

"Not exactly."

"I knew it," he sighs. "Why does trouble seem so determined to dog your every step?"

"I don't know," I say in a very small voice.

Pause.

"You only need one more bash in the face and then we'll be quits!" I quip because I'm pretty eager to get off the subject of Lizzie and exactly what my role was in the whole debacle.

"Your incidents were complete and utter accidents, whereas somehow you're involved in this."

"Do you think it will bruise?"

"At least we'd have matching injuries."

"But you and Fleur won't next weekend. The color will proba-bly clash horribly with her dress."

"Don't worry. It won't bruise." This seems significant in a funny sort of way.

Fleur arrives. "Darling, I've been looking all over! How is it now?" She looks a bit annoyed at finding us together so I make my excuses and leave them.

My parents and I say our goodbyes to our hosts and, just like the musketeers, our number is down to three as we climb into the car and make our way back to my flat. Alastair and Lizzie were still locked in the study when we left and I presume he will give her a lift home. My mother mercilessly pumps me for information on the evening's events and I gleefully relate them, thankful for something else to think about.

The rest of the weekend drags by as though time is playing a sick joke. I go through simultaneous agonies of longing for the next week to be over and yet dreading the time when I won't see James any more. My mother is fantastic. She refuses to let me mope around the flat and insists we go for a bracing walk by the sea and then for tea in a local hotel on Sunday. But everywhere I look I am reminded of him. It's like a record going around in my head that can't be turned off, and even I'm getting a bit sick of the tune. When we return home, I call Lizzie for the umpteenth time since the party. And for the umpteenth time since the party, the phone just rings.

Just when I was beginning to think it wouldn't, thankfully Monday morning dawns. I dress with great zealousness and Tristan and I set off eagerly. The journey takes a short time and I soon find myself bounding up the steps to the police station.

"Morning Dave!" I greet my new friend (formerly the-grumpy-git-desk-sergeant).

"Good weekend, Holly?"

"Yeah, fine," I say brightly.

"This is your last week with us, isn't it?" I nod and smile in answer. "Bet you won't know what to do with yourself afterward!" I grin again and think to myself that he doesn't know just how true that is.

As I arrive in the office, the night shift is finishing putting up a huge great banner across the office. It reads: "JAMES SABINE'S LAST WEEK OF FREEDOM! MARRIAGE IS NOT JUST A WORD, IT'S A SENTENCE!"

I grin up at them all as they stand on top of the desks. "That's great!" I exclaim.

"Took us all night to make!" one of them tells me.

"Quiet was it?"

"Very."

I settle down at my desk and try to ignore the giant swatch of fabric hanging above me. I get out my laptop and collect my e-mails. There's one from Joe asking me to come in tonight to discuss my "next assignment." I sigh and wonder if the mayor's dog has died and he wants me to cover it. The rest of the day shift filters in and gradually the office fills with noise and the smell of coffee. Phones start to ring and people begin to yell. A cheer breaks out from across the office and I look up. James has come in and is staring at the banner. I try to arrange my features into a suitable grin and watch him as he ambles across.

"Morning," he says.

"Morning, how's the nose?"

"Sore. How's your head?"

"Fine."

"And the toe?"

"Fine."

"Have we covered everything?"

I pause for a second; "I think so." I carry on tapping away as he gets us some coffee from the machine and then goes through his in-tray.

"Anything?" I ask after a while.

"A rape, unfortunately. I just need to get hold of a WPC and then we can go and interview her." He makes a few calls and then gets up. "Come on, Colshannon, time to go."

We meander down to the car pool, a journey we must have made at least fifty times over the last five weeks. I decide against calling Vince and asking him to join us on this one as I think the case might be too sensitive. The last thing this poor girl needs is

Vince snapping away at her and saying, "Could you do the crying thing again, ducks?" We're just going to have to use some library photos. Once in our familiar gray Vauxhall, we zoom round to the front of the building where a WPC is waiting on the steps. Conversation thus avoided between the two of us, I spend the twenty-minute journey talking to the young female officer about rape cases and dig up some fascinating facts for today's diary edition. The morning passes quickly and I am horrified by the rape case, so much so that James repeatedly asks me if I'm all right. We all return to the station and I busy myself by writing up my notes. At about four o'clock I have finished for the day, so as James is still busy on the phone and with paperwork I decide to play devil's advocate and wander down to see Robin.

I pop my head around her door and she looks up from her desk.

"Hi! Fancy a cup of something?" We meander down to the canteen. We chat about this and that on the way and it's not until we are sitting down with our drinks that I ask, "Robin, do you remember you once said I didn't know the whole story about you?" She looks at me hesitantly but I continue regardless. "Do you think you could tell me it now?"

She looks at me a while longer and then nods. "I suppose if I can't trust you by now," she sighs. "It's really hard to know where to start. But do you remember, when you first came to the station, I was quite new?" I nod. I remember it well. "Well . . ."

Oh my God. Poor Robin. Poor, poor Robin. When I first met her, I wondered how on earth someone as glamorous as her had ended up working in the PR department of a police station. Well, all is revealed. Basically, she has been poo-ed on from a very great height. Possibly rivaling that of the Eiffel Tower. She came down from London to be with her boyfriend, Mark. Apparently he had been begging and pleading for her to join him here in Bristol for months.

You know the stuff. He called her every day, told her of his plans for them, the great stuff they could do at weekends instead of commuting between here and London, blah, blah. And then one day she watched a program on old people and what they wished they had done with their lives and she said the whole thing was so poignant, so powerful, that she went back to her incredibly high-powered and successful job the next day and gave in her notice. Just like that. Apparently they were furious because they were in the middle of a campaign or something, but Robin said that she was afraid if she didn't do it then, she would never do it at all. But when she arrived down here a day early to surprise Mark with her news, she found him in bed with another woman.

Can you imagine that? Literally caught in the act! Practical old me instantly wondered what happens then. I mean, does he get dressed first and then the shouting starts? And what happens with the other woman? Do you address her or ignore her? Anyway, Robin then immediately (well, not immediately, obviously; the shouting bit came first) rang up her boss to ask for her old job back and he was so narked with her for leaving in the first place that he refused.

"Why didn't you go back to London and just get another job?" I queried.

"It would have meant I had failed. Failed with Mark, failed with my big, bold move to Bristol. I'd already sublet my flat as well. I had nowhere to go."

"What about your friends? Couldn't you have stayed with them?"

Robin looked sheepishly into her coffee. "I haven't actually told them yet." She must have looked up and seen my horrified expression—I couldn't go and buy a bagel without telling my friends—because she hastily added, "I just couldn't. I mean, I'd given in my notice at my glamorous, highly paid job to be with the supposed love of my life, only to find out he had been cheating on me for God knows how long. And then I couldn't even get my old job back! I felt stupid. I couldn't return to London and say, 'Hey everyone! You know that momentous, life-changing decision I made? Well, it was the wrong one. And you know that wonderful, gorgeous boyfriend I was always going on about? Well, he was shagging someone behind my back.' My friends have always looked up to me and they thought everything had turned out perfectly for me. I didn't want to drop in their opinion." She shrugged. "So I stayed here and tried to make a go of it. I found the most challenging job I could. I knew that if I turned this place around, leaving London would just look like a diverse career move on paper."

She stared back down into her coffee. "And then I made the mistake of getting involved with someone from work."

"Did that start after Mark?"

She nodded. "I was at a really low ebb. We went out with the rest of the department for drinks after work but we got on so well together that things progressed, well, to the bedroom, I suppose." I felt my insides lurch. "It was just so nice to be with someone but then even he dumped me."

"So that's why you want to go back to London?"

"Yeah," she shrugged again. "I've had enough of it down here. I want to go home."

"Are you coming to the wedding at the weekend?"

"James insists." I reached over and patted her hand and we both stared into our cups, lost in our own thoughts.

At the end of the day, James and I say our respective goodbyes and I make my way over to the paper. Joe, for once, is the bearer of glad tidings!

"Congratulations! Judging from the number of calls, e-mails and faxes we have had over the last few days, it seems your diary is a big hit! People are wanting to know what your next diary is going to be about! Any ideas?"

"What for?"

"Another diary, of course! I want to start trailing your new one by the end of the week!"

"You're not sending me back to covering pet funerals?" I say in surprise.

"Of course not! Also"—he leaves a dramatic pause—"someone from the *Express* has called. Wants to serialize this diary in the national press."

"You're kidding?"

"No!" A broad grin covers his face and he shakes his head from side to side. "And when I explained you had another diary idea up your sleeve they wanted an option on that too!"

"Oh God!"

"So you need to come up with an idea quickly! I'll give you two weeks to set it up after this one has finished. Come up with some thoughts and pop over tomorrow after work to discuss them."

I smile all the way back to Tristan. Who would believe it? The *Express,* too! I can't wait to tell my parents and Lizzie. I put Tristan into first gear and zoom off to do just that.

twenty-seven

———————

I've been home less than twenty minutes when the intercom buzzes angrily. I pick it up.

"Hello?"

"Holly! It's me!" Lizzie's voice crackles. I buzz her up and wait at the top of the stairs. I don't have to wait long until she bounds energetically into view. She exudes happiness and excitement. She grins widely at me and exclaims, "We're engaged!"

I give a gasp of excitement and lead her by the hand into the warmth of my flat, asking on the way, "So how did it happen?"

"Lizzie's engaged!" I announce to my parents before she even has time to answer. Amid the cries of congratulations, I go through to unearth a bottle of champagne I won in a raffle a few months ago. I stick it in the freezer to chill for a while and then eagerly run back into the sitting room to hear the story. Lizzie is half laughing and half crying.

"You see, I concocted a little plan that I would send myself some flowers and pretend to receive calls from a suitor in order to make him a bit jealous!" she says by way of explanation to my parents. My father looks a little mystified at this apparent recipe for disaster but my mother nods understandingly. "We were going through a bit of a bad patch and I thought the relationship needed some help to move it along. The result being he was so jealous he refused to talk to me! He somehow got it into his head that I was seeing Holly's detective! So he followed me that day we all went to the drinks party. He said he caught sight of James when he came into the room and just saw red, so he punched him! Anyway, he proposed last night. Said he never realized until then how much he loved me." Lizzie has the grace to blush and together we go through to the kitchen to get the champagne and some glasses.

"So it worked after all, Holly!" She is standing in the kitchen with me as I twist the foil off the bottle.

"What worked?"

"The plan. OPERATION ALTAR worked! He was mad with jealousy all along!"

"He punched James, Lizzie. I don't think that was part of the plan," I protest.

She airily sweeps James' hemorrhaging nose aside with a brush of her hand. "He said he was trying to work out who I was seeing and the only person he kept coming back to was your detective. He said every time he walked into my office I was reading your paper!"

"Did he not know James was engaged?"

"Well, you never mentioned it in the diary."

"Why did he follow you that day we went to the party?"

"He kept popping round to see if I was back at the flat and of course that was the one day I went home to change. So when he saw me emerge in my red dress he presumed I was on my way to meet someone and he trailed me!" She giggles to herself. "He had to wait ages at the front gate of Fleur's house to follow someone in!"

"Pity he didn't have to wait longer. He might have cooled down a bit."

"You will say sorry to James, won't you?"

"I'll try."

I put four glasses onto a tray along with the bottle. "Alastair must love you an awful lot, Lizzie, to go through all that caper," I say, a touch wistfully. "Waiting outside your house, following you to parties, smacking other men on the nose." Don't get me wrong, I'm absolutely thrilled for her. It's just more lonely being broken-hearted by yourself. We walk through to the sitting room together and I place the tray on to a small table and hand the bottle to my father.

"He promises he won't work so hard from now on. We're to spend lots of time together! That, after all, was the problem to begin with!" She hugs herself with happiness. The bottle bursts open and, when poured and duly handed out, we make the appropriate toasts.

I sit cross-legged on the floor. "Actually, I have some news too!"

"What is it?"

"They want me to do another diary! And the *Express* has bought the rights to serialize this one and an option on the next one!"

Lizzie stares at me open-mouthed. "Fantastic! Let's drink to that!" We all raise our glasses.

"To Holly's diary!" proclaims my father.

"To Holly's diary!" my mother and Lizzie echo.

"So what's the next diary going to be about?" asks Lizzie, settling into the sofa.

"We were just talking about it before you arrived." I pause, wondering how to break the news. "I actually thought I might go away somewhere," I say casually.

"Where?" says Lizzie in horror. "What about my wedding?"

"You haven't even set a date yet! Besides, it won't be for long. Just a few months—I think I want to get out of Bristol for a while after James' wedding."

"Do you promise it won't be for too long?"

"I promise."

Lizzie nods understandingly. "What do you think you'll be doing?"

I lean forward enthusiastically, anxious to share my new idea. "Well, I thought . . ."

"Mountain rescue?! Are you mad?" James cries. We are driving to a veterinary practice to investigate a suspected arson attack on the surgery.

"I think it will make a great diary," I say defensively.

"I'm sure it will! Posthumously!"

"I'm not going to die," I say dismissively.

"You. Have. To. Go. Up. Mountains!"

"I know that. I can go up mountains, you know. People do go up mountains. That's the whole point of mountain rescue," I explain impatiently.

"Holly, you have trouble making it down to the car pool without a packed lunch. How do you think you'll manage twenty thousand feet up in the freezing cold? It will get painful!"

"Oh, I'm getting used to pain," I mutter. Actually, the physical fitness side had crossed my mind, and the pain side also. But I think it will go some small way to driving out the other pain, the one that can't be alleviated by a hot bath and a plate of pasta. Sheer physical exhaustion might also help me to sleep at night. I can only have had about four hours so far this week and I would rather be on a mountaintop faced with a yeti and with only a torch and a jar of lip balm for protection than have to go through that every night.

There is a slight pause as we both stare grumpily out of our respective windows.

"Where are you going to go to do that?" he asks suddenly. I'm starting to get cross. He has completely cabbage-ed up (inadvertently, I'll give him that) half of my life and now he's rowing with me and doing his best to wreck the other bit.

"Somewhere with mountains," I say sarcastically.

"Why? WHY would you want to do that?"

"Because I am absolutely and completely in love with you and have no wish to remain in this town after your marriage as every single little thing I see reminds me of you and the fact that the closest I ever got to you was when I was knocked out and not even conscious to appreciate it."

OK. I don't say that. I wanted to, but what I actually say is, "Why not?"

"We could think of plenty of things to report on around here. What about . . ."

He flounders.

". . . the sherry-making industry!" he finishes triumphantly, picking on one of the only things that Bristol is famous for.

"I've made up my mind."

"So what does your boyfriend say about this mountain rescue thing then?" Blimey, he just doesn't give up, does he?

"We've split up."

"Oh Christ. Sorry."

"S'OK. I broke it up."

"Any particular reason why?"

I look fixedly out of the window. This conversation is too close for comfort. "No, no," I murmur. Subject closed. We both sulk for the rest of the journey.

We arrive at the practice. Vince is waiting for us, leaning against his Beetle and looking pretty in pink jeans and a crisp white shirt. We both get out of the car and walk toward him.

"Ooooh. What is wrong with you two? You have faces longer than a wet weekend in Scarborough!"

"You try and talk some sense into her. She wants to cover a mountain rescue team for her next project," snaps James.

"What's wrong with that?" asks Vince.

"Holly and mountains? One of them is going to come off worse."

"What are you trying to say?" I snarl.

"Oooh! Handbags at dawn!" squeals Vince, looking from one to the other of us, clearly thrilled to be in the middle of such a row.

James disappears into the entrance of the surgery.

Vince and I wander slowly after him. "He's so masterful," sighs Vince. "Oh to be in his fiancée's shoes next weekend."

The comment hits home and I wince slightly. Life gets so complicated. I wish I could go back to the time when happiness was a cup of hot chocolate and a video of *The A-Team*.

Vince playfully gives me a couple of pokes in the arm. "I think the detective might be quite fond of you," he says and waltzes into the reception.

"I think he might be quite fond of Man United too but I doubt he's going to call off his wedding for them," I murmur to myself and follow them both inside.

You may be wondering why I am not just coming straight out and telling James how I feel. Well, I'm wondering the same thing. I think he is quite fond of me in the way you get quite fond of a pair of slippers, or perhaps more like the way I tried taramasalata a few times and hated it and then started to quite like it. But the point is, I don't think he feels the same way about me as I feel about him. If you put the whole thing into perspective, which believe me I have struggled to do over the last few days, then you can see he has asked this beautiful, kind girl (with a few rubles to her name to boot) to marry him. At this point I am already seeing the "happy ending" signs. Then I pop up six weeks before the big day and I cause him nothing but aggravation. We row endlessly but get on quite well toward the end. Would you call off your big day on the strength of that? No, quite. So I really can't see the point in telling him and there is also the fact that I don't want to be laughed out of town. He obviously has loads of

gorgeous women after him. Robin for one. That's the other thing
which seems to be making me overly cautious. I've now felt first-
hand what it's like to have someone cheating on me. If James
wasn't faithful to Fleur, what chance would I have?

My mother and Lizzie, bless them, have been trying to make the
week better for me but in fact have only succeeded in making it a
lot worse. My mother is utterly convinced there is a way to rectify
the situation and has spent her time hatching dastardly plots with
Lizzie. Coming from someone who spends most of her time immersed in fiction and not fact, and another who is viewing life
through her own rose-tinted, definitely prescription, loved-up
glasses, I'm not holding out a lot of hope for them. My mother is
insisting on meeting me for lunch today, despite my protestations
of work/James/a hernia.

At noon I realize I'm going to be late for her. I look across to
James who is immersed in the paperwork from the arson attack
at the veterinary surgery. We have a very strong lead on the case
and he is hopeful of making an arrest this afternoon, which
would also perfectly round off the diary with a triumphant ending. Everything is wonderful, bar the most important.

"James?"

"Hmm?" He looks up distractedly.

"I'm going to have lunch with my mother. Will you come and
get me if you're going to make that arrest?"

"Where are you going?"

"Browns on Park Street."

"Yes, you go. Enjoy yourself while us poor police officers
slave away trying to protect the country. Don't give it a second
thought." He smiles suddenly. "Say hello to your mum."

"I will."

* * *

Tristan and I make our way through the city center lunchtime traffic and I try not to become agitated at being away from James. I walk into Browns, ten minutes late, to find my mother smoking a cigarette and with half a bottle of Chablis on the table in front of her. A group of admiring waiters are clustered around her, but they quickly disperse as soon as her scowling, not-quite-as-attractive daughter turns up.

"Darling!" She kisses me firmly on both cheeks and, while holding me at arm's length, looks me up and down. "What on earth are you wearing?" I look at my flowery A-line skirt and frown. I've always quite liked this skirt. "Your grandmother used to have a sofa made out of that material," she continues when the look on my face should have told her to stop. "Are you sure you didn't whip off the loose covers when she wasn't looking?"

"Quite sure." I splosh some wine into a glass one of the waiters has just brought me. She lights another cigarette and settles down.

"I want to talk to you." A waiter comes over and hands us two lunch menus. In order to avoid the oncoming subject, I study it intensely and make my choice of a sandwich. My mother doesn't give the menu a glance but just says, "I'll have the same," and hands it back with a beaming smile.

"I'll have an orange juice as well," I tell the waiter. "Do you want one too?" I ask my mother.

"God, no, darling." She drags heavily on her cigarette. "I don't want anything with vitamins in it. Now," she says decisively as the waiter scurries away. "Have you told him yet?"

"No, I haven't and I have no intention of telling him anything."

"Don't you think you should?"

"NO!" I say hotly, my temper flashing into life under the strain of it all. "Why does it have to be me? If he felt the same way and, by the way, that's a very big 'if', then wouldn't *he* say something? He is getting married on Saturday. He doesn't love me. End of story. What you are doing is really painful." I take a huge slurp of wine.

My mother edges her chair a little closer to mine and looks with concern into my face. "Darling. You're my only daughter."

I fix her with a sardonic look. Even with my mother's penchant for exaggeration this is going a little far. "Mother, I have a sister," I say patiently.

"Of course you do." She tries again. "Darling, I only have two daughters. Er, of which you are one." She pauses. "You see? That doesn't run quite as well, does it? Anyway, my point is that I only want to see you happy."

"I know you do. Look, I've only been friends with James for a short amount of time. I don't see what I can do. I think I would know if he loved me back; there would be—something. Signs. There would be signs." While I am gesticulating madly, I notice Joe strolling up to the table. I stop mid-gesticulate. "Joe!" I exclaim. "What are you doing here?"

"Looking for you. I called your detective and he said you were here having lunch with your mother. So I couldn't resist coming down myself!" With an exaggerated swirl, he bows to my delighted mother. I tut loudly.

Joe pulls up a chair and plonks himself down. Our sandwiches arrive and my mother graciously shares hers with Joe.

"Did you want me for something?"

"Yeah, I wanted to know if you're going to make an arrest this afternoon."

"I hope so. James said he would come and get me."

"And Amy has been contacting mountain rescue teams for you. She thinks she might have one in Scotland. Would that be all right? She needs to get back to them."

I glance over to my mother who is carefully not looking at me. I nod firmly. "Scotland would be fine." We eat in silence for a few minutes.

"Speaking of Scotland, is Buntam playing the Saint Andrews course this weekend?"

I nearly choke on a piece of lettuce. In fact, I should have tried a little harder.

"Er, Buntam? No, he can't. He's allergic."

"Oh no! What to?"

"To, er, haggis, of course. That's why he can't go to Scotland." I groan inwardly. To HAGGIS? What am I thinking? Couldn't I come up with anything better than haggis??

"Buntam," echoes my mother. "Who's Buntam, darling?" I look in alarm from Joe to my mother to Joe again. Surely he couldn't fire me now? Now I have the diary?

"Buntam is Holly's cousin, Mrs. Colshannon. He plays championship golf," says Joe seriously. I briefly toy with the idea of my mother having senile dementia.

"Cousin? Championship golf?" echoes my mother. "I very much doubt it—the only allergy our family has is to fresh air. Besides, I think I would remember a relation called Buntam. The name has a peculiar resemblance to Oscar Wilde's—darling, why are you kicking me?"

I cover my face with my hands and sink down into my chair with a soft groan. I hear a snort of rage from Joe and peep through my fingers. I frown to myself—he looks as though he's having a fit. His eyes are bulging, his face is puce and he seems to be stuffing a napkin into his mouth while making strange hiccuping noises.

I sit up swiftly. "Joe? Are you all right?" He seems to be having some difficulty speaking. There are . . . tears running down his face.

He pushes some words out. "Oohh, Holly." His face is screwed up with laughter. What the hell is he laughing about?

He squeezes some more words out. "Oohhh, I knew Buntam was made up."

"You knew? And you just let me carry on?" My voice is incredulous with disbelief. Joe is unable to speak through his laughter, so I carry on.

"I had to watch golf at the weekends; do you know how mind-bendingly DULL watching golf is?" OK, this is perhaps not the appropriate response for someone whose job is on the line but I'm having a difficult week.

Joe goes into fresh convulsions of laughter. He pats my arm. "Don't be too cross, he's the only thing that got you the job. I knew he was made up as soon as the first syllable was out of your mouth. But anyone who could tell such imaginative lies, I wanted working for me." He pats away as I stare incredulously at him. He starts laughing again. "Besides, do you know how amusing it has been to ask you about him and watch you scrabble around for excuses! I think the best one was when Buntam was staying in the hotel that had the power cut and . . ."

"Hello Holly," says a familiar voice behind me. I look round and then jump in surprise.

"Hi Ben," I say nervously. "How are you?" From the look on his face, I start to feel unaccountably worried.

"I'm fine. I was just having lunch with some work colleagues over there and thought it would be churlish of me not to come over and say hello," he says coolly.

He smoothly shakes Joe's hand and introduces himself as Holly's ex-boyfriend, then turns to my mother, shakes her hand and murmurs, "So nice to see you again, Mrs. Colshannon." It is as though a complete stranger has taken over his body. I don't feel I know this person at all. An awkward atmosphere hangs over the table. Ben sits down.

"I've been thinking about some of the things you said the other night, Holly. I have to say it has been bothering me who this stranger with short hair and green eyes could be." He turns to my mother and Joe. "Who is this man that my wonderful ex-girlfriend has fallen in love with?" Joe's mouth is open wide and I sink down in my chair once more. "And then, guess what?" He rather unsportingly doesn't let me guess but continues regardless. "I turned on the television last Friday night and who did I see there?"

Ben doesn't go on to tell us his sensational revelation because two things happen. Firstly my mother faints clean away underneath the table and secondly James Sabine turns up.

twenty-eight

"She's too heavy to lift," I say loudly. My mother's eyes faintly flicker. See? I knew she was faking.

"Holly!" says James, shocked. "Your mother has fainted. Could you get some water instead of making unhelpful comments?"

I sulkily pour some water from a carafe on the table and give it to him. He has rolled his jacket up and placed it underneath her head. A small crowd has formed around us which I would imagine is the reason for some of the more dramatic noises my mother seems to be making. She's like Peter Sellers' bugler who just won't die.

"So *this* is . . . ?" Ben says loudly from the front row. I had forgotten he was there.

"BEN!" shouts Joe. "Come and tell me all about your rugby team; could we do some more coverage for you in the paper?" Joe loops his arm around Ben's shoulders and Ben allows himself to be led away. I breathe a sigh of relief at a small crisis averted and turn my attention back to my mother, who mysteriously seems to be regaining consciousness.

"It's a miracle," I say sardonically.

James shoots me a glare. "Wasn't that your EX-boyfriend?" he hisses. "I thought you were having lunch with your mother?"

"I was. He turned up."

"Aaahhhh," says my mother. She sits up slightly, hand to her forehead.

"How are you feeling?" James asks anxiously.

"How many fingers am I holding up?" I ask, placing the V-sign in front of her eyes.

"I'm sorry, I don't know what came over me. It must have been the feng shui in here or something," my mother exclaims.

"Holly, take your mother out to the car. We'll run her home first. It's parked around to the right," James snaps, holding out the keys. "I'll just settle up your bill."

I slowly lead my mother out of the restaurant, supporting her around her waist. I drop her as soon as we get outside. "I don't believe it!" I rage.

"Darling, I *know*, neither do I. Ben upstaged me so badly—I couldn't believe it myself when he walked straight across me like that. Absolutely unforgivable."

"No, I mean you," I spit out. "Why did you have to faint?" I start off toward the car.

My mother looks a little shocked. I suppose to her it was a natural reaction. "Because Ben was about to tell everyone that you love James, of course! I could see James walking across the restaurant."

"I thought you wanted James to be told!"

"Not like that, darling, with Joe there as well. It would have been awful. Besides, as I remember, you didn't want him to be told. I did it for you."

My steps slow down slightly. I might have been a little uncharitable.

"Oh yes. Er, sorry. So, do you think Ben is going to spill the beans?"

"Nooo. Joe will persuade him somehow. Coverage for his matches or something. There is no way Joe is going to let any paper but his own upstage your diary."

The week passes as though time is in an egg-and-spoon race. Spurts of speed and monotony by contrast. My memories of my

last few days at the police station are all out of focus and linked by
a swirling cacophony of emotions. Every time Fleur called James
I could almost feel myself falling into the precipice. Fleur. (Fleur.
I find if I say her name quickly enough, I can make it sound as
though I am being sick.)

Lizzie and Alastair are still cocooned in their happiness. I think
a lot about Teresa and Ben together, and when I really want to
play the masochist I picture James and Fleur or James and Robin
together. I have a heightened sense of awareness of James. I know
where he is at all times and how close he is to me. Sometimes I feel
the warmth of his body and the electricity in his hands if they occasionally brush me.

The two last evenings, while wallowing in good old-fashioned
self-pity, I have been going through my CD collection and pulling
out every song I know will make me cry. George Michael, U2—
even good old Robbie and Take That have played their part. I
thought it might exorcise the pain somehow but all it has succeeded in doing thus far is to give me puffy eyes and several soggy
handkerchiefs.

But I do have some happy memories too. Today lots of happy
things happened and today was my last day of the diary. It is
Friday.

I got down to the station at the usual time and was greeted not
only by a series of whole sentences from Dave-the-not-quite-so-
grumpy-desk-sergeant, but also by a rip-roaring department
send-off party for both James and me. Let me tell you, it's quite a
surreal experience to eat cake and set off party poppers at eight in
the morning but I rose gallantly to the challenge. In fact, I think
all mornings should start like this from now on. Of course the rest
of the day was very busy, what with trying to tie up the arrest
from the arson case at the veterinary surgery and writing the last
episode of the diary. James offloaded all of his cases onto an increasingly pissed-off Callum.

At five-ish I made a move to go and file my final diary copy at the paper. I said my goodbyes to the various people in the department I wouldn't be seeing at the wedding tomorrow. James helped me carry all of my stuff in cardboard boxes (WHERE had it all come from? Where?) out to Tristan. We stood awkwardly after he had deposited the last box in the boot.

"So," I said.

He looked at his hands. "So . . ."

"I'll see you tomorrow."

"Yes," he said slowly. "I'll see you tomorrow. You know, I would have suggested going out for a drink together, it being your last day, but the boys have laid on a sort of stag do—"

"It's OK," I butted in quickly. He held the door open as I packed my tired limbs into Tristan.

"We'll see each other again, won't we, Holly?"

"I don't think that would be wise, do you?"

He frowned. "I don't know what you mean."

"I don't suppose you do," I said in a small voice as I pulled shut the car door, waved at him and drove off before he noticed the tears streaming down my face.

At the paper, some of the folks wanted to go out for Friday night drinks but, to be honest, I simply couldn't face it. So here I am, back at home, being fed vodka and tonics by my mother. She is full of news of the wedding, having had lunch with Miles today. The front door buzzer blasts out. My mother answers it and shouts through to me that it's Lizzie. Lizzie has been around almost every night this week to cheer me up. The problem is she is so happy that she can't resist talking about her own wedding when she is with us. And apart from my mother's spurt of effort to get James and I together at the beginning of the week, she seems to have finally come to respect my wishes and there has been absolutely no mention of it since.

Lizzie bursts through the door. "Holly! How are you?" She

can't help herself; love and happiness are gushing out of every pore.

"I'm fine," I answer and smile. It's great to see her like this after so many weeks of unhappiness but I wouldn't be human if I didn't admit it chafes a bit.

"Last day today, eh?"

"Yep, last day." Riveting conversation.

"Holly, Lizzie and I spoke on the phone earlier and we thought we would just pop into town," says my mother.

"Now?"

"Well, I need some tights for tomorrow and . . ."

"A new wedding mag is just out and I want to get that," says Lizzie.

"You're going to leave me tonight? Of all nights?"

"Don't be silly. We won't be long. Your father's here anyway."

I sigh and look over to my father who winks at me. "Oh, all right."

They quickly gather their bags and, chatting excitedly, go off without so much as a backward glance.

My father and I are just about to settle down to supper and an old episode of *Dad's Army* when the phone rings.

I answer it.

"Holly? It's Fleur."

"Hi Fleur, how are you?" I ask slowly. Why on earth is Fleur phoning here?

"I'm fine. Listen, I wondered if you wanted to pop over tonight. You know, for a drink."

"Tonight? But you're getting married tomorrow!" say I, rather stating the obvious. "Haven't you got tons to do?"

"The wedding coordinator is doing most of it. Can you come?"

"Well, not really," I say, looking over at my plate and my father. "How about when you get back or something?" With any luck I'll be up a mountain by then.

"I'd really like to see you tonight." Her voice sounds a little strained. "Will you come? For me?"

"Er, OK."

"I'm at my parents' house. Do you remember where it is?"

"I think so. I'll be over in about half an hour."

We say our goodbyes and I replace the receiver thoughtfully.

"Dad, I have to go somewhere . . ."

twenty-nine

Nervously picking up my bag, I bid a hasty goodbye to my father and scurry down to Tristan. I fumble with the keys and frantically wonder why Fleur wants to see me. Dropping the damn things at my feet, I bend down to unearth them and inadvertently catch sight of what I'm wearing. I recoil in horror. I look like an advertisement for the grunge movement. I came in from work and crawled into my oldest, most comfortable clothes. These just happen to be a pair of ancient, faded combats complete with interesting tie-dye effect from a time when I was making very free and loose with the bleach on a cleaning spree, and my oldest jumper, which has been handed down from brother to brother to brother to sister so that now even Oxfam would turn their nose up at it. Said jumper is dotted all over with holes from where some grateful moth has feasted on it and my brilliant white T-shirt underneath is dramatically highlighting its meal venues. Damn. I look at my watch; no time to go and change. Fleur is just going to have to make smug comparisons, isn't she?

I put Tristan into gear and we whizz off, the miles starting to clock up as I make my way toward Fleur's country house. Why on earth has she rung *me*? Is she lonely? Does she really want me to come over for a chat? Why does she want me to come over for a chat? What has happened to all her hen do pals? Not to mention Mummy and Daddy and the legions of staff that seem to be permanently camped up there? Couldn't she chat to them? The wedding coordinator must be a friendly sort of chap. Besides, she has only just met me and so I'm hardly a friend. And while we're on that, why was she so eager to make me a friend? Why go to all that trouble? Uncharitable child that I am, I don't really understand it.

Maybe she wants me up there for a more sinister reason. A quick scene change and I picture the dark, brooding mansion house. There seems to have been a power cut and all the staff I just mentioned have mysteriously disappeared. I picture myself walking into the study and seeing Fleur's pretty, impassive face flickering in the candlelight. She moves toward me and, shock, horror! in her delicate little French-manicured hand is an axe! I involuntarily clasp my hand to my not-so-delicate neck and pull my stomach up from out of my shoes where it seems to be happily nestling. Just a chat, I murmur to myself, just a chat. No need to overdramatize.

Twenty minutes or so later, I pull up to the huge iron gates and press the buzzer. In a faltering voice I tell the intercom who I am and the gates slowly open as though welcoming me into Hades (don't overdramatize, don't overdramatize). I travel timidly up the drive, noticing the huge marquee sitting quietly to one side of the grounds like a white blancmange, and park in the driveway in front of the house, now devoid of all the BMWs and Audis that had adorned it so capriciously last weekend. The engine shudders to a halt and I look out. Right. The electricity's on. That's a good start.

I walk up to the front door and ring the bell. To my surprise, Fleur herself answers it.

"Holly! How are you? Thanks for coming!"

"No problem." We air-kiss a good three feet from each other's faces and she leads the way across the massive hall. Her Manolo Blahnik heels click softly on the wooden surface while my huge clogs (an absolute necessity when it comes to choosing accessories to complete the grunge look) clomp along behind her. She opens the door to the study, the very same room where James, myself, Lizzie and Alastair were the weekend before. The fire is lit this time though. It crackles in the hearth and bathes the room in a soft, mellow light.

"Would you like a drink?"

"Thanks. Whatever you're having."

She goes over to a corner of the room, pours an amber liquid from a cut-glass decanter into a solid crystal glass and then refills her own. She's obviously been on the juice while waiting for me to arrive. As she's doing that I have a quick look around the room for concealed weapons. Behind the sofas, up the chimney, nestling behind the clock in lieu of the party invitations. You know, the usual places.

I hastily fling myself down into a corner of a sofa as she comes back carrying both the glasses. She hands one to me and then daintily sits on the edge of the second sofa, tucking one slender ankle behind the other. Damn. That's what happens when you don't go to a Swiss finishing school. You end up charging about like a baby elephant. Fleur looks like a panther.

"So?" I say, sensing a lull in conversation. "Are you excited?" I try to inject some semblance of feeling into my words but they almost stick in my throat as she fixes me with her blue eyes. Funny, I'd never noticed how cold they are.

"I don't think you should come tomorrow, Holly," she says calmly, looking down into her drink.

There is a pause as I try to comprehend this rapid shift in mood. I take a quick gulp of my drink. Flaming whisky burns down my throat, giving me a welcoming reminder of what warmth feels like. "Why not?" I whisper, voice hoarse with the fiery spirit. I don't need to ask because she is going to tell me anyway.

"Oh, I think you know why not. I saw the TV thing and I've

read your diaries." She gets up suddenly and walks over to the fireplace. Her hand on the mantelpiece, she turns back toward me. No doubt another pose they taught her at school. "Pathetic, like little love letters. Do you really think he would prefer you to me?" Her eyes are steely as she looks me up and down. Ah. I can see her point on this one and it's actually the very thing that has been giving me a lot of jip over the last week. A not-so-natural-blond reporter, a few pounds the wrong side of nine stone, complete with family armed with personality disorders. Yes, I can see where she's coming from all right, it's where she's going with it that worries me. She doesn't keep me in suspense very long.

"You see, I think it would embarrass both of us tomorrow, you being there. It's our special day and I don't want it marred with memories of you looking all cow-eyed." I flinch as this one hits home. "But he doesn't want to be unkind; he didn't want to say anything to you."

"You've discussed it with him?" I say in a small voice. A very small voice—barely discernible, in fact.

"Often. Don't get me wrong, he doesn't dislike you or anything. Now, what did he call you the other night?" I don't know. Fat? Stupid? Clumsy? Her tinkling laugh rings out and grates over me like broken glass as she remembers their obviously amusing conversation.

"Quirky! That was it, he called you quirky!" I shrug inwardly to myself. Quirky isn't so bad! In fact, quirky is quite good. Now did he mean quirky as in unique and interesting or as in loopy? I wonder if she would notice if I was quietly sick in my lap, or better still in hers.

She turns away, bends down in front of the fire and picks up the poker. Ahhh, exhibit A. She turns back to me, poker in hand. "You see, Holly, I love him. I love him desperately and I don't want our wedding day ruined by you." She waves the poker around liberally in order to illustrate her point. It's having a strange hypnotic effect on me as she waves it back and forth, back . . . and . . . forth.

"Yes, it will be a very happy day for you tomorrow," I jabber frantically, still mesmerized by the swaying piece of ironware. "You met James at your charity, didn't you? After Rob died."

Her face softens and she smiles slightly as she looks over my shoulder and into the past.

"Yes, he came in every week for two months. On his last visit he left his wallet behind. I could have run after him with it, but I decided to call instead and offer to bring it round. So I dropped in after work one day and naturally he took me out for a drink to say thank you. The rest, as they say, is history." She kneels down and starts poking the fire. I breathe a sigh of relief at her choice of poking matter. She leaves the poker leaning up against the wall; no doubt it will come in handy should I start to prove difficult.

She continues her tale. "He was quite reticent at first; he was coming out of another recent relationship." Robin perhaps, I think to myself. "And he didn't like all this." She waves her hand airily around the room. "But I changed his mind. You see, someone grieving as he was is actually in a very vulnerable position." My stomach tenses at the very thought of James in pain. "They need lots of care and attention and I knew just how to handle him, having worked at the charity." She gives me a little smug smile and a metaphorical pat on the back for herself.

"So you 'handled' him?" I ask indignantly. Ah, a little too feisty. Her hand inches toward the poker. I relax my face into an inquiring look.

"Holly," she says in her best condescending manner, "I don't just handle *him*, I handle everyone. Do you think it's easy being rich? Do you?" I open my mouth to answer that not only does it look quite easy but that I'm certain I could do it standing on my head with both my hands tied behind my back, but then hastily close it again lest I get the poker shoved in.

"It's not like the good old days when everyone bowed and curtsied to you. Gave you respect just because you had money. Nowadays you have to *justify* why you have money. I blame it on the Lottery." She walks in agitation over to the window. "People think you don't have problems just because you have money. You can't say a cross or unkind word to anyone without RICH BITCH being branded across your forehead." She shrugs. "I got bored with it. So one day I decided that I would be sweetness and light to everyone."

"Hence the bereavement charity?" I murmur.

"Yes, actually. Hence the bereavement charity." She stares at me, challenging me to protest. I don't; her trigger finger is twitching and I don't fancy being on the receiving end of it. "I was bored with the Hooray Henrys my father used to undisguisedly throw in front of me. What I wanted was a really good man but I just didn't know where to meet him. There were only a certain number of jobs I could take without qualifications—the charity was my third attempt but it certainly paid off. Good men are hard to come by, Holly. You should know that."

I nod numbly; actually I did know that. And her particular "good man" is a once in a lifetime opportunity as far as I am concerned.

She reaches up and twirls a strand of hair around her finger, looking dreamily into the distance. "And one so kind and honest." She seems to snap to and her eyes lock back on to mine. "And he's dynamite in the sack."

I drop my eyes first. This one hits me squarely in the stomach and damn well nearly doubles me over. Golly, dynamite eh? Not that he'll ever be blowing up my quarry, but still, nice to know what I'll be missing. She turns her back to me and stares out of the window.

"We'll be spending a lot more time together as well when he finishes his work."

"Finishes his work?" I echo.

"Daddy's going to offer him a nice little position in the company."

"But James will hate that! He loves his job!" I exclaim.

"We'll see." My mind reels with this simple phrase. How on earth could she persuade James to give up his work? I don't like to think of the many devious possibilities.

I stand up to leave. I have as much information as anyone can handle. Quietly replacing my glass on a side table, Fleur hears the gentle clink and spins around.

"Don't think you can run and tell him all this, Holly. He's on his stag do somewhere, you won't find him. And don't bother turning up tomorrow because I'll have security throw you out. Even with your lust for publicity you would find that distasteful."

Incapable of saying anything, I shake my head.

"And don't even consider contacting him after the wedding. I'll tell him you're a compulsive liar. He'll believe me over a reporter any day." There is a pause as her eyes challenge me to make a rebellion. Seeing there is none, she shrugs to herself and turns away again. "It wouldn't make any difference at any rate. James is a man of his word." A small smile plays around her lips. "That's the great thing about good men; once he's made a commitment, he'll make it for life."

"Why on earth did you try to make friends with me?"

She shrugs to herself. "I wanted to keep you close. You . . ." her eyes wander slowly downward, ". . . used to be quite attractive."

I stumble blindly from the room, tears blurring my vision. I tug frantically at the huge oak front door, slip out and run to Tristan. Wonderful Tristan. Fumbling with the key, I finally thrust it in and pray. My rock in a sea of despair. Make that a lightly slipping sand structure, I add to myself as the starter motor chugs over and fails to make the vital connection. Come on Tristan! I angrily bang my hands on the dashboard. Get me out of here! I can almost feel Fleur's eyes on my back. I try again and he apologetically hums into life. Ramming him into first gear, we hurtle down the drive and out on to the country lane.

I ease up a bit as we put the miles between us and Fleur. No wonder that bitch is friends with Teresa the Holy Cow. A match made in heaven, the two of them. There is no doubt Fleur is one hell of an actress—she had me completely and utterly duped. Her acting skills would put my mother to shame any day.

I have to tell James. I have to somehow get to him and tell him all this. My mind resolved by this rather flimsy mission statement, I put pedal to the metal. The hedgerows whizz by in a blur and are gradually replaced by increasingly urban scenery. A thought filters through a tiny chink in my brain and I let up on the accelerator a tad. What if James doesn't want to know all this? Let's face it, it's the last thing you want the night before your wedding. Some daffy blond riding up like the cavalry, blowing her bugle or whatever, proclaiming she's here to save you. And don't think, Holly Colshannon, that he'll thank you for bringing him this spot of bad news, give the travel agent a quick call and jet off with you on the honeymoon. You can stop right there with that little fantasy; he thought you were quirky, remember? And Fleur, with all her talk of commitment, is right about one thing—James takes it very seriously. Surely he'll feel he's already committed? That a slight technicality of fifteen hours or so won't make much difference?

I mull these things over in my brain and come to one conclusion. James needs to know. Even if he never speaks to me again, even if he decides to go through with it anyway, he still needs to know. For once in my life I am going to do something right. Tristan and I accelerate toward the city center.

thirty

S tag dos. Stag dos. Where on earth would you go on a stag do? I speed into the center of town, park Tristan at a rakish angle and dive into a nearby pub. The Friday night punters don't give a second glance to the rather tatty, wild-looking blond staring frantically about. Instead they set about the serious task of getting profoundly pissed, their faces set determinedly. I can't see James or anyone else from the department so I dive back out and continue down Park Street. Like a whirling dervish, in and out of pubs, clubs, wine bars and any other watering hole you care to mention I go, getting more and more distraught as time goes on. Cursing what I had previously considered a blessing—Bristol's extremely wide and varied choice of drinking venues—I come to a screaming halt outside Wedgies nightclub. "I'm looking for a stag do," I say to one of the bouncers standing outside.

"We've got plenty in here, love. Take your pick."

"No, no. A particular stag do. He's tall with . . ."

"Are you the stripper?" he interrupts.

"I certainly am not!"

His glance strays to my extremely inappropriate choice of clothing, finally coming to rest on my clogs. "No, no. I can see that," he murmurs.

I draw myself up to my full height and stick out my chest. I am just about to ask why not when the clock on the Wills Memorial Building chimes ten. Realizing I haven't really got time to debate my suitability as a stripper with a bouncer on a pavement on a

Friday night, I make to walk past him. He puts out his hand to stop me. "It's five quid to get in, love." Clearly my appearance belies the fact I am earning a wage packet. "That's fine," I reply as haughtily as I can and strop into the nightclub. A bored woman behind a plastic screen holds out her hand.

"That's a fiver please."

"I'm just looking for someone. I'm only going to be a couple of minutes."

"That's what they all say. It's still a fiver." Her hand clenches persistently. I sigh and get out my wallet. I have twenty quid. This is going to prove to be an expensive evening.

A quick look around confirms the fact that I am wasting my time and I walk back out into the evening air, giving the lady and the bouncer a backward wave as I continue down the street. Girls dolled up in their finest party gear and tottering along on high heels stare and giggle as I clomp by in my clogs. In and out, in and out, I weave.

I pass a cash point and empty my virtual piggy bank, giving me a total sum of another forty pounds to spend. I eventually zigzag into town, my pockets considerably lighter, and eye the Odyssey nightclub. My feet are beginning to blister inside my clogs and my ankles are bleeding from where I keep catching them on the side of my wholly inappropriate footwear. Sinking down on to a nearby bench, I morosely study the ground. Scenes from my future life play before me. Will I be left an old maid? Playing mother to Lizzie and Alastair's gorgeous posse of children? Will I meet James again? I look about despondently until my eyes spot the police station. Of course! I leap up with renewed energy and purpose and, with a hop, a skip and a jump, bound over to the doors. I burst through the entrance, questions already on my lips. "Dave! Do you know where . . ." I slow down and slide to a halt as a complete stranger looks up at me inquiringly.

"Where's Dave?"

"He finished his shift at seven o'clock, miss. Can I help you with anything?"

"Do you know Detective Sergeant Sabine?"

"Erm, the name's familiar. Is he a day shift officer?"

"Er, yes."

"Well, I wouldn't know him then, miss. I'm night shift only." He looks dismissively down at his pile of papers.

"Could you possibly buzz me in? You see, they're all out on a stag do and I thought I could just call . . ."

"Can I see your security pass?"

I rather needlessly pat my various pockets. "I've left it at home, but . . ."

"I can't let you through then."

"I rather need to get hold of Detective Sergeant Sabine. Is it possible you could just look up a couple of officers' details on the computer? I thought I could ring their wives and ask them if they know where they might have all gone."

"I couldn't possibly hand out an officer's personal phone number to anyone." He silences me as I start to protest. "Even if I wanted to. I can't access that sort of information on the computer here. You need to go upstairs to do that. Which you, young lady, are certainly not doing." My shoulders sag as I frantically try to think of a way around the problem. My brain clouds as panic sets in and, without any further explanation, I turn on my heels and run out of the station.

I make my way back to Tristan and together we zoom into another part of Bristol. It's half past eleven now. The pubs will be emptying and the nightclubs filling up so I am better to start concentrating on those. Abandoning Tristan, I start my search on the triangle and then move on to Whiteladies Road. Nothing. I'm running out of money and places to look. Two more clubs left and I only have a fiver. I take a gamble on one and pull a blank. He's not there. Sinking on to another conveniently placed bench, I put my head in my hands and start to cry. On and on I weep, tiredness and despair adding their eyefuls. Someone's warmth touches my hand. I look up.

"Here you are. Get yourself some food." Someone presses a pound into my bewildered hand. I start to cry even harder and my breathing comes in short gulps and gasps. Another person comes forward and presses a coin into my hand. I just sit and stare down at the money. One pound and fifty pence. I look quickly over at the last nightclub. I need another three pounds fifty to get in. "Can you spare any change?" I ask a passerby, grateful for the first time this evening of my choice of outfit. They ignore me and pass on by. "Can you spare any change?" I plead and beg, eyeing a genuine homeless person watching me incredulously from the sideline. I stare at him, challenging him to step in and queer my pitch. What on earth have I descended to? He walks away muttering, knowing a genuine nutcase when he sees one. I silently apologize to him and pledge a pound to every homeless person I see from now on if only I can gather enough money together to get into this last nightclub. I just know James will be there.

I soon have my required five pounds and run into the nightclub, leaving my last donor staring after me in disbelief, doubtless thinking me a no-hope alcoholic. I eagerly hand over my ill-gotten gains and walk through the doors. Music booms at me and my eyes take a few seconds to adapt to the dim light and flashing strobes. I walk around, looking desperately from person to person, my eyes constantly roving. Suddenly I spot a broad back I think I recognize. Yes! A crop of short sandy hair. I dart after him. "James!" I call. I catch up with him and lay a hand on his back. He turns around. "James! I've been . . ."

A complete stranger looks me up and down. "Sorry . . . I thought you . . ." I stutter. Without waiting for a reply, I turn blindly away and walk out into the night.

I drive slowly home, unwilling to give up but also defeated. My parents are anxiously waiting for me as I walk into the sitting room. "Where the hell have you been? It's two o'clock in the morning! We've been worried sick!" My father goes on to expand upon this comment with further recriminations, doubtless all justified, but my mother, seeing my tear-stained, dirty face, silences him. Unquestioningly, she undresses me and puts me to bed. Expecting to lie awake, I surprise myself by instantly dropping off to sleep.

I wake with a start the next morning, my heart racing. The clock says eight. The wedding is at twelve-thirty but I still have a few hours. Throwing yesterday's clothes back on, I hastily go through to the kitchen. No sign of life from my parents' room. Not wanting to wake them after their fraught evening, I leave a note propped against a milk bottle, grab my keys and run out to the car, only pausing to grab my bag containing my security pass and my wallet.

Once down at the station (still no sign of Dave), I am admitted through the security barrier and bound up the stairs, intent on making a few phone calls. A few officers I don't know are on duty but listen patiently as I trot out a convoluted story I made up in the car on the way down about needing to get hold of James Sabine on urgent police business. They nod understandingly and one of them obligingly logs on to the computer. "You're out of luck, love," he says after a few minutes of tapping. "Detective Sergeant Sabine's on annual leave. All calls should be routed to Detective Sergeant Callum Thompson, it says here."

"Could you try him please?"

He taps a little longer. "You're unlucky today. He's not on call and he won't be available until tomorrow. Would that do?"

I shake my head. I need to find out where Callum and James spent last night. Would they have gone home or stayed in a hotel?

The officer looks at me inquiringly. "Could someone else help?" he asks.

I shake my head again. "I'm afraid only James Sabine can." Tears fill my eyes and the officer pats my arm. "We'll track him down, love. Don't you worry." And with this he gets on the phone. He's back off it two minutes later after calling one of the detectives from the department. "Gosh, you're unfortunate aren't you, love? It's Detective Sergeant Sabine's wedding today apparently; that's why you can't get hold of him!" He grins at me, apparently pleased with his Sherlockian deduction. I nod wearily and the smile on the officer's face fades. "Aren't you the reporter . . . ? You and James Sabine . . . ?" I nod again. Words are now beyond me and slowly the penny drops. The officer stares at me. "Right," he says decisively and gets back on the phone.

Together we call and call until our digit fingers are nearly falling off. Again and again people aren't sure where Callum and James are. I speak to the officers themselves, their wives, children, great-aunts, anyone who happens to answer the phone. Most of the officers who were out last night seem to have extreme cases of amnesia. I do find out that Callum and James were staying in a hotel somewhere together but no one can remember the name. They can't even tell me where it was as they packed them both into a taxi at about one this morning.

"Where did you go for the evening?" I ask casually when I manage to get hold of another officer called John.

"Weston-super-Mare. Callum thought a bit of sea air might do us all some good!"

"Weston-super-Mare?" I cry somewhat hysterically, thinking of my exhausting night traipsing the length and breadth of Bristol, freely handing over my hard-earned cash to fat nightclub owners.

"It was fantastic! You should have been there!"

"Hmmm."

"Anyway, I think Callum said they were staying somewhere like, em, the Pacific?"

"Right. Thanks John."

I get off the phone and pass this piece of precious information on to my new partner. We bring up everywhere with "Pacific" in its title in the Weston-super-Mare area on the computer. We both take a deep breath and start phoning.

I look at my watch. It's a quarter to twelve. Countdown is forty-five minutes. I wearily replace the receiver and gently put a hand on my partner's forearm. He looks up from dialing in another number. I shake my head. "Don't worry any more. He would have left for the ceremony by now." The officer (I never even found out his name) slowly replaces the receiver and looks at me. He smiles sympathetically as I get up. "Thanks anyway," I add before sluggishly weaving my way through the maze of desks and down the stairs.

Time seems to be running on slow for me. I watch a flock of birds as they fly in perfect formation across the blue sky and mindlessly think the weather has turned out well for them. I notice a building I've never seen before and wonder if it's always been there or whether someone else had an evening as busy as my own last night and knocked it up while we were all still asleep. Will James notice I'm not there at some point? At the buzzing reception, will he frown to himself and think he hasn't seen Holly? I'm too exhausted to cry, I just want to get into the car and drive and drive until I reach the end of the earth. I have no wish to go home either, so I fish my mobile out of my bag and call my own home number to speak to my parents. The phone rings and rings; I stupidly and belatedly realize they'll both be on their way to the wedding. The answer machine clicks on and I press the cut-off button on my mobile. I sit for what seems like hours, trying to think of what to do and where to go next. I consider calling Lizzie but as my finger hovers over the digits I realize I am not really feeling up to coping with their happiness right now. I know that sounds completely horrible of me but I'm not. I just want to get as far away from here as I possibly can. I think wistfully of Cornwall, of the green fields and the blue sea. Cornwall. I'll just drive down to Cornwall, to my parents' house. I have a key to it on my keyring which has always hung there. I call my home number again and this time I leave a message on the answer machine.

"Hello. It's me, Holly. I've decided to go down to Cornwall for a few days. To home. I know you are coming on tomorrow after the wedding so could you bring some clothes for me? Just make sure everything is off and slam the door on your way out. Thanks. See you tomorrow."

With a marginally lighter heart, I leave a message for Joe saying I am taking a few days' holiday at my parents' house and set off toward the M5 south and home.

I try to keep the tears at bay by talking out loud to Tristan about everything and anything that comes to mind. I jabber about the weather, the holidays I fancy taking, the books I'm going to read. Anything to keep my mind off the wedding which I know will be over by now. Little thoughts come bumbling in of their own volition. Mr. and Mrs. James Sabine. Sounds nice, doesn't it?

At about junction twenty, Tristan starts to judder. "No, nooo. Tristan, please, not now." He practically starts to pant and I reluctantly pull over on to the hard shoulder. I turn off the engine and sit immobilized for a few minutes. Tristan shudders alarmingly every time a lorry goes past. This had to happen today of all days, just when all I wanted was to reach home and collapse. Another ironic indication that sometimes life isn't fair. Muttering madly, I drag myself out of the car and start the long hike toward an orange emergency phone. I glare ferociously at every passing motorist who looks with interest at the loopy bag lady hiking up the hard shoulder.

"Just let any rapist or murderer come within an inch of me," I mutter savagely, "just let 'em try." I tell the polite operator I am a woman on my own, request her to call the RAC and stomp back to the car in a thoroughly bad temper.

Twenty minutes later, which to be honest was plenty of time for any accomplished axe murderer to have had his wicked way with me and then chopped me up into little bits, a familiar squad car pulls up. I smile at them in the mirror. Pete and Phil, my usual muses, beckon me into their car, the usual formalities dispensed with.

"Hello Pete, hello Phil!" I mutter as I clamber in the back.

"Are you all right?" Pete asks, swiveling around in his seat and frowning at me.

"Fine, why?"

"You just look a little strange, and a little ..." His eyes wander down my strange apparel.

I sigh. I can't be bothered to explain. "Gin rummy anyone?"

They grin and Phil reaches into the glove compartment for the pack of cards while Pete pours me a cup of coffee from the Thermos. Two hands later, the radio buzzes to life and Phil takes the call. I sip my coffee and wait for him to finish.

"Holly, we're going to have to go. Urgent call. You'll be OK. The RAC won't be long now."

I sigh, say my goodbyes and then am thrown out with great expedience on to the hard shoulder. I walk back to Tristan, give the boys a wave and climb in. I am just berating my fate quietly to myself when I notice a red car has pulled up behind me. Oh, terrific timing. The axe murderer has arrived. Bloody marvelous. I look hastily around the car for a weapon and seize upon a rather timid-looking ballpoint pen that is quietly nestling underneath a crisp packet. Someone raps on the passenger door window. I lean over, brandishing my pen at them, and say, "Now look here . . ."

James Sabine's face stares back at me.

I gape at him and the adrenaline hits my stomach and starts slushing the sparse contents around. Not content with wreaking havoc with my digestion, it then proceeds down to my legs and turns them to jelly. I shift position rather quickly as he pulls open the door and climbs in. "Where the *hell* have you been? The station said you've been trying to get hold of me and we've looked everywhere for you."

I take a quick squint at the car behind. Is Fleur in there, complete with four large suitcases, ready to jet off to the Maldives? "I, er . . ."

"The paper said you were going to Cornwall."

"I'm allowed to go to Cornwall," I say a tad defensively, but he's too busy staring at my rather attractive outfit.

"What on earth are you wearing?"

"Erm, my clothes," I mumble.

"You actually paid money for these things?"

"James, what do you want?" I ask impatiently, the waiting carving small holes in my heart.

It's his turn to look a bit sheepish and confused. "Well, in a word, I want you."

I look at him in astonishment. "Me?" I echo.

thirty-one

—

"**M**e?" I ask again.

He nods slowly, his green eyes fixed upon mine. We stare at each other until he hesitantly moves his head forward and kisses me. A brief, warm kiss. He sits back and looks at me again.

"I hate to seem pushy, Miss Colshannon, but could you tell me whether it is at all reciprocated? It's just that I think Callum"—he gestures with his head to the red car behind—"might be wanting to get back."

I rush to get the words out. "It's reciprocated. Very reciprocated. It couldn't be more so, in fact," I whisper.

"Good." He opens the passenger door and leans out, giving Callum the thumbs-up sign. The red car flashes its lights and hoots as it pulls away.

I still stare incredulously at James, not sure whether this is some sort of huge practical joke and Jeremy Beadle is about to leap out from behind a tree. He leans forward again and kisses me. Wave upon wave of beautiful, sweet kisses. His hands move up my arms and reach my face. His thumbs linger around my cheekbones and then plunge into my hair.

"Hmmmm, arhhmmm!" I murmur. Not in careless, gay, abandoned passion but due to the rather unattractive thought that I haven't washed my hair since the day before yesterday and my teeth since early this morning. He breaks apart in surprise. "What?"

I wrinkle my nose apologetically. "I don't feel terribly clean, that's all. Don't want you going off me within five minutes."

"No danger of that. Been having impure thoughts about you for weeks." He grins at me but draws back a little nonetheless at my request and takes both my hands in his.

"Really?" I ask in wonder. I hesitantly lean forward and touch his face, still unsure about the reality of the situation. I double-check to make sure I'm not dreaming.

"The wedding?" I ask simply.

"Didn't go ahead, needless to say." Not needless to my ears. I want to hear every single gory detail, and anything with Fleur in it I want to go over twice.

"When? How?"

"Mixture of things, really. We went on my stag in Weston-super-Mare as you know. I spent the whole time in a confab with Callum. The rest of the department had a delightful night getting uproariously drunk while Callum and I debated my future. I didn't know what to do, Holly. I was so confused. I knew something was definitely up when I found myself getting into the passenger side of the car when you weren't there just to smell your perfume on the seat belt. I found myself wanting to call you up to talk to you at all hours of the night. You made me feel something I thought was dead, something I thought had died with Rob. But I couldn't see clearly, I thought it might just be last-minute nerves. You see, when I first started to date Fleur, she was a ray of light after all those months in darkness. She was beautiful and charming and just what I needed then." He pauses for a second and looks down at our intertwined hands.

"Go on," I urge, anxious to get to the bit where it goes wrong.

"Well, I guess she was a bit pushy and to begin with I didn't seem to have room to grieve for Rob and love her. I thought the love for her would come in time. To get married seemed the natural progression; my parents were thrilled and I suppose I hoped in some small way it would start to heal them. You know, a wedding, grandchildren in time, things to look forward to."

"But Fleur didn't want children," I interject.

"I know, she mentioned that a few months ago. Though after the marquee had been booked, the caterers vetted and the church reserved, I might add. Maybe that was when the cracks started to appear. I don't know. At the time I smoothed over it, thinking I could change her mind later on. And then I met you . . ." He smiles slightly and looks into my eyes. I smile back. Ahhhh, now we get to the good bit. I settle down into my seat and await Jackanory.

". . . and your arsey attitude." I frown a little to myself; this wasn't quite what I had in mind. "And I started to look forward to my days at work. I glimpsed something pre-Rob that I vaguely remembered."

"How did you call it off with Fleur?"

"Well, when your mother found us at the stag do—"

"My mother?" I interject.

"Yes, your mother," he repeats patiently. "Lizzie was with her too."

"Lizzie?" So that's where the two of them got to last night, and I believed them when they said they were stocking up on tights and wedding mags.

"Well, they turned up at about eight-ish. They had been down to the station and caught Dave coming off duty and he'd told them where we were. He even drove them into Weston-super-Mare because he was so anxious for them to get hold of me. Must have second sight that man! Your mother had had lunch with Miles yesterday. He'd told her all about his plans for me in his firm. In the end that's what finally convinced me." He looks at me and grins. "It also gave me a very good reason to call the wedding off."

"I saw my mother last night though; why didn't she tell me?"

"To be honest, she probably didn't know what I was going to do. I wasn't exactly forthcoming about how I felt about you. I just said I was going to sort things out with Fleur. I've been up all night with her. Talking," he adds hastily as he sees my raised eyebrows. "I called your house this morning but you'd already gone."

"I was trying to find you."

"I know. I found messages on my mobile from the station. Urgent police business, was it?"

"Very urgent. I saw Fleur last night."

"She told me all about it."

He kisses me again and my insides squirm with longing, hunger and God knows what else.

"Was it awful? Calling it all off?"

He winces. "It was quite bad."

"Were your parents upset?"

"Not as much as I thought they were going to be."

"What about Robin?" I ask suddenly.

He frowns. "What about her?"

"You're not still seeing her?"

"What you mean 'seeing her'?"

"Well, you and she were having a thing, weren't you?"

His face suddenly relaxes and he laughs. "A thing? God, no. It was Callum; Callum and she split up."

"Callum?"

"You thought I was . . . ?"

"But you had her in your arms when I first saw you together."

"I was comforting her. Callum, callous sod that he is, had just dumped her. I should have told you at the time but I didn't trust you because you were a reporter."

"Was that what you and Callum had a row about?"

James nods and smiles wryly. "He thought I was taking her side too much. She'd had a really rough time—did she tell you how she came down from London and found her boyfriend in bed with someone else?"

I nod faintly. "I'm sorry. I didn't know what to think."

"I felt kind of responsible for her. You know, her being new and Callum being my best friend. Well, she's seeing your doctor now anyway."

"My doctor?"

"Doctor Kirkpatrick. She met him at the hospital after you were knocked out, remember? They've been out once this week already. She was supposed to be bringing him to the wedding."

I smile suddenly. "How wonderful for her. She might not go back to London now."

"I'm not interested in Robin," he murmurs, leaning forward again. "Promise me you won't go up mountains now? Shadowing some poor bloke from a mountain rescue team who doesn't know what he's let himself in for?"

"No, no. Too boring anyway. Sherry-making will be much more interesting. The RAC is turning up in a minute, by the way."

"What an exceptionally good purchase this car is turning out to be," he whispers, reaching for me again. We melt into our kisses and wrap our arms around each other. A flash of light jolts us suddenly and we both look up in alarm. Vince, armed and dangerous, is grinning through the window.

"That's a front page exclusive!" he yells at us and makes a run for it.

about the author

SARAH MASON is a full-time writer and lives in Cheltenham with her husband and her West Highland Terrier. This is her first novel.